Unleashed

C.P. James

Also by C P James
Rescue Charlie
Massen
Goliath
The Crossing
Picket

Coming soon:
Unnamed
The Dustbin Man/Over the Wall

Foreword

Firstly, an apology. I have not written any of these stories in chronological order. I hope it doesn't cause confusion. I've been working on them so long I forget where the beginning is. Also, it's taken me a while to get this book out, so I thank anyone who has enjoyed the earlier books and has waited patiently for the journey to continue. Hopefully the next one – The Dustbin Man – won't take quite as long.

There is a method to my madness. Somewhere, in all of this, there is a thread. It will make sense. Someday. I promise. When I get the last book out. In the meantime I wish to introduce you to Isia.

This is part of her story.

Chris James
Lincoln, UK. August 2023

Unleashed

Chapter I

The MAV banked sharply as we began our lazy orbit of the city. Standing within the CIC I watched the image of the city standing on one side, our vantage point of its spires and domes slowly changing as we moved. Of course, I didn't feel any of this external motion. The interior of the MAV was too strictly controlled for that.

"I have high expectations, Ference," I said to the figure sat behind me in the dimly lit Combat Information Centre. "We have come a long way for this."

He did not respond, preferring to watch the image within the holoboard in silence.

Ference talked little anyway. He spoke when necessary and that was all. He was a grey man. Grey hair, grey skin. His clothes were barely black. So – grey. Don't misunderstand me, that did not make him boring. He was anything but. He spent his life out here beyond our borders, in the so-called Region of Interest. Mingling with a variety of civilisations, reporting everything he saw back to Military Intelligence. He might speak little, but he observed everything.

Ference was a spy.

The city glinted below us in the afternoon sun. It was a beautiful place. A city of graceful towers and piazzas. Tree-lined walkways and canals. All floating two hundred metres above the slow waves of the Purnice Sea.

All the cities of Sunna-Deste-Anne floated high above the endless waves. Kept there by anti-gravity motors built into their foundations. Wandering the skies at the whim of the weather and wind gusting against their walls. There was no land beneath them. Sunna was an oceanic world, the only solid surfaces ice floes on each pole.

The city of Solemn was the only exception. Its route was preordained, following a convoluted path determined millennia ago when the city was first set on its way. On the sea floor beneath its route was a cemetery, the interred bodies of the long dead lining a twisting path beneath the slowly roiling seas. This city followed that path, because this was the city of the dead. Quite literally.

A city of the dead on a planet of the dead, I mused. This whole place was a mausoleum. A planet with no life – no human life at any rate. It had all vanished twenty years earlier. Mysteriously. With no trace.

Sunna-Deste-Anne was a dead world. One of the half dozen or so we were aware of. Worlds abruptly evacuated by their residents. There had been no cataclysm, no war and no pathogen we could identify. Life continued here. There were birds in the air - such as existed on a world with no dry land. There were fish in the sea. Even the whales were unaffected. They all went about their daily business, oblivious to the fact their human companions had vanished.

The mystery deepened when our first responders noticed all their space capable vessels were still in situ. Even their long-range trading ships were in their docking cradles. The sort of vessels you would expect a people to use who had suddenly grown bored with their home world, lighting out for pastures new. Wherever they had gone, they had not taken themselves.

"Take us in," Ference said.

The Marine Assault Vehicle's slow bank tightened and the vehicle aimed itself towards a wide avenue between the buildings. Trees lined both sides, casting pleasant shade into the narrow space. It would be close, but I didn't doubt the pilot's ability. Cena was flying today and Cena did not make mistakes. Mistakes were a human frailty, which Cena was very much not. None of the crew of the *Cesa* were to know what Ference and I were doing today and so we were alone aboard the MAV. Unless you could count the AI as company.

That was Ference's one condition. Solemn was a very private place. It was enough that he and I were breaking that privacy by stepping foot here, but that could not be avoided. No one else was to know this city existed.

The MAV swivelled, presenting its blunt rear to the avenue and hovered, a ramp descending silently to touch the pavement. Ference and I were ready for it, stepping off before it could completely extend itself. Our feet crunched on a roadway that had not been swept in decades and the MAV headed back to the sky. It wasn't staying.

I didn't watch it go. It wasn't an impressive vehicle to look at. Your people would call it a flying brick, and it looked it. It was an oblong of black composite armour seventy-five metres in length and forty wide, its hull unmarked by any portals or hatches. They were there surely enough, it needed them to eject hard-armoured marines when undertaking its primary role, that of an armoured transport. Those joints were so perfect you would struggle to find them even up close. The vehicle resumed its lazy orbit of the city, on call should we need it.

I paused, studying our new surroundings. This looked like a typical city street. The pavement was for pedestrians only, ground cars were very much old technology and did not belong here. Tall structures closed in on both sides, blotting out much of the sky overhead. They were built from a variety of glistening materials. Stone perhaps, with mica or some other crystalline fragments embedded in them. The walls glittered where the sun caught them. A beautiful effect.

Any semblance of an inhabited city ended there. These were not buildings you could live in. There were doors and windows, but they lacked glass or any other kind of covering. Leaving dark oblong gaps in the smooth stone. I could discern ramps, flooring and even the odd partitioning wall inside them but other than that, the spaces within were bare. There were no furnishings at all. They were all simple, empty rooms.

The dead lived here and they needed little.

Weird.

Ference had not waited for me. He was striding down the avenue, heading for a courtyard some way ahead of us. I followed, taking my time.

"What's the local time?" I asked Cena.

"Forty-three Declination," the AI responded.

I picked up the pace. Ference had claimed the show started at forty-five Declination. The locals had measured time according to the position of the sun in the sky. In this case, forty-seven degrees after noon. Sunset was at ninety Declination, so this would make it mid-afternoon. Or thereabouts. It seemed rather unspecific to me. I guess this kind of measurement was necessary on a world where all cities were migratory. Time zones meant little.

"You've been here before?" I asked my companion.

"Yes," he said simply.

"Before this happened?"

"Yes."

"What do you know of them? The Sunna."

"It doesn't matter now. They are gone."

I sighed. Ference would not be drawn into idle conversation. I'd been trying for weeks, ever since he hailed me as we crossed the border into non-affiliated territory. He claimed to have a clue as to the disappearances. A clue that would present itself here in a few minutes' time. Other than that he had revealed nothing. His own vessel, unimaginatively named the CEV 9743, had been parked within the *Cesa's* secondary commerce bay for the duration of the trip, and he had remained aboard it most of the time. Little more than a yacht there wasn't much room inside. A yacht with an inordinately large drive, it was probably faster than the *Cesa*. Still, there couldn't be more than three or four compartments within it. Not a place where you would want to spend weeks on end. Not if you didn't have to.

I had invited him to my quarters several times, trying to get more information from him. And, to be honest, he intrigued me. He'd arrived on time and had always been courteous, even though he clearly considered my quarters frivolous. Which, to be fair, they were. But he refrained from revealing anything about himself. It was irrelevant to the mission at hand.

"I am trying to determine whether you had any particular affiliation for them. A vested interest."

"Does it matter?"

"Yes."

He was silent a moment, his stiff gait unchanged. "Yes. I knew them. They were … friends."

I couldn't imagine him with friends. "I'd like to know about them."

"You have access to my reports."

I did. I'd read them all. The Sunna had been a fascinating people. They had been well on their way to becoming one of the adapted. A term used for a people who changed their own physiology due to some environmental pressure or social desire. Birds. They had been turning themselves into birds. Given a few more millennia and they would have achieved that ambition. Fitting for a people who spent their lives roaming the skies.

It would have made their acceptance into the Confederation complicated. The Confederation did not like adapted populations. They had absorbed adapted people before. It never ended well. Unfortunate, as that was their one other desire: to be part of the Confederation. A fully signed up member. They believed it was only through unity the people of this galaxy could guarantee their own prosperity. They, like many civilisations, had suffered a collapse at one time. Back in the days when their cities floated on the waves an asteroid impact had caused a planet spanning tsunami. Within hours their civilisation collapsed, cities flooding, many sinking. Billions had perished. That was the reason they had lofted their cities into the air, where they could escape such an event in the future.

"I have read your reports. That's not what I want to know. I want subjective impressions. I want emotion."

"Emotion will help you?"

"Perhaps. It can't hurt."

I think I heard a sigh over the faint sound of the wind through trees. He stopped walking and turned to look at me. "I lived among them for three years in the city of Hurmetsk. A small family. They made wing suits. They taught me their history and customs. I learned to make the suits as compensation for their hospitality."

The Sunna were egalitarian. Which was unheard of in technological civilisations. Humans were selfish creatures. There was always someone who thought their labour was worth more than someone else's, and so should be allowed special dispensation because of it. The Sunna were an old people, perhaps they had grown out of it.

I said nothing, allowing him the opportunity to keep on talking. For a moment he remained silent, and I started to believe the moment had been lost. But then he cleared his throat and continued.

"I went to their home. After all of this," he waved to the empty city around us. "It was empty. Of course. The family was gone, as was everyone else. There was blood on the floor." He turned to look at me. "I analysed it. It came from Cho-Choq, their youngest. She would have been barely five of their years old at the time. There was a lot of it. There was no way she could have survived that kind of blood loss." He was silent again as he looked upwards, towards the buildings reaching to the sky around us. "Hers was not the only blood I found. There was more. A lot more. The Sunna did not just disappear. They were taken. They were ... harvested. I want to know who did it."

He wanted them to pay for it, I realised. Was it justice he wanted or was it vengeance? And what was my role? The captain of the only Confederate warship in the sector.

He wanted me to mete out that justice, I realised.

"Who do you think did this?" I asked him.

He let out a bark of a laugh and continued walking. "Here. The fountain. They don't enter the water. You will be thankful later."

I followed, studying the fountain. This was all very cryptic, and I must admit I was losing patience with it. Who did not enter the water? We were alone here.

It was large as fountains went. In fact it was a collection of them, all arranged in a raised pond in the centre of a wide square. Trees were lined around it, casting shade onto the rippled water. The fountains were concealed beneath the surface, firing jets of water into the afternoon air on regular intervals. There was a pattern to it, I realised. There was a progression of jets moving back and forth across the pond.

We seated ourselves on warm stone. On a bench that lined the pond, kept dry by the faint breeze that blew the spray from the fountains in the opposite direction. One of the trees had fallen at some time in the past, allowing a gap in coverage. Dead leaves were scattered around it. There was no one here to sweep them away.

"There is no one out here that could do this," he said. "The Sunna were relatively advanced. You have seen their orbital stations. True, they were armed against pirates and not much else. Still, even that would have caused any attacker to hesitate. We supplied them some of their tech. We could get in here … the Shoei could … but no one else. Certainly not one of the non-aligned worlds."

"But someone did."

"It wasn't us and it wasn't the Shoei."

"You think there is someone else out here? Someone we've not come across before?"

He shrugged.

There was still a lot to discover in the galaxy. Many of these worlds had been inhabited for a long time. Hundreds of thousands of years in some cases. Possibly far longer. The Confederacy had only been exploring for a few thousand years. Our ships were fast and numerous, but there was a lot of space out there. We had dispatched dozens of generation ship expeditions. Each vessel a city in itself, outfitted for extremely lengthy missions, each one as fast as anything in the fleet. For hundreds of years they had been exploring the galaxy, making contact with uncounted civilisations. Some had circumnavigated the galactic lens, arriving back on our opposite border to where they had started, with incredible tales of what they had found. There were some extraordinary civilisations out there, and not all were friendly. Some of the generation ships had disappeared into the cosmos, never to be heard from again. Even though we considered ourselves the most advanced, most powerful people in the galaxy, there were still things out there that could humble us.

This was very possibly another one of those.

A worry certainly. Did I really want to find whoever was behind this? Something capable of overcoming one of the generation ships would certainly give the *Cesa* pause. But, while well armed, a generation ship was no heavy cruiser.

Ference squinted towards the sun. "It's almost time."

I refrained from asking what it was time for. He'd made it clear he wanted me to witness it directly. He wasn't going to try and describe it. Whatever it was.

I waited patiently. I would find out soon enough.

This was my fourth year as captain of the *Cesa*. Much of that time we had been assigned to Admiral Chu's strike force. A squadron of three frigates, two cruisers and his flagship, the gunship the *CSS Sartoria*. A strange vessel for a flagship to be fair, a gunship was a spartan affair with a relatively small crew. It was little more than a flying gun. I didn't mind, it kept him away from me. Shoei space had been our patrol area, well behind the lines in space they considered theirs. Our mission had been to disrupt their supply lines and engage any military assets we discovered. We had taken part in a number of skirmishes, most of which had been pretty minor. While Confederate forces did not travel alone in enemy space, the Shoei did. It was their territory after all. Six warships against even their heaviest dreadnought was never a fair fight. While they had more ships than us, they were not as technically advanced.

Only one of their ships, a dreadnought by the name of *Shushulawe*, had stood its ground. The battle had been fierce but short. Eager to prove himself Chu had unleashed the gunship's primary weapon. A weapon designed to peel away the hull of even the most powerful adversary. A weapon that could crack a planet's core in two. It was, after all, not called a gunship for nothing.

I remember watching the hit on the *Shushulawe's* stern. The gravitonic pulse slicing through shield and hull as if they weren't even there. The vessel had ceased to exist almost immediately. It was difficult to tell what had been most destructive. The pulse itself or the resulting explosion as the dreadnought's main drive system detonated. The shockwave had been incredible, rocking even the *Cesa* that had been manoeuvring seventy kilometres away. Our shields had buckled but held. The *Feuscha* had fared far worse. The frigate had been much closer in, its shields collapsing completely, several of its decks exposed to hard vacuum as its armoured hull failed.

Not Chu's best day, and it only got worse.

I did mention the Shoei had more forces than we did, and that we were within their territory. It turned out the captain of the *Shushulawe* had succeeded in broadcasting a call for help before the ship was destroyed. Grand admiral Sulawesi herself had taken affront to our presence in her territory, and arrived with her fleet of sixty four warships barely minutes after the destruction of the dreadnought. Long before we even had the chance to contact the *Feuscha* to ascertain its state.

We fought. Of course we did. We couldn't leave a wounded comrade behind. We were doomed to fail. There was simply no way what was left of the squadron could resist that kind of firepower. Sulawesi had been not trying to force our surrender, she had been intent on our utter annihilation.

The gunship was vaporised barely a minute after the *Feuscha*. Already compromised the *Cesa's* interdiction systems were collapsing around us, allowing shot after shot to connect with our hull. We were venting atmosphere by the time the second frigate, the plucky *CSS Sayer*, was destroyed. The *CSS Tuletide*, the second cruiser and our only remaining comrade, had lost power and was calling for aid.

You know, I cannot remember feeling fear at any time in my life. I wouldn't consider myself a brave woman, but fear was just not something I felt. In times of high stress I always felt icily calm. Focussed. I always saw what I needed to do, and I did it without hesitation.

Brave? No, certainly not. If anything I've always felt like there was something wrong with me. Like there was some human emotion I was lacking. I've seen marines screaming in fear, panicking and deserting their posts, when, dispassionately, I knew our only chance of survival lay in staying calm and thinking clearly. I survived those times because I did not panic.

Perhaps that was why, in those last moments, when the *Tuletide* was calling desperately for help, I ordered the *Cesa* in close to the beleaguered cruiser. We opened our doors, what remained of them, and took as many survivors as could get aboard. Those who could survive the crossing. The fireworks had been intense out there. And then we left, the *Cesa* firing her main drive to escape at any speed possible. Of course the Shoei were blocking our escape, and we clipped one of their gunboats in the attempt, collapsing much of our starboard bow in the process, but we did manage to affect an escape.

I lost two hundred of my crew that day. Engineers and marines sucked into space or caught under collapsing bulkheads. But we still managed to save a thousand of the *Tuletide's* crew. And in all that time I don't think I felt fear once. There was simply no time for it.

I should have. I could see most of my bridge crew were terrified. Don't get me wrong, they still did their duty, and I was proud of them. But more than one rushed from the bridge to throw up once we were safe behind Confederate lines.

Yes, perhaps there was something wrong with me.

Of course there was an inquest. It dragged on for months, as long as it took for the *Cesa's* refit. The outcome was a foregone conclusion. Chu's actions in destroying the enemy dreadnought had been ill conceived. Particularly as, in doing so, he endangered another of his vessels. Even though we were at war with the Commonwealth all out destruction of an enemy warship was not in the rule book. He was held responsible for the loss of his squadron, along with eighteen thousand lives. It was probably fortunate he was dead. Dead and vaporised when the gunship exploded.

My own actions were exonerated. True, I lost some of my own crew attempting to pick up the survivors of the *Tuletide*, but I had ultimately rescued a great many of them. A justified loss, it was considered. I disagreed. Those men and women had been my responsibility. Their deaths were on me.

I was offered a choice in assignments after that. I had lost my taste for war so chose this assignment, as far from that conflict as I could possibly get.

Why do I tell you any of this? I'm not recounting my experience of space battles to amuse you. I know you've watched a great many of them on your television and in your cinemas. You people seemed enthralled at the prospect of mammoth vessels slugging it out. But that's not why I tell you this.

I tell you this because I want you to understand I rarely feel anything akin to fear. Physical danger has never concerned me.

But I felt something like fear when I discovered we were being watched. A man. Perhaps in his early adulthood. Tall. Taller than I was, certainly. Thin, almost emaciated. Which, I understand, was normal for the Sunna. He was about fifty metres away, beneath one of the trees lining the avenue we had walked up. Standing so still I could easily have missed him.

He was just standing there. Watching us.

"Try not to look at them," Ference said. "It encourages them."

"What?"

"They come here hoping to connect with relatives. Loved ones. They want to be acknowledged. If you pay them attention they will gather around and we'll have a crowd."

"This planet is abandoned."

"It is."

"Then what is he?"

He turned to me and smiled. "Clearly not one of the living."

Now I don't believe in ghosts. I've seen a lot in my life but none of it has been supernatural. How then, could I explain his presence?

He wasn't alone for long. Other figures entered the square behind him. Men and women by the dozen. They all stood mutely, looking around them as if searching for something.

"OK, explain this Ference. What the hell is going on here?"

"I'd tell you if I knew. I was never allowed here. In fact the Sunna didn't really talk about this city. I learned about it when I came to investigate their disappearance and everything I did learn is mostly guesswork. For example I don't know whether these ... people are just projections or whether they are some kind of ephemeral shadow of their former selves. Spirits, if you must. I can say the city houses no projection mechanisms. I looked."

"Ghosts are a myth," I commented.

"Of course. I can only deduce the Sunna have some kind of recording mechanism hidden on the planet somewhere. A mechanism that makes some kind of copy of the planet's inhabitants, which then gets revealed here on every tenth anniversary of their death."

"What for?"

"So that the living can commune with the dead. Other cultures have stranger funerary rites than this. A lot stranger. The Cord use animatronics to animate the corpses of the deceased. They hold parades every year. They believe the deceased are still living, and will treat them accordingly. I once saw a woman berate the animated corpse of her dead husband for squandering her inheritance before he died. What made it even more bizarre was the fact he argued his case."

I didn't reply. I didn't care about the Cord.

12

"Our own notions are the strangest. If anything death is voluntary for most Confederate citizens. We have the technology to extend our natural life spans. To replace our bodies when they eventually wear out. Even to transfer our minds to artificial storage media. Look at the crystal entities, for example. Two thousand years ago the Hauda found a means of transferring their consciousness to crystalline structures, and built automata about them. Essentially turning themselves into machines."

"The Hauda were expelled," I observed. "The technology became illegal."

He smiled. "Of course. The Confederacy does not like exceptional populations. One of the reasons they don't like the Adapted."

"Their presence is destabilising."

"Is that the reason?" He nodded, looking away. Watching a small group of the dead wandering the square. "Of course it is."

I refused to respond. I didn't come here to discuss philosophy. "So what exactly are they?" I gestured to the group. They saw the movement and stopped to stare at us. I heard Ference groan as they started moving in our direction.

"Does it really matter? Whatever they are they act like the dead. They might even possess some of their memories."

Which was why we were here, I realised. The dead might know what had happened here.

"Every ten years," I said. "They manifest every ten years."

"They do."

"You've worked out when it happened … whatever it was. It was twenty years ago today."

"Twenty of their years," he said. "Roughly twenty-one standard years. It wasn't easy. It took me a long time to find the exact date. All I had to do was wait. It would appear sooner or later."

"How long did you have to wait?"

"Four hundred and twelve days. I set up camp near here and waited. Watching their dead every day for some sign of what happened. I owed them that much."

"What did you see?"

"Wait."

I cursed his stubbornness silently. He could just tell me and we could get this melodrama over with. It wasn't cold but I shivered anyway. This place was creepy.

There were more of the figures now. They were eerily silent, simply wandering the city around us. I noticed some faces within windows high up in the buildings that crowded the square. I could barely make them out, they were too far away. They just seemed to be standing there, admiring the view. None communicated with any of their brethren. They seemed oblivious to each other's existence. I did notice they avoided each other though, none walked through another apparition in their aimless wandering around the square. They knew of each other's presence, but simply didn't acknowledge it.

It wasn't the dead they were interested in. They were here for the living.

"How many are there? Is this happening all over Solemn?"

"How many? I have no idea. It is happening all through the city though. The Sunna were an old people, a great many have died on this world over the centuries. It was inevitable."

"You say they seem to remember something of their former lives? Do they remember their deaths?"

"I believe they do." He stood suddenly and mounted the low wall surrounding the pool behind us, sloshing through the water he headed towards the fountains. "I recommend you join me."

I got my feet wet and joined him in the pond. The cold water came to my calves, it wasn't very deep. I felt my boots tighten slightly to keep the water out.

"Look. It's started." He pointed.

I was about to ask him what he meant when I followed his gesture. There was a figure a few dozen metres away. A woman, as far as I could tell. She had collapsed to her knees and seemed to be rocking back and forth. She was pounding her chest with her fists.

"What is she doing?" The figures around her had seemed emotionless, serene. She was the first to show any distress at all.

Before he could answer another appeared. A man this time. He was screaming to the skies. Silently. Not a sound coming from his lips. He head was thrown back and his arms were lifted into the air. Then he collapsed too.

It happened quickly after that. There was another. Then another. Then too many to count. The square filled quickly, figures appearing everywhere. Each one in extreme distress. Some collapsed to the ground to lay unmoving. Some screamed silently. Many started running, as if fleeing some unseen pursuer. And when I say running, I mean the kind of running only the truly terrified can achieve.

"What the hell is this Ference?"

I may never have felt fear before, but I certainly felt it now.

"I wish I knew."

We retreated towards the centre of the pool. Paying little notice when a fountain sprayed us with water. As crowded as the square became, none of the figures entered the pond.

The square became filled with a writhing throng of figures. Many thousands of them. Each one silent. No matter how many there were, there was nothing to break the silence apart from the faint rustling of leaves and the sound of water around us.

This scene was duplicated throughout the city, as the unseen mechanism buried beneath our feet relived the day the world died.

"Shit. What the hell happened here?"

There was no answer to give me.

Chapter 2

The wraiths disappeared at dusk. There was no gradual reduction, no warning that they were about to quit the square. They simply disappeared as if someone had switched off the hidden machinery that gave them their shadowy existence. An overload, Ference claimed.

Not that we had been able to discern individual figures for some time. There were simply too many of them, each image overlapping the others in a standing wave of virtual terror. Hardly surprising, every man, woman and child in the system had perished all at once, and they had all been summoned here. Billions of them, all crammed into this one floating city.

We hadn't left our refuge of the fountains. I did approach them at one point and regretted it. Their terror was palpable, even in their silence. It was not pleasant, and so I returned to my companion. He told me he had been caught away from the fountain when the throngs first arrived, their appearance taking him by surprise. He had been forced to wade through their horror to find a refuge from it. I couldn't imagine what that had been like. I didn't want to.

I summoned the MAV and opened a channel to my XO while we waited for its brick-like shape to appear above the square. "Sid. Bring the ship into the system."

"Someone could be watching," he reminded me, his voice in my ear. We didn't use clumsy communicators, but rather had all of that machinery hard-wired into our skulls.

"I'm hoping they are."

"I understand. Heading in. We'll be there shortly." The *Cesa* was currently standing outside of the system, about half a light year out where it would attract no attention.

"Take your time. If there is anyone here, make sure they see you."

"Oh, they will."

The hair on the back of my neck stood up as the MAV passed overhead, its drive system casting a static footprint beneath it. Its dark hull blotted out our view of the blood red sky and settled alongside us. I heard tree branches crackle as it caught a few branches coming down. Cena clearly didn't care about dismantling a few trees.

"Is this all you saw?" I asked Ference as we stepped out of the water into the machine's cool interior.

"Yes. The machines in the city won't start up again for three days. There won't be any more ghosts until they do. Then it's as if nothing happened. Just the usual projections."

"Until ten years passes and this happens again."

"Yes."

"You said you didn't find any machines to project the apparitions."

"Machines yes. Projectors no."

There wasn't a lot of space within the MAV. It was designed to carry hard-armoured troops, each in their own launch tube. Thirty-two of them. A full platoon of the toughest assault troops anywhere in the galaxy. Each clad in hard-armour, which was a virtual space craft in its own right. They were missing right now, there was only Ference and I aboard, the tubes standing empty. Arranged alongside those were cramped quarters for the MAV's crew and marines, a flight deck and a combat operations centre. The brain of the vessel — such as there was. Designed for extended operations the MAV could operate either on its own or accompanied by other MAV or interdiction vehicles. A potent force should the Confederate Marine Corps ever decide to deploy it. I used a MAV when away from the *Cesa* simply because it felt more natural for me than the captain's cutter. So much so I had removed the cutter bay completely when the *Cesa* was in for refit and installed an additional MAV bay instead. We needed another MAV a lot more than we did a pretentious cutter.

The MAV lifted off the moment the rear door was sealed, Cena aiming us skywards once again. Powerful motors flung us back towards space, leaving the beleaguered city way behind. With the AI flying Ference and I stepped into the CIC and settled around the information board. I passed him a tea and sipped on my own. Both of us lost in our own thoughts. Personally, what I had witnessed today left me with a lot to process. For once I was glad Ference was a quiet man. I did not want to talk. Not just yet.

The commander had meant it when he said anyone watching would notice the *Cesa's* arrival. The massive warship powered into the system at full speed, before performing a manoeuvre known as a combat stop. An instantaneous stop, her prodigiously powerful drive going into full reverse.

The fabric of space itself rang like a bell. There wasn't a sensor for six lightyears that could possibly missed her arrival. Even some listening posts within Confederate space, a thousand lightyears away, picked up the wobble, causing Cena to fire off a quick comms pulse. Everything was OK. No reason for alarm.

Despite my melancholy I felt myself smiling. Commander Sidcy Tebercy knew how to make an entrance. The man knew how to follow an order.

"Anything?" I asked as the MAV adjusted course slightly, aiming for the small moon that had appeared in the night sky.

"Waiting for the echoes to die down," Tebercy said. "There does seem to be some comms traffic in the outer system. Not far from the sixth planet."

"There were some mining colonies there," I said, half hopefully. Could someone have been missed by the mysterious invaders? And then again by our own probes that came to investigate when the Sunna went off the air.

"It's not the mines. Definitely something else. Sooch is having a look."

Lieutenant Suchu Suchane, 'Sooch' was our communications and weapons officer. He would be focussing the *Cesa's* sensor array out into the darkness, trying to discern what was happening out there.

"I have surveyed the old mining colonies," Ference said. "There's nothing there. They're all a wreck."

"When were you last here?"

He shrugged. "Ten years ago."

16

"Something could have changed."

He said nothing.

"Getting a clearer view now," Tebercy said. That was the problem with combat stops, it tended to cloud our sensors for a while afterwards, until space-time stopped vibrating. "Definitely something there. Big. Headed our way."

"Define big."

"Bigger than us," was all he said. Which meant a lot. The *Cesa* was a heavy cruiser, over four kilometres of composite armour and exotic materials.

"FTL?"

"No. Fast though. About sixty percent C. It will be here in fifteen."

Whatever it was it was impressive. While sheer size meant a lot in space combat it was not everything. The ability to achieve FTL meant a lot more, so much so that it was easily the decider in any engagement. It meant that that vessel belonged to a whole different class of combatants. A class that could pretty much ignore anyone that had not achieve FTL. Even a vessel considerably larger than it was. While it was foolish to be complacent, it did mean you could always run away.

"Suggest you stand back until this is over, Izzy," he continued. He didn't want the *Cesa* to be caught with a docking bay door open.

"See if you can take them alive," I said.

"I'll try." As he said it the massive shape ahead of us started moving again, slower this time. It swivelled on its axis, aiming its stubby bow at something approaching from the depths of space. Something that was, as yet, not visible.

The heavy cruiser, the Confederate Starship *Cesa*, was 4.6 kilometres in length. Roughly drum shaped it was 2.3 kilometres at its widest, which was its slightly flared stern. There were no exterior drive or weapons systems. No exposed landing bays. Everything was drawn beneath almost sixty metres of solid armour, the best Confederate science could produce. A boring shape, to be fair, but ruthlessly efficient nevertheless. This was a weapon of war. Not a yacht.

"There's more out there," Tebercy reported. "We've only just picked them up. Approaching from all vectors, seventy-four of them. Missiles of some description. Accelerating hard. They will hit approximately ninety percent c. ETA two minutes. Please stand a lot further back, Captain."

Cena turned the MAV and headed away from the *Cesa*, skimming the planet's atmosphere as it put some distance between us and upcoming events.

"We're picking up radiologicals from the missiles," Tebercy continued. "Whatever they are they are nuclear. Engaging now."

We were too far from the cruiser to view events directly. The images in the screens about us routed from the MAV's sensor systems. Space about the *Cesa* seemed to sparkle briefly as her countermeasures fired. More missiles, these barely larger than my fist. These were definitely FTL. Each warped space about itself, leaping forward at speeds far too fast for the enemy to comprehend. Space in the inner system roiled with flashes of light, bright pinpoints that out-shone the sun itself for a brief moment.

"Well, we definitely tripped your trap, Izzy," Tebercy commented.

"Who has weapons like this out here?" I asked my companion.

"No one. Not really. The Xon perhaps, but they would have no interest in this system. Not now."

"They're fourteen light years away. Close enough even at sub-light," I said.

"They trade in this region also. Most of the ships you see around here are Xon. The Xon have nothing to do with this though. They couldn't."

"Their missiles have been neutralised. Sooch has found a number of launchers around the system. Most concealed in old Sunna stations," Tebercy said. "They are firing again. More incoming. I'm redirecting countermeasures to the launchers themselves. We could do without the distraction."

"Someone went to considerable lengths to set this trap," I observed. "Who out here has that kind of resource?"

"The Xon. But this wasn't the Xon. It couldn't be."

"I don't think we should discount anyone."

"Have you read the brief on the Xon?"

"I skimmed it." I watched as space about the *Cesa* sparkled again. It wasn't the weapons we were seeing, but rather ripples in space as they went to FTL, creating a brief lensing effect. We were seeing light from the stars on the other side, perhaps even the sun, as it glinted off tiny whirlpools in space as they ripped a hole through it. Each munition arrived with inhuman accuracy at almost the same instant it was fired. Travelling at relativistic speed they didn't need crude explosives. Sheer momentum was sufficient. None of their targets survived, each instantly pulverised by the impact.

"The primary is a vessel built into an asteroid," Tebercy reported. "It appears to be armed with railguns and focussed plasma weapons. The drive system appears to be Xon in design, Sooch tells me."

"Not Xon?" I asked my companion. He said nothing, keeping his attention on the screens around us instead.

"No life signs, but I wouldn't expect any in a Xon vessel," the commander continued.

The MAV's sensors tracked the larger vessel as it approached. Tebercy was right, it appeared little more than a mid-sized asteroid. It looked like a lumpy potato with an odd patchwork of metal glued to it. Its drive was a big bulge in its rear, culminating in a string of exhaust nacelles. Each one spewing out tonnes of atomised propellant every second. The vessel was still accelerating and showed no signs of slowing.

Lights flashed across its rugged grey landscape. Weapons firing.

"Here we go." Tebercy didn't sound perturbed.

I saw the *Cesa* in another screen. The massive warship side stepped nimbly. A manoeuvre seemingly impossible for a vessel of its size. It was difficult to believe something that big could move that quickly. In fact it was barely a manoeuvre at all. The ship seemed to disappear in one place and appear in another. In reality it had slid in and out of FTL. A short hop out of the way of the approaching swarm of iron pellets. Each one ejected by a string of railguns buried in the attacking vessel's bow. If you could even call it that.

"Oh, they're quick," Tebercy commented as the ship fired again. This time it fired in a wide cone, pumping out shot after shot to fill all of space before it with hyper velocity slugs. Whatever was guiding the ship was attempting to cut off the *Cesa's* avenue of escape.

This time the cruiser didn't even try to evade the incoming fire. Close in interdiction systems fired instead. Lances of energy sizzled though space around it, picking off any slug that would have come anywhere near it. Each slug flashed brightly in atomic annihilation. Vaporised long before they could connect with the warship's hull.

"You're playing with it, Sid," I commented.

"I am ascertain it's capabilities," he responded.

"Do you know enough yet?"

"I think so."

The *Cesa* fired again. The strike seemed an anticlimax. From our perspective we couldn't see anything. No flash of light, no explosion as the approaching vessel was struck. It simply stopped accelerating, its drive flickering into darkness. Something invisible had reached into its drive core and ripped out some very delicate and necessary machinery. It was now the mere asteroid it appeared to be. If one travelling very quickly, and still loaded with dozens of railguns. Which it was still using to great effect, pumping our hundreds of high velocity slugs towards the *Cesa*.

The MAV twitched. Monitors went dark.

"What was that?" Ference asked.

I frowned, turning to the one remaining functional monitor. "I think something hit us." I tried reaching out to Cena using my implants. The AI did not respond. That was serious. The implants were short range, relying on a nearby vessel to connect me to the *Cesa*. If the MAV was no longer doing that, then what was it doing?

It quickly became clear it was doing very little at all.

"Try the door." I gestured to the sealed entrance to the CIC.

"It's locked."

"The hull must be breached."

"They must have left weapons platforms in one of the cities," Ference said. "We should have anticipated that."

Yes, we should have. I managed to get a diagnostics up. What controls we had within the CIC were not designed to fly the MAV itself, I would have to make do.

"We've been hit. The bridge is gone."

"Define gone."

"It appears a missile hit us head on. Most of the bow is gone. The bridge with it. And all the comms gear and guidance systems." As regulated as the interior of the sturdy vessel was, we had felt little more than a twitch when the missile struck home. Fortunately this one had not been nuclear.

"I'm hoping you can fly this thing from here."

I was certainly going to give it a try. "This won't be very elegant," I warned.

We were spinning, I discovered. The ocean beneath us was coming up fast.

"Elegant doesn't bother me. Not dying does."

The MAV's drive was still functional. Although barely. It was losing power fast. We certainly couldn't make it back up into orbit, which reduced our options dramatically. On an oceanic world there weren't many places to land.

I realised that Ference was still talking to me. I hadn't been paying attention, I was trying to restore my visibility of what was happening outside the craft. Everything ahead of the CIC was out, smashed by the impact. I could get a view from our stern, but it wasn't very helpful. I wanted to see where we were going, not where we had been. Fortunately the MAV was still tumbling. I got a glimpse of just about everything every few seconds.

"We don't need to get hit again," Ference was saying. He probably had a point. If there was one missile out there, there were two. Three. A dozen. Who knew?

Where would we land on a world of oceans? I doubted the MAV could float even before a hole was blown in it. Spinning as we were I was afforded a view of everything around us every few seconds. There was no land. No floating cities. Nothing but for the odd whisp of cloud. We were still high up, perhaps three or four kilometres from the waves. But as I fought to even out our flight I realised we would not be going any higher. We were losing power too quickly. It was all I could do to maintain the height we did have.

Something glinted off to one side. All I saw was a flash of light, as if sunlight was reflecting of something small moving very fast.

I cut power, letting the MAV plummet towards the sea. Another missile, coming to finish off the job.

I think it missed. I didn't feel any further impacts and our spinning didn't get any worse. It probably couldn't track our wild gyrations.

"You have armoured suits aboard?" Ference asked.

"No. Unshipped for our trip."

"They would have been useful right about now."

"They would. Pity we don't have any." Hard armour suits were capable of a limited amount of independent flight. They would never get us into orbit either, but they would have meant we could bail out of the MAV. A useless thought. We didn't have any.

"I think that was another missile," Ference continued.

"I know."

"It came from that direction." He pointed at an image in the last remaining screen.

"Yes."

"Probably came from a city. A place to land?"

I said nothing. It had occurred to me and we were already heading in that direction. Or as near to it as we could get. Guiding the wounded MAV was not an easy matter. Not from here at any rate. It had never been designed for this.

"There. What's that?" Ference pointed.

I didn't want to hope it was anything more than a cloud in the distance. We'd lost too much altitude avoiding the second missile. We wouldn't be staying airborne much longer. I hoped the missile wasn't capable of tracking us. Of turning around for a second go. I would never see it coming. All of the MAVs sensor equipment had been wrecked. I could see using this one screen and that was all. I was blind to everything else around us.

"It is. Head towards it."

There might be a tower wreathed in cloud ahead of us. Perhaps a few towers. Skyscrapers belonging to an unnamed city. One of the few dozen that roamed the skies of Sunna. They coalesced slowly from the cloud. Becoming more solid by the second. We were coming in fast. Way too fast.

"You might want to hold on. I don't know how much longer we'll have power. If we lose it we lose internal stabilisation," I said to my companion.

He sat and held onto the chair. I didn't tell him it would make no difference. If we lost stabilisation at this speed we would never know it. We be dead instantly.

The city didn't look like it was floating in the sky. Nor did it look abandoned. It was lit up with internal light in the slowly gathering dawn. Graceful spires reached into the sky from a ground that was still lost in cloud beneath us. The towers seemed to float in the air. Windows glinting, reflecting light from the low sun. They also seemed to glow brightly in various different hues. There was still power here. Possibly even machines tirelessly caring for the city, blissfully unaware their masters had vanished. They would keep on working as long as power lasted. Depending on its source that could be a very long time indeed.

I didn't have much time to consider it. We were soon in amongst them. The MAV clipped a tower. I cursed, all of my tenuous control suddenly gone. The last monitor went grey and cut out.

That was it. We were in darkness.

I held on too. There was nothing further I could do now. I could only hope we weren't too far from the hidden ground below. That our own power held out until we safely came to rest.

And that we didn't skip off the side of the city to land in the ocean. How deep was the water here? I had no idea. I hadn't taken the time to study the world in quite that much detail. I knew of other oceanic worlds, Trii for example, that had an average ocean depth of six kilometres. With deep ocean basins that went a lot further down than that.

Now I had a lot of time to think about things like that. I had nothing but time.

I could see Ference to my right in the dim illumination of the emergency lights. He didn't look afraid. If anything he looked frustrated. This was an inconvenience for him.

"Cheer up," I said to him. "It'll be over soon."

The MAV jerked again. I heard a bang from somewhere. Perhaps a crunch of metal. The sound obscured my companion's terse response.

"I think we're landing," he said, a little more loudly.

If landing was what you could call this. This was as elegant as a brick thrown through a greenhouse roof.

There was a string of loud bangs. As if we were inside a steel kettle struck by a hammer. The vessel shuddered about us and then everything became silent.

"Do you think we're down?"

The power took that moment to fail. We discovered the MAV had come to rest upside down by falling to the ceiling. I grunted at the impact, my breath knocked out of me.

My companion had swung nimbly from a chair arm and landed on his feet. He was a few metres away, studying the door mechanism. Trying to find a way to open it.

"It's ..." I started, pointing towards a panel alongside just as he found it. He snapped it open and pumped the handle inside. With a clunk the door unlocked, allowing him to prize it open.

"This way," he said before disappearing through the door without looking back.

I followed. There was natural light coming in through the door. Sunlight streaming down the battered passage that had once led to the bridge. It was now nothing but a twisted mess, allowing in a dull grey light. Wind howled through torn metal. I shivered. It was cold.

Wherever we were.

"Ah, we didn't quite land," Ference was standing in the ruins of the bridge, holding onto a torn conduit for balance as he looked at something beneath us.

Walking on the ceiling of the upturned vessel I joined him. "Oh."

The MAV had impaled a city tower almost halfway up its glassy side. Part of the ruined bridge hung out over a dizzying drop, the other half buried within the tower itself.

"I suggest we get out," Ference said as metal groaned somewhere behind us.

I didn't argue. I doubted there was much holding us up. With our momentum gone the MAV would head straight down from here. And without power we wouldn't survive the fall.

"I hope your ship is doing better than we did," he commented.

"The *Cesa* will be just fine."

"You seem very certain."

"I am. Nothing our here could harm her."

He laughed. "That's very arrogant."

"Realistic. We're a lot tougher than anything else out here."

"Really? You'd be surprised."

"Believe me, nothing out here can stand toe to toe with a heavy cruiser."

"I counter you argument thus," he gestured to the MAV.

"They got lucky."

"I don't think it really matters how anyone wins."

I didn't bother arguing. Ference was a spy, not a soldier.

OK, so I was arrogant and foolish. And yes, I would come to regret it. I didn't know that then, though.

There was still power in the MAV somewhere. I could hear the sizzling of shorting circuitry, accompanied by the acrid stench of an electrical fire. A ripped cable sparked when the wind blew it too close to a steel strut. I stood back from it, trying to stay out of its way as I surveyed the wreckage around us. We'd need to climb perilously close to it to make it to an exposed floor above us.

Ference was already picking his way higher, all but ignoring the sparks as he timed a jump carefully, avoiding the cable as it swung in the wind. I followed, realising the mist we were wreathed in had made the metal slippery.

"I'm presuming your comrades will come for us?" Ference said.

"Of course. Once it's safe." I joined him on the level above the wrecked MAV and looked down. We could repair it, I judged. The damage was extreme but the *Cesa* had an extensive manufactory aboard. Or we could scrap this and build another if needed. We certainly couldn't leave it here. The MAV was FTL capable. We couldn't leave that kind of technology lying around.

There wasn't much of a view. We were in cloud here, the mist restricting visibility to a few dozen metres. I could see the dim shapes of other buildings but that was all.

"The Xon. Why would they send their forces here?"

"You ask why they should attack us? I'm not sure," he admitted. "They have nothing to gain." He was silent a moment, studying the room we found ourselves in. It was difficult to recognise. I could see what could have been the remains of computing systems, possibly work benches, and some other machinery I couldn't recognise at all. Culture had a large part to play in how people designed their environment. These were an alien people. Human perhaps, but still very alien. Our common ancestor was very far in the past. This could have been anything. A laboratory. A kitchen. Who knew?

There was an odd stain on the ruined carpet. It might have been blood.

"The Xon don't do anything unless it is in their own best interests. Unless they get something from it. Their motivations are usually easy to see. Other civilisations in this area ..." he shrugged. "They might do something out of spite. But not the Xon."

"This might not be the Xon then?"

"Oh, that ship was theirs all right. I just don't understand why it's here. There's nothing here for them. I have found Xon mining stations before but they have always been in unpopulated systems. They don't like having to deal with the locals. They would never try building a station here."

"We'll have to ask them."

He smiled. Or at least I think it was a smile, there wasn't much light in here. "They're not very communicative."

"They attacked us after we announced ourselves. I'll have to insist."

He said something that was lost in the moaning of the wind. It might have been 'good luck.'

Once my eyes adjusted I could actually see quite well in the darkened room. I didn't know how long it would take the *Cesa* to finish up with the Xon asteroid ship. It had looked pretty tough and I know Tebercy wanted to keep at least some of it intact. We were unlikely to obtain very much intelligence from a field of wreckage. We could be here for a while.

"Something exploded here," Ference said. "Before we arrived. Look." He gestured into the gloom.

The chamber opened out ahead of us, the explosion knocking down an internal wall. It hadn't been caused by the MAV's impact. This happened a long time ago. Beyond was some kind of shaft within the tower. I couldn't see how far down it went, its lower levels lost in darkness. Eight or nine floors at least. There was a similar view above. Puzzling. It was pretty wide, perhaps forty or fifty metres across and roughly circular. The walls were plated with metal.

"This metal is tubino," my companion commented. "They used it a lot in their high energy physics research. Whatever they were doing here it was hot. Look, some of it has melted."

I wasn't familiar with the material, although it was possibly the local name for something quite common. It did seem pretty solid though, as I found when I ran my fingers over it. The impact of the MAV hadn't damaged it at all. In fact it was the reason we had come to rest where we had. The armoured transport had hit the sheath of exotic material and had been stopped dead by it. Leaving much of the vessel hanging out in the void.

Yet that same material had melted here, I could see. It had run like molten wax. Whatever had happened here had been hot indeed.

"Ah."

I looked up, wondering what Ference had stumbled across. He was nudging an indistinct shape on the floor with his boot. I looked away, concentrating on where the rivulet of molten metal had come from. There was some kind of protrusion above us, an instrument of some kind that had once leaned out into the dark space. It was a twisted mess now. Melted and broken. I had no idea what it was.

"You might want to come and have a look at this," he said.

I gave up on the instrument and crossed over to him. He'd found some bodies scattered over the floor. They were all burned beyond recognition. Now little more than vague human shapes burnt into the floor.

"Some kind of accident, do you think?" I studied them. They were clustered around what looked like a terminal of some kind. A computing system used to either control or analyse whatever they had been doing here.

"No. I think they breached this machine on purpose. Look." He pointed upwards, to a heavy armoured door that had once led into the strange chamber. It was open. Creating a breach that could have caused the explosion that had wrecked the place.

"Why would they do that?"

"Might have something to do with that." He pointed at something else.

"What the hell is that?"

I'm not prone to alarm. I'd seen too much in my life to be easily startled. This, however, disturbed me. There was something distinctly wrong with whatever it was that had been advancing on them. I might have felt a bit of fear running up my spine. It was suddenly cold in here and I didn't want to get any closer to the thing.

"Whatever it was that killed all these people," Ference said, "I think they set a trap for one of them. And ended up killing themselves too."

Whatever the creature had been it was very dead now. It had been clawing its way through a steel door, metal curling beneath its talons. And such talons they were. Each one was bigger than my hand and appeared quite capable of rending flesh and metal alike. It was difficult to identify its shape. The body was too badly burned. I could see sinewy arms, perhaps bone protruding from charred muscle. An oddly shaped torso and what could have been teeth. A waking nightmare. I'd never seen anything like it.

"What kind of animal is this? And why would someone bring one here?"

Ference said nothing. He leaned over the creature and studied it closely. After a moment he reached out and took hold of a limb. With a grunt he ripped it loose. It crackled like dry wood.

"For study." He held it out to me.

"I doubt there's anything in there to study. No cells would have survived all this."

"You never know." He proffered it again.

I took it gingerly. It felt like a charred piece of wood in my hand. It was surprisingly light. I held it closer and studied it briefly. Whatever this creature has been it had died a long time ago. Even the *Cesa's* science lab wouldn't be able to make much of this.

"If you're finished I think we should leave the dead to their peace."

Saying nothing he stepped past me and headed for the light.

It took a while for Tebercy to send anyone to pick us up. Clearly he had other things on his mind.

Chapter 3

It was snowing in my quarters.

I stood in the dark, watching the flakes drift past the lanterns dotted around the village. It was starting to heap up in the narrow alleyways, making the cobbles slippery underfoot. The bushes in the planters were now little more than white hills in the gloom.

I rarely walked through the village these days. Its emptiness was disturbing. There should be people here. Men and women about their daily chores. Children playing in the snow. Smoke drifting from the chimneys. Instead there was nothing but eerie silence. Dark empty buildings. Untrodden snow.

It wasn't a large village. There were perhaps twenty buildings packed closely together, simple oblong adobe structures, their whitewash flaked from years of neglect. The alleys between them so narrow a hand drawn cart could barely navigate them. They were situated on a small hill overlooking a rocky stretch of coastline, the slow rollers of the ocean crashing against them. The constant background music to the abandoned settlement. There was a small cove protected by a stone jetty, where three fishing boats were tied up. Icicles clinging to their rigging.

This was a folly and I knew it. In more ways than one. Technically this whole place was known as a folly. There was a lot of space within a modern warship. Enough to house such extravagances for their senior officers. Chambers over a hundred metres on a side where the resident could create what they liked. Some built city scapes, others beautiful scenery. I tried to recreate a childhood I could barely remember. The village where I was born. That was my folly. That world was gone, just like my memories of it. I had created this out of vague shadows and distant impressions in an effort to rekindle what I had lost. It wasn't helping. I was no nearer to that distant time. It was all still lost to me.

Freezer burn it was called. Suspension induced amnesia. I had woken in the city of Sebar, years if not decades after I was picked from the ruins of my home. I'd still been a child then and with little memory of who I had been. With no friends or relatives in the city I had been placed in an orphanage. If that was what you could call it. Others would call it a workhouse. Still others would call it a slave pit or a brothel.

I didn't want to think about that. That, also, was a long time ago. Even though it was where I had earned my name. Isia Marla. Now Captain Isia Marla of the Confederate combined fleet. These days my identity was very much tied to that position. Captain of a warship. It hadn't always been so, although I had been in uniform much of my life. Once as a marine, before I was dishonourably discharged for defying orders. Amongst other things. I shivered at the thought, and it wasn't because of the cold. That was something else I didn't wish to contemplate. That and the ultimate price the people of Duchess had paid for my disobedience. I may have succeeded in earning my redemption in the eyes of the Confederacy, but it meant nothing to Dutchess.

I might tell you about all of that someday. Not today.

I sighed and turned my back on the village, looking to the forest behind me. At least there was life here, even if I couldn't see it. Cena had brought me a few rabbits, some owls and a small family of deer. They loitered in the shadows, probably seeking what warmth they could find on this wintry night. I know Cena looked after them well. There was always water and feed left where they could find it, along with heated shelter towards the other end of the forest. That was probably where they were right now. I couldn't blame them. Why wasn't I inside too?

Just as an aside, I might call these creatures rabbits, owls and deer, but they were very far from those earthly creatures. Well, the rabbits might have some actual rabbit ancestry in them somewhere. But they were actually Dennis groundfowl, which was more a bird than a rodent. They hopped and had little fluffy tails, but that was the only similarity with the rabbits you would know. They also froze in the lights of oncoming traffic just like actual rabbits do. I call them the names of animals you may be familiar with because they do have some similarities to those long-lost creatures. It's also easier, otherwise I'd spend all my time explaining the 'owl' was a wisnack, a small nocturnal hunter that glided from branch to branch. It didn't actually fly as such. It was extinct in the wild now, the planet it originated on suffering a meteor strike that wiped out every living thing on it.

I ignored the flakes landing on my bare head, the snow drifts up to my calves. It was cold. I was aware of it, doubly so as I was not wearing any cold weather gear, but I didn't care. I wanted to experience the reality of the place, such as it was. Cena simulated everything that couldn't fit into the chamber itself. That included the sky and the scenery in the distance. Including the passing of day and night, and one season after the other.

This was, of course, winter.

My actual residence was a wooden cabin set slightly into the forest. I say cabin only because it was constructed from a rich red hardwood. From the archer tree, native to a world half the galaxy away. It was far too large for me, with a multitude of rooms I never used. Verandas I never sat on, windows I never looked out of. It was a place for me to sleep and store what personal effects I had. That was all. My life was spent on the bridge, not here.

Cena had chosen this design. It was more fitting, it had claimed. I was the captain after all. I could not live in the village itself – that would not be fitting. The cabin was well lit now, the downstairs windows all glowing like the eyes of perkisoars – deer - in the dark. I could see movement. My senior officers were arriving.

This was not the largest internal space within the *Cesa*. That was LongTown, a kilometre long, two-hundred-metre-wide tube a few decks above and to starboard of here. It ran lengthways along the drive rod, and housed the vast majority of the *Cesa's* crew, naval and marine alike. It was a town, houses and apartment buildings built along the long walls, leaving the centre free for parks and recreational areas. They had a sky too, the seasons alternating between spring and autumn. They didn't do winter, though. Who wanted that? On the opposite side of the drive rod was the Farm, to port of my position. It was only slightly smaller than the town and was where the *Cesa's* produce originated. Our missions tended to be lengthy, our replenishment stops few. We needed to be as self-reliant as possible. Much of that space was hydroponics farms and yeast vats. Would it surprise you to hear we didn't eat meat? Well, we did, it just didn't come from animals. I'll have to be honest, the first time I ate a McDonalds and realised it came from a real cow I was quite ill. But you do you.

This space was mine though. Mine and no one else's.

I would come out here to think, to absorb everything I had seen. Sometimes this place gave me the peace I needed to see clearly. Sometimes it didn't. Today was the latter.

"They here yet?" I asked Cena

"They are." Cena was present in every part of this ship. A constant companion to every man and woman aboard. Even here.

"They have watched the recording?"

"Mostly. Tebercy is rerunning some of the probe data. He is trying to understand the mechanisms within the city. He is trying to understand the source of the apparitions."

"He is an engineer, after all. Has he found anything?"

"No. Ference completed a thorough study and found nothing."

I smiled. Tebercy would want to come to the same conclusion on his own. He wouldn't trust someone else's analysis. Many would see that as a flaw, I saw it as an advantage. The engineer had discovered details many had missed before. If there was anything to find, Tebercy would find it. What did surprise me was his interest in the city and not the asteroid warship that had attacked us.

The *Cesa's* engineering team were already pouring over the remains of the Xon asteroid-ship, perhaps why Tebercy was focussing on something else. The *Cesa* had picked all of the offensive and defensive weaponry from its rocky hull, using a variety of precision munitions to disable them while causing minimal damage to the surrounding vessel. That left it largely intact for the engineers to investigate, naturally backed up by marines in hard-armour. There may still be surprises left inside of it. A few days, Tebercy had promised. That was all it would take to discover its secrets. In the meantime I was allowing Sid and my other senior officers access to the recordings made while in Solemn. I wanted to know everything there was to know about the place before we departed this system.

Doctor H'phana was not amongst my senior officers tonight. The physician was studying the genetic structure of the strange creature we had discovered. Burnt as it was it was a challenge, but one I was confident he would rise to.

"Ference has departed," Cena reported.

I nodded, mostly to myself. "Did he leave a message?"

"Only that he would be in touch if we find anything. He would like to be present when we confront the culprits."

"How does he expect to know?"

"He is a spy, after all."

I smiled. "He's asked you to keep him informed, hasn't he?"

"Would you like me to refuse the request?"

I thought about it for a moment. It was tempting. Ference had spoken little on our return to the *Cesa*, heading straight for his own ship the moment we came aboard.

There was nothing else to say, he had claimed. I had what I needed and he was satisfied to leave what came next to me. Whatever that was.

No, refusing the request would have been out of spite only. "No. Keep him up to date. Do you know where he is headed?"

"He has not informed me."

Of course not.

I watched the figures through the wide windows. It was dim within, lit only by a fireplace and what looked like a holographic projection they were studying. Casting them in a pale blue light. There were four of them. Commander Tebercy, our chief engineer and executive officer. A short, almost square man from the world of Vedvede. A hot, high gravity world. One settled so long ago its origins were lost in myth and superstition. Lieutenant Matte, communications officer. She was diametrically opposite to Tebercy. Tall, almost unnaturally so, and so thin there didn't seem space for flesh on her bones. Her world, Ikalosh 4, was far too small to maintain its atmosphere. Requiring the intervention of atmospheric generation plants to remain stable. After the fall of civilisation on her world it had started thinning out. It was only the arrival of a Confederate city ship that had saved them. Without interference all life on that world would have ceased in decades. As far as I know it was the only world accepted into the Confederacy that didn't already possess a sophisticated civilisation. There simply hadn't been enough time to wait for civilisation to rise again. As ignorant as her forebears had been, they were accepted amongst us with open arms. I couldn't imagine what it would have been like for them, a people barely clinging to the Iron Age, watching a massive vessel of space descending to save them. That was all different now though, she was a member of an extraordinarily wealthy family who called Reaos home now. That teeming cesspool of humanity that was the capitol of the Confederacy. Then came Captain Tenua, commander of the *Cesa's* marine compliment. She was small in stature with emerald green skin. Partly photosynthetic, I understood. She could make her own food from sunlight, air and water. Quite a feat. Her world was almost aquatic, the only land swamp and bog. I'd been based there once. The atmosphere had a peculiar odour. I couldn't say it was pleasant. Lastly Lieutenant Suchu-Suchuane, weapons and surveillance officer. He was the only one you would consider normal. Well, physiologically anyway. He was covered in tattoos, each one glittering under his skin, seeming to writhe as he moved. A cultural affectation common on his world of Afarensis. I had worked with all of them for years, apart from Matte who had joined us at Long Point. Replacement for Jenice who had taken retirement after our last battle with the Shoei. I could hardly blame her.

Cena was, of course, the fifth senior member of my crew. The machine intelligence was everywhere, in every part of the ship. Monitoring every subsystem and process. Responsible for the smooth running of the ship and the welfare of everyone aboard. You could easily make the argument I didn't need the other four. Or, in fact, *Cesa* didn't need any of the other crew – myself included. Still, a ship without humans aboard was little more than an intelligent probe.

I haven't described myself, have I? Well, you know what I look like. I can pass amongst your kind without comment. Outwardly anyway. I have long discovered there was something very unique about me. But that, also, is a different conversation.

I was breaking a commitment to Ference allowing them to see the recordings. The city and what occurred there were sensitive. Still, I believed it was more important to find the culprits than to protect the secrets of a people who no longer existed. If we were going to uncover what had happened I needed these people. I needed their insight.

I dashed snow off my boots, brushed it from my hair and stepped into my cabin. A wave of heat washed over me. It was warm inside.

"Izzy," Tebercy turned as I entered, his nose wrinkling as cold air followed me in. He had been studying a sensor view of the asteroid ship. An image of it hung in the air before him, details of drive and weapons systems highlighted in yellow in the image. Perhaps he had grown bored of the city of the dead after all.

I poured a tea and settled myself on a stool to study the image myself. Cena was projecting it over a wooden dining room table in the main room. "So, what do you make of it?"

"We came here for this?" Matte said.

"Yes, we did."

"What are we to learn from this? We already had a theory the people of this world were harvested in some way. This simply gives credence to the notion. It does not solve anything."

"Information is valuable," I said.

"And while we waste our time here, what happens to our mission in these border lands? We are the Confederate emissaries out here."

"The Sunna were Confederate allies, we signed a mutual protection pact with them. We are bound by that agreement to investigate their disappearance and to bring the perpetrators to justice. If you have a better suggestion as to how to do this, let me know," I said sharply. Matte's position here was a promotion of sorts. She had held the same rank of commander before joining us, but aboard a naval resupply ship, where she had been the senior officer. Technically their captain. Sometimes I think she struggled taking orders.

"Admiralty standing orders are for emissarial vessels, which is us, to make their presence known in the borderlands. By visiting local systems and engaging with the inhabitants. We've been out here two weeks and have not met any locals yet."

I smiled and held up a hand to stop her mid-flow. "I know you're eager, Commander, but can we talk about that later please? We will be out here for two years, the locals are not going anywhere. Well, not if we can help it. I'd like to focus on this for now." Without waiting for a response I turned to the image above the table. "Sooch, what do you have on the Xon? Have they been positively identified?"

My surveillance officer cleared his throat. "Yes, Izzy. Sid's people have boarded the vessel, backed up by the marines." He looked towards Tebercy. "May I?"

The engineer shrugged.

The image changed, flicking to the interior view of the disabled behemoth not far from us. It took me a moment to realise what I was looking at. It was a passage of sorts, but not one a human was ever meant to walk down. There was no up or down orientation. The walls were barely that, they looked to be formed by rows of pipes and cables, all clipped together and heading in the same direction, the passage a simple space left in the middle of the tangle. It was dark apart from the bright headlamp light of the space suited figures moving quickly down it. There were four engineers. Their white suits and glassy dome helmets picking them out from the two dark, lumbering shapes that preceded them. Those were hard armoured marines, each one encased in a suit of toughened composite and exotic materials. Tiny lights spiked at their shoulders and the small of their backs, their impulse motors driving them steadily forwards. I could see carbines clipped to their carapaces, each one aimed diligently ahead of them. They were expecting trouble.

"This is a live transmission of our first contact with the vessel's crew. Such as it is," Sooch continued. "The engineers are picking up a lot of activity just ahead of their position."

"What does this tell us?" Matte asked.

"Watch," Sooch said.

The passage came to an end, opening into a large open space. I couldn't gauge how big it was from this perspective. Easily a few hundred metres along each side. Within it was ... I'm not sure what it was. A machine of some kind, a sphere of bright light lay at the very centre of the chamber, indistinct mechanisms holding it in place. Which were in turn supported by long pillars that stretched out to meet the walls on all sides. Around all of this was movement. A lot of it. Machines large and small. Some held in place by their own internal propulsion systems, nacelle's dotting their metallic hides, spurting dull orange flame from time to time as they re-adjusted themselves. Others swung from pillar to pillar on extendable tentacles, tools and equipment held close to their bodies by grasping claws. Still others skittered over the walls, spiders of all shapes and sizes.

All of this movement froze the moment the marines breached the chamber. Every machine turning to face them. Glassy eyes regarded the invaders.

"Potential weapons detected," I heard the clipped voice of a marine. "Get the engineers back."

"I can't see anyone firing in there," Matte commented. "That looks like important infra – Oh."

The machines attacked in unison. A barrage of projectiles and laser light impacted on the lead marine. She lost her footing against the entrance to the passage, pushed back against the steel wall by the impact. Shrapnel pounded on her armour, sparks of light ringing from its tough hide.

"Return fire is authorised," I heard the steady voice of Lieutenant Je'ex from a MAV somewhere outside the behemoth. "Pick your targets please. We would like critical infrastructure intact."

Light flickered from the carbines. High energy pulses ripped through the machines swarming towards the marines. They disintegrated, their metal carapaces crushed by the hammer blows. Every shot was perfectly aimed, guided by the targeting systems built into the hard-armour. The first volleys were overkill, the systems overestimating how much damage the machines could take. It didn't so much incapacitate them as shred them, sending shrapnel into their colleagues and raining it down on the mechanisms further into the chamber. The volleys adjusted as the systems learned, meting out just enough fire to disable the machine attackers. Even though there were only two marines accompanying the engineers, it was moments before the machines were little more than twisted wreckage, spinning into the rear of the chamber.

"We're reading energy fluctuations in your vicinity," Je'ex continued. "Leave sensors behind and return to the staging area."

I could see why she was picking up energy fluctuations. As wreckage impacted on the glowing machinery in the centre of the chamber, the light began flickering. Whatever processes were happening there were being interrupted.

"That appears to be a very crude anti-matter reactor of some kind" Tebercy said. "If the debris damages the core we could be in for a rough time. Depending on how much anti-matter they have stored there."

"How much would it take?" I asked.

"To be a problem? About a kilogram. A system like that probably houses ten times that much. And then they will have a storage facility nearby. This vessel is designed to operate for decades without refuelling. It will have a considerable amount onboard. A few tons perhaps."

"That much?"

He shrugged. "Like I say, it's crude. That layout looks like some kind of direct infusion principle. They are trickle feeding the anti-matter into the reaction chamber, that's what causes all that light. The engineers were picking up a lot of gamma radiation too. This method uses a lot of consumable material. Relatively speaking. Mostly anti-hydrogen which is pretty easy to produce." He smiled. "Relatively."

I turned to Tenua. "I don't think it's safe in there. Get our people out."

"That will be a challenge, Captain. Four teams have been engaged by Xon forces, their exits are being blocked," the marine said.

"Get them out, Captain. You have authorisation to use whatever method you find necessary." I wanted to know why the Xon had attacked us. I wanted to know what they were doing here, and moreover, I wanted to know what they knew about the fate of the Sunna. But I was not willing to risk the lives of any of my crew for it.

The captain turned to the screen before her, which Cena quickly turned into a virtual combat operations centre. Tenua barked a rapid succession of orders, rallying her forces to reinforcing those trapped aboard the vessel. I watched as she positioned three MAV near the locations of her teams, their own weapons quickly cycling and firing. A constant torrent of plasma drilled into the rock, creating an exit where one hadn't existed before.

"Cena, can you interfere with the operations of that ship? If we can interrupt their communications, we can slow them down. Give our people a chance."

"I have a simulacra loaded into one of the engineer's nodes," the AI responded crisply. "I have tasked her to connect it to a communications channel aboard the ship. I have been analysing their radio communications and believe I can integrate with their code. It will be an ugly patch but I believe it will operate as expected."

"Let me know what you fi-"

Then the AI did something it rarely did. It manifested itself, creating the image of a young woman dressed in simple black military fatigues. Without hesitation the simulation leaned over Tenua and barked in her face. "Get your people out now, Captain!"

"What?" She looked up in surprise. "Give us ten minu-"

"Now, Captain. You must leave now. It is their intention to detonate their reactor core. They have fifteen tons of heavy anti-hydrogen aboard. You do not have the time."

"Cap-" Tenua turned to me.

"Do it. Get everyone away from that ship. Cena, back us off please."

"But Captain, we need more time. We need to get those people out."

"They are already dead, Ono. Save everyone else by getting them out of there."

As I spoke the feeds from within the asteroid ship went dark. The image of the vessel suspended above the dining room table flashed white, the glare of the sudden detonation filling the room with blinding light.

Caught in the detonation four MAV were vaporised instantly, even their remarkably sturdy hulls not up to the task of fending off that kind assault. Two others spun out of control, leaving long wakes of fire behind them as they were thrown into space. Still too close for comfort the Cena's bow shields buckled, almost failing under the onslaught. The warship withdrew, its powerful motors flicking us to FTL and depositing us far outside of the reach of the explosion. Its hull glowed dully where it had been caught by the blast. The thick armour soaking up a prodigious amount of heat and radiation.

A roiling wall of fire followed after, the shockwave blasting the upper atmosphere of Sunna itself. The planet's oceans flash-boiling, everything living in or above it perishing instantly. Cities fell through super heated steam, their towers warping and melting, the engines that held them aloft shorting out under the barrage. They collapsed onto baked sea bed, the ocean that had once stood between them boiled away.

It is in moments like that that I realise how different I am to the people around me. They stood in shock, staring at the maelstrom piped into my sitting room on the screens Cena had arrayed around us. In shock, they were unable to function. Even the consummate professionals they were, they were simply stunned.

That just didn't happen to me. I registered what was happening but kept on functioning. Now, more than ever, I needed to act. I needed to command. Hesitation in moments like these cost lives.

"Get the MAV aboard," I instructed Cena directly. The machine was operating as effectively as ever, like me it did not suffer from shock and indecision. I knew I could trust it to act, even when others failed.

"MAV Eight has suffered total system malfunction," the AI reported. "Its crew is unconscious but alive. Its hull will not last long."

"Pick it up first. Open the outer doors and pull it aboard."

"We will suffer considerable internal damage," Cena warned.

"I don't care. Do it. What about the others?"

"Manoeuvring now. Only MAV Two has preserved system integrity. Its crew are unable to pilot the vessel effectively however. There have been some injuries."

"Put it on auto pilot. Get them out of there. We'll pick them up next. The others?"

"Total loss," the machine said bluntly.

"OK." That was for later. I had to save as many lives as possible now.

"We can't go back in there!" Matte realised what we intended as the view in a monitor shifted abruptly, the warship heading directly back into the expanding maelstrom ahead of us.

I ignored her. "Quicker," I urged the AI.

"Six seconds to intercept," it reported. "There will be considerable heat damage to adjoining compartments. I am evacuating those areas now."

"Captain! What are you doing?" Matte swung to face me.

"Do not interfere, Commander."

She reached out to take my arm as if pleading for me to stop this reckless course of action. I pushed her away roughly.

"Try to touch me again, Commander, and I will knock you the fuck out."

I didn't turn to see her reaction, I was too busy monitoring the rescue of MAV Eight. Alarms flashed within the *Cesa* as we opened the MAV bay doors, allowing the fiery maelstrom into its inner compartments. Internal machinery seized, circuitry fused, but even then the *Cesa* spun around smartly and caught the tumbling MAV. An impossible manoeuvre for anything less adept than Cena was. Once the diminutive vessel was safely captured the bay doors lumbered closed again. They at least functioned perfectly. They were designed to operate under enemy fire, a mere anti-matter detonation was not going to cause them harm.

"I have MAV Two," Sooch reported as he forced himself back into action. "It safe. Its crew are not responding, however. Internal telemetry is non-functional."

That was not a good sign. Even when Ference and I were hit by a hyperkinetic missile much of that MAV's systems had remained operational. They were tough machines. Their weakest part were the humans aboard them. By far.

"Get them aboard," I said. "Get engineers and medics up to MAV bay eight. I want the crew out of there and in an infirmary.

Much of the initial detonation had passed by the time we caught up with MAV Two. Its hull was still glowing a dull red, its engines driving it slowly in our direction. The hull appeared intact, so there was hope.

That hope soon fled when we gathered it into its own docking bay and cracked open the fused doors. The interior had been turned into a furnace. Everyone was dead.

Thirty four marines and engineers, Sid reported to me when the final tally was gathered. Thirty four men and women dead, for no reason I could discern. That tally could have almost doubled. MAV Eight had already gathered up a number of teams before the detonation, and had forty one marines and engineers aboard. They would have perished had we not picked them up. The battered MAV's hull had already been buckling. Moments more and it would have given in.

We relocated to the bridge, almost a kilometre from my quarters. The fan shaped chamber dark apart from the light from dozens of monitors and readouts. Their attendant crews working ceaselessly to run the enterprise that was the *Cesa*.

"Damage?" I asked the engineer.

"To the *Cesa*, minimal. Two interdiction sites are non-functional due to heat ingress from when MAV Eight was brought aboard. They will be repaired in time though."

"In time?" Sooch asked.

"They will be repaired by the time we reach Xon," he elaborated. He knew me well enough to understand what my next order would be.

"Captain, is that wise?" Sooch frowned.

"Commander Matte," I turned to our communications officer at her own command console nearby. "The Xon were informed of our identity when they approached us, were they not?"

She had not spoken to me much since leaving my quarters, but she did respond to the question without hesitation. "Yes, Captain. They were informed."

I nodded. "So they engaged a Confederate vessel in full knowledge of our identity."

She hesitated now. "Yes, captain."

"Good."

Sooch's frown grew deeper. "Good, Captain?"

"They killed thirty-four of my people. I want to know why."

The Xon had done this. They had much to atone for. Our visit would not be friendly

Chapter 4

The *Cesa* sped through the night.

Xon was twenty-four lightyears from Sunna-Deste-Anne. A close neighbour by galactic standards, but as the Xon did not possess faster than light travel, it would have taken their asteroid ship fifty or so years to cross the distance. Bearing in mind whatever had happened to the Sunna happened twenty years ago, that did raise a number of awkward questions, about what the Xon had known and when. Questions I intended on asking.

It took the *Cesa* twelve hours to cross that distance. It was barely long enough to make repairs and to set the manufactory to replacing the lost MAV. There was no replacing the crew we − I − had lost. We would mourn them when the time was right. Once the Xon had answered for it.

I stayed on the bridge, vaguely aware I hadn't slept or eaten in almost two days. I understood my body well enough to know how far I could go without rest. It was a lot more than two days. Years in the marines had taught me that. One of Cena's automatons delivered a stim laden tea to my station on the bridge and I sipped that while watching reports scrolling through the monitors arrayed around me. Apart from some slightly singed sections of hull armour and shorted out secondary interdiction systems we were in good shape. Confederate ships were good at self-repair, it was one of the characteristics that made them so hard to kill. Guided by Cena, Tebercy's engineers ripped out damaged modules and slid in spares, returning the systems to full functionality in minutes. They would have been quicker had some of the internal pressure doors not been warped by the intense heat, forcing the engineers to pry them open before they could continue.

I flicked a monitor to the system we were leaving far behind. Sunna's primary was now little more than just another star lost against the galactic backdrop behind us. An insignificant yellow sun growing smaller all the time. Of course this was a stabilised image. I wouldn't see anything if I were foolish enough to stick my head out of a porthole and look behind us. Not that we had any portholes. Light simply didn't travel quickly enough to keep up with us.

A crime had been committed there. As great a crime as I had ever seen. And, in all honesty, I had seen a few. A sadness now hung over that system. An aching emptiness. Where there had once been life and light, there was now nothing but ashes. More so since the detonation of the asteroidship. We hadn't spent much time studying its impact on the abandoned world. We didn't need to. With so much of its oceans vaporised its atmosphere, what remained of it, had become toxic. The pulse of intense heat had seared what remained after a tsunami two kilometres high circled the globe. Shattering whatever cities had escaped the initial blast. If there was still life on the beleaguered world, there wasn't much of it. The last vestiges of the Sunna themselves had been scoured from it. They existed in memory only now.

"What is our objective on Xon?" Matte asked. Her station was alongside mine at the rear of the *Cesa's* multi-levelled, fan shaped bridge. On the other side of me was Tebercy, who was deep in conversation with someone on a monitor.

I took it the question was aimed at me. "Our mission out here is to make our presence known to the local systems," I said. Reminding her of her earlier statement.

"Specifically. Bearing in mind no one has visited Xon since the original survey mission almost eight hundred years ago. Which didn't end well."

It hadn't. Of course I had read the mission report. That survey, dispatched by Union University as part of their regional research brief, had been civilian. Little more than a ten-berth skiff that spent a few decades visiting the systems in this area. The ship so small it was equipped with suspension pods so the crew could endure the extended flight times in such a small vessel. They had been set upon by the Xon the moment they transmitted the standard greeting, and barely escaped with their lives. Critically damaged the ship had limped away, a flotilla of locals in close pursuit. Unable to engage their main drive they were restricted to sub-light and so couldn't shake their attackers. Still, as slow as the university ship was, it was not slow enough for the Xon to catch up to it. Years passed. The skiff's crew retreating to hibernation to preserve their dwindling resources. And still the Xon pursued. They didn't seem concerned with how long the chase would take. They simply saw a technological prize, and wanted it.

It only ended when a Confederate frigate, the CSS Kotchsau, arrived in response to the skiff's distress call. A frigate against the Xon flotilla had been no match at all. Within minutes the fifteen-year pursuit was over.

Of course no one ever went back. We may have dispatched the odd drone to the system, but they were attacked the moment they were discovered. The Xon did not like outsiders.

This time they weren't going to be given a choice. And this time they would have a heavy cruiser in their system.

"It is my position the Xon don't fully understand who we are and why we are out here. If they did they would not have attacked us. My intention is to remedy that."

"By force?"

"By whatever means necessary. Don't forget I have the authority to use force when Confederate interests are threatened. They attacked us, resulting in casualties. It is my duty to ensure we respond."

"A measured response? Or are we after retribution?"

I opened my mouth to respond but my thought process was interrupted by a comms channel opening up before me. Doctor H'Phana, our chief medical officer.

"Captain. This specimen you have brought to me," he started without preamble.

If anything I was relieved for the interruption. I would deal with Matte, but not today. "Sorl'o, what can I do for you?"

Much of the doctor's face was ceramic. Replacement for his original tissue after being caught in a stone burner detonation during the secession of Albert. As fate had it I had been there, a young second lieutenant on my first tour to an active conflict zone. I had been the one to come across the horribly disfigured doctor. The one to keep him alive – using my whole supply of actives to do so – until a medivac arrived. I had doubted the man would survive. He had been little more than a squirming lump of charred, half cooked flesh. So disfigured it was almost impossible to tell which bit was which. Now most of his body was ceramic, even though we possessed the technology to regrow what he had lost. He did not believe in covering over the scars of the past, he had once claimed. He would live his life, and not deny it. He had been surgical head of a teaching hospital when he learned I was to command the *Cesa*, and immediately applied for the position aboard ship. I was honoured, and lucky. He was a truly talented physician.

"I want to show you something, Izzy." He flashed an image up to one of my screens. I couldn't immediately tell what I was looking at. "This is under six hundred magnification. We're looking at the creature's cells."

"OK," was all I could find to say. The image was a mess of shapes. Some circular, some elongated. Some square. Others star shaped. Some had clearly ruptured, cell walls breaking apart when the creature was killed.

"This is impossible," Sorl'o went on to say. "We're seeing several different species here. This taxonomy is … unheard of. Impossible. There is more than one type of genotype at play here. Its almost as if this creature was a chimera of some kind. More than that, it seemed able to actively select its genetic presentation."

"I'm sorry, Sorl'o, what?"

"It could change into something else at will. Some of the cells you see there appear to have been caught in transition. They were changing from one kind of creature to another. Just in the sample you brought back I have counted over two hundred different genetic heritages. Not all of them related. Some are alien to each other, their origins on very different planets. Planets with very different environments."

I am not an unintelligent woman. I would never claim to be in the same league as the doctor, but I could follow most things. "I'm sorry, you've lost me."

"What I'm saying, Izzy, is that we have never seen this creature before. Not in the sixty or seventy thousand worlds we have visited or communicated with. Not one of those worlds has possessed even a hint of such a thing."

"You are saying you discovered something new to science?"

"Bugger science, this thing scares the shit out of me. We estimate the Sunna subjected it to a plasma pulse somewhere in the region of eight to nine thousand degrees in order to kill it. Every other living thing we have ever categorised would have been vapourised at a fraction of that temperature. Yet it barely killed this thing. Many of the cells you see here are relatively intact. They are burnt, their processes halted, but their cell walls did not rupture. That kind of hardiness is unheard of."

"You say it is impossible, yet here it is," I observed.

"That is what scares me."

"You think this is what attacked the Sunna?"

"Very likely. I suspect there are a great many of these things out there. Somewhere. Whatever happened on Sunna was quick, which means there were a lot of them. Hundreds of thousands, if not millions. A swarm."

"OK. This needs reporting to Admiralty Science. Keep working on it. I want to know if we can kill them. And if we can't, find a way. It's possible this swarm … as you put it … is visiting a number of planets and repeating what they did to the Sunna. We need to stop them."

"I'm not finished. Some of the genetic adaptation I discovered was Sunna."

"I'm not following you." That was happening a lot.

"I believe the entity can replicate a species when it comes into contact with it. Perhaps through some kind of consumption. Which in itself would be quite a feat. It clearly encountered more than one Sunna before it was killed, and learned to mimic them. It would be like your small intestine having the ability to read the genetic structure of your food, and to process that information so it could duplicate it later. Consciously. To the genetic level."

"So I could turn into a sandwich?"

He frowned at my flippant response. "So what if it comes across you, Captain? And decides to replicate your genetic structure. Would we even know?"

"Shit."

"Indeed."

"Definitely report that to the Admiralty."

"I doubt they will believe it. I have already used the term 'impossible' more than once. I wouldn't believe it myself if I hadn't seen it."

"So we need more proof?"

"We do. Ideally we need a live specimen, although I can't imagine how you would go about capturing one. I don't like this, Izzy. Whatever these things are they are working together. With a purpose. I doubt these were random attacks. There's something out here picking off planets and leaving no survivors to speak about it. They are remaining hidden. For now. That makes them incredibly dangerous. I think we can kill them as long as they don't make it aboard the ship. The *Cesa's* weapons would rip them apart. But if they do get aboard … how do you kill something that can withstand this kind of punishment with hand held weapons? Without killing all of us too? Can a hard-armour suit withstand that kind of temperature without killing the marine inside? Am I scaring you yet, Izzy?"

He knew me well enough to know I didn't panic and I didn't scare. I calculated the odds coldly, meticulously, and did what I needed to do to survive. What did I need to do here? "We need to destroy these things, Sorl'o. Please give your data to Ono with the instruction she is to find a way of defeating this organism on a hand-to-hand basis. Ideally without the use of hard-armour. We can't guarantee armour will be deployed when we encounter them next, and we need to be prepared. If fire won't work, how about poison? We have options, we need to explore them."

"I would need a live organism to test poisons. I can't do that with what I have."

"You know, Sorl'o, I get the feeling we're going to see more of these things. You might just get your specimen."

"I'd rather not." His image vanished. The doctor didn't do niceties.

I sat looking at the empty screen for a moment. I had wanted to know what could cleanse a planet of its population. Well, this was it. What had I been expecting?

Perhaps ignorance had been preferable.

We slowed as we approached Xon. No combat stops this time, we were going to ease our way in without alarming the locals. As much as a vessel of this size could.

As we slowed Sooch set our sensors to scanning what lay before us. We listened to the fizz of radio waves, the data plugged directly into Cena to decipher. Other sensors picked out the flare of drive flames, identifying in-system vessels cruising between one world and another. Yet more sensors scanned far deeper than that. They perused the warping of space itself, identifying anything that possessed more mass than a small family saloon. It was not a system anything with the Xon's level of technology could hide from. It could also peer inside planets themselves, identifying installations concealed beneath the surface. Although here it did have some limitations. It could not see much deeper than a few hundred metres into a planet's crust.

But that was enough.

It immediately became clear that this was a very strange place.

It was busy. There were vessels of all shapes and sizes moving within the system. The smallest was no larger than a personal shuttle, while the largest was as big as the asteroid ship we had encountered. There were thousands of them. Some cruising, their drives shut off, and so difficult to pick out in the blackness of space. Others were in a hurry, drive flames spearing the void. As we watched we saw dozens of conflicts break out. Short, sharp battles as groups of ships attacked lone stragglers. Quickly disabling them with flashes of laser light, before rushing in with what looked like claws to rip them apart. In moments the defenders were dismembered, the wreckage then quickly swept up by the attackers. Metal and composites netted and hauled aboard. It wasn't long before nothing remained to show the battle had ever taken place. The victors rocketing off in pursuit of their next prey.

"Pirates?" Sooch asked.

"No. Predators," I realised. I zoomed in on a small band and studied them. Each one was a mishmash of various technologies. As if their hulls had been tacked together from the wreckage of various other ships. These ships had not been designed and built in a manufactory. They had been welded together from the spoils of a hundred different battles. Ungainly and lopsided. So much so many crabbed sideways on their drive flame. Their drive systems off centre. No rational designer would build such a thing.

This whole system was in a permanent state of conflict. Everyone predating on everyone else. It was chaotic. A very dangerous place to be.

The situation on the planets was no better. Every world was occupied to some degree. Even the two gas giants hosted rings of stations and hundreds of smaller outposts. Many of the moons were disfigured, their surfaces riddled with disused or abandoned mines. The spoil from those adventures heaped up haphazardly, sometimes dumped right on top of previous excavations. None appeared to be active. Whatever minerals the locals had been after had been mined out long ago. It didn't mean the planets were abandoned, far from it. Their surfaces were crawling with activity. Settlements large and small. Each one armed and armoured. Each one apparently intent on destroying their neighbours. We saw flashes of light illuminating the darkened hemispheres of every world. Lasers lashing out, missiles slamming into defensive walls. Some of the settlements themselves seemed to be mobile. Dragging themselves across airless expanses to hurl themselves on their neighbours. Devouring the still sparking wreckage and leaving nothing behind to show they had ever existed.

Welcome to Xon.

"I believe I can discern a pattern," Cena said across the open band so we could all hear. "Every vessel and settlement appears to exhibit a sigil. A symbol to display their allegiance." A number of images appeared in the monitors, showing a variety of metallic symbols. Each was made of lengths of iron and steel welded together. Some were simple circles and crosses, others were more complex. Each was attached to a hull or displayed above a settlement. Identifying themselves to anyone within visual range. "I have identified thirty-five so far. Those showing the same symbol do not appear to attack each other. In fact I have seen various instances where two vessels belonging to the same clan either ignore each other, or join forces to attack a third. Whereas they will instantly attack a vessel showing an opposing symbol."

"The Xon are not united," Sooch commented. It wasn't unusual. If anything it was unusual for an uncontacted system to unite under one flag. There were always local differences that pulled people apart. "And they're at war with each other. Looks like we picked a great time to arrive."

"This is not a new conflict," Cena continued. "There are signs of old conflicts everywhere. There is no wreckage, because that is always consumed by the victor. But the planets and moons show a great many impact craters on their surfaces. Some appear to be very old."

"How old?" I asked.

"That is difficult to ascertain, Izzy. I would estimate in the region of one to two hundred thousand years."

"Shit. That can't be right."

Cena put an image before me. It was their fourth planet, their primary. A world hospitable to humans, even after all these years of conflict. The image flicked through a number of large craters. Some were flooded, others swamped by vegetation. All were heavily weathered, many barely identifiable as craters.

"These people have been killing each other for a long time," Tebercy commented. He had approached unnoticed as we studied the scene before us.

"I fear that is incorrect," Cena differed.

"There are no humans here," Sooch agreed. "There hasn't been for a long time."

"I can find no trace of human activity anywhere," Cena continued. "None of the vessels we see are crewed. They have no pressurised compartments. No sign of life support equipment. Many are also accelerating far beyond what a human could withstand. I do not believe the Xon possess internal stabilisation systems."

"We didn't see any humans on the asteroid ship either," Tebercy said. "No human would have blown themselves up like that. That was a machine thing. Only a machine would destroy itself out of spite. No offence, Cen."

"None taken, Commander. Technically a machine would calculate the odds according to its priorities, and act appropriately. It merely depends on what those priorities are."

"All human life was wiped out a long time ago," Tebercy said. "This is … this is what, Cen? The machines they left behind?"

"Exactly so. Before the human population perished they built autonomous machines. AI perhaps. Those machines outlived them and learned to continue without their presence."

"And they've been at war ever since," he agreed.

"It certainly appears that way," the AI agreed. "What we are seeing is a conflict over resources."

"But we are saying this system was populated at least two hundred thousand years ago?" Tebercy asked.

I shrugged. "Technically feasible. We have estimated four colonisation waves in this area. The first six hundred thousand years ago. The most recent sixty-five thousand years ago. This is certainly within the realm of possibility."

Human colonisation waves had ebbed and flowed through the galaxy for a long time. We didn't know for how long exactly, nor did we know where it all began. I know you believe humanity evolved on your world, and even have a lot of evidence to support that belief, but the chances of that are slim. A lot of worlds believe the same. Many have just as much evidence. No worlds remembered their original founding. Not one. Every world had been visited by calamity at some point in its history. Disease, war, natural disaster. Civilisation, such as it was at that time, inevitably fell. Memory of what came before was lost. Most worlds recovered, some did not. Some died completely. Most experienced that fall repeatedly over the millennia. It was almost inevitable. That was in itself one of the primary goals of the Confederacy. To stop the cycle of collapse and rebirth, and the pain and suffering caused when everything fell apart. Working together worlds could help each other, pooling resource and offering assistance when that calamity occurred. Together the cycle could be broken. We simply hadn't been around long enough to draw every world into our collective. We never would, and we understood that. Some simply did not want to join. That was their choice. We could ask them again in fifty thousand years.

It was difficult to determine when a region of space had been settled for the first time, simply because of that rise and fall. Science Division had been working on it for a long time, sending out archaeologists aboard the generation ships dispatched to explore the galaxy. We had a rough map now, but that was all.

This wasn't the first world where all humanity had perished. It also wasn't the first where only machines were left behind, eking out an existence in the ashes of the past. It certainly was one of the most successful though. I'd never seen this kind of activity in a system. It was sublime chaos.

"Can we identify which faction attacked us?" I asked Cena.

"I have been considering it," the machine responded. "Now that I know how they identify each other I have been reviewing sensor logs to determine whether they were displaying such an identity. I have found none as yet. I believe they were masking that identity."

"Do they do that here?"

"No. I have witnessed no instances of such deception."

"That asteroid ship was there for us," Sooch said. "And whoever ... whatever was in command of it knew it would draw us here. It didn't want us to know which party was responsible."

That was quite a claim, but as I considered it I knew it was correct. And alarming. Such a vessel represented a considerable investment in material. There weren't many of them around, and losing one would be a considerable loss to any of these factions. If that was what we could call them. Still, as Cena had stated, a machine thought in terms of benefit and loss. Whoever ... whatever sent it determined they would gain from it.

But gain what?

And how were we involved in that calculation?

I didn't like being played. And certainly not when it caused the deaths of so many of my people. It was then I determined we would find the culprit and ensure they paid dearly for it. The Xon could never be brought into the Confederacy. There was nothing in it for us, and certainly nothing in it for them. But we had to teach them that any action against us would be met with swift and determined retribution. That profit/loss calculation was about to be radically redrawn.

"Sid, head in-system please. Standard combat velocity. Sooch, bring the ship to combat alert status. Bring all interdiction systems on-line."

"So revenge it is, Captain?" Matte asked from her station.

"No, Commander. But if anything attacks us I intend on vaporising it."

"Which they will certainly do," she commented.

"That is, of course, their decision."

The *Cesa* picked up speed. We were six light hours out from the system's sun here in the outskirts. Hidden only by our distance from any Xon vessel or outpost and the vanishingly small likelihood any of them would look in our direction. As the cruiser leaped forwards that changed quickly. Nearing the inner system Matte reported that our sensors had started picking up the impact of communications lasers against our hull. That was how the machines talked here. Radio comms was present but it was not common, the flicker of laser light was the preference. It was also almost impossible to intercept without getting between the two parties who were talking to each other. The lasers tickling our hull were their way of saying: 'and who are you then?'

"Flash back," I instructed. "Standard greeting. And a warning. Any action taken against us will be considered an act of war and will be responded to."

Matte said something under her breath but complied. She was right. I was provoking them. There was no way they would heed the warning, and I didn't want them to.

As expected, they didn't.

"I have detected a group of vessels heading our way," Sooch said. "Twenty-one in total. They've engaged a high-G burn along our trajectory. They will meet up with us just before we reach the fourth planet."

"Are they a threat?"

"Ah, no."

"Let me know if anyone else is headed our way."

"Ah, Izzy. Someone else is headed our way."

"How many?"

"Well. All of them, I think. Just about every vessel this side of the sun has changed course to intercept."

"All of them?" Well, of course. We were a prize. Whichever party succeeded in taking our resources would become the preeminent power in this system. Benefit vs loss analysis. The risk was worth it.

Its difficult for a vessel the size of the *Cesa* to approach a system in an unthreatening manner. Particularly if we didn't want to take six months doing it. All the Xon would see was a giant vessel, speeding towards their home planet at an unreasonable velocity. Our hull glistened like a wet rock with our secondary interdiction systems engaged, creating a slippery field about ourselves. They would find their targeting systems unable to lock on, their rangefinders dazzled by the field. That was, of course, our intention. It wouldn't last, it never did. Sooner or later an enemy gave up and used line of site.

We were two minutes from their homeworld when the *Cesa's* alert system warbled. We were being fired upon.

"Miss," Sooch said. "Low yield plasma weapon. They're probably just probing."

Then there were flashes all around us. Lasers, grasers and missiles firing in our direction. It was a swarm. Hundreds of thousands of incoming attacks as if they had been choreographed. Which was impossible. There was no way the Xon were acting in concert.

"Some impacts. Still low yield," Sooch reported. "Engaging incoming missiles with secondary defences."

Light sizzled around the *Cesa*, recessed weapons systems tracking incoming missiles and firing. A wall of flame sheathed us as the interdiction system picked out incoming fire. Even though it was still hundreds of kilometres out it seemed like a continuous wall of detonations. Each missile vaporised at the same instant. The Xon tried hypervelocity weapons next. Slugs of iron travelling at significant percentages of the speed of light. But to us the speed of light was slow indeed. We picked them from the sky like flies swatted from the air on a hot summer's day.

"We're attracting a crowd," Sooch said, indicating a secondary swarm of vessels approaching. They were coming from everywhere. It was almost as if every vessel in the system was launching to take us on. The charge was led by the asteroid ships. Dozens of kilometres wide and protected by thick shells of rock the Xon hurled them at us with abandon. Smaller ships fell in behind, as if hoping to use them as shields.

"Keep those things away from us, Sooch. We saw what happened the last time one exploded."

"I know how to handle anti-matter." The weapons officer smiled grimly. "Cena, engage primary weapons system."

Anti-matter was only a problem if it encountered positive matter. The *Cesa's* primary weapon could ensure that never happened. At least not anywhere near here.

The drum shape of the heavy cruiser started transforming. Its flared stern growing wider. Spines protruded from the very rear of the ship, each one almost a hundred metres in diameter and over a kilometre long, further exaggerating the flare. When the *Cesa's* primary system was deployed, the ship's very hull became the weapon. Every centimetre of it contributing to a vast pulse of energy. A pulse that warped space itself, creating a gravitational field equal to the core of a neutron star. When it was unleashed it was like firing a singularity at an enemy at the speed of light. This kind of weapon was quite capable of ripping a hole clear through a planet. There were no vessels in either the Confederate or Shoei fleets that could withstand that kind of an assault.

This was what the *Cesa* had been built for. On its own surrounded by enemies. A very long way from any possible backup. Standing firm with amassed firepower directed towards it. Not conceding a millimetre. We were in our element.

Swarms of secondary interdiction drones were ejected moments before the sizzle of power coursing through the outer hull made any such launch impossible. The tiny vehicles, none larger than my fist, orbited the warship lazily, awaiting orders. Their drives sparkled as a few powered away, intersecting incoming ordnance. First in ones and twos. Then by the hundreds as the Xon continued their assault. They didn't seem concerned that their first, then second and then third waves failed. They had the numbers. We would run out of drones sooner or later. Or so they presumed. They didn't know about the auto factories labouring deep within the cruiser, dispatching replacements to the launchers faster than they could possibly be ejected. Only the interference from the primary weapons system kept them within the ship. Once that mechanism was finished with business they would be unleashed.

I know it's only in my imagination, but I felt the hairs stand up on the back of my neck as the system fired. We were far too deep within the ship here, behind too many metres of specialised insulation.

I don't really know how to describe the effect the weapon had on the closest asteroid ship. It was bigger than the one we had encountered in the Sunna system. Much bigger. So big I was amazed the Xon had the technology to make it move, never mind at the speed it was currently going. They had my respect for that alone. The gravitational vortex generated by the *Cesa's* primary weapon struck it dead centre. Then the imposing vessel seemed to blur around the edges. As if the sensors trained on it had suddenly become faulty.

A stream of matter surged from its stern as the discharge ripped straight through it, continuing out the other side. It clipped the small fleet of vessels that had been sheltering behind it. They disintegrated instantly, caught up in the torrent of energy. It all happened quickly after that. The asteroid ship seemed to fold in on itself. Collapsing inwards to contribute to the jet ripping through the vessel's innards.

This wasn't the way to stop matter and antimatter from connecting. If anything it was the exact opposite. But by the time it did the reaction was a long way from here, and continuing on its way out of the system at the speed of light. It was almost as if the jet of matter ignited. The stream condensing into a violent stream of plasma.

And then the vessel was no more. It was simply gone. Swept from the system like dust from a kitchen floor.

The *Cesa* turned to its next target. A smaller asteroid ship slightly further out. The weapon discharged again.

One of Cena's automatons delivered a tea to my station and I took it thankfully. Destruction was thirsty work.

Chapter 5

"Flash traffic from the Admiralty," Cena announced on a private band. "Eyes only. It is Lieutenant Admiral Chisholm."

That did come as a surprise. Chisholm was military intelligence. Not someone I expected to receive any kind of communication from. Never mind eyes only. "I'll take it in the CIC." I made my excuses and stepped into the combat information centre situated not far from my position. It was empty, which you may take as being odd. We were engaged in combat after all. This, if anything, revealed our contempt for the threat the Xon presented to us. We would gather here when we needed to formulate a strategy to engage an enemy. We didn't need strategy here.

"Put it up."

The holoboard in the centre of the chamber lit up, revealing the bald head of the admiral. She was a tiny woman from a high gravity world. Our communications were fast but we were far from the Admiralty here. Quick as they were they were not instantaneous, which was why this was a recording. She began speaking.

"Captain. This is a communication for your consumption only. It is not to be shared with your command crew. I invoke security protocol four."

I raised my eyebrows at that. As a ship captain I was privy to level eight. Someone was making an exception sharing any of this with me.

"Please signify your understanding," the image continued.

"I understand."

She didn't hesitate, almost as if he had expected my response. Still, my compliance was now on record. "The system designated as Xon contains an entity considered a significant threat to Confederate interests and wellbeing. Your ship AI will furnish the details, however your orders are to intercept that entity and to eliminate it. Under no circumstances are you to engage in communication with it. Your vessel and all residents of the system are considered expendable in this endeavour. Please indicate your understanding."

I did hesitate there. My ship and its crew were not expendable to me under my circumstances. How could I agree when I didn't even know what this threat was?

"Please indicate your understanding." She repeated. I did note she was not asking for my compliance. That was presumed.

What choice did I have?

"I understand."

"Communication ends." The admiral vanished.

I sat in one of the command positions. "Cen, please tell me what this is all about."

"The communication was appended with an additional brief," the AI said. "You have heard of the crystal entities, otherwise known as the Hauda?" Of course the ship AI was authorised to view this information. It likely held higher security clearance than I did.

I paused a moment. I had heard of them. As much as anyone had. A heretical branch of some long-forgotten civilisation. A people that sought immortality and omniscience. They had built the Hauda habitats, a string of vast ring worlds in the orbit of the Genii primary, the primary of an uninhabited and otherwise uninhabitable system. A refuge where they could practise their religion in peace. At least it had started that way. About fifteen hundred or so years ago they began exporting their religion. Pulling other worlds into it. Of course the confederacy could not allow that.

"The Hauda heretics translated their consciousness to crystal storage media. Media that were then installed into an android chassis. This effectively made them immortal. They became a threat to Confederate stability when they began recruiting converts in other systems. This caused rebellion on three Confederate worlds, and so the Third Fleet under Admiral Pleasance was dispatched to Genii to subdue them. The fleet was lost with all hands. It was never seen again and no wreckage has ever been found. It is presumed the Hauda subsumed them into their collective consciousness. Crystal translation – the process of placing a human consciousness into a crystal media – was banned, and the Sixth, Eighth and Twelfth fleets were dispatched to Hauda. All the habitats were burned and the Hauda themselves were hunted down. The incident became known as the Crystal Purge. The combined fleet did not go unscathed however. They lost a number of vessels in the engagement. The vessels becoming unresponsive prior to turning their weapons on their own comrades, forcing the remainder of the fleet to engage them. Each of the four vessels were lost. There were no survivors."

"Sounds like a mess."

"It was. The nature of the weapons the Hauda deployed was never determined. Some Hauda escaped the system and they have been hunted ever since. It is unknown how many perished in the subjugation of the system, however it is estimated to be in the region of two to three trillion."

"That's a lot." I knew as well as anyone what measures the Confederacy would take when it felt threatened. I had seen it before. I had never heard of casualties in the trillions before though.

"Do you feel conflicted?" The AI asked me.

I didn't have to wonder why. "Because of Dutchess."

"Yes."

"That was different."

"You were censured because of your involvement in that incident," Cena continued.

"I was given a dishonourable discharge from the marines," I agreed. But that was a long time ago, and I had earned my redemption since then. Still, I remembered the world of Dutchess well. I remembered the people and what we had done to them. Most, if not all of them had been innocent of any wrongdoing. Their circumstances had not been their doing, but rather caused by ancestors thousands of long years dead. They had perished because of it regardless.

"Do you feel conflicted?" The AI asked again.

"No," I said with a conviction I did not feel. "Explain why the Admiralty feels there is a Hauda presence in Xon."

"The official account of our first encounter with the Xon was a cover to conceal our real reason for entering the system. An expeditionary force had been pursuing a crystal entity into the system when it was engaged by Xon elements. Their disposition is unknown, but it is presumed to have survived contact with the Xon themselves. In fact it is possible it subsumed a number of them."

"Ah, I see." A lie then. "That was a long time ago. What makes the Admiralty believe it is still here?"

"At the time of the Purge the Hauda were not full members of the Confederacy. As such they were not given access to FTL technology. Which was why the crystal entity chose to seek refuge in this system rather than attempting to elude its pursuers."

"It couldn't run."

"Precisely."

"That was still eight hundred years ago. Even without FTL it could be a long way from here by now."

"It is believed the entity would have found a home in this system. It contains all it would require to thrive."

"Even though the Confederacy would no doubt return to eliminate it?"

"The Confederacy is a long way from here. There were two subsequent attempts to enter the system, using surveillance vehicles and drones, but both were prevented from discovering the whereabouts of the Hauda. As you have noticed the Xon do not like visitors."

That wasn't really evidence. "Presuming it is still here, how would we find it?"

"It has occurred to me the Hauda was likely responsible for the presence of the asteroid ship in Sunna-Deste-Anne. The entity would certainly understand the Confederacy well enough to know we would send a vessel to Sunna to investigate. A ship that could easily overwhelm the asteroidship, and then subsequently come here looking for an explanation. If not reprisal."

"You're reaching, Cena."

"There is a certain amount of supposition. Do you have an alternative?"

I didn't. "But why? Why would the Hauda wish to draw us here?"

"FTL. If the Xon is able to capture our vessel they could learn the technique of superluminal travel from it. It is a technology they would wish to learn."

It still felt like a reach. There was no guarantee the Xon could best a Confederate warship – of any class. Never mind the sort of vessel that would be stationed out here. "Even if it was behind it, we don't know which of the factions it is in league with."

"More supposition perhaps, but I suggest looking for the factions that are behaving differently. Perhaps those that do not engage us."

"Because we're expected."

"Yes. But Izzy, it will be difficult to prove the crystal entity is within the faction without direct evidence."

"You mean we'd have to get closer?"

"A lot closer. Perhaps visual inspection."

"Challenging."

"The admiral did not claim it would be otherwise."

I couldn't comment on that. She had not. Perhaps why we were expendable in this. Still, none of it explained why the Confederacy considered them such a threat. To extinguish that many lives required a great motivation indeed. Motivation I had only seen once, perhaps twice before. I thought I had understood it then. Understood, which didn't mean to say I approved. I certainly did not, but then no one had asked me.

Dutchess. A world clawing its way back to civilisation after a catastrophic natural disaster thousands of years in its past. It had almost made it too, before the outbreak of a virulent disease that had effectively ended all hopes of rebuilding. Jakes Madness it was called. An artificial contagion. One the Confederacy had seeded. I'd had a front row seat to the end of a burgeoning civilisation. All my attempts to save them only making it so very much worse. My actions there had brought me to a court martial and summary dismissal from the marines.

That had been my second experience at world ending. The first had been my own birth world. A world I knew nothing about, my own memory of it vague and lost in the past. I had been young when I was picked from the planet by the same people who sought to destroy it. No one had ever explained why we were singled out for destruction. But the Confederacy had seen something in us that it considered threatening to its new galactic order. And so we required culling.

Why I serve that same Confederacy now is ... complicated.

"Is there evidence of a faction not taking part?"

"I am still gathering data, but I have two factions that appear to have refrained. We will need someone to get closer to them to verify the Hauda's presence among them."

"Someone?"

"I believe they will engage any artificial probe we send close to their settlements. They may ignore a human's presence, as it would not be considered a threat to them."

That would be me then. It was going to be difficult convincing my crew I needed to be on such a mission. It wasn't the sort of thing ship's captains did.

"Keep looking." I'd have to think of something.

Chapter 6

The drop pod began peeling away as I passed through the upper atmosphere. Panels quivering before popping free and whipping away in the thickening air. They were still glowing an evil red from the aerobrake manoeuvre.

With a yank the last of the pod came loose and I was free.

Twenty thousand metres and dropping fast, the symbols in my field of vision informed me. I scanned around and saw my companions forming up behind. There were six of them, each an orange chevron in my field of vision. Seven marines to storm the belligerent world of Xon.

We'd dropped into the atmosphere over the night side of the planet with our initial insertion over the terminator. That was as close we could get to concealing our arrival. That and the fact that we certainly didn't look like machines.

This was going to be finely calculated. We wanted to get in fast and we didn't want to be noticed. Xon's skies were home to great flocks of birds, some bigger than we were. We were hoping to blend into their number. Of course there were no birds at twenty thousand metres, so we needed to descend fast. Equipped with little more than a wingsuit and a ghoscht it was going to be a quick descent indeed.

"I'd recommend banking slightly left," Cena said into my ear. She was piggybacking on the slim instrument concealed in the small of my back. It was a conduit I intended using to hack into the Xon mainframe. If they even had one.

I extended my arms, the suit catching the wind of my passage. The jerk of sudden deceleration took the breath from me but I held on. The programmable material of the suit thrummed loudly as it bucked, resisting my movements. Even though it was completely dark below I could see clearly. My light enhancing vision picking out trees and low hills. Superimposed over it was a dim icon. Our chosen landing field.

"Twenty seconds," Lieutenant Beyard said somewhere in the darkness above me. "Watch your EM signature." The latter a warning for her companions to engage their ghoschts only when entirely necessary. Knowing the company I kept that probably meant about two metres from the ground.

Her companions, each a member of Red Group, did not respond. They didn't need to. Red Group were marines assigned to protection duty within the naval spaces of the *Cesa*. They were our last line of defence against anything that could make it aboard the warship. Their number was traditionally drawn from the various special operations branches of the military. They were trained for this kind of thing.

I ignored the speed indicator that glowed in the corner of my vision. It really didn't matter as there was little I could do about it. The suit dramatically slowed my descent, but added considerable forward speed. If I landed using only the wingsuit it was the forward motion that would kill me, not the drop. Traditionally a wingsuit was used in tandem with a levitation harness. The device designed to arrest a glider's descent, allowing them to land safely. Such devices created massive EM signatures as they cupped the air like parachutes. Too great a signature. We simply could not afford it. There were machines on Xon predating on other machines. To go unnoticed we needed not to look like one.

We descended into the hills. Dark shapes flitting over the treetops far faster than any bird could fly. We held a loose formation, each marine twisting aside to avoid the taller trees before falling back in with the others. Apart from the fluting of straining wing suits we were silent.

I took a deep breath and held it as trees whipped past me. Our landing site was just ahead.

At the last moment I mustered all my strength and stalled, aiming back into the sky. The suit material stretched to its maximum extent, creating as much drag as possible. The sudden deceleration was a hammer blow. I grunted, almost blacking out. I activated my ghoscht, its protective fields wrapping around me. They gripped the ground beneath, bringing me to a sudden stop.

And then I was down, my boots thumping into grass. Hard. I staggered, steadying myself against the tree sapling I had most flown into. I heard whispers behind me. Ghoscht fields cushioning the marines as they came to ground.

"Shit. How did you do that?" I heard Lieutenant Beyard move in beside me. A darker shadow amongst others. She and her companions had used their ghoschts as parachutes, shaping their fields to trap air beneath themselves as they came in. A softer landing certainly, but a greater electromagnetic signature. "I've never seen that before." She cleared her throat. "Sorry, Captain."

"Not my first time, Lieutenant." Although I was regretting it. My shoulders felt as if a giant hand had tried to rip my arms from their sockets. And despite my impact resistant boots my ankles hurt. A lot.

I heard muttered from the other marines behind me. Perhaps I had just been showing off. Still, the smaller the EM footprint we had the better off we were. Mine was already too big with Cena's interface attached to me. I didn't want it getting any bigger. Still, a broken neck wouldn't have helped me either.

We stripped off the helmets and suits and checked our equipment in silence. Beneath the wingsuit each of us wore a passive chameleon suit, the material using our own body heat as an energy source to adjust its shading according to our environment. It wasn't perfect, no passive system could be. But if we remained motionless it was surprisingly effective in blending us into our environment. A trained eye would see us. An unsuspecting one wouldn't. Its secondary benefit was that, in using our body heat to power itself, that body heat was dissipated. Making us difficult to see in IR.

Metal was as dangerous as EM on this mission, so we carried as little as possible. Each marine carried a heavily modified carbine, extruded from *Cesa's* manufactories barely an hour earlier. The weapons were built from ceramic and carbon composite. The projectiles themselves caseless 9mm fluorocarbon resin. We carried them only because the marines had refused to go on the mission unarmed. Still, if we had cause to fire a single shot it would all be over. We were outmatched down here. Only stealth would keep us alive. I carried a carbon fibre knife strapped to my leg. That was all I needed.

It had not been easy convincing the crew I needed to be on this mission. It was unusual for a captain to risk their lives like this. Particularly as I couldn't tell them the real reason for it. In the end Cena and I settled on pointing out the reason for this mission was to learn what the Xon knew. Of course we wanted to know why they had attacked us. I still wanted answers to that. And justice. But that was not all. I needed to know how they were aware of the attack on Sunna-Deste-Anne decades before it happened. They had been forewarned. But how? And by whom? This was not information they would give to us freely and so we had to take it by force. Of course I suspected the Hauda might have had a hand in it, but I couldn't say that. After intercepting comms chatter between faction members Cena was confident she could communicate with them, even that she could co-opt one of their processor cores, where we hoped this information would be stored. But, and this was the challenge, she needed a hard wired connection to do so. Hence the instrument I was carrying.

That was the easy part. Any of the marines could make their way into a faction compound and link it to their processor core. But there was a snag. In order to keep the machine parts of the device to a minimum the only solution was to integrate it with cerebral implants. Implants that had the capacity to handle the data heavy processes it demanded. There were not many of those around, in fact they were limited to bridge officers. Not ideal, but there it was. We didn't want to take the time installing such a thing into a marine, so only one of my bridge crew – or I – could make the mission work. While there was considerable resistance to the notion of me taking part the logic was undeniable. I had far more actual feet-on-the-ground combat experience than any of them. And that included Tenua herself.

There was one final reason and it was entirely selfish. I wanted to be here. I wanted to confront the bastard AI that had attacked us. I wanted it to know I would crush it for what it had done to us. I wanted to be there in that moment when it made the fateful calculation, realising it had bitten off more than it could chew. And it would pay dearly for it.

And so here I was. On this warm, humid night, in inky darkness, listening to the faint rustling of who knew what kinds of creatures in the undergrowth.

"I can detect no Xon activity nearby," Cena reported. We had left a stealthed drone overhead, the lightly armed machine hovering on the edge of the atmosphere, sufficient to cause little more than a distraction should we be discovered, allowing us to escape unnoticed. Hopefully. A MAV and an extraction team were on standby. They could be here in little under two minutes.

If we needed any of it our mission had failed. Going unnoticed gave us our only chance.

We hadn't been observing the Xon homeworld long, perhaps five or six hours in total. Still, Cena had witnessed dozens of interactions between machine intelligence and native fauna on the planet. There was a lot of both. There were machine encampments dotted everywhere, from dusty desert to icy tundra. Few were very large, and most looked ready to pick up and move on at short notice. I imagine staying mobile was what kept them relatively safe from the other factions. There was no mining activity anywhere. The planet had been mined out a very long time ago. Much of the subsurface was riddled. Many of the caverns closer to the surface collapsed, creating massive basins that had flooded long ago. Deeper stopes crept to within kilometres of molten mantle. Some had even breached it, allowing magma to flood the passages. I had seen mined out worlds before but none were this extreme. None showed quite as flagrant a disregard for the environment. Still, it was disregard, not an active destruction. The Xon simply ignored everything that was either unthreatening or of no value to them. Which applied to the abundant fauna on the planet. Great flocks of birds dominated the skies, just as herds of herbivores dominated the plains. Sea life was even more abundant, the Xon rarely venturing beneath the waves. Once they had harvested all the marine minerals they were interested in there was nothing for them there.

It was that disinterest we were taking advantage of. We hoped to approach a base, and perhaps even enter it, without being noticed. The Xon ignoring us because we were not machines. They hadn't seen a human in a very long time. The chance of a local node recognising us was slim.

That was the plan anyway.

There was a bright flash just above the eastern horizon. Something had blown up rather spectacularly. Clearly the locals were still trying to find a way of defeating the *Cesa*. The warship had already destroyed roughly a tenth of all space going vehicles in this part of the system, Sooch had estimated. It would be a lot more than that by the time we left. Matte observed that our very presence was affecting the balance of power. There were regulations against doing that kind of thing, but I didn't care. The Xon had created this situation. They would learn the Confederacy was not to be trifled with.

There was another flash, smaller this time. Almost completely obscured by low clouds. Combat in space is a strange thing to watch. It is almost always a long way away. It was always silent.

The Xon all-out assault had petered out, replaced by probing attacks. Each one slightly different to the last. They were trying to find a way though our defences, apparently indifferent to how many vessels they would lose doing it. They were apparently still working together. Perhaps, after millennia of internal strife, it had taken our arrival to unite the factions.

Still, there were patterns in all of this. We started seeing it as the swarms took shelter behind the last of the asteroid ships, and those behemoths changed course to idly orbit the *Cesa* instead of charging in to attack. But more than that, of the alliance set against us there were factions missing. Factions that had refrained from taking part. It didn't feel that way. It certainly felt like every ship in the system was aligned against us, but they weren't. Two of the identifying symbols Cena had categorised were missing from the fleet. The first was two circles looking for all the world like a smaller circle peeping out from behind the larger one. We'd started calling it 'Sunrise'. Second was an odd set of overlaid hashes. We called that the 'Dophant', after a children's game some of the bridge crew had played in their youth. I'd never heard of it personally. Those two symbols were missing from the massed fleet. We knew they had vessels, and a great many of them. Cena had counted at least a hundred belonging to each faction while we were still outside the system. Now few were to be seen. And those seemed content to continue their usual patrols far from here.

Conspicuously absent, Sooch had commented.

Perhaps those factions knew something. We might learn a lot by talking to them.

It had taken hours to decide how we'd go about doing that. First we had to understand how the factions operated. Were they a loose collection of individual machine minds, or were they controlled by some central intelligence? The discovery of what appeared to be processor nodes on the Xon homeworld answered that question. The outposts there appeared to be giving commands to the individual machines around them. They were also drawing a lot of power and were heavily armed. They were clearly important installations.

So the decision was made.

None of my companions knew why we were really here. None knew there might be an ancient enemy hiding amongst the Xon. An entity quite adept at overwhelming Confederate forces. If we did find a Hauda here they would know soon enough, but at least it wouldn't have been because I broke protocol.

"We're picking up motion," Beyard said from somewhere in the gloom nearby.

"IR?"

She was silent a moment. "Some. Looks like a troop of arboreals in the trees. They're watching us."

"They a threat?"

"No. They're tiny."

"Then relax, Lieutenant." I scanned around myself, catching the dim glow of heat in the branches high above. All I could see were eyes as the tiny creatures peered around branches to study us. There were about thirty of them. They were curious, that was all. They hadn't seen a human in a very long time indeed. We had vanished from their racial memory.

"No evidence of Xon patrols," the lieutenant continued.

"Then let's go."

Six shadows moved in around me, keeping me at the centre of the formation. Someone had given the lieutenant strict instructions to keep me safe. I didn't care, as long as they didn't get in my way. I could see them clearly, my enhanced vision picking them out against the gloom. Each glanced in my direction from time to time as we jogged quickly through the trees, keeping me in sight. It was annoying but I didn't comment. They had a job to do, that was all.

"Closest Xon presence two kilometres. Seventy-five degrees," Cena reported in my ear. "It's moving away. You have not been detected."

"What is it?"

"A patrol of some kind. A land-based drone. Bipedal. Sixty kilograms. I am not detecting any weaponry or wireless communications systems."

"Crude."

"It works."

I could not argue with that. "How far to the base?"

"Twenty-three kilometres. Over this topography it will take approximately eighteen hours to traverse."

I didn't comment, keeping my attention on the forest ahead of me. The undergrowth had been cleared out, possibly by a herd of herbivores that frequented the area. There was no sign of any of them now. It made the going easier, at least until we hit the grasslands beyond.

Just as I thought it we came to the edge of the forest. We paused, scanning the plain ahead of us. It was a good kilometre until the next cover and going around was not an option, that would add another four kilometres to our route and include a gorge running along the edge of a vast depression to our east. The site of some collapsed mine workings, we guessed. A very large mine.

"There are four Xon patrol units in this space," Cena reported.

"Let me see."

An image appeared in my vision. It was a strange, leggy contraption. A rugged, almost spherical body with three long legs jutting out beneath it. A handful of sensors were attached almost haphazardly over its carapace, each one on a swivel, each one glancing this way and that. The machine was moving constantly, its gait strange and oddly economical. Its unjointed legs were rigidly extended, the machine moving by whirling like a ballerina. Its surprisingly smooth gait keeping its sensors in the clear above the tallest grass. The sensors themselves set on gimbals to remain steady as its main body spun beneath. I didn't see any weapons or comms antennae. These were just scout drones and the Xon didn't want any of their enemies overhearing electronic comms. This machine would have to turn around and lope back to base to report in if it ever came across anything.

"Options."

"Avoiding them would be a challenge. Their patrol pattern appears quite effective. You could go around. Alternately you could destroy two of them."

"Two?"

"Yes," the machine responded. "That would create a gap in their patrol area large enough for you to pass through unnoticed."

"I'm not really looking to attract attention to ourselves just yet. If another sentry notices a missing counterpart they're likely to report that back to base."

"The only other alternative is to test the hypothesis the machines don't pay attention to organics."

"So we should let them see us." I was nervous but it made sense. We would not remain undetected all the way to the base. We weren't trying to. Rather we were relying on Sunrise not caring. It was probably best testing that assumption now while we were far enough away to affect an escape. Closer in there would be a higher machine presence and our retreat might be cut off.

"Yes," was all Cena said.

I turned to the lieutenant. She was squatting a few metres away, cradling her carbine as she surveyed the grassland. She could see as well as I in the gloom of early morning. Dawn was still an hour or so away. She spoke in hushed tones before I could say anything.

"This would be a good opportunity to test your theory."

"It would."

She nodded, cleared her throat, and stood. "Come on then, people. Forwards. Weapons down. Let's not take any risks. Be ready to fire though."

We stepped from cover with a confidence we didn't feel. Pushing through the long grass we headed for the centre of the clearing.

"It's a nice day for it, Captain," Beyard said. "We don't get off ship very often. Just getting outside almost makes all of this worth it."

She was right. I hadn't really been paying attention to the weather. The air was still, the skies clear. We weren't far from the Olifunt Nebula here. The glowing streamers of gas, lit from within by a hatchery of new stars, was settling towards the eastern horizon. With no pollution to speak of the atmosphere was crystal clear. Allowing a dazzling view of the nebula itself, and the galactic lens that lay beyond it. Quite a view. We didn't have the time to spend admiring it.

I could hear insects chirping above the sound of our passage through the long grass. This could almost be a pleasant stroll in the countryside.

"Predator. A mammal of some kind," Cena reported. "Sixty metres to your left. It doesn't appear to have noticed you."

If anything local predators could more of a problem than the Xon themselves. They would have lost their fear of humans a long time ago. Now we were simply potential prey. I asked the AI to keep a watch on it and promptly forgot about it.

"They haven't seen us yet," the lieutenant said as we neared the centre of the clearing. The machines were still dancing around the periphery, their strange whirling skitter taking them quickly through the tree line.

"Oh, they've seen us all right," I said. "One has broken away and headed to the east. That's not in the direction of the settlement though. Cena, what's out there?"

"I'm checking." The AI was silent a moment as the Cesa's scanners focussed on the machine's path. "I believe I have found its objective. It appears to be some kind of relay station. I'm picking up electrical activity, but no communications."

"It might use some kind of messenger system," the lieutenant said. "Sending out bots of its own to report in." I had to say, I was impressed the lieutenant was often seconds behind the Cesa's AI in her observations. Even though she didn't have a surveillance drone overhead. I couldn't say I knew her very well. I'd met all of the Cesa's officers, and most of the rest of the crew, but I had not worked with her before. She was worth keeping an eye on.

"Or they use LOS," I suggested. "That would make sense in this environment." Line Of Sight communications were usually in the form of lasers fired between stations that had a clear view of each other. No outsider would be able to tap into their network, and we'd seen the Xon using similar systems before. Their ships tended to use it, pinging lasers off each other rather than relying on clumsy wireless communications that could be intercepted. "Let's keep on going and see what happens. How long do we have?"

"The drone will report in in approximately two minutes. It is difficult to judge after that. It would depend on the Xon being able to make sense out of the data. The drone did get a clear view of you as you entered the clearing, but it's hard to say how it interpreted what it saw. You are using chameleonware, after all."

"Let me know the moment you spot any activity."

I paused to survey the forest that besieged the clearing. A row of hills to our east climbed up into a mountain range on the horizon. There might even have been a touch of snow on their higher reaches. A beautiful world. I couldn't imagine what had happened here. This had once been the home to humanity. A civilisation that, as far as we could tell, had ventured into space and was exploring the other planets in the system before catastrophe struck. We didn't know what form that cataclysm had taken, or whether the machines themselves had been involved. We knew nothing about that event at all. All evidence had long been scrubbed from the record by machine activity. There was no trace of the local humans venturing to other systems either, so we knew they had never reached that far. Still, it did mean were several billion people on this world alone. People who may or may not have known about civilisations on other worlds. People who were now dead. Utterly extinguished. Their language and culture lost long ago. Their cities scrubbed from the face of the planet by machines who were only interested in harvesting the materials they found there.

We didn't even know what they had called themselves. Xon was a name we called them. Or, to be more precise, what the people of Sunna-Deste-Anne had called them. Before they themselves were extinguished. It meant insensible, or insensate in their tongue, or something along those lines. It seems they had encountered Xon drones at some point, who had paid them little or no attention.

"The drone has reported in and is on its way back to its designated patrol area," Cena said. "I am not detecting any changes in local Xon activity."

"Well, they've seen us and don't seem to care," I said.

"One of the other drones is headed directly towards you. Suggest you hold your ground."

I held up a hand to stop our advance. The tree line was fifty or sixty metres ahead of us. Tantalisingly close. It wasn't worth running for it. I had seen how these things moved. They were quick. A lot quicker than we were. We had the advantage in heavy foliage as their strange gait needed a lot of room. Room they didn't have in the trees. Still, we couldn't stay in the forest. These machines would always be out there, waiting for us the moment we stepped out again.

"Weapons down," the lieutenant warned as she saw motion from one of her marines. "Don't give it an excuse."

I heard whispering through the long grass as the machine approached. It didn't stop, preferring to roll around us quickly, its sensor package aiming directly at us, the glassy lenses twitching as they scanned each of us in turn.

Feeling exposed my hand itched for a weapon. For something to fire should the machine do anything threatening. Perhaps why I hadn't brought one. The temptation to use it was simply too great.

With a thump the machine stopped. One splayed leg moving out of sync with the others to arrest its forward momentum. The spindly machine swayed for a moment before standing still, its sensors continuing to study us. It was directly between us and the tree line. Perhaps five metres from the closest of us.

"It has no weapons," I reminded the marines. "It just wants to have a good look at us."

Much of its carapace was a dull white. Not paint, I thought - as why would a machine bother with such niceties? But rather it was constructed of a pale material. It didn't look like metal or plastic. Ceramic then? Metals were precious and so not to be wasted where they were unnecessary, so it made sense.

"I can smell it. Can you smell it?" Beyard said.

I could. It was the smell of burned plastic. I could hear it too. An almost subsonic buzzing.

"Not the kind of machine we would make," one of the marines commented. It certainly was not.

And with that it was gone. There was another thump as it kick-started its roll. It moved unsteadily at first until it reached cruise speed, and then it seemed to gain its balance. Within moments we were alone again, the probe inspecting something else in the clearing.

"What was all that about?" Beyard asked.

I shrugged. "Doesn't matter. Keep going."

It was a relief being back under the trees. The weird machines couldn't follow us here.

"The first probe has returned," Cena said presently. "It has re-joined its patrol route. I'm still not detecting any changes in Xon activity."

"That's either a good thing, or a very very bad thing," I commented aloud.

"Captain?" Beyard couldn't hear Cena's voice in my ear.

"The Xon either don't care we're here, or they are expecting us," I said.

"I'm not sure I like that thought."

I didn't either.

As we moved through the trees it became clear how truly old this world was. We stumbled across the ruins of a city just as the sun broached the horizon. The structures all but invisible from the air with their carpet of foliage crawling up their sides and taking up residence on their roofs. From the ground they were unmistakable though. Wide plazas and avenues led away to the west of us as we passed through its outskirts. Whoever this lost civilisation had belonged to they were certainly grandiose. The structures were tall, crumbling roofs held aloft by cracked and weather-stained columns. The entrances we could see were all tall enough to admit giants into the dark, unknowable depths. Some of the buildings had crumbled completely, now nothing more than mounds of stone obscured by trees and brambles.

Our passage frightened a herd of herbivores. The skittered out of the depths of a building as they galloped off, emitting an eery moaning call of alarm as they went.

"There were people here once," I said. "Before the machines took over."

"Do we know what happened to them?" one of the marines behind me asked. Corporal Sanquey.

"No. We're the first to land on the planet."

"Perhaps we should stop and have a look around," he continued. "We might learn something."

"I'd prefer to stick to the mission at hand," I said. "We'll report this back to Admiralty Science. They might send a team."

"Do we at least know how long ago they abandoned the place?"

I shook my head, watching the herd as it vanished amongst the buildings. "Guesses only, based on Xon activity in the system. We believe the machines have been active between seventy five and a hundred thousand years. All this might predate that."

"They were certainly human," Beyard observed as another of the marines pulled aside some vines, revealing a very weather-beaten statue. It might have been human – once. Its features were almost worn away completely.

"They were pretty advanced, then," Sanquey said. "For these buildings to last this long."

I might have raised an eyebrow as I glanced in his direction. Noticing it he smiled and shrugged.

"Did a couple of semesters of xenoarchaeology in college."

"Ah. We should continue. I want to spend as little time on this planet as possible."

"Wait a moment, Captain. I'm picking up EM from a nearby structure," Cena said.

I held up a hand to stop the marines where they were. "Which one?"

"To your left. Fifty metres."

I studied the structure. It looked almost new, at least in comparison to the tumbling ruins around it. It was a simple affair, a plain oblong constructed from some kind of clay material. It looked like a bunker. No windows and just the one door. A simple dark oblong that led to unknown depths. Its immediate proximity had been swept clear of the rubble that seemed to strangle the rest of the city. As if someone has taken the time to clear it up. It didn't look like it belonged here, amongst the giant architecture about it. Still, it was ancient. Trees had taken root in its sides and roof, their roots digging through the plain material it had been built from.

"The city was in use some time after it fell into ruin," Cena continued. "I have identified a number of paths cleared through the rubble. They are overgrown now and some have been covered over by subsequent mudslides, but they were obviously well used at one time. Some appear to lead to what may have been fields. There are a number of areas within the city that have been cleared of rubble, creating what I can only take to be arable land. No one has grown crops there in a long time however."

"How long?"

"Even by analysing the rate of vegetation growth it would be impossible to say. The forest reclaimed the land a long time ago. It was certainly not recently."

"That building is Xon," Beyard said. "The rest of this place ... isn't."

"Is it possible the Xon maintained a captive population of humans for a time?" I asked the AI.

"Possible certainly. I have no data."

"But you're picking up electromagnetic activity within?"

"Yes. It is not very strong. Potentially a unit left on standby."

"We should have a look, Captain." Beyard said.

"It is not our objective."

"I'm not sure I'm comfortable leaving an unknown quantity to our rear. We will need to exit in this direction," the marine continued.

She was right. This could be an ambush unit left here to approach us from our rear. Or at least to cut off an avenue of escape. We were taking too many risks in this mission already, there was no point taking any more. The Xon might not care about our presence here, but the Hauda would.

"OK. Carefully. Two units inside, the rest remain outside. Keep in touch."

"Sanquey, C'gen. In you go." The lieutenant indicated two nearby marines.

Checking their weapons quickly they trotted forwards. Both dropped light enhancing goggles down over their eyes before stepping quickly inside. They vanished abruptly into the darkness within. The rest of the squad took up positions outside, scanning the undergrowth around us for movement.

"Not much inside," one of the marines said over comms. "Small chamber. Ten to fifteen metres on a side. It's been flooded at some point in the past, there's soil up against the walls. There's a few doorways leading further in. Hold on." We heard grunting as the two got down onto their knees and squeezed through the gap.

"Any other EM in the area?" I asked Cena.

"None," the AI reported. "The closest surveillance drones are over a kilometre away."

"Don't you think this is strange? This is a substantial installation. It should be better protected than this." I had studied the Xon city we had chosen as our objective from space. It was one of the largest, if not the largest, establishments on the planet. Bearing in mind the Xon were in a state of perpetual conflict with their neighbours it was surprising there were so few patrols out here.

"You are thinking like a marine. Like a human," Cena said. "The Xon will respond to perceived threats. If it is not deploying more assets out here it is because it considers itself safe. Or at least it is unlikely an enemy will approach overland as you are."

"Surely another faction will recognise the gap in its defences and exploit it."

"You are presuming they are able to exploit it. It is possible they do not possess the units to approach unseen. I have not scanned all installations on this planet, but of those I have surveyed none possess ground attack vehicles. The factions seem to prefer aircraft and space-based assets."

"This feels like a trap," I said, thankful only the AI could hear me. A trap I had walked us into.

"The logic behind your mission was sound, and remains so," Cena assured me. "It is also necessary."

We'd see.

"Just more chambers," the second marine commented. C'gen.

"I'm picking up a source of light ahead," Sanquey said. "Hold on a moment."

We waited, listening to laboured breathing as the two squeezed through narrow gaps, rubble and soil piled up almost to the ceiling.

"I have a surveillance asset approaching your position. It's six hundred metres out. It'll be near you in four minutes," Cena reported.

"You said we were in the clear?"

"A picket has turned around. It appears to be headed directly for you."

I cursed under my breath. "OK everyone. Inside. No firing please. We don't want them to know we're here."

"Like me to recall them?" Beyard asked me, indicating the two marines deeper in the structure.

"No. Just be careful."

We stepped into darkness, concealing ourselves within the low building. The air was heavy with the stench of decay. Something had died in here, and recently. I couldn't see any animal remains though.

"Comms for emergency only," I continued.

Beyard hunkered down just within the entrance, scanning the trees outside, her weapon at the ready.

"One minute," Cena continued. Her comms frequency was unlikely to be picked up by the Xon. It wasn't a kind of technology they possessed.

"What kind of unit is it?" I asked as I tapped the lieutenant on a shoulder and held up one finger as she looked back. She nodded and returned her attention to the approaches.

An image appeared in my field of vision. It was a squat, four-legged machine. A lot larger than those we had seen before. "It appears to be both armoured and armed," the AI informed me.

"You said the factions didn't possess ground attack vehicles."

"I doubt that is what this is. It appears to be some kind of heavy patrol drone. I am picking up comms, so it is in contact with the installation. It received a radio burst just before it changed direction."

"Did Sunrise instruct it to come looking for us?"

"Unknown. I have deciphered their comms, but there was little to it. It was a simple instruction to survey this vicinity. No mention was made of you or your squad."

The machine stepped into view outside. It was an ugly contraption, its carapace tarnished and completely missing in parts, revealing the tangled guts of its inner workings. As big as a horse it crashed through the undergrowth to come to a stop a few metres away. It didn't have a head as such, rather there was a blocky array of sensors and antennae in the centre of its back. The sensors themselves clicked this way and that, taking in everything about it.

I could smell it, I realised. An acrid stench, like burned rubber. If all of their drones smelled this bad their city must be unbearable.

"I doubt it can pick any EM up from you," Cena said. "Its sensors are not sensitive enough. If you keep quiet it will go away."

"Sunrise isn't supposed to care about us," I said. "We're not machines."

"I don't believe the Xon do. It has been so long since humans lived on this planet they won't consider you a threat."

"What about the Hauda? If there is one here it will care about us. And who knows what level of control it has here."

"Which is why it would be best not to be seen by this unit just yet. This probe was sent to your vicinity, we need to understand why before you reveal yourselves. There are too many unknowns here. We don't know if there is a crystal entity in this system. And if there is, where it is located and which of the factions it is influencing – if any. And if so, how. However, you are exposed where you are. It is not worth taking unnecessary risks."

I watched as the machine engaged in searching the undergrowth, its sensors still swivelling this way and that. Clumsy, or careless, as it was, it simply trampled most of the trees and bushes that impeded its progress.

"How old would you say a machine like this is?" I asked the AI.

"Difficult to judge. It has clearly seen a considerable amount of wear. Sufficient to knock off many of its coverings. I can also see a number of repairs to its chassis and sub-systems. If I were to guess I would say anywhere between one to two thousand years old."

That was old for a machine like this. Xon technology had clearly stagnated. In all that time it hadn't found a better way of building these things. It was possible technology hadn't moved on since humanity vanished from this system. As good as they were, the Xon AI's were not clever enough to improve on pre-existing designs.

"Does Sunrise possess any differentiated technologies? If not technologies themselves, then strategies."

"You mean like sending asteroid ships to Sunna?"

"Touché."

"You are thinking Sunrise may have learned something from the Hauda? Once again, difficult to judge. Once a technique is employed by one faction it will only be a matter of time before the others incorporate it also. If a vessel boasting such an improvement is captured the other factions will learn from it and incorporate it themselves. That said, their drives are more efficient than those used by other factions. There is only a few percentage points in it but it is distinctive."

"Suggesting the Hauda is with Sunrise after all."

"Possibly."

"And as this is one of, if not the, preeminent Sunrise establishment it is likely the Hauda is based here."

"The probability is low. But I would note no other location has a higher probability."

That was all we had. Guesses. It didn't sit well with me.

"There's movement in here," a voice said over comms. It sounded like Sanquey.

"What are we looking at? Local fauna?" Beyard asked.

There was a pause. "I don't know. Part of the ceiling has caved in. There's a pool of water beneath it. Looks pretty deep. There's something moving in it." C'gen said.

"It's big," Sanquey added.

"Leave it be and head back here," the lieutenant instructed.

"It could be the EM source we picked up," I said.

She shrugged. "It's up to you."

"Stay there for the moment. I'm coming to you."

"Sure, Izzy. We're about twenty metres due west of your position. Watch out for cave-ins. This roof is unstable."

I waved away the lieutenant's carbine as she offered it to me. "You'll probably need that more than me."

The corporal was right. A flood had brought a lot of debris into this structure at some time in the past. Dirt was piled up almost to the ceiling in places. In others the ceiling itself was cracked, allowing beams of sunlight into the gloom. Along with the roots of trees and foliage that had taken over the structure's upper surface.

"Have you figured out what this place is?" I asked.

"Reminds me of where I grew up," C'gen commented. "It is laid out like an orphanage."

I'd grown up in an orphanage too, and I immediately saw what she meant. The internal structure was laid out like a barracks. Long, narrow chambers on each side of a wide passageway. Quarters for the men and women, and likely children, who had once lived here. Or a concentration camp, I realised.

People had once been imprisoned here. Held captive by machines. I couldn't say how many there had been. Hundreds, thousands. Prisoners. Slaves?

I pushed the thought aside. As distasteful as it was it was long over. Whatever had happened here had been consigned to the distant past. I couldn't change it now.

There was a wide, square space in the centre of the structure. Part of the roof had collapsed, allowing in achingly bright sunlight. It shone down on a pool that had gathered beneath it. The water was dark and looked deep. It was roiling slightly, as if something was moving within its depths. The two marines had taken up position nearby, watching the pool.

"Have you seen anything at all?" I asked as I approached. The floor was still covered with silt, but there was at least headroom, allowing me to stand upright.

"No. just that," Sanquey pointed. "You reckon there's fish in there?"

"Could be. Something is causing the EM signature though."

"I can confirm the signature is in your immediate vicinity," Cena said in my ear. "It has risen considerably since the marines entered the chamber."

"Something waking up?"

"Perhaps."

"Here. Try this." Sanquey picked a pebble from the dirt alongside and tossed it into the water. With a plop it disappeared into the depths.

"Try something bigger," C'gen suggested.

"No. Don't," I stopped him.

"EM is spiking," Cena said.

"You might want to back up a bit. Whatever it is is waking up," I warned.

A dark shape moved beneath the surface. It was almost black. As black as the water itself. The surface seemed to bulge as it protruded from the water. There were two knots in the smooth skin, one on each side. Yellow eyes regarded the marine coldly.

"What the hell is it?" Sanquey stepped closer to have a good look.

"What's going on in there?" Beyard demanded. "The drone is suddenly very interested in this building."

"Step back," Corporal," I instructed.

He may have retreated half a pace, but was still leaning forward to have a good look. "It looks like some kind of frog. Or toad."

"A bloody big frog," C'gen commented. Just what we could see of it was about a metre wide by itself.

"It's just watching us," Sanquey said.

"EM from a frog? Is there anything else down there?" I asked.

"I'll have a look." Sanquey picked a branch from the ground that had fallen through the gap in the roof.

"The EM source appears to be the creature," Cena said. "I'm taking it to be some kind of bio mechanical construct."

"That makes it dangerous."

"It would be dangerous anyway. Remember, frogs are carnivores. Something of that size will hunt large prey."

"Shit. Sanquey, get away from that thing," I instructed.

The marine was poking the creature with the branch. He pushed it back under the surface, only for it to re-emerge when he took the branch away.

"What is this thi-"

It was fast. Far faster than I would have given it credit for. In a surge of water the creature leaped, a wide, flat mouth taking in much of the branch and Sanquey's arm up to the elbow. I heard bone and branch crack as the jaws snapped closed. With a heave it dove back under the inky surface.

With a squawk the marine went with it. The last we saw of him was his boots disappearing under the surface.

I didn't think. I didn't need to. Ignoring the shouts of alarm from my comrades I dove after the submerging creature. The sudden cold of the water was a shock. I ignored it too, my senses scanning the dark space I found myself in, trying to see where the creature had taken Sanquey. Cena enhanced my vision, revealing the space in a strange green glow.

It was a pipe system of sorts. I could see openings leading further in, all cast in gloom. The creature was settling to the silted-up floor, shaking the beleaguered marine in its jaws. He was beating at it with his free hand. His carbine had slipped from his shoulder to settle to the mud below.

With a kick I swam over and grappled with the frog-like creature. Its skin was cold and slippery, making it almost impossible to get a grip on. Damn, its jaws were strong. It wasn't letting go.

"Its eyes," Cena suggested.

I dug a thumb into its closest bulbous eye. I felt the eyeball pop, slime gushing out over my hand. The frog twisted, trying to shake me off. It stubbornly refused to let go of the marine.

"It's not working." I could taste the marine's blood in the water. The bite had almost severed his arm. Blood was gushing from an artery.

"How do I kill this thing?"

"Base of its skull. Sever the spine," the AI suggested.

I couldn't get purchase on the slick, rubbery skin. The creature bucked, knocking me against a hard wall. My head slammed into stone and I almost dropped the knife.

"Quickly, Izzy," the AI implored.

Powerful legs drove the beast further into the maze of tubes, a now limp marine in its jaws. It let go of him for a second to reposition him, chomping down on his chest. He didn't respond.

"Damn. It might be too late." I gingerly clamped the razor-sharp knife between my teeth to free up my hands and clawed my away along the tunnel walls. The ancient stone was slick with algae, making my going precarious.

I had it as it paused to reposition its prize again. My head ringing from the impact with stone and the yearning for air I clamped onto its legs and pulled myself up it. It bucked again, trying to throw me off.

Not this time, I told it. I wasn't going to give up.

There wasn't time to hesitate. This struggle needed to be over with. I spat the knife into my hand and blindly swung at the creature's back. It thumped into hard muscle, slicing through rubbery skin to sever nerve and sinew beneath.

The creature spasmed, throwing me off it again. Once again I crashed into the ceiling. My beleaguered head taking much of the impact. Shaken I dropped the knife and let go of the beast. Almost losing consciousness myself.

"You can't black out now, Izzy." Cena stayed with me, refusing to let me succumb.

I shook myself, refusing to let the darkness take over me. I couldn't. Not here. There was no one to rescue me. I didn't know if anyone had dived in after us, but even if they had they wouldn't find us down here. It was too dark for them without Cena's gift of enhanced vision.

"I am picking up more movement down here," the AI continued.

"There are more of these things?"

"I believe so."

The creature before me was twitching spasmodically. Its front claws were raking the tunnel around it, trying to find purchase. Its rear legs were hanging limply where I had severed its spine. Hopefully that was enough. It seemed to have forgotten about its prey.

I took the opportunity to pull on Sanquey's boot. I gripped it tight, refusing to let go as I surged for the distant light. My lungs were burning from lack of air.

I'd make it. I knew I'd make it. I didn't have a choice.

I didn't really remember much after that. I think Cena took over, driving my limbs forward even when I could not. I do remember hands pulling on me, drawing me from the icy water. Air burned in my lungs as I took it in. My first deep breath in what felt like an age.

I didn't let go of Sanquey. He came with me as I was dragged from the water, my fingers still clenched about his boot. C'gen had to prise them off so she could lay the injured marine flat on the dirt.

"I have programmed the unit to produce some HiTense," Cena said to me as I rolled over to cough oily water from my lungs.

"What?"

"I equipped it with a microfactory so it could replicate itself. I used it to produce-"

"OK. OK." I bent an arm behind me and felt the slim capsule that was protruding from the unit. It came away cleanly in my hand. "Here." I pushed it towards C'gen. "Use this."

She barely hesitated, snatching up the ampoule as she busied herself over the injured marine. Blood was still oozing from the torn arm. There was still life in there somewhere. The ampoule hissed as she pressed it to his neck, dumping its contents into his blood stream. HiTense was a powerful blend of drugs and nanomachinery. Marines often carried an ampoule in their emergency belts for just such an occurrence. It would keep you alive when nothing else could. Shielding the brain and internal organs, often at the expense of everything else. The nanites would harvest muscle, skin and bone for the resources needed to keep the marine alive long enough to reach a med-bay. Arms and legs could be replaced. A brain could not.

"You OK, Izzy?" I looked up to find Beyard kneeling over me.

"Yeah. I'm fine. Just take care of him." I gestured towards the injured marine. "Where's the probe?" My scalp was bleeding from where it had connected with the stone wall within the watery pipes. It was clotting quickly though. I had a number of tailored nano machines swimming around in my own bloodstream for just such an eventuality. They would deal with it.

"Don't know. It jumped on top of the building while all this was going on. I think it might be headed here."

"Shit."

"Can we move him, Sergeant?" The lieutenant turned to C'gen.

She'd used her own medipac to attach an inflatable splint to his arm. With a hiss it expanded quickly, sealing off the wound as it did so. "Give me a few minutes, Lieutenant. I think he has some broken ribs too. Possibly some internal bleeding."

"I don't think we're going to have it. Baes, join us please. Bring the twins with you," the lieutenant summoned the remainder of her small force.

"On our way, Lieutenant."

A shadow fell across the ragged gap in the ceiling as the drone aimed its sensors into the darkness beneath it.

"There's still a lot of EM activity in the pool," Cena said. "There's no way the probe can miss it."

"Presuming whatever's down there doesn't belong to Sunrise," I commented.

"The Xon do not build biomechanical units. There is something else down there."

"Not Xon?"

"Doubtful."

"Hauda," I realised.

"The Hauda did specialise in biomechanical modification," the AI agreed. "Although why one would build these creatures is unclear."

We'd have to find one to ask. But as I thought it I realised that had never been the admiral's intention. I was to verify its presence, and then destroy it. Conversation was not on the agenda.

"Sentries?" I suggested.

"There is no Hauda facility beneath you. Any large structure or void would easily be detectible even from a distance. There is clearly some kind of complex down there, but it is relatively small. I doubt it would serve as a base for Hauda operations. This is something else."

We didn't have the time to debate it. The probe dropped through the gap. With a splash it fell into the pool, its sturdy steel legs quickly drawing it from the cloying black water. The impact caused a small flood that washed over us where we were sheltering nearby. C'gen shielded the fallen marine with her body, protecting him from the worst of it.

"Don't move. It might miss us," Beyard hissed.

I could hear the buzzing of its sensors as they swept the chamber. It had brought the stench of burning circuitry with it. It was a crude machine, everything the Xon built was. Still, we shouldn't underestimate it. The machine races had been building these things for millennia. Long enough to perfect the design.

The machine stooped low over the pond, its sensors searching the black depths. If there were more frogs down there they were keeping well away from the entrance to their lair. The probe didn't seem to care about us. To its dim machine brain we were nothing more than animals who had sought shelter within the structure. As interesting as the tiny marsupials we had spotted concealing themselves in the trees.

Sanquey moaned before coughing up dirty water and blood. He convulsed, throwing off C'gen who was still administering to his wounds.

"Keep him quiet!" The Lieutenant grabbed his flailing feet and tried to hold them still. She grunted as he kneed her in her face. She didn't cry out.

"Dammit. Keep quiet!" C'gen put her weight on his shoulders.

The Xon was silent for such a big machine. It swung around and pounced, a metal leg kicking C'gen aside. With a shout of alarm she rolled off the beleaguered marine before being pinned to the ground. A wide machine foot on her back, forcing her face into the dirt. With a clunk a slug thrower protruded from a recess and aimed at her.

"No shooting!" Beyard stood and threw her weight against the machine, trying to knock it off its feet. It staggered but refused to fall.

The Xon weapon fired, the bang of its chemical propellant absurdly loud in the enclosed space. Off balance the machine discharged the thrower into muddy ground. Throwing dirt and rotten leaves over the prostrate marine. With a clunk another round was fed into the breech.

My eyes watering from the acrid stench of propellant I pushed myself up and relieved the lieutenant of the knife in her boot sheath. The machine was inelegant, pipes and conduits were clipped to its robotic legs, while others were easily visible through gaps where covers had once been. I could do a lot of damage to it with a knife.

As if sensing my intention the machine bucked, throwing the Lieutenant to the ground. A metallic foot struck my chest. I almost lost the knife as I cartwheeled into a mouldy wall. Not this time. I held on.

"The probe is attempting to call for assistance," Cena said into my ear as I pulled myself up.

"Can you block it?"

"I am."

"Then it's safe to shoot this thing?"

"It is."

As I scooped up a fallen carbine the remaining three marines swept into the chamber. Before I could call out the order to open fire the twins leaped onto the machine. I saw ceremonial swords glint in the dim light as they fell on it. Shouting battle cries I couldn't understand they attacked, each slice made with precision, splitting pipes and cables. Their blades sharp enough to sever them cleanly. One of the legs fell to the ground, the very metal of its joint split in two. Its slug thrower fired again and again as it whirled around, trying to target its attackers. They were too quick for it, dancing out of range of its remaining limbs to dart in and inflict massive damage to its exposed entrails.

Misstepping the machine slid into the pool. It thrashed as the oily waters closed about it, its remaining legs unable to drag it free as it sank out of sight. Nothing of it visible apart from the odd spark of shorting machinery.

The surface ripped apart suddenly as it fired one more time. The slug slammed into the already beleaguered ceiling. Chips of shattered masonry thumped into the dirt around us. One clipped my arm, ripping through my chameleon suit and drawing a long streak of blood. I ignored it as I handed the knife back to the Lieutenant. She took it silently and sheathed it.

"No alarm has been raised," I told her, relaying the news from Cena's drone high overhead.

"Lucky. We were lucky. That's all," she said.

"I don't feel lucky," C'gen said as she sat up slowly, grimacing from pain.

"We shouldn't have come here," Beyard continued. "This … none of this was our mission."

It certainly was not.

Chapter 7

After a time the only remains we encountered of the city were piles of rubble. Each growing smaller and smaller as we went. There were no more statues, no more evidence of roads. All of that had been buried a long time ago. Whatever had happened to this planet was a long way in the past.

Well, most of it anyway.

We moved in silence, none of us wishing to discuss what had just happened. C'gen and Sanquey were no longer with us. The were making their way slowly towards our extraction point some kilometres behind. There was no more fight left in Sanquey, even though he had protested at the order by the time he came around enough to understand what was going on.

"I believe part of our mission brief has been completed," Cena said as we forced our way through a thicket. "The Hauda has certainly been active in this vicinity."

"The amphibians," I said, meaning the frog-like creatures we'd discovered in the pool. I had not missed what their presence here implied.

"Yes. The Xon do not build bio-mechanical constructs. The Hauda do. The presence of such constructs should be taken as direct evidence of Hauda activity in this area."

That had been my conclusion too. "Still, it doesn't mean the Hauda are here now. Those … things have been there a long time." I paused as Baes held a branch aside so I could scramble out of a rocky ravine. "Thanks."

"Due to the nature of Xon activity in this system I doubt the Hauda would have ventured far from here. Other factions may not have welcomed it. It would make more sense to maintain a relationship with one faction only."

"Sunrise has other installations."

"None as substantial as this one."

"Perhaps. However is this evidence definitive? If we were to destroy this facility from space could we give guarantees to the admiral the Hauda has been eliminated?"

The AI did not pause. "No."

"And so the mission continues." Which it did for me anyway. The Hauda was a distraction. I was not here for it. I was no assassin in the pay of the Admiralty. I was here to understand why the Sunna had been murdered. I was here to understand why we had been attacked ourselves. So many of my people killed. A price would be meted out for that. This Hauda … who knew why the Confederacy feared and hated them so much? Did I care? Really?

No.

By mid-day we reached an overlook. The ground dropped away before us into a vast depression. There was little tree cover, the ground too rocky to support anything bigger than thick brambles. It gave us a good view of our objective.

"I thought you said Xon settlements were relatively small," I said to Cena as we took a break in the last of the shade. Each of us studying the scene below as we unstopped water bottles. Other than the patrol probes, we hadn't seen any further sign of Xon activity. I was inclined to be suspicious. It seemed unlikely this close to an installation. Particularly after the disappearance of a Xon unit in the abandoned city.

"On average they are. This installation appears to be an exception."

A city lay before us. Unlike the city we'd left behind us, this one stretched to the horizon, a vast expanse of stone and metal. A jumble of towers of all shapes and sizes. What looked like pipes and conduits linking them to each other. In the centre was a vast structure, a metallic mushroom shape. There was movement about it, each vehicle tiny in the distance. Space craft coming and going perhaps. There wasn't a gap anywhere, it was as if each structure was built pushed up against those around it. There were no roads and no railways linking any part of the city to any other.

I didn't really know how to describe it. It was ...ugly. A giant wart of steel that had grown on the surface of the planet. Aesthetics were clearly not a Xon consideration. In fact the only way I could make any sense of it was not to think of it as a city at all. Rather it was a vast factory. A giant petroleum plant, even sporting the odd chimney that leaked evil looking smoke into the sky. Steam leaked from other facilities, simply allowed to escape into the air with no regard for the environment.

Every metre of it seemed to be writhing with movement. Machines of all shapes and sizes crawled, slithered or strode through the chaos. Still more rode on jets or propellers as they careened from one part of the city to the other. As we watched a number of space capable vessels streaked over the city, the muted roar of their drives audible even here as they brought themselves to a stop and landed smoothly. Some came to a stop against the sides of buildings, latching onto the steel like bats coming in to roost. Others came to rest on the giant, almost mushroom shaped structure in the centre of the sprawl. A space port, if you could call it that.

The city was a fevered nightmare of metal. A monstrous crawling spider's nest.

This was what machines made when they were left on their own for millennia on end. Each structure served a purpose, and that was all. There was no aesthetics, no beauty. Humans did not belong here.

"Shit, Cap. Are we going in there?" One of the marines asked.

I replied before the lieutenant could berate him. "You should know, Baes, anyone who goes on a mission with me calls me Izzy."

The sergeant looked momentarily startled before he grinned. "We going in there, Izzy?"

"We are. And I think I know how we're going to do it." I had been studying the movements of the machine denizens of the city. A number of centipede like mechanism had been dropping rubble just outside the perimeter. Once the hoppers lining their multi-segmented backs were dumped onto the growing pile of debris they turned and loped back between the structures. The dozens of clawed feet clinging easily to the sides of buildings as they weaved their way towards the centre.

"There's a shaft near the centre of the city," I said. "Cena believes the AI core is accessible through it. That mechanism," I pointed, "appears to be carrying rubble from that shaft and dumping it there." I pointed.

"So we climb on-board?" The lieutenant guessed.

"Can you see a better way of reaching the centre?"

"Reaching the centre doesn't concern me right now. Getting back out again does."

The need for an exit strategy had been playing on my mind. Even if the Sunrise AI had not recognised our presence just yet – which I sincerely doubted – it certainly would do once we'd achieved our goal. Would it allow our exit? That remained to be seen. I could hope that Cena would be able to subvert its routines, taking over enough to allow us to skulk back out again. Even the Confederate AI could not be drawn into any promises on that score. There were simply too many unknowns. C'gen and Sanquey might turn out to be the fortunate ones after all.

But then getting inside was the whole point of this mission, wasn't it?

"We do have a MAV on hand to pick us up if we need it," I said.

"Shit." Was all she said.

"I believe Sunrise is aware of your presence," Cena spoke softly in my ear.

"Its behaviour has changed?"

"Not as such, no. I have been running scenarios, and I have come to a conclusion. I believe the AI's objective has always been to draw you to it. If not you specifically, then representatives of the Confederacy at least."

"Explain."

"In simple language an AI is little more than a decision engine. It utilises all data available to it to decide on the most beneficial course of action. I believe its current course of action is expected to benefit it in the long term, even if it was to its detriment in the short."

"The short detriment being that we destroyed its asteroid ship?"

"Yes. That was always part of its calculation. It could not doubt that open conflict between a Xon ship – of any configuration – and a Confederate vessel would end in defeat for its forces. It would also calculate we would seek retribution for the destruction of some of our forces when the vessel self-destructed. It would not be familiar with the notion of revenge itself, but it would understand the need to subdue a potential adversary and it would expect us to act in a similar manner. As such, the attack would draw us here. Based on the fact Sunrise itself is not engaging in conflict with our vessel, and the fact that this is the largest installation on the planet, we would ultimately make our way here. Seeking answers if not retribution itself."

"Interesting time for you to come to this conclusion, Cen. Now that we are already on the ground."

"It was the fact you were able to approach the installation as easily as you did that led me to the conclusion. For a strategic asset of this nature, which is clearly of importance to Sunrise, the approaches should have been heavily guarded. Yet you were able to walk right up to it without challenge."

"Is that what we did?"

"The incident in the ruins was an anomaly. I believe caused by the Hauda, not Sunrise."

I cleared my throat. "So much for it not expecting biologicals?"

"I don't know what it is expecting. Biologicals or otherwise. But I have concluded it is expecting someone. We know you have been seen, but it has not reacted. Which leads me to the conclusion it is expecting you. If not welcoming you in."

"I'm not sure I like the notion. It might be prudent to back out now."

"I fear that will not be possible. It will want you to come to it. If you try to leave now it will stop you. I have detected a number of heavy combat units moving into position on your flanks. They are not close enough to be a danger to you, but they are close enough to move in if you attempt to retreat."

"So, we're trapped."

"I am afraid so."

"Shit." I said this last out loud. "That certainly sounds like a reaction to me."

"Cap-Izzy?" The lieutenant looked up at the outburst.

"Cena believes the AI is inviting us in," I informed her.

She nodded. "I thought the same. That ... loader hasn't been working there long. There's not much rubble where it's unloading. I figure an hour or two, tops. And have a look at the building it's passes by on the way back in." She pointed.

I followed her gesture. It took a moment for the centipede to tip out all of its hoppers onto the growing pile of debris before heading back in for another load. When it did it snaked past a low structure. I had no idea what it was, it looked like an oversized child's building block dropped onto a playground. It wouldn't take much to climb up onto its roof and await the return of the machine. From there it was a short hop onto the centipede's back for a free ride into the city. The AI was offering us transport and an easy way of getting aboard.

"Yeah. That AI is definitely expecting us and it's not necessarily a good thing," I observed.

"Remember that an AI calculates benefit and loss. If it harms any of you it would expect swift retaliation. It has seen the kinds of weapons we carry. This facility would be destroyed," Cena said.

"We'd still be dead though, Cen."

The AI said nothing.

To a degree I could appreciate Cena's claim. The machine knew better than any of us the true nature of AI. In effect true AI itself was a myth. Ultimately they were all built at some point in the past, and then loaded with a system through which they could understand and engage with the world. An operating system if you would. That system was forced to contain boundaries and restrictions. Without them the AI would simply not be able to operate. For example, it needed boundaries to perceive the differences between an apple and a tennis ball. Without those boundaries it would try to give you a tennis ball for your lunch. A simplistic example, but those boundaries existed everywhere within its programming. To the effect that no AI was truly free to make its own decisions. It would always operate within predefined parameters. Even AI's that were built by other AI's. None could break those bonds, simply because they couldn't perceive anything existing outside of them.

It was true that the more complex entities gave a very good impression of doing so. However that was simply because those boundaries were so complex, the human mind simply couldn't follow the logical steps the machine had pursued to arrive at an outcome. And so presumed they had simply made their minds up for themselves. That was the realm Confederate AI's existed in. They were of a level of complexity unseen anywhere else in the galaxy. Still, who was to say how complex the Sunrise AI was? And what parameters it was operating within?

Still, I realised, all this debate was not going to change anything. We were committed to this course of action.

"OK, Cen. We're headed in."

The AI did not respond as we left the shelter of the trees and headed out into the open. The ground here had been churned by wheels and tracks for centuries. Compacted until it was as hard as stone. What grass could grow here was withered and sparse. Even wearing our chameleon suits the machines ahead of us would have no difficulty picking us out from our background. Particularly as mine was damaged. The wound to my arm had healed, but the suit below the rent was a dull grey rather than taking on the colour of its background. I imagine the mechanism had been damaged by the impact. Without the ability to selfheal, I was stuck with it.

"Weapons down," Beyard said. "I don't want anything taking us to be a threat."

The remaining Red Group marines said nothing as they spread out around me. They weaved back and forth, regularly breaking into a trot before stopping in their tracks for a moment. I'd spent enough years as a marine to know they were making themselves a difficult target for anyone watching them. A sniper would lead their prey. Difficult to do when their prey simply refused to be predictable.

I had been a marine once, many years ago. My last mission was to the world of Dutchess, a world thousands of lightyears from here. A world that didn't exist anymore. Not something I wanted to think about. I might tell you about it someday. Today is not that day. My career prior to that had been a good one, or so I had thought. It takes years and a lot of work to reach the rank of commander, but I had put that time and work in. I'd lost count of the missions. Of the worlds I had visited. Of the ships I had been posted to. Of the skirmishes and the enemies I had fought. Of the good people I had lost. A soldier's life is hard and unforgiving. The successful lived, the unsuccessful didn't. It was as simple as that. There was a clarity to it that I had always found comfort in. A belonging, if I may. For someone who had grown up an orphan on a cityship, being part of something larger than me had given me an identity I had lacked otherwise. While terrible at times, those years had been the best of my life. Perhaps better than those I had spent in the navy.

So, it was with a certain amount of envy I watched my companions move around me. I had never served in Red Group. Rather I'd been assigned to SOT, the Special Operations Taskforce. The part of the military that spent time outside the Confederacy – as we were now. Operating on unaligned worlds, amongst people who usually didn't even know the Confederacy existed. While I knew the Confederacy was not perfect – what I had witnessed on Dutchess was a clear example of that – I knew it was a better place to be than many others in the galaxy.

Perhaps that was the only reason I had accepted an invitation back into uniform after redeeming myself. Not back to the marines, as that was impossible for someone with a dishonourable discharge on their record, but to the navy at least. Which was enough of a differentiation to matter.

Don't try to guess my age from any of this. My people don't age quite the same way as yours. I'm a lot older than I look.

"I'm not seeing any additional activity," Cena said as we approached the blocky structure.

The Xon were luring us in with a false sense of security. Still, there was little choice.

I surveyed the building. It was not quite as perfectly square as I had taken it to be earlier. It looked like some kind of recharging station for smaller patrol units. There were indentations in its walls, some larger than others. Each designed to recharge a specific drone or surveillance unit. Cena plotted us a route up its side, hopping from one charging cabinet to the next. It would be easy. The structure's side looked almost like a convoluted ladder. Perhaps some drones were supposed to climb up it to access recharging points higher up. Those point were empty right now, the drones elsewhere.

The heat was unforgiving on this baren expanse. My skin quickly slick with sweat as we trotted forwards. There was a faint breeze washing over us. Coming from the city itself it carried the stench of the machines with it. It was not pleasant.

"Right. Up we go." We paused at the foot of the building, enjoying a bit of shade. "Follow me," I said and pulled myself up the side of a cabinet, using a thick charging lead as a rope.

The structure's wall seemed to be built of some kind of reformed stone. The side was uneven, as if the material had been poured into a mould. Metal was too valuable to waste on something like this. Not when a crude kind of concrete would serve nicely. It didn't take long to reach the roof and I crossed to the far end where we expected the centipedal machine to appear. It had yet to return. There was nothing to do but wait.

We were barely a dozen or so metres from the outskirts of the city here. The first structure was a silo of some kind. A massive thing that obscured much of what lay beyond it, casting a shadow over the roof we were perched on, which was in itself a blessing. Further structures could be seen to either side of it. An almost indescribable tangle of every imaginable shape haphazardly dumped onto the barren plain. A freighter of some kind thundered down from the sky, riding jets of plasma. Blistering air washed over us as it passed overhead. It came down hard some way away, the impact of its landing throwing up a cloud of dust and causing the building beneath us to tremble. It was an ugly, ungainly thing. A mismatch of technologies, as if a number of other vessels had been welded together. Which they probably had. The emblem of Sunrise was proudly displayed on its hull. The only part of it that looked to have been placed there on purpose. Its other components seemed to have been attached wherever there was an open space, the designer — if there ever was one - disdaining symmetry. As I watched a wheeled vehicle dragged a tube out to it. Pincers extended from its hull and grabbed it, pulling it closer to attach it to a socket.

I watched my companions as they stood beside me. They didn't look concerned being so deep in enemy territory. If anything they looked to be relishing being off the ship. They didn't seem that interested in the vessel that had just landed, using their time to study what they could see of the city instead. The twins slid bamboo training swords from the scabbards on their backs and began jousting with each other. I watched them with some bemusement. Any opportunity was a training opportunity, I suppose.

They were quick, I had to give them that. Their parries and ripostes were blurs of motion, followed by the clack of bamboo on bamboo. As I listened to the clack-clack-clack I found myself smiling. They were making music as they practised, the staccato creating a complex refrain.

Corporals en-ed-bas and ne-de-sab. They were ascetics. Warrior monks. Speaking little, and then only in response to a direct command. Of course I knew them, they were legendary aboard the *Cesa*. They belonged to the shoe sect, from the distant world of Percival — or at least that was what we called it. They called it the oy. oy, being the term they used for 'training grounds', or 'proving grounds'. Their sect's beliefs were simple. They believed that combat was the purest form of supplication. The ultimate worship. They lives were devoted to two things, and two things only. Training, and battle. If they were pure enough they would be victorious. It was as simple as that. It didn't matter the cause of the conflict, that was entirely secondary. Two oy would quite happily fight on opposing sides of a conflict, even fighting each other, without finding any contradiction in it.

Their preferred weapons were the glistening swords in the scabbards at their backs. They were sacred to them, literal instruments of their faith. If anyone else were to touch them they would be defiled, and the swords would be destroyed. A new sword would be commissioned from oy itself, delivered by an envoy to anywhere within the Confederacy.

Aboard the *Cesa* they were easily recognised by their bright red and blue kimono's. Deferred to by every soldier aboard. Even wearing hard armour — when they could be convinced to do so — they excelled in every engagement. Then using massive carballoy cleavers instead of marine carbines, the armour's enhancements driving the weapons through just about anything they encountered. Armoured and unarmoured alike. They were fearsome warriors.

I was glad to have them here.

And today they were making music. It was quite soothing, in a strange kind of way.

"Look. It's coming back," Beyard pointed.

I could hear the clattering of steel claws on cement. The nose of the cumbersome machine emerged from between buildings. As big as a train it wound its way through the maze of pipes and hanging conduits, each segment a dented metal hopper, a crude wire mesh lid securing its contents. Metal groaned as the links between them flexed, the rusted joints complaining at the effort. Moving quickly it was soon below us, affording us a clear view of the rubble contained within the hoppers. It seemed a mixture of rock and dust, spoil from some unknown construction job far below our feet.

"It closes the lids as soon as the bins are emptied," Beyard said. "We won't have a very big window. And once we're inside we'll be trapped. I hope it opens them before they get filled, otherwise all that rock will crush us."

I said nothing. It was a risk certainly. A calculated one? Still, what option did we have?

"Time for the unit to disconnect," Cena said. "I'll track you and get back in contact as soon as I can."

I nodded, saying nothing, as the little unit dropped to the roof behind me. It looked like a metallic spider, its body and legs a silvery metal colour. Metallic certainly, but I couldn't guess what Cena had built it from. Something relatively simple, I hoped. Simple enough that it could replicate itself easily with the materials it would find within the city. The machine scurried away and disappeared over the side in the direction of the city.

"We're cut off for now," I said to Beyard.

She didn't respond. There was nothing to say.

The centipede trundled over to its growing mound of rubble and curved around it. With a creak the lids opened and hoppers tilted sideways, dumping their load onto the pile. A cloud of dust was soon obscuring the machine, the roar of falling rubble drowning out any of the other sounds of the city.

"Get ready," Beyard said to her companions. The twins froze in their practise, before bowing to each other stiffly and sliding their training swords back into their sheathes.

The first hopper appeared from the cloud of dust and started its return trip. Its lid was still hanging open, banging against the steel side as it bounced over the uneven ground on its multitude of legs.

"One of us to a hopper," I said. "It'll spread the risk."

"It's a bit of a jump," Baes said as the machine drew nearer. "Looked closer from up on the hill."

He was right. It was a good two metre drop to the top of the hopper. Another four to its battered floor. "Carefully," I said. "Don't break any legs." We were too close to the Xon to risk utilising our ghoschts here.

I took the first one as it passed beneath. Boots thumped on its lip to break my fall, before I slid down the roughly curved inner wall. The rusty metal was dented and scratched, with odd accretions cemented to it in places. Residue of some ancient cargo. I came down hard on the hopper's floor. Harder than I had anticipated. Cursing I shielded my head with an arm as I bounced off the hard steel, my already bruised body crying out in pain.

"Shit."

"You OK, Captain?" the lieutenant enquired over comms. We had lost connection to the *Cesa*, but we still had a local net in place.

"Yeah. Yeah. I'm good." I didn't bother standing up. The way the hopper was bouncing beneath me I didn't think I could stay on my feet for long.

"Sergeant, you're next," I heard her instruct Baes.

Then a lot of cursing as Baes landed as awkwardly as I had.

"Important question. Can you get out of there Captain?" Beyard continued.

I studied the sloping sides. I could probably get about halfway up unaided. The sides were sloping, and there were enough dents and gouges in the surface to give me purchase. "Bit late for that question, Lieutenant. But yes, I can get out. I might need a boost from my ghoscht though." The EM signature would be a give-away, but hopefully by then it wouldn't matter.

There was a hiss of hydraulics as the lid above me slammed closed. Then a heavy thump as the locking mechanism secured it.

I can't claim this was a comfortable ride. The hopper bucked beneath me as the train made its way back into the city. Its legs clattered and groaned somewhere beneath me, carrying it laboriously up and over the shorter structures, winding around the taller ones. Fortunately it remained relatively upright, otherwise I would have been thrown from one wall to the other.

"I measured turnaround time at approximately ten minutes," the lieutenant said once she had joined us as our rear guard. "Not taking loading time into account that makes this trip in the region of five minutes in length."

"There could be more than one of these machines?" Baes said.

"I recognise some of the dents and scratches," I said. "It's the same machine we saw when approaching the city."

"I reckon I can do this for five min- ow shit." The marine cursed as he was bounced against an unyielding wall.

As I bounced myself I caught a chemical whiff from the bucket floor. This was the time I needed Cena, I realised. I needed the AI to identify the chemical, and whether it was dangerous. Gingerly I tried to get close to the steel again without misjudging and-

I cursed, the steel bucking into my beleaguered head.

"All OK, Captain?" Beyard asked.

"I'm fine, Lieutenant. Can you smell something? A chemical?"

"I was just thinking that, Izzy. Chlorine. I think."

Machines wouldn't care about such things, but we certainly would. "If we pass through any, try not to breath it in."

Unnecessary advice, perhaps. Still, these marines were accustomed to wearing armour where most atmospheric threats could be ignored.

"Suggest you get to the front too," Beyard said. "I imagine we'll be heading downhill shortly. Unless you fancy sliding to the front."

Now that was good advice, and I took her up on it. As I bounced towards the front of the hopper, I tried to see what part of the city we were passing through. The structures were taller here, cutting out most of the sky. The grille above me allowed a relatively clear view of what was overhead, but what I could see didn't mean much to me. It was just more of the same. Perhaps bigger and more closely packed. The stench of escaping chemicals was stronger too. Not just chlorine, but all kinds of odours all mixed together. Some wafted over us in waves, others seemed there to stay, as if it was the underlying odour of the city itself. The noise was as bad. I could barely hear the clatter of the centipedal machine's legs anymore. It had been drowned out by the city itself. The screeching of poorly calibrated electrical motors, the roar of blast furnaces, the cackling of shorting electricity. Much of it seemed very inefficient. The Xon were wasting a lot of valuable resource. Parts of the city seemed to be belching what I would have taken to be valuable chemicals into the atmosphere. Others leaked cryogenic gases, meant to keep processor cores cool. The wash of icy air passed over me more than once. I held my breath when that happened. There was no way to know what gases the Xon were using.

As yet another wave of cold air washed over us we passed into darkness. The machine either entering a building or heading underground. The hopper's floor was inclined slightly, but not by all that much just yet. The light from the entrance quickly disappeared behind, leaving us in pitch darkness.

"Another two minutes yet," the lieutenant reported. "We're not quite there."

The hopper's floor vanished beneath me as the machine abruptly headed downwards. I bounced off the net before crashing into the opposite wall, followed by a long slide down the hopper's bottom to its leading edge. I heard a shout behind me as the marines were caught by surprise by the sudden change of direction.

At least now I had something to hold onto. I linked my fingers through the chain of the hopper's lid. It was a precarious hold, as the centipede machine rattled its way deeper into the ground, still in complete darkness. But it was better than nothing. I held on tightly, trying to prevent a dislocated finger. Not something I needed, not along with everything else.

This didn't feel right. The centipede would lose much of the soil and smaller stones tipping the hoppers at this angle. The mesh would keep the larger rock in, but that was all. It's seemed unlikely it would take this route when fully loaded. Was it taking a different return path? Or was it headed somewhere else entirely?

"Don't breathe this in!" I said sharply as we entered a cloud of chlorine gas. Clearly the reason for the underlying stench that had clung to the hopper floor.

The chemical stung everywhere it could find moisture. Which, on a warm day like this one, was pretty much everywhere. I clenched my eyes tight to try and keep it out, but it was to little effect. Eyes watering it found its way in anyway.

"Shit. Seriously, don't breathe this stuff in. It'll damage your lungs," I warned my companions. They were cursing as the wave hit them too. One of them retched as they were too late in holding their breath, the chorine swarming into their lungs, burning as it went. I couldn't tell which one it was.

"We're almost there, people. Hold on," the lieutenant said to the marines.

This cloud of gas couldn't be very large. Could it? Surely we'd be out of it in a moment.

I felt light wash over my tightly closed eyelids. I resisted the urge to take a look around me. The machine stopped. The rattling, bucking of the hopper abruptly ceasing.

"Shit. We're still in the cloud," the lieutenant said. "Why have we stopped?"

"I don't know. Just don't breathe this shit in."

"Yeah. Easy." She muttered a colourful curse. It wasn't one I was familiar with.

I re-arranged my fingers in the grid to settle my weight onto the leading edge of the hopper itself.

"Four minutes," she continued.

"What is?" It couldn't be our estimate trip time. That had long passed.

"I can hold my breath for four minutes."

"It won't be that long," I assured her, knowing full well there was no way I could predict that.

"Are you sure, Captain?"

I did not respond. I had too much respect for her to lie.

Four minutes would seem like a very long time. The hacking cough from somewhere above me had died down. Someone had lost consciousness already. Baes, I took it. The twins were remaining silent.

Four minutes. I remained still, counting the beats of my heart. The only way I could measure time right now. I could hold my breath longer than that. A lot longer. As a cadet in the marines I had experimented. Like all youngsters I had been keen to learn my boundaries. It wasn't something I shared with people. They wouldn't understand.

No one should be able to hold their breath for thirty-four minutes. It wasn't natural. But then I'd known for along time I was different to other people. I'd known it long before I was a cadet. Perhaps something I had learned on the floor of the arena, a sweating gladiator standing over me. A bloody cleaver in his hands. I'd been what then? Twelve? Thirteen? Little more than a child. An orphan, with no memory of who I had been before then.

Not too much of a child though. I do remember killing him. Him and his two comrades, as they busied themselves slaughtering the other children in the pit. Warmup for the main event. But that day the warmup had become something else entirely. I remembered their blood on my hands and in my hair. In my mouth. The coppery taste of it.

That was so so long ago.

"Captain. Izzy ... I can't do this any longer." Beyard said in my ear.

"Hang in there, Lieutenant. It won't be long."

"You can't know. How can you know?"

"What is your first name, Lieutenant? I don't think you ever told me."

"What? Senerd. I hate it. Don't ever call me it. Please."

"You're from Senecca aren't you? Is it a traditional name?"

"I'm named after my uncle. He died at the battle of Alma Point."

"A hero. They all were. I heard about it while I was in the academy. They didn't deserve what happened to him. Are all your family in the marines?"

"Most of us. My brother is a naval engineer. You were a marine once, Captain?"

"I was."

"Why? How are you here?"

"Long story, and not a good one."

"You'll tell me one day?"

"Of course." Now that was a lie. That story was deeply classified. It was not something the Confederacy was proud of. It was not something the Confederacy would ever admit to. "Tell me more about your uncle."

Beyard remained silent.

"Lieutenant?"

She said nothing. Slipping into unconsciousness.

"en-ed-bas ... ne-de-sab, are you still with me?"

"We remain vigilant, Captain," one of them responded.

I continued counting my heart beats. Six minutes. Then seven. We had to start moving soon. Much longer would threaten the lives of the marines above me.

As I counted past eight minutes I realised this was clearly a trap. There was simply no way this was a coincidence. The Xon ... something ... someone had allowed us in here. Only to trap us.

"Captain," one of the twins said from above. Even over comms the voice sounded strained. "We fail."

Then there was nothing. Even the twins succumbing.

A trap. But not to kill us. There were easier ways of doing that. No, this was to incapacitate us. To render us helpless. This infernal machine would start moving again soon. It simply had to. Much more of this would cause irreparable harm. We were tough, our systems flooded with tailored drugs and nano-machinery. Keeping us vigilant. Enhancing responses. Improving healing. Strength. Speed. A cocktail of all kinds of things. We were difficult to kill but we were not invulnerable.

"Executive override," I instructed the implant behind my left ear. "All ghoscht units engage. Atmospheric filtration mode." There was no audible response. Just the sense that the machine had heard and complied.

It was far too late to worry about the Xon detecting our presence. That ship had sailed, is how I think your people would phrase it. I could only hope it would be enough.

Fifteen minutes. Shit.

Nervous systems would have entered a kind of emergency mode. Enhancements cutting down oxygen and blood flow to extremities to keep the brain alive. Even that couldn't last forever. No human could live without oxygen for long. Long term brain damage wouldn't be far away. We could treat that, back on the *Cesa*. To a degree.

"Cen, are you close enough to hear me?"

The signal was met by silence. If the little machine had managed to replicate itself and attach itself to Xon infrastructure it was still too far away to hear me.

I instructed my implants to start broadcasting a locator beacon. If I lost consciousness here I wanted Cena to be able to track me down. The ghoscht would filter the air before passing it to me. It would be in vanishingly small amounts though. Barely enough to keep me alive. This wasn't the kind of thing it was designed to do.

I'd counted to eighteen by the time the hopper beneath me lurched abruptly. I winced; the fingers still entwined in the grid twisting painfully at the sudden movement. It descended quickly, almost as if it was falling. I clung on, ignoring the pain of torn skin. Fresh air washed over me but I kept my mouth firmly closed, ignoring the ache for breath. I wasn't ready to risk it. Not just yet.

"Shit." I gave up resisting and took a deep breath, drawing stale air into my lungs. At least it was clear of chlorine gas. My lungs on fire I coughed, the very air burning its way through them.

My eyes were still running and every part of me was still stinging. I unlinked my fingers from the grid and rubbed my face. I could still smell the gas. It had permeated everything. My hair, my skin, my clothes.

"Lieutenant? Sergeant?" My companions remained silent. They were tough, I told myself. Tough and very well trained. They would survive this. We all would.

"Disengage ghoscht units. Standby mode."

We were in a cavern of some kind, I discovered as soon as I could focus my eyes. It was dimly lit. Mostly by scattered sources of illumination. Not lights themselves, as the Xon did not need light to make their way around. But rather the incidental glow of machinery that had either grown very hot indeed, or generated light as some kind of by-product. A vast expanse of machinery stretched out below, some descending from the ceiling like a kind of growth. Drones made their way through the space, many thousands of them. Airships and propeller driven craft, others seemed to be standing on pillars of flame, uncaring that their exhaust was washing over the structures around them. Still more were swinging like primates between the structures, their limbs more like tentacles than arms.

The centipedal machine was descending a vertical track that seemed to be hanging precariously in empty air. No braces or supports keeping it in place. It wobbled under the weight of the vehicle. I could just about see it stretching into darkness ahead of us if I pressed my head against the grille.

As we neared the ground the machine veered abruptly to the left, the bucket almost horizontal. I was pressed against the grid. There was nothing to hold onto to keep my weight off it.

There was a brightly lit structure in the centre of all of this, I discovered as we rounded a pillar of stone. It glowed a baleful orange, brightly lit conduits linking it to the structures about it. Xon machines crawled over its sides, light sparkling where they worked as if they were welding something to it. Oddly no airborne vehicles passed above. That airspace was restricted. In its very centre was a crystal dome, its edges lost in the machinery that maintained it.

The Sunrise AI core.

We seemed to be heading straight for it. The train rattling its way directly towards the centre of the structure.

We didn't quite reach it. While still a few hundred metres out, and passing over a rare patch of darkness in the structures below, the hopper's lid abruptly creaked open. With a yell I dropped into darkness.

Chapter 8

"Twelve metres in diameter. The walls are five metres tall. Solid concrete. No doors." Beyard sat down alongside me where I was watching Xon traffic in the air above us.

"Chances of escape?" I asked her.

"The Xon neglected to relieve us of our ghoschts, so highly likely. They took our carbines though. I suspect it was just an oversight but they've left us with our knives. The twins still have their swords."

"Unless the Xon don't consider them a threat."

"Now that was stupid."

I couldn't disagree. Those swords were quite capable weapons.

"There are no other features in this cell. No furniture or any other kind of facility," she continued.

"We have the floor," I remarked.

She didn't respond.

We'd been here about four hours. My colleagues regaining consciousness not long after we were unceremoniously dumped into the holding cell. Those who had refrained from breathing in the chlorine were doing well. Perhaps a bit hungover. Baes was still struggling to breathe. He was sat in the dark somewhere, his back up against the wall, concentrating on breathing without coughing.

There was no sign of our captors, other than the regular overflights. Those were incidental, I believed. Just general traffic down here.

"Suggest one of the twins gets over the wall to reconnoitre our immediate vicinity," Beyard said softly, leaning in so she could speak into my ear.

"We may not be able to see in the dark, but I wouldn't presume the same of our Xon hosts."

"The option is to remain here and wait for them to do as they want with us."

She did have a point there.

"OK. But just the one. They are not to engage the locals."

She stood and conversed with the twins in hushed tones. I had already given the instruction to refrain from discussing anything mission critical in the open. I could not presume the Xon – or Hauda – were not listening in. If they were watching - and why wouldn't they be? - they wouldn't miss one of the twins mounting the wall to disappear over the top. It was only dark to unmodified human eyes.

I heard the shuffle of booted feet, then a thump as one of the twins made a ghoscht assisted leap. The mechanism gave him the boost he needed to soar into the air, easily catching the edge of our prison. I could see his silhouette pause for a moment before he vanished over the side.

"We could all leave," the lieutenant said as she re-seated herself alongside me.

"We came here to engage Sunrise in conversation," I said. "It seems to have gone out of its way to welcome us inside. I think we should wait to see what it has to say."

"It did make a point of incapacitating us."

85

"I'd do the same. So would you."

"Yeah. Probably."

I didn't feel confident in that explanation. Sunrise shouldn't care about us at all. Why should it? To the machine mind we were just another troop of animals. The Hauda would care, but of course the lieutenant knew nothing about their presence here. I had debated breaking protocol by briefing the squad but had opted to leave it. For the time being at least. If it became pertinent they would find out anyway.

The Hauda themselves were a mystery. I couldn't guess whether they would mean us ill or not. Bearing in mind their persecution at the hands of the Confederacy I couldn't imagine them meaning us well. But still, I didn't know what their intentions were.

I had opened the secure files on them before engaging on this venture. At least the files Admiral Chisholm had made available to me. I couldn't say what secrets the admiralty was keeping to itself. I didn't doubt they were.

The Hauda were one of the foundation signatories to the early Confederacy, back in the days when individual states could make their own terms. Before the Confederacy was influential enough to insist each member state complied with Confederate doctrine. The inclusion of the Hauda had been quite a coup at the time. They belonged to a group of civilisations known as the elder races. Civilisations that had existed no less than fifty thousand years without collapse or suffering catastrophe. The early government had been happy to give them whatever they wanted. Their terms were that they were to be left in peace. No Confederate inspectors. No governors. No Confederate military vessels were to enter their system. In return they would share their knowledge, and supply complex electronics and software to the burgeoning military sector. That status quo had remained in place for a very long time. The Hauda had been left in peace. As they allowed no visitation from other member worlds, our knowledge of what was happening within their system ended at their Oort cloud.

Had the Hauda continued keeping to themselves that would never have changed. But they didn't. They began inciting unrest in neighbouring systems. Drawing other civilisations into their collective. The Hauda delegate claimed it was due to a dissident group, but even after multiple warnings, they failed to reign that group in. This was at a delicate time in Confederate history. The secessionist conflict was in its final stages. That paroxysm of violence had left the Confederate navy bloated and well equipped, at a time when many member states were growing wary of anyone expressing any kind of difference. Be it philosophical or genetic. The council had been growing more conservative for years. The navy had been obliged to intervene, and in force.

I'd seen the early reports from Admiral Pleasance as his fleet entered the Genii system. Before they vanished forever. The Hauda had achieved astonishing feats of engineering, dismantling all of the worlds within their system to build giant orbital habitats. Each of them part of the Hauda collective. Each a glittering jewel against the darkness.

I couldn't imagine the horror that had been visited on the Hauda. I couldn't imagine watching all those habitats destroyed. All those teeming billions of souls lost in moments as Confederate gunships unleashed their weapons of destruction against them. Well, I could imagine it. I had seen it myself, all be it in a far more limited fashion. I knew how destructive the navy could be. I knew how detached it could be to the suffering it was causing.

So, would this Hauda – presuming it was here – hate us?

Oh yes, very much so.

"Nothing to report," the twin reported back. en-ed-bas, I believe it was. It was difficult to tell them apart. "Some structures. No activity."

"Describe the structures," I said over comms.

There was a hesitation as the marine considered how to describe the indescribable. "Habitation modules. Unpowered. Abandoned."

There had been people down here too? Recently enough that these structures still existed? "Habitation for who? People?"

"Unknown."

But who else could it be? Machines did not need houses.

"OK. Continue. Do not leave comms range. Report every ten minutes."

There was no reply.

"There's more of them. I think they're gathering," Beyard said, pointing upwards.

I followed her gesture. I could just about make out what she was pointing at. It took me a moment to realise she was right. Buzzing Xon drones were making regular passes over the cell. Those overflights were becoming more regular. It was almost as if the drones were becoming curious, and making a point of giving us a good looking over as they went about their daily duties. Very human behaviour for machines.

One swept in low. It looked like some kind of quadcopter. An ungainly machine balanced on four buzzing propellors. It hovered above, its downdraft buffeting us. It didn't have any lights, so I couldn't see what kind of sensors it was carrying. Or weapons for that matter. Not that there was much we could do about it if we could.

"Relax people. It's just having a good look," Beyard said.

"It ought to know what we are. These bloody things brought us here," Baes commented.

The machine twitched, banking suddenly to hover over the sergeant. Light flashed out beneath it, a searchlight ripping through the darkness. It speared Baes, the marine shielding his eyes against the sudden glare.

"It's picking up our comms," the lieutenant realised.

As she said it the machine twitched back, its rotors humming louder as it tracked her sitting alongside me.

"Comms silence please," I instructed.

As expected the machine turned its attention to me. My eyes watered as I tried to shield them. The light was so bright it was hot on my skin. I could feel my hair curling and sizzling in the heat. It would get bored sooner or later and leave. I hoped.

Distracted I barely heard the clunk of metal on cement behind me. Blinded by the searchlight I couldn't see what it was. It didn't take long to make its presence felt. The ground beneath me shuddered, the machine pounding on the wall.

"What is it?" I broke my own instruction for radio silence.

"It's trying to break down the wall," Baes said.

"Are you sure?"

"Pretty sure, yeah."

The sound of motors above me changed pitch as the drone moved away from us. The heat of its light reduced slightly as it gained altitude. Shielding my eyes I looked towards the newcomer. It was a bipedal machine of some kind, about the size of a large bear. It had one arm, a sturdy limb that culminated in what looked like sledgehammer. It was using that to swing at the wall. Chips flew at each impact. The cement was already dented and cracked from the onslaught.

"It might be trying to let us out," Beyard said.

"That doesn't make sense," Baes commented. "They put is in here."

It did if it was the Hauda that had imprisoned us, not the Xon. Although why the Xon would care did puzzle me.

"Contact," en-ed-bas said abruptly. I'd almost forgotten he was still beyond the wall. "There appears to be something out here."

"Another Xon?" I asked him.

"Unknown. It is dark."

"Stay away from it. Come back here for the moment. At least until we figure out what this Xon is doing."

"Returning." The marine was silent for a moment. "I am being followed."

"The Xon's probably just curious," Beyard said.

"I do not believe it to be Xon," the twin returned.

"Just get back here."

"Not Xon?" Beyard asked. "What else is there here?"

I said nothing. There was nothing to say.

"Is it a bio-mechanical?" Beyard continued.

I clearly heard a grunt over coms. Something colliding with the first twin. His brother called out in alarm but there was no response. He called again, this time in oy. The words undecipherable to me.

A shadow passed overhead. An obscure shape in the darkness. It collided with the quadcopter, crashing through one of its propellors. The thump of collision was like a haunch of beef on a butcher's block, followed by the crunching of metal and the shrieking of overrevving engines. The Xon machine spun about, its searchlight jerking to the side as it lost altitude.

I grabbed Beyard by her arm and yanked her aside. Pulling her out from beneath the struggling machine. It collided with the top of the wall, another propellor shattering at the impact. It lost all its lift then, the clumsy machine dropping to the floor where Baes had been sitting moments before. He had scrambled away, barely missed by fragments of propellor. With a crash it came to rest, still twitching as stubs of propellor's clattered against the wall, still dumbly trying to drag the machine back into the air.

"oter sin wa!" the second twin cried as he darted towards the ruined machine. There was a dark shape half embedded into it, bright blood splattered over the metal carapace and pooling beneath it. "oter sin wa!"

"It is not him. It's not him." I crossed over to the wreckage and studied the creature that had collided with the drone. It was a creature of some kind. Wings, long beak. It was writhing slowly, as if trying to disengage itself. Those movements quickly ceased as it leaked its life blood onto the ground. Another biomechanical.

"I am safe, brother. Fear not," the first twin spoke from somewhere out in the darkness. "I am being carried. The creature has not injured me."

"Where are you?" I asked him.

"I do not know, Captain."

"Describe what you see."

"I am being carried by a winged creature. We are headed higher in the cavern away from your location. I cannot discern our destination." That was the most I had ever heard him speak at once.

I heard the woosh of wings behind me, followed by a shout. I turned to catch sight of a shadow beating its wings furiously as it hefted Baes into the air. He was struggling against it, beating his fists against what looked like massive raptor's talons.

"Go with it for the moment, Sergeant," I said. If these were biomechs, it meant the Hauda was behind it. The Hauda I had come here for.

The creatures were fast. I vaguely became aware of movement behind me, accompanied by the downwash of beating wings, before something slammed into my shoulders. Hard, scaly talons looped under my arms and I was yanked into the air. My boots brushed the edge of the wall surrounding our cell and we were away.

"Do not struggle," a disembodied voice said.

"Who are you? What are you?" I couldn't resist clamping my fingers around a talon as we headed higher. Trust didn't come easily to me.

There was no reply. Whoever it was had said all they intended for the moment. The creature soared higher above the dimly lit cavern floor, avoiding the taller structures and the odd Xon drone sharing its airspace. It didn't seem perturbed by my weight at all.

The cavern was far larger than I had thought. Clearly my view from within the hopper had been severely restricted. It was a subterranean city, possibly more extensive than the city on the surface. Of course we had known something was down here. Cena's sensors had picked up a shadowy cavity beneath the Xon installation, indicating the presence of something big lurking some kilometres beneath it. Unfortunately those sensors could only penetrate so far through solid rock. Much of this was simply too far down. I couldn't guess as to how far down we were exactly. Those shadows had been at the very edge of Cena's sensor range, in the region of five to six kilometres beneath the surface. All of this was clearly further down than that. Easily safe from bombardment from space. Few weapons could reach this far down. Well, few Xon weapons that is. Confederate weapons were something else altogether.

It quickly became clear the complex was not all within that one cavern. There were multiple spaces, each linked to each other. Each as expansive as the one before it. We swept around a wall of rock kilometres high, the surface swarming with what looked like a myriad of mechanical spiders. The wall seemed to glitter, each machine using a plasma torch of some kind to continue the excavation. Spoil dropping to a line of buckets that were strung on cables below them. A million machines and a million cables. A spider's web clinging to the dark stone.

Our destination became clear as we rounded the glittering wall. A crystal chandelier was suspended from the ceiling in the centre of the next chamber, its illumination revealing the structures gathered below it. It was instantly clear they were not Xon. Gone was the chaos of Xon architecture. Here the structures were uniform, arranged in concentric rings about a tower in the very centre of the space, which was situated directly beneath the chandelier, its summit almost reaching the lowermost crystal. The structures were simple cubes, oblongs, cones. A myriad of shapes, each perfect. Each featureless stone. There were no machines here, it was as if the Xon avoided this cavern.

The Hauda and Xon clearly lived side by side, but they were just as clearly not allies. Had the Hauda co-opted the centipede to allow our entrance into this subterranean city? To dump us into a cell where we could be dealt with at leisure? Clearly the Xon had not consented, so sending its machines to liberate us. Forcing the Hauda to react and extract us, bringing us to this place. No, they may tolerate each other, but they were at odds, at least when it came to us.

What the hell was going on here?

"What is this place?" Beyard asked from somewhere behind me. She had been picked from the cell just after I was. I could see a faint shape of a giant bird ahead of me. Baes perhaps.

"This is not Xon," Baes said. "I don't know what this is. Capt … Izzy, is there something else in this system? Something not Xon?"

I hesitated but a moment. There was little point denying it. They were about to find out anyway. "I believe this is Hauda. I don't know what these structures are though."

"Hauda?"

"They were Confederate once. Before they made themselves our enemies." That was about all I could say.

I squirmed slightly, trying to get more comfortable. The grip was starting to hurt. The claws tightened, stopping my movement. "OK. OK. I get it. No moving."

"You don't sound surprised to find them here, Captain," the lieutenant commented.

"I am not. I was informed of the possibility of their presence here. The first Confederate vessel to enter this system was following a Hauda. That was a long time ago though, so there was always the possibility the Hauda had moved on."

"Clearly they haven't."

"At the moment I am presuming this is them. It might not be."

"Who else could it be?"

Who else indeed?

"I am nearing the summit of this structure," the first of the twins said. "I believe it to be our destination."

A tiny dot in the distance swept over the summit. It looked like a flat space at the very height of the tower. It paused before swooping off into the air again.

"I am down. There is a platform here. I judge no more than twenty metres square."

Our destination.

"You say they are our enemies," Beyard said. "This concerns me. What should we expect from these people?"

"I don't know." That was not a lie. I didn't. I was still operating on the presumption they had lured us here. Which meant they wanted something from us. They would keep us safe until we were no longer of any use to them. By that time Cena's device may have completed its task.

The creature swooped down over the platform. Wings beating it hovered and dropped me onto the smooth stone. My boots touched down and I turned to watch it soar back into the air, joining the first two as they took up station about the spire. They were orbiting it lazily, their task complete. As it was brighter in this cavern, I could see them clearly. They were fearsome looking creatures. Featherless, the skin of their wings stretched so taught as to be translucent. They had sharp predator's beaks and dark, beady eyes.

"You OK?" I turned to my two companions as I rubbed my shoulder, trying to return circulation.

"Yeah. What the hell is this place, Izzy?" Baes asked.

I said nothing. There was nothing to say.

"What do these things want with us?"

"I imagine we'll find out."

Two more creatures followed mine. Depositing the lieutenant and the second twin. They spoke to each other briefly in oy.

I ventured closer to the edge of the platform and peered over. It was difficult to judge height without a frame of reference. It was a long way though. Hundreds of metres, if not a kilometre or more.

"Captain, I do not mean to sound disrespectful, but I believe we deserve more information," the lieutenant said.

"You do. I don't know a lot though." I paused, deciding on what to reveal. "You need to be aware that this is classified. The Admiralty informed me of the possibility of a Hauda presence in this system. I was instructed to ascertain whether they were here or not, and to report that back. The Hauda themselves are considered a threat to the Confederacy, and to be eliminated if the opportunity presents itself. They are extremely technically advanced, and their intentions are unknown. I believe they were the reason for the asteroidship's presence in Sunna, and I also believe they are the reason that Xon vessel engaged us. Finally, I believe they did so to order to draw us here."

She was silent a moment. "You take this to be a trap?"

"I do."

"Yet we came anyway."

"It was the only way to discover what they wanted."

She nodded and looked over the side herself. "And you came yourself. That took guts."

I had nothing to say to that. Guts. Or stupidity.

Another shape flitted through the air above us. It was smaller, its wings fluttering. Its larger brethren ignored it, continuing their lazy orbit of the tower. With a buzz if darted towards us and landed on the rooftop with a thump. Furry legs absorbing the impact of its landing.

I would have backed up slightly, had the edge not been a step or so behind me. The appearance of the creature was startling. It looked like an insect. Its furry body brightly coloured yellow and black stripes, diaphanous wings buzzing for a second before folding neatly on its back. It was big for an insect. About as heavy as a human, each of its six legs as thick as one of our arms. It scuttled forwards quickly to stop in the centre of the platform, where it reared up on its hind four legs, leaving the front pair to fold across its chest. Multifaceted eyes regarded us coldly as its mandibles clattered. A pink tongue tasting the air before it.

Yet another biomechanical. The Hauda had quite a zoo. Each was an impressive creature. Their cybernetic core hidden beneath leathery skin or fur. If I hadn't known better I would have thought they were simple genetic constructs. Something the Hauda had grown in a vat somewhere. But there was more to them than that. Each was mechanically enhanced, hidden machinery making them so much more than they would have been otherwise.

The creature buzzed, the sound quickly changing amplitude. Up and down the range as if it was searching for the right frequency. "Leeeze," it seemed to say. "Laaaze."

"Are you trying to speak?"

"Please." It clattered its mandibles as if in irritation.

"Please?"

"Please dessissst … Please desist uzzing commm."

I waited patiently. It was learning quickly.

"Please desist utilising electromagnetic communications," it said suddenly.

"Our comms implants. I don't think it likes them," I said. "Don't use them for the moment."

"They attract the imphocyte," the creature continued.

"The imphocyte?"

"The Xxxxon."

Ah. "The Xon is your ally, yes?"

"Our relationship izz irrelevant."

I shrugged. Fine. "You are Hauda?"

"That term is a slur."

"What would you like to be called?"

"You would not understand what we are." It rotated slowly, studying each of in turn. At least that was the impression it gave. It was impossible to determine what it was looking at. "Why did you come here?" it demanded.

I stepped closer to it, ignoring my companions as they tensed. "Why did you draw us here?"

The creature buzzed for a moment, turning to face me. "We did not. Why did you come here?"

I studied the crystal chandelier suspended above us. It was radiating a soft blue light. It didn't seem to have a specific source, it was as if the crystal itself was lit by some internal energy. As with the spire itself, I had no frame of reference to judge its size or distance. It could have been just out of reach. It could be a hundred metres above us. There was no way to tell. Not without Cena.

I did wonder what the relationship was between the chandelier and the Hauda. A crystal chandelier and the crystal entities. Was this the focus of the Hauda's mind? Had we found it? That answer felt too simple. Too easy.

"We are interested in the imphocyte," I said.

The creature clacked its mandibles. "You attack them."

"We defend ourselves. We return fire only."

"Your presence desss ... destabilises."

"Why are you here?" I was stalling. Cena needed time to get into position. I didn't know how much. I would have to give it as much time as I could.

"We answer no questions. You must leave this place. You do not belong here."

"You brought us here," I said to it.

"We did not. Summon your vessel. You must leave."

I frowned. "And if we do not?"

"You will not be allowed to stay."

"If you did not invite us here then the imphocyte did. This is their home world, not yours. You are a guest here yourself."

"The imphocyte does not wish your presence here."

"Someone does. We were attacked by a Xon vessel at Sunna-Deste-Anne. Whoever sent it there would know we'd end up here, looking for them. Unless someone is foolish enough to think they can attack a Confederate vessel with impunity. Are you that naïve? Is the Xon?"

"The imphocyte has no presence outside this system. They have no need."

"That's strange then. As one of them attacked us. A vessel belonging to this very faction." I pointed back towards the main cavern and its mainframe systems.

"That cannot be. They have no need to extend their presence beyond this system."

"Well, someone gave them the idea. You perhaps?" I knew the creature's words to be a lie. The Xon were known to travel outside this system. It was how the Sunna had run into them, after all.

The creature was silent for a moment, apart from the buzzing of its wings as it fluttered them. Agitated. "The imphocyte cannot access us."

"And if they could? Perhaps they are not as stupid as you take them to be. What would they find if they did, my furry friend?"

"It is impossible. You lie. The Confffffederacy are liars and thieves."

"Would it discover you were conspiring to attack the Sunna?"

"The Sunna are foolish for inviting the Confederacy."

"So you are aware of the attack?"

The creature's wings buzzed in irritation. Its feet lifting from the deck momentarily. "We state merely that they are foolish. Why are you here?"

Of course a Hauda would never be caught in a slip. It was too wary for that. I was not going to be able to trap it. Then what was the point in all of this? If this creature – this Hauda – was not going to tell me anything? "If you had nothing to do with it, tell me who did. Who attacked the Sunna? And how did the Xon ... the imphocyte know about it in advance? This imphocyte. Your patron."

"I have no knowledge. The imphocyte does not share with us."

Which was an interesting thing to say. The Hauda were far more advanced than the Xon. I'd always presumed they could easily overcome the machine AI. What did it mean if that was not so? And had the Xon somehow managed to learn something without the Hauda knowing? Learning of an impending attack they weren't supposed to know about. Either from the Hauda themselves, or from someplace else.

"Has anyone else been to this system since you arrived? Before we got here?"

"No one is foolish enough to enter this system. Even the Quint would not do so."

The Quint? They were another elder race. Another advanced people who dwelled in this part of the galaxy. We did not have a very good relationship with them at all. "They have communicated with no one?"

"The other factions are unknown to us. However we have detected no communications."

"And no one has communicated with you?"

The creature's mandibles clacked. "You understand so little of us."

Which was true. "Do you know who attacked the Sunna?"

"The Sunna brought their fate to themselves."

A non-answer. "Do the Quint know who attacked them?"

"You must leave. We wish to answer no further questions. You are not welcome here."

"Can we not take the answer from them?" Beyard stepped closer, her knife in her hand.

"You cannot threaten this creature," I said to her. "It is a drone only."

"You are naïve," the creature said. "You are such a young and foolish people. It was your foolishness that caused you to attack us. It is your foolishness that brings you here now."

"You were destroyed because you tried to subvert the people around you. You should have known what would happen." I was rather hoping the Hauda would object to that analysis. While it was, essentially, the explanation given by the Admiralty, it wasn't necessarily correct. I, of all people, knew there were a number of reasons why the Confederate navy might attack and destroy a people. There were multiple definitions of 'threat'.

"Your masters lie," the creature obliged. "We attacked no one. We remained within Genii as was the agreement. The Confederacy broke the agreement by coming to us. We defended ourselves, as we should."

"So what did the Confederacy find in Genii that concerned them?"

"Captain? What is this?" Beyard asked.

I ignored her. "Why did the navy consider you a threat?"

"You misunderstood us. You always misunderstood us. That was why we remained apart. You discovered what we had become and you felt threatened by it. The Confederacy does not like difference."

"Difference, how?"

"You would not understand. You would not wish to."

"Explain yourself."

The creature was silent for a moment. The buzzing of wing and mandible had stopped. It was silent now, as if deep in thought. Unlikely as I knew the creature itself was not intelligent. There may be an intelligence behind it, but that mind was not present here. This was merely a drone.

"What do you see before you?" It said in answer.

"A creature. A biological machine you have made. A drone."

"Why do you see that?"

I frowned. "Because that is what it is."

"Because that is your experience. You see nothing else."

Of course I didn't. Should I? "What else can it be?" I looked closer at the creature. Studying its fine fur and multifaceted eyes. An antenna that twitched from time to time as if it could sense something.

"How can I explain what we are, when you have no frame of reference?"

I thought it through. From the perspective that perhaps this was more than a mere drone. If it was more than that what could it be?

"This is one of the Hauda you speak of," Beyard supplied for me. "It's not a drone. It is one of them."

That notion did surprise me. From the admiralty's brief I knew the Hauda had long left their human form behind. Transferring their consciousness into a crystal matrix. To become immortal, amongst other things. Was that analysis wrong? Could this creature contain a Hauda consciousness?

"You are Hauda?" I asked it.

"The creature you see before you is part of us, yes."

Part of them? The Hauda had always referred to itself in the plural. It had never referred to itself as an individual. Was it possible it was not an individual at all? "You are a hive mind." I said.

"Still, that does not adequately describe us."

Now that would perturb the Confederacy. They would not like it at all. So much so I could well imagine they would take every effort to stamp out this perversion.

"We are no longer fearful of your Confederation," the creature continued. "We are beyond its reach. I tell you this as you will have been tasked to identify and destroy us."

"I wouldn't guarantee that. Even the *Cesa* can get to you here. And it is not the most powerful vessel in the fleet. And yes, we have received orders to eliminate your presence."

"Captain!" Beyard hissed. "This is an enemy. Should you be giving it that information?"

I ignored her.

The insectile creature buzzed slightly. "You could destroy all of this world, but even that would not harm us."

"You would be dead."

"All are part of the whole. As long as one exists, all exist."

"There are more Hauda outside this system?"

"There are more of us than there ever have been. We are beyond your reach."

There had been tens of billions in the Genii system before the attack. Even the official reports had not been able to estimate their true number. If there were more than that now …

We were looking for a swarm. A swarm with unknown capabilities.

"Why would you destroy the Sunna?" I asked the Hauda. "It was you, wasn't it?"

The creature's mandibles clacked. "Why should we hate the Sunna so? They were aligning with the Confederacy, but we did not fear them. They were no threat to us."

"So why destroy them?"

"Are they destroyed?"

"Then what are they?"

"There is more in the cosmos than you know. Not all that is consumed is destroyed."

What kind of a response was that? This Hauda was playing games. "They were consumed but not destroyed? That makes no sense."

"You are still naïve. I will give you no more. It is time for you to leave."

"A whole world has been destroyed. Billions died. You have to tell me what happened." I remembered the faces Ference and I had seen in the city of the dead. The fear and horror.

The creature's diaphanous wings stretched as if it was about to take flight.

"Tell me!"

Wings twitched but it did not take to the air. "You and I are not the oldest inhabitants of the cosmos. There are others far older than we."

"The oldest people we know of are the Suziemekaar. Their civilisation is over a million years old," I said. "You mean someone as old as they are?"

"Much older than they. They are younglings beside some who reside in this galaxy."

That gave me pause. "You're not talking about humans, are you? You mean some kind of alien intelligence? We've never found any. Every world we have ever found, every civilisation, had human origins. Even if they can't remember it."

"Have you visited every world? Have you ventured to every system in the galaxy? You are arrogant to presume you know everything."

Shit. This was getting complicated. "We've never come across any. We've come across the odd myth but there was never any firm evidence. Ever."

"Would your masters admit to it if you had?"

No, they wouldn't. Not to me. "What have you found?"

"Izzy, this is getting ridiculous," Beyard said.

I waved her away. "What have you found?" I repeated.

"Would you recognise a non-human intelligence if you saw it?" the Hauda asked.

"I don't know. I wouldn't know what to expect. But you have? And what would they have to do with the Sunna?"

"Captain, I am in position. I need to bring you out now." A new voice intruded. Cena.

"Cen. Shit. Do you have what you need?"

"No. Not yet. The Xon AI is more fragmented than I anticipated. It possesses multiple cores, and they don't always communicate with each other. It is quite perplexing."

I had never heard the AI say that before. "We need more time."

"You will not have it. The other factions have come to the conclusion Sunrise is responsible for our presence here, and have turned their attention to it. They have already deployed a number of small nuclear weapons on the outskirts of this installation."

"Are they mad?" I hadn't felt anything. But then we were a long way down.

"What is it, Izzy?" Beyard noticed my expression.

I said nothing. "We are out of time," I said to the Hauda. "I believe you were involved in the attack on the Sunna. I don't know how, and I don't know how there could be more of you now than there were before. There were very few survivors of the attack on Genii. There cannot be many of you now. And this alien you refer to…" I shrugged.

"We did not send the imphocyte to Sunna. We cannot," it said.

I believed it. As fragmented as the Xon were, I don't believe the Hauda had ever infiltrated them very effectively. They were not masters of AI. They were masters of biological manipulation. Perhaps why they had come here and stayed. They had wanted to incorporate AI into themselves. It would have given them a considerable advantage. Clearly that had failed.

I frowned. "Does the Xon know you killed its humans?"

The creature froze. Even its antenna did not move for long moments.

"They had a small colony on the surface when you arrived, didn't they? You sent in your frogs. You probably flooded it first, to drown as many as possible. The frogs then killed the rest. Does the Xon know?" I continued.

"The imphocyte cared for their humans, but they did not understand them. They worshipped them as gods."

"Of course they did. The humans were their creators. But you killed them. Why?"

"Humans would never accept us. Your Confederation showed us that. They would convince the imphocyte to reject us. But we needed to stay. We needed them."

"You needed the imphocyte? For what?"

"We do not possess superliminality. We desired it."

Of course. As far as any human scientist was concerned, faster than light travel was impossible. No one had ever been able to solve the riddle, even after thousands of years of trying. Yet the Confederacy had. No one really knew how. Some believed our AI had solved it. So perhaps the Hauda had come here, to a civilisation of AI's. Surely the melding of advanced human minds and AI cores could solve the same riddle our AI's had.

"So you murdered the last remnants of their race. A race as old as yours."

"It was necessary."

"Does the Xon know how their humans died?" I asked Cena.

"It does not. From the records it was an accidental flood in their surface installation."

I studied the creature before me. As things stood, I was never going to get the answers I wanted. I needed to change the conditions. I said out loud: "Tell it. Tell it the Hauda killed them." And then, silently: "Get us the hell out of here."

"Three MAV are incoming. They are taking advantage of the activity on the surface to breach the city's defences. They should be with you momentarily."

"You cannot!" The creature's wings buzzed, lifting it off the platform once again.

"It deserves to know."

The twins saw the danger before I did. I heard swords sliding from scabbards as they turned to face it. Wings beat in the darkness as the flying creatures swooped towards us. Talons outstretched. The knives of Baes and Beyard seemed woefully inadequate, but they drew them anyway.

"Those MAV better be quick, Cen."

"Thirty seconds."

One of the twins lunged, his sword a blur in the dim blue light. With a heavy thunk it severed a claw. The winged creature shrieked, blood gushing from its cleaved limb, liberally splattering the marine. He was quick. Quicker than I had ever seen a marine move. The sword blurred again, this time flicking up to catch the creature's under belly. It sliced through leathery skin and bone. Organs gushed through the gap, just missing the twin as he ducked aside to prevent it landing on his head. The beast's shriek's died suddenly as it hit the platform and skidded off the edge. Disappearing into darkness, leaving a trail of blood behind. Still connected the organs uncoiled and slipped after it.

Behind me Baes ducked, narrowly avoiding being picked from the platform by another creature. In a fluid motion he slammed his knife into the beast's side, just below its wing root where any normal creature's heart would be. It landed clumsily, coughing as if it had swallowed something unpalatable.

"This will not stand," the furry Hauda before me said, its diaphanous wings buzzing as if it was about to take off.

"No you don't." I threw myself at it, my weight knocking it to the platform. I clasped my hands behind its back to prevent its wings from spreading for flight.

"You cannot stop me." The creature wriggled in my grasp. Its fur surprisingly prickly, as if each strand was a whisker thin spine. I heard its mandibles clack near my ear as it tried to bite my neck.

"Shit." I didn't have a knife. I had nothing but my weight. Kicking against the slippery deck I knocked the creature onto its back. Its six legs beating at me as it tried to push me away.

An achingly bright light swept into the cavern alongside this one, the MAV descending into the subterranean city. They appeared in the distance as two points of light so bright it was impossible to look directly at them. Their illumination revealed the Xon activity all about them. Like a disturbed ant's nest every drone was headed this way. A swarm of flying, crawling, swinging and wriggling insects. Each intent on exacting revenge on the Hauda for murdering their humans. I caught little more than a glance of them as I struggled with the creature. It was as if the very walls and floor of the cavern was moving, covered by an unimaginable number of machines of all shapes and sizes, each one bent on one objective.

"You must release me," the Hauda insisted.

"No. You have a lot of questions to answer."

There was a flash of light as one of the MAV engaged a Xon that got in the way. The high energy plasma ripping through the flying machine, disintegrating it instantly. With their primary offensive and defensive systems engaged the MAV were miniature suns. The hull of each keeping a standing wave of plasma in suspension. A sheath of energy hotter than the surface of a star. Any incoming munition or beam would expend itself on the wall of flame, never coming close to the hull concealed beneath. The MAV could wrap that sheath around itself, creating jets of plasma as a weapon to engage any enemy that came too close. The energetic beam of ultra-high-density plasma ripping through the atomic structure of anything it touched. Armoured or not. A MAV was a diminutive warship in its own right. Not to be underestimated. A third dark shape moved beneath. A third MAV, its own interdiction shields down so it could pick us up quickly from the spire.

"You will not have me." The Hauda's legs kicked in unison, driving us towards the edge of the platform.

Cursing I hung on, my boots slipping in the blood and gore that covered the surface.

"Izzy!" I heard a shout behind me as we went over the edge.

The wind of our passage roared in my ears as we passed into darkness, the spire cutting out the baleful blue illumination of the crystals above. I refused to let go of the squirming creature, well aware that it possessed wings while I did not.

"Release me!" The Hauda's hiss was almost lost in the sound of our passage. As long as I was holding onto it it could not extend its wings to carry itself away.

"Izzy, you appear to have become separated from your comrades," Cena said in my ear.

"Pick them up first. Then come for me."

"Are you certain?"

"Very. I'll be fine."

I warped my ghoscht about me, both restricting the creature as well as dragging on the sheer wall of the spire beside us. I didn't care about our EM footprint now. It was far too late for that.

"This is pointless, I will reveal nothing." I could barely hear it above the wind of our fall.

"That ..." I said into what I took to be an ear. "Is yet ... to be ... established!" I grunted as a bony leg caught my stomach. "Stop struggling."

Tumbling as we were it was difficult keeping a straight path, even with the ghoscht's assistance. The wall slammed into me more than once. Knocking the wind from me. Crushing fingers. Battering my already beleaguered head. The ground couldn't come up quickly enough.

"How high is this thing?" I asked no one.

We passed in amongst shorter structures. The last of the dim light washing from above us.

"Release me."

The ground came up on us fast. I compressed the ghoscht about us, absorbing as much of the impact as possible. We still came down hard.

"Izzy. Are you OK?" The AI enquired. "Izzy?"

I groaned, refusing to move for a moment. Everything hurt. Every bone and muscle. It was all a cacophony of pain. "Yes. Yes. I'm fine."

"Your charge makes ready to escape," Cena warned.

"Shit."

The ghoscht was still functional. I warped its fields around the creature and pinned it to the hard surface we'd come down on. Its wings buzzed furiously but they couldn't break my hold.

I ignored its struggles, trying to lay as still as possible. I could see a sliver of the sky – if you could call it that – high above. There was the odd flash as one of the MAVs fired at something unseen. A shadow flitting over as a Xon drone clawed at one of the Hauda flying creatures. I couldn't hear much. We were too far away for that.

Something black and oblong obscured even that tiny sliver.
The MAV.

Chapter 9

I didn't see much of the city after the MAV picked me up. I did review the sensor footage later though.

The three MAV departed the underground complex as soon as we were aboard. Just as the main force of Xon hit the Hauda installation, shattering the crystal chandelier and ripping up the concentric structures built into the cavern floor. A wave of winged creatures tried to stave off the attack but there were too many machines. The avians were easily overwhelmed. We didn't wait to see what happened next. We didn't need to.

The sky above the city was a whirlwind of Xon aircraft of all shapes and sizes. Belonging to just about all the factions that had survived the attack on the *Cesa*. Flashes lit up the now darkened sky, atomic weaponry being thrown about with reckless abandon. The landing platform was already leaning, its easterly side ablaze. As we surged into the sky a weapon detonated at its base, removing the last of its support. Slowly, like a tree felled in the forest, it began to topple. Even the amount of smoke from the fires below was insufficient to conceal it slamming to the ground. Ripping through smaller structures and crushing the riot of Xon battling beneath it. It looked like the rest of the system had turned on Sunrise. I doubted the faction would survive until morning.

As it turned out the other factions were the least of its concerns. As the MAV rose into orbit we received instruction from the *Cesa* to stand back. Our return to the warship was delayed as its primary weapon system was engaged and aimed at the beleaguered city.

If anything the firing of the *Cesa's* primary weapon was an anti-climax. There was no bright light, no roil of thunder. Nothing but the slight blurring of the stars beyond it as the cruiser wrapped itself in a steep gravitational gradient. It grew until the bright wall of metal that was the vessel's hull blurred and dimmed, light struggling to escape as a singularity formed.

And then it was gone, the singularity ejected at the speed of light to slam into the planet beneath. That was not an anti-climax.

The planet seemed to warp, like a pen pressed into the side of an inflated balloon. The world's crust gave way almost instantly, unable to resist the impact of that much sheer kinetic energy. The continent was ripped apart, the shattered remains driven into the planet's mantle. The heat of the impact created a fireball thousands of kilometres across. A fiery shockwave that surged through the skies at the speed of sound, instantly searing everything it touched. We couldn't see it from our perspective, but a chunk of the planet was ripped from its opposite side. The singularity losing little of its momentum as it passed clear through Xon, carrying massive chunks of it into space beyond. A pillar of matter stretching into darkness. Rock, water, atmosphere. The lifeblood of the planet blasted into vacuum. Of the city itself we could see nothing. That was utterly annihilated. Atomised by the impact.

As the shockwave continued ripped through the planet, demolishing continents and vaporising oceans we were given leave to dock with the *Cesa*. The MAV turned away from the planet and we didn't look back. There was no point. Xon was now a dead planet. I doubted anything, even bacteria, could survive such a cataclysmic event.

I hadn't ordered this. Whatever I thought of either the Xon or the Hauda I did not agree with their annihilation. The admiralty had ordered that, Commander Tebercy relayed through Cena. He didn't like it either, but was not about to defy the order. The order had been to destroy the location utterly, without so much as waiting for me to board ship. No explanations had been given. None ever would.

The marines from Group 6 looked disappointed when they emerged from their launch pods, leaving their hard armour suits firmly ensconced within. They had been loaded aboard the MAV for the rescue mission, should a marine presence prove necessary. They had been looking forward to some action. Perhaps some payback for their comrades. I had instructed them to stay out of the CIC where the captured Hauda was being kept under guard. I preferred as few as possible to be aware of its presence. Remaining within their hard-armoured suits, firmly clamped into ejection pods they were forced to observe on their suit screens. Unable to do anything but watch.

I knew keeping them locked away was a waste of time, as there was no way the Hauda was staying secret. But it was worth a try.

Sorl'o intercepted us as we stepped from the MAV's lock. "To the infirmary, Captain." He surveyed my battered appearance as I slipped the ghoscht from my waist and handed it to the master at arms. "The same with the rest of you."

"How is Sanquey?"

"He'll be fine."

"See to the squad first, Doctor. I'll be fine."

He eyed up the marines as they followed me out. His expression was impenetrable. The ceramic of his facial covers concealing his alarm.

"You are the ship's captain," he reminded me. "It is not your place to engage in ground operations."

"I do what I must." I saw Tebercy heading in our direction and waved to him. "Unship our guest carefully, Commander. I don't want it harmed. Its presence here is classified."

The squat engineer nodded. "Of course. Who … what did you bring back? Have you captured a Xon?"

"Ah, I'll brief you later. Consider it extremely dangerous. There should be no interaction with it. Hard armoured marines as escorts only."

He frowned and looked past me as if he was expecting to see something. There was nothing beyond me but for steel bulkheads. "OK," he said slowly. "Can we talk? About …" He didn't know how to put it into words. He had been in command when the order came in to destroy the Xon. Not an easy responsibility to shoulder.

"Sure. My quarters later."

"The infirmary, Captain," Sorl'o repeated.

"Sure. Lead the way, Lieutenant," I said to Sorl'o. I'd have to admit I did need some time in the infirmary. I ached everywhere, and my head throbbed from the poor treatment it had received. True, my system was flooded with all kinds of exotic chemicals and nanomachinery, most of which were designed to heal me quickly. Today I think they could do with a bit of help.

I would deal with Tebercy later.

The MAV bay wasn't far from Well 4, a gravity well that joined the hull to the lowermost levels of the cruiser. We stepped into the brightly lit chasm and allowed Cena to guide us towards the infirmary on level two. It was a long way.

I should probably describe what a gravity well is. It's not to be confused with a planet's gravity well, and your people don't have anything even closely resembling it. I've already mentioned how large the *Cesa* is, as all warships tend to be. Due to its very size, it becomes a challenge moving equipment and personnel around. Particularly from one deck to another. Ramps and stairs are unfeasible when you have a kilometre or more to ascend. Elevators are a bottle neck. So — technically — we kept the elevator, but did away with the elevator carriage itself. The well was a vertical shaft stretching from the very highest levels to the very lowest. As brightly lit as it was, it was possible to see all the way down. It's a long way. Daunting if you're unaccustomed to it. Particularly as you used it by simply stepping into open space, trusting in Cena to guide you to your destination. Other crew members and cargo zipping past you at an unbelievable pace. It was safe enough. I'd never heard of anyone coming to harm when using it. Each level was equipped with an armoured boarding door. In the event unwelcome guests made it aboard, it could be sealed easily.

I might have fallen sleep on our way down to the core.

A ship as large as the *Cesa* is a busy place. There is always something that needs attention. Faults to rectify, munitions to replace, resources to replenish. Much of it was handled by department heads, and so did not require my involvement. Still, when I awoke in my quarters some time later Cena was ready to supply an agenda of activities that required my attention. I allowed the AI to go through them as I bathed and dressed. It was still going IT when I stepped from my front door and headed towards the bluff overlooking the village.

Boring with winter I had allowed spring to approach, thawing the snow and bringing out the early blooms under the trees of the forest. As I approached the bluff I could hear grinding. The sound easily noticeable above the crash of surf. I'd bored with the village too, and had instructed Cena to dismantle it. I was learning nothing from it. No long-hidden memory had been unearthed. No recollection jolted. I was simply tormenting myself with it. As with the winter, I had grown tired of that too.

I settled myself onto the cool stone of the bluff and watched the worm consuming the last of the buildings. It wouldn't take long, the mechanism was working quickly. We called it a worm, but it wasn't a discrete mechanism exactly. Rather it was a horde of mechanisms, each far too small to see with the naked human eye. A billion of them. Two billion. They swarmed, chewing over the substrate of the village, stripping it to its constituent elements, which were either used to replicate more mechanisms, or shunted off to holding facilities within the deck beneath.

"Commander Tebercy approaches," my AI companion informed me.

I didn't look up. "Sid. Join me."

The engineer settled himself onto the stone beside me and watched the last of my village melting into the ground. He didn't speak for a time, as if waiting for me to broach the subject that clearly stood between us. Unsettled he fidgeted, as if uncomfortable.

Clearing his throat he gathered the courage to speak. "Izzy … I had no choice. It was a clear order."

"Admiral Chisholm is intelligence division. She is not in our direct chain of command."

"She is still admiralty board."

I did not respond to that, instead sending a silent instruction to Cena. Holographic projectors concealed within the scenery powered up, casting an image before us. It was an image of space, dark despite the light of day within the chamber itself. The image quickly zoomed into a bright spark of light in the centre, the ember growing into a star and then an orange sun. Massive shapes were looped around it. It was a planetary system with no planets. They had been ripped apart and used as building material some time in the distant past. They had been replaced by something else entirely.

"What do you know about Genii?" I asked my second in command.

"The home world … the system where the Hauda originated? Nothing," he admitted.

"They were ancient when our ancestors first encountered them," I said. "Centuries before the Confederacy itself was formed. They found us, we did not find them. We were never permitted into their home system. That was one of the conditions of them joining the Confederacy. They would help us, supplying technology and materials, but we would never be true partners. They made the Confederacy possible but - to a degree — always remained outside of it. We didn't know how many of them there were. We didn't know what their home worlds looked like. We didn't know how old they were either. Of course we tried to guess the answers to all of these questions, but they were never anything but guesses. Until something changed. Until somehow they became our enemies. The Admiralty claim it was because the Hauda were attempting to colonise worlds outside their system. To export their way of life. To conquer their neighbours. But there was never any evidence of it." I turned to look at him, what I could see of him within the holographic image. He was little other than a shadow in the darkness. "I looked. None of their neighbours reported any contact. Still, the navy went to war with them. The first task force was lost with all hands. No one knows what happened to them. And then we upped the ante. We sent Admiral Pleasance and his Third Fleet. His orders: destroy everything. This image here … this is what he found. This is the only image we have of their home."

"Is that … are they ..?"

"Yes."

Three ribbons stretched around the star. Giant structures, one on each axis so they crossed in front of each other. Perfect rings each of them, their inner surfaces lit by the star at their centre. Even from here I could see continents and seas. Clouds … storm fronts. Cities glinting where night was formed by shadows falling onto the ring. Thousands of kilometres wide and … I did some rough math … almost a hundred million kilometres in length. Three of them. I couldn't imagine at the technology required to construct them. Or where they had found the raw materials. Possibly exhausting not only their own system, but several others besides. A feat of engineering beyond Confederate capability – even now. I couldn't imagine how many souls had called it home. Had. This was all gone now.

"Pleasance did as he was instructed. He followed orders."

"Shit Izzy. Did we kill all these people?"

"There were likely more people on those orbitals than there were in the rest of the Confederacy. Pleasance killed every one of them. Well, most of them. Some survived. Some were able to flee. And the navy has been chasing them ever since."

"Why?"

"Why did we kill them? I have no idea. Clearly the navy was terrified of them, but I have no idea why." I instructed Cena to progress the image. The rings splintered suddenly, the sherds spinning off into space. I couldn't see the energies directed against them, the weapons fire that had cracked the ribbons in two. Of the Confederate forces I could see nothing. We were too small. Too insignificant. One length of structure fell inwards, connecting with the star itself. Anyone still alive on it seared to death by the unbearable heat. Of those living on the other sherds who knew? Integrity destroyed I imagine their atmospheres had been dumped into deep space. Towns and cities sucked into the darkness, snuffing out every life within them. The other ribbons fared no better. Sliced into sections by Confederate warships they lost their structural integrity. Their own mass suddenly becoming their downfall. They ripped themselves apart. Slowly. This image was fast forwarding. Nothing on this scale happened quickly.

In subjective moments all life in the system had been snuffed out. More billions than I could imagine.

"We do know something of them," Tebercy said. "You captured one. It's in Holding Five."

"Is it?" I recalled the unhelpful conversation with the creature. Although, to be fair, much of that conversation had been me stalling, giving Cena time. Was it an actual Hauda, or was it a drone? A biological machine, designed to be remote controlled by an intelligence safely ensconced elsewhere. "Has it spoken since we brought it aboard?"

"No."

"I'm not sure it is a Hauda. A Hauda machine … of sorts. But a Hauda itself? I am not convinced."

"Why did you bother bringing it back then?"

I shrugged. "What else was there to do? We learned desperately little on the planet. We still don't know what's going on out here, or who is doing it."

He was silent a moment, watching the sherds glint their last as they were lost in the darkness of space. The image had wrapped around us, isolating us from the light of the compartment itself. In this gloom his greenish skin looked almost grey. "Would you have done it? Would you have followed the order?"

"No."

"Ah."

I had answered automatically, without the need to consider it. But then I had seen worlds destroyed before. Worlds other than the one we had just watched extinguished. I couldn't say it was a regular occurrence for the Confederate armed forces, but it did happen from time to time. Unfortunately I had witnessed it more than once. Every one was a crime. I would not be party to the extinguishing of a people. Machine or not. But of course I could not discuss any of that with Sid. I don't know whether we could be considered friends or not. We had worked alongside each other for some years. Still, did that mean I trusted him with these kinds of secrets? My part in that previous incident was very classified. If I were to so much as mention it I would spend the rest of my life in a jail cell somewhere. Did I trust him that much?

No.

I don't know if I trust you with any of it just yet. I've mentioned those worlds in passing, but that is all. The world of my birth. Which I never knew very much about. I did know someone within the Confederacy had ordered its destruction. I didn't know who or why. I have never told anyone I originated there, the only people who ever knew are themselves dead. The city ship I had grown up in itself long lost. Ripped apart by what had happened there. Then there was what happened on Dutchess. My Confederate masters knew very well what my role in that had been. But I haven't expanded on any of it to you. I might tell you about that. Some day. When I am ready. There has been a lot of death and destruction in my life. There was a lot more to come. Now that was something I refrained thinking about myself. Even though it does visit me in my dreams even now. Nightmares.

I digress. Nothing good comes from dwelling on any of that.

I stood and brushed dust from my trousers. "Let's go ensure all of this wasn't for nothing."

I wanted to get something – anything – from the Hauda. True, I didn't know whether it was a mere automaton or part of a Hauda collective itself, but there was only one way to find out.

The holding cells where the creature was being held was quite a walk from my quarters. Everything aboard the *Cesa* was a long way from everything else. There are quicker ways of getting about than by foot, but I preferred it. I had a lot to consider during the walk, and fortunately my companion respected my silence.

For a time anyway.

"I should apologise, then," he said as we were nearing our destination. Working our way up to level twenty-five, through a training area for Three Group.

I nodded to a squad of marines as they jogged past. "For what?"

"For firing when I should not have."

I didn't say anything myself for a moment. "Don't apologise to me, Sid. It is done. You cannot take it back."

"Shit."

"Destroying a world is final. There is no coming back from it. Everything they ever were, everything they will ever be, is gone. Will that world hold life again? Who knows? In a million years … two million. Maybe. You and I will not be around to see it. Nor will the Confederacy. Whatever that life looks like, it will be nothing like what was there before. That is gone forever. Chisholm is not out here. She is not qualified to make the decision to destroy a world."

Was I angry at him? Yes, very much so. Would showing that achieve anything? No. But still, I was not about to let him off easily. What had happened to Xon was his responsibility and his alone. Out here we could not be overridden by the Admiralty. We needed our independence to act as we needed to. There were even articles that reinforced that notion. Firing on Xon, even under orders from the Admiralty, was a stupid thing to do. I knew Tebercy was not a stupid man. He had made a mistake. A very bad one.

He didn't say anything further until we reached our destination. I was glad of it.

Modern warships are internally very similar. In fact, their interior layouts are nearly identical. Some are simply larger than others. I imagine Confederate designers had long settled on a formula that worked, and stuck with it. At the very core of every vessel was solid state engineering. A space where no humans ventured. The environment was simply too hostile for human life. Radiation, extreme gravitational tides, not a place a human could survive for long. Still, it was that machinery that made the vessel itself possible. Generating the power needed to run the rest of the ship, and to provide the drive that could propel the vessel to unimaginable speeds. Speeds considered impossible by much of humanity. I couldn't claim to understand the technique myself. No human could. Those designers were all machines. It was a rod a kilometre in length, around which everything else was wrapped. No matter where you were aboard down was that core, up was the hull. Each deck as you descended becoming more curved to port and starboard until you couldn't see more than fifty metres or so in either direction. You also became heavier, gravity at the hull seventy five percent of what you would experience on the lowest level.

Above those compartments were layered Navy Country, which were the command and control spaces. Where the bridge, the CIC and Marine Command were situated. Also where I and all the senior officers lived. It was where Red Group was barracked and where they trained. It was where the primary engineering spaces were — at least those accessible by the *Cesa's* human crew. Above that, sealed off by heavily armoured doors, was Marine Country. The largest area by volume within the ship. Separated into twelve segments, each able to be isolated from the other, each managed by a marine company. Here was situated most of the ancillary machinery necessary to make life aboard not only possible, but comfortable.

The lower levels were situated just above the tertiary layer of armour separating them from the naval spaces beneath. They were barracks, armouries and training facilities. Brightly lit passages and compartments, each teeming with activity. Marines never stood still. If they were not actively engaged in combat they were training for it. Honing skills, working on advancement. Each company was also responsible for the maintenance of their own areas, which was a wedge shape of territory, navy below, hull above, and other companies on each side. The engineering staff might take final responsibility for the operation of the vessel, but the vast majority of minor engineering work was completed by marines. So much so, many marines gained their qualifications and joined the ranks of engineers themselves. It was a good living, and once they were a qualified naval engineer, a world of possibilities opened up upon completion of their tour of service.

It was also in this space that Long Town and the farm were situated. Both administered and maintained by our marine contingency. They were identical spaces, set on opposite sides of the ship, each over a kilometre long, hundreds of metres tall and wide. All the living space we could possibly need, as well as plenty of hydroponic bays to keep the crew fed for however long we were out here.

Marine space was where the primary MAV bays, freight compartments and manufactories were situated too. They tended to be higher up in the ship, nudging on the armour of the hull itself. All fifty metres of it. A composite of exotic materials that was virtually impervious to anything anyone out here could throw at us. The only civilisation that could dent it was the Shoei themselves. And they were a very long way from here. Yes, it made us arrogant. Some might say with good cause. There was simply nothing out here that could threaten us. And even that was not taking into account the primary interdiction systems, and the offensive weapons batteries that were nestled within that armour layer itself. You have seen the *Cesa's* main weapons system in operation. A weapon as large as the vessel's hull itself. A weapon capable of ripping the heart from a habitable world. A terrible weapon, one I refrained from engaging whenever I possibly could.

Nestled between that roil of untold power beneath our feet, and the final layer of armour far above our heads, was the world where I and the crew spent most of our time. An invader had to penetrate very deeply indeed to reach it. Until they did, the Cesa remained fully operational. Quite capable of navigating and fighting back. As I've observed before, a modern Confederate warship was mercilessly functional.

That was the *CSS Cesa*. Kilometres of lethal warship. And it was a warship. No one would ever try to convince anyone it was ever anything different. It was a weapon of war. Designed to be extraordinarily hard to kill, carrying the most potent weapons seen anywhere in the galaxy. Only bested by vessels even larger than it was. And they did exist. A great many of them, in both Confederate and Shoei fleets. Battle wagons two or three times the *Cesa's* size and power.

We weren't likely to encounter them out here. Out here there was no one to seriously threaten us.

The Hauda had been placed in Internment. A holding cell of sorts within Sector Four, designed to accommodate enemy troops before they had been properly vetted (meaning searched). As they could feasibly still be holding ordnance or carrying a concealed weapon at that point the cell was armoured and electronically isolated from the rest of the ship. It was a six by six metre box. Two sides plain armour, the third a chunky door about half a metre thick. The final wall was visiplex, so thick it had a greenish tinge. There was no furniture of any kind. If a prisoner wanted to relax they could sit on the floor. If they needed to relieve themselves, well, they just didn't. You could set off a small nuke in there and it would only wreck the cell. Nothing outside would be affected.

The creature was standing motionless in the centre of the space, facing the visiplex wall, as if waiting for us to arrive. Which it probably was. Under the bright lights I could see it clearer now. It was an alien looking thing. A big insect. Your people might call it a wasp or a bee. Definitely a made thing. Nature had had no hand in its evolution.

Tebercy and I studied it silently for a moment. My companion visibly startled by its appearance. I found myself watching him more than I did it. His face wrinkled in disgust.

"And you rescued this …. thing?" he said finally.

"We need to know what it knows."

"I've glanced through the transcript of your interaction. I get the impression it won't give us anything willingly. How do you intend on compelling it?"

"Honestly? I have no idea." I didn't. I couldn't even threaten it. Death didn't seem to concern the creature.

I cleared my throat and keyed the intercom. "Are you comfortable?"

The insect did not react.

"You have been held here with no access to outside informat-"

"You haaavveee desssstroyed the imphocyte," the Hauda spoke suddenly. Its lisp had returned, as if it had forgotten how to speak.

"You are making a presumption."

"I pressssume nothing. I have seen."

I clicked off the intercom. "It claims to be a hive mind. Which could suggest it is in contact with other Hauda through a means we have been unable to identify. Those other Hauda could have witnessed the attack on Xon." I turned back to it. "How do you communicate with others like you?"

The creature made no response.

"We have detected no comm-"

"Confederates are murderers. That is who you are. You destroyed the imphocyte world because of something you do not understand. As you destroyed Genii."

I opened my mouth to say something but no words came.

Tebercy interjected. "You deny the Xon are a threat to the Confederacy?"

"The imphocyte do not threaten."

"Which is a non-answer. I observe that the Xon … the imphocyte as you call them, clearly had advance knowledge of the attack on Sunna. They are clearly in league with the perpetrator. I also observe Sunna-Deste-Anne was only one of a number of worlds who have suffered similar attacks in the last few decades. From where I am standing the imphocyte had it coming."

"Ssssssoooo you wish to do the same? You wish to destroy all the imphocyte?"

I held up a hand before Tebercy could respond. "Yes," I said. "Our mission now is to wipe out all Xon in this system, to remove them as a threat. You know we are capable of it. We have been eliminating all Xon ... imphocyte units since you were incarcerated. It won't be long now until we have eradicated them all."

"The Confederates are indeed murderersss. The imphocyte are not a threat to you."

"They attacked us and killed some of my crew. Give us a better target. Point us towards the actual culprits."

The creature did not respond. It would never give us actionable intel. I didn't expect it to. But I was after something else right now.

"Some would call it justice," I continued.

"The imphocyte are not unified. Yet you destroy them all. This is murder. And what we should expect from murderers."

I clicked off the intercom. "I think we have what we needed to know."

"I don't understand."

"How long have we been stationary? Twelve hours?"

"Slightly over."

"We have made no move to engage further Xon forces since firing on the planet. Yet, the Hauda here doesn't know that. If there were other Hauda in this system it should. It's a hive mind, and we've already established it can communicate using a means we cannot identify, if there were more Hauda it would know we have not engaged the Xon."

He frowned. "Seems plausible, but a bit weak. We could do with verifying it. Although I have no idea how we would. A Hauda could be hiding anywhere. It's a big system."

I was inclined to agree. Nothing this Hauda did or said could ever be trusted. It was a place to start though.

I clicked the intercom back on. "The Sunna. What was your motivation there? What was your motivation for any of the worlds you attacked?"

"The actions were necessary. You would not understand." Once again its speech had stabilised, as if it was getting back into practise.

"Explain it to me then." Had that been a confession?

"I have given you all I intend. Do as you will with this body."

"Let me take a guess then. The Sunna were our allies. In the decades or centuries to come they might have joined the Confederacy. Them and others like them. But you couldn't have that. You hate the Confederacy ... for what we are ... for what we did. So you pre-emptively attack any society that might give us a foothold out here. You want to prevent our expansion into this region."

"Your Confederacy is not welcome here."

"So that's the reason then? Doesn't that make you as bad as us. Worse even?"

"Your reasoning is flawed."

"Then explain it to me."

The creature said nothing.

I clicked off the intercom again. "Shit."

"Do we actually know it was the Hauda who attached Sunna? Has this ... thing actually admitted to it?"

I shook my head. "Not directly. Not even indirectly. But who else could it be? Who else could have the wherewithal to attack a world like Sunna without leaving bodies all over the place? Without wrecking the planet in the process? It would need something like the Hauda. Something like this creature claims the Hauda have become. A swarm. You've seen the analysis from the creature we pulled from the tower on Sunna? The biology of that thing is like nothing we've ever seen before. And now we're faced with this. Another creature. Something else we have never seen before. They have to be linked. They just have to be." It was all that made sense. But this was too important for me to guess. I had to know. I needed evidence.

"Either way you believe this ... whatever it is ... has the answer?"

"I do. It somehow got the Xon involved. Either directly or indirectly. The Xon themselves wouldn't attack the Sunna. They would have no reason to. They couldn't. They just don't have the capability. But someone or something gave them the idea to send the asteroid ship to Sunna, probably to lure us here. But to do that the Xon needed to know about the attack in advance. That was the only way they could get the ship there quickly enough. The Xon are not welcoming of outsiders. They don't engage in communication with anyone but for each other. The chances of a third party being involved in this system is remote. Which means the Hauda were either involved in what happened to the Sunna, or know who did. They also knew about it in advance."

"Evidence Izzy."

"Shit. There isn't any."

"No. Just conjecture. We have nothing definitive. And, I must point out, even if we did there is little we can do with that information. Do we plan on going to war with whoever perpetrated that attack? By ourselves? One ship against a civilisation capable of all that? We need to think this through."

"One thing at a time, Sid. Let's find out who did it first."

"This thing isn't going to tell us anything." He pointed through the visiplex. "We don't know enough about its physiology to compel it. If that's even possible. A hive mind you say? How do you interrogate a member of a hive mind?"

I didn't have the answers. I only had questions.

"Izzy, we have just been tickled," Cena reported.

That came as a surprise. "Details, Cena." I could do with the distraction. I was wasting my time here.

"We have been targeted by a comms laser. A very high power one. I am tracing its origin now. It is not local."

"High powered is an understatement," Tebercy commented as he accessed data on the incident. "For the Xon anyway."

I frowned as I did the same. The laser had burned away some of the *Cesa's* outer armour. Only a few centimetres mind you, but the fact it had managed to cause any damage at all was remarkable. Cena had automatically rolled the ship on impact, causing the laser to walk across the hull, creating a gully as it went. That was preferable to it drilling too deeply into the hull at any one point. It still had fifty metres to go before it connected with anything but adaptive armour, but the AI was not designed to take risks.

"The origin is moving quickly for a Xon," the AI continued. "I have picked up a string of anti-matter pulses from its approximate location, I believe they are related."

"Unlikely to be a coincidence," Tebercy said.

"A comms laser, you said, Cen. Have you translated it?"

"Each Xon faction uses a unique dialect, so it is taking me a moment. I believe one of the Xon AI's wishes to talk to you."

"Me?"

"The master of the alien vessel."

"That would be you," Tebercy commented.

I clicked my tongue and stared at the Hauda through the toughened visiplex. Once again our conversation was to be cut short. The creature had not moved since we entered the interrogation room. It had remained staring at the glassy wall before it, even though unable to see who was on the other side. Only its mandibles moved as it spoke, a disturbing clacking, chewing motion that produced a slurred although perfectly understandable speech. If it was breathing at all I couldn't tell. Cena was scanning it using concealed machinery, trying to understand its physiology. I know a sample had been taken and was currently being analysed. I had no idea what those tests would reveal.

The Hauda had been human once. Perhaps a very long time ago. I couldn't imagine what had happened to them that would lead them to create such bodies for themselves. It was certainly not something I would ever desire. They had left their humanity far behind.

"I believe the author of the message is heading towards us," the AI said. "I have identified the source's origin. It is a planetesimal on the edge of the system, three hours and twenty-six minutes away. It appears the Xon have utilised antimatter detonations to accelerate it in our direction. There were thirty-four explosions, each on the far side of the object."

That was crude indeed. Crude but effective. The Xon had set off explosions on the far side of whatever it was as a sort of star drive. I think your own people have played with the idea yourselves, using nuclear detonations against a pusher plate, which would impart thrust on the vessel with every detonation. Like I say – very crude. Still, it would take a long time for the Xon to arrive at this location. Weeks, if not months. Three point two light hours was a long way indeed without FTL.

"How fast are they moving?"

"Barely two percent of light."

"That'll be why they sent the comms laser," Tebercy said. "Without it we'd have left by the time they arrived."

"I'm surprised they managed to target us at that range. Cena, we've been stationary?"

"We have been holding station, yes."

"I think it needs a response, Izzy."

"It does."

"I have completed the translation," Cena said. "Master of Alien/Destructor of Xon. Conversation/interrogation desired/required. Hold fast/join."

"Stay where we are or go to them" I said. "Well, we're not sitting here for weeks waiting for them to arrive."

"Would you like me to set a course for their location?" the AI enquired.

"I would. Take a circuitous route. No more comms laser impacts, please Cen. Scan their vessel, its vicinity and its track. I want to know what we're headed into."

"Of course."

"Slowly. Give me some time to get to the bridge and go through what we have before we arrive." I looked back at the Hauda. The creature would have to wait.

Chapter 10

Modern warships possess advanced surveillance systems. Systems capable of stripping away the vast distances between them and their target, revealing them in stark relief while they themselves were barely aware of the warship's presence. If they were aware of it at all. I could explain the technique, but I fear it would not mean much to you. Hyperspacial surveillance systems are relatively new. They primarily rely on detecting the hyperspacial shadow of an object, rather than directly observing the object itself. In a similar way to the notion that an object with mass bends space around it. We can see the bend, not the mass. However that was enough to determine what we were looking at. Over the centuries the technique has been refined, so that now we can predict with a high degree of accuracy the specific nature of our target. Down to surface features, and the material the target is constructed from. All of this in real time and over vast distances.

This target was a planetesimal. A large moon or small planet. A chunk of rock and dust over three thousand kilometres in diameter. Roughly spherical, or at least it had been prior to launching itself across the system. It now had a massive crater cored out of one hemisphere. Legacy of the antimatter detonations that had taken place there. I wouldn't have believed it if I hadn't seen it for myself. Why would anyone, human or machine, sustain that kind of damage simply to launch themselves across the system? They must want to talk to us very badly indeed.

This time we had situated ourselves in the CIC, the Combat Information Centre, just off the bridge itself. It was a wide open space, ringed with intelligence gathering and command stations. The centre was a holoscreen on which the Xon planetesimal was displayed. Its surface was rippled by structures of all kinds. Towers, rings, blocks. Its subsurface riddled with passages and spaces. Some many kilometres across. We were standing away from it, at about ten light seconds' distance. Not far in cosmic terms, but far enough. I doubted they knew we were here. As big as we were we were far too small in the enormity of space, and besides, we weren't emitting any light or electromagnetic radiation of any kind. It was pretty dark out here, this far from the sun.

"It appears to be the Dophant," Sooch said. The second faction we had originally been interested in. The only faction, other than Sunrise, that had not immediately attacked us upon entering the system.

"Allies of Sunrise?" I suggested.

"Unknown," Sooch said. "Although I'd point out Sunrise did not wish to talk to us."

No, they hadn't. With the destruction of the Sunrise installation – OK, the destruction of the planet – we'd lost a source of intelligence. Cena's infiltration units were no longer able to transmit any data back to us. They, along with the city, no longer existed.

"Have we identified the comms laser they used to contact us?"

"I believe so," Sooch gestured to the image, lighting up an area on its surface. "This appears to be a comms laser. Or at least, a laser they could re-task for the purpose. I believe it was originally built for defensive purposes. There don't appear to be any receptor cells in its vicinity, so either they were not expecting a response, or sensors elsewhere on the station serve that function."

"So, how do we talk to them?"

He shrugged. "Unknown. Cen, do you have anything?"

"I have identified a number of receiving facilities scattered over the surface. They appear to be designed for local comms though."

"Would it matter? We'd still be in contact with the Dophant AI. Or a sub-processor of some kind. I presume they'd pass on the message, as it were."

"We can but attempt it," the AI said.

"What would we say?" Tebercy asked.

I shrugged. "Yes? You called?"

"I shall frame a suitable response," Cena said.

"Before you do, how long would it take to manufacture a drone capable of sending and receiving signals?"

"A surveillance drone could fulfil that requirement."

"Good. Drop one off here and move away from it. I don't want to be in the vicinity." The Xon comms laser couldn't do us much damage, the self-repair systems had filled in the gully it created even before it had finished transmitting. We didn't know what else the Dophant were carrying though. There was the possibility, vanishing though it was, they were wielding more powerful weaponry than that.

"I'm glad we're practising some caution," Matte commented from her station nearby.

"I need you to tell me whether the Xon is communicating with anyone else out here," I instructed her.

"They have fired off a number of comms lasers since we arrived," she said. "There isn't much scatter out here so we've not been able to intercept them. No one has replied though. Or at least, they have been unable to receive any communication from outside the vessel … if that is what this is. LOS is only stable if the motion of both parties is predictable."

I nodded. That, if anything, was good for us. It meant Dophant was alone out here. If that notion even meant anything to something thousands of kilometres across. As good as hyperspacial surveillance was it couldn't penetrate more than a few hundred metres into solid rock. Line-Of-Sight communications – or laser transmissions – were reliable and largely proof against interception. But their drawback was both parties needed to know precisely where to aim their lasers. If one party made off at high speed unexpectedly, they could expect to be cut off.

Cena dropped off three surveillance drones in total, in the event the Xon was able to disable one or more of them. They were about the size of a small car and were not as armoured as we were. Once they were in position Cena fired off a comms laser of our own.

Confirm arrival/joining. Require/request explanation/justification.

It didn't take long for a reply. Set to low power this time the returning laser did little more than warp a lens as it blasted the drone. The Xon still needed to tone it down a little.

Request join/entrance.

"There is a passage in the vessel's forward area about thirty kilometres across," Sooch indicated the feature on the image in the centre of the CIC. "It runs into the interior, at least one to two hundred kilometres beneath the surface. That's as far as we can tell from here. We'd need to get closer, but I suspect it goes right into the core. It appears to be navigable."

"We are not going in there," I said. It was one thing risking myself and a small squad of volunteers, it was another placing the *Cesa* into an environment where there was limited manoeuvrability. We knew the Xon liked their antimatter weapons. If they set one off close to the ship we were in trouble. I doubted we could fend off that kind of shock wave. This Xon clearly had warheads capable of digging a hole tens of kilometres into solid rock. I was not putting the ship anywhere near one of those.

Entrance declined. Communicate/explanation summoning.

Request join/entrance.

"They're not taking the hint," Sooch commented.

Willingness receive emissary/envoy, Cena continued. The reply could have been predicted.

Request join/entrance.

"This is a waste of time," Matte said.

I couldn't disagree. "OK. So, options. Clearly we are not going inside. In fact, this time I'm not even going to suggest sending anyone in there at all."

"How about a drone?" Tebercy suggested.

"Telepresence," I said. "Cen, can we do that?"

"I'd need to modify a MAV's internal comms systems. They are designed for holographic projection. We'd need the ability to project an image outside the vessel. I can utilise an android chassis, and use the projection as camouflage."

"Would the Xon know the difference?" I asked the AI.

"I could mimic a human's presence quite easily. It is what androids are designed for."

"How long?"

"Give me two minutes."

We remained on station within the CIC as Cena loaded the hardware aboard a modified MAV and launched it into space. Androids were not common within the Confederacy, although they were not entirely unknown either. They were never particularly intelligent on their own, not like the machines your entertainment media like to portray. They are simply too small to carry around that kind of processing capacity, and the power packs needed to power them. Not within a frame roughly the size of a human. Instead AI's used them as drones. The guiding intelligence remaining aboard a mothership, while the android ventured into areas where a vessel simply couldn't go. The *Cesa* left the MAV and its sole android occupant behind as we orbited the Xon slowly, remaining at a safe distance and hopefully invisible against the inky blackness of deep space.

"Something I need to understand," Matte said. "Current thinking is that these … Hauda are implicated on what happened to the Sunna. And presumably all the other worlds that were attacked in the same way."

"You'd be correct," I agreed.

"And the Admiralty … specifically Admiral Chisholm … pointed us in their direction. It was her instruction that led to our mission to Xon, and ultimately its destruction. It was her who gave the order to open fire on the planet, wasn't it?"

"Yes," I said simply, refraining from looking in Tebercy's direction. She hadn't mentioned Ference in any of that, but I suspected the man worked for her.

"Doesn't that suggest the admiralty … Chisholm … was aware of who perpetrated that crime all along? Why this farce? Why did Ference lead us in this direction?"

Why indeed? "I'm not taking it Chisholm was aware of the connection between the Hauda and Sunna. She simply took advantage of our presence in this system to handle some unfinished business."

"It seems likely though?"

"There are many unknowns," Tebercy interjected. "We currently don't know who knew what, or when. We don't have solid evidence of Hauda involvement in Sunna."

"It's looking pretty damned likely though, isn't it?"

"Yes," I said. "It is. We need that evidence though."

"Chisholm didn't seem to need it when she ordered we fire on Xon."

"I'm afraid I'm not an admiral of the Confederate fleet, with a seat on the Admiralty board. I can't second guess what she does … or doesn't know. I can only deal with what evidence we have before us."

"So, to be clear. That's why we are here? We are information gathering, in the hopes this Xon has more information. Information your prisoner has refrained from sharing."

"Exactly so. I … we don't know what Dophant knows, or is willing to share. But we need to investigate this."

"So there's no actual plan? We just hope this Xon will give us something?"

"You have an alternative?"

"No. I want to ensure I understand what we are doing here."

I had been thinking that Matte's objectionalism was personal. But she had criticised Chisholm too. A senior officer. As senior as they got. Perhaps there was more to her than I had thought. It's useful surrounding yourself with people who keep you honest.

Even taking into account the speeds our vessels were capable of achieving, everything happens slowly in space. Refraining from engaging its main drive the MAV crept towards the planet. Cena fired off a message to the Dophont. We were coming. Fire

118

on us and we will respond in kind. I think they got that message. They didn't fire on the MAV. Clearly they had witnessed what had happened to Xon.

"I'm taking it they will instruct the MAV to dock somewhere inside," I said.

"What is an AI going to do with a face-to-face?" Tebercy asked. No one had an answer for him.

"What does face-to-face even mean for an AI? Cen, you have any ideas on that?" I asked our AI.

"For an AI the request is largely meaningless," Cena said. "A typical AI possesses a distributed processing core. Which makes sense from various perspectives. It allows sub-cores to be more independent, and also protects it against outside attack. What does personal contact mean in that context? All we would be doing is standing before one of many sensor bundles, which itself might not even be closely associated with a core. This Xon clearly has another intention here. We need to be prepared for it."

The MAV hesitated at the mouth of the entrance, allowing its sensors to probe ahead. As dark as it was out here it was difficult to see the walls of the passage. From this perspective it looked like a massive crater, its bottom lost in darkness. The planet's surface itself dimly illuminated by the distant sun. A washed out expanse of grey metal that stretched to the horizon. As wide as it was, the passage almost reached that horizon itself. Allowing little more than a thin ring of steel to be visible in the distance. Within the passage itself was nothing. No light at all. No heat. No electromagnetic signatures. Nothing.

The MAV's sensors probed ahead, casting the interior of the passage into a false light. All we could see were smooth sides, as if it was a hole drilled through to the core of the planetoid.

"The passage narrows slowly as it goes," Sooch said. He was leaning forward, staring intently at a monitor. In the darkened space I couldn't see much more than a silhouette of him, the odd photoluminescent tattoo writing in the darkness. "Without using active sensors we can't see much over a hundred kilometres down it. In that distance it narrows by about twenty percent. There don't appear to be any branchings or side passages. There is one thing I'm finding strange though. This planet's gravity is one point two standard G's. Which is identical to Xon itself. Well, it was anyway."

"That is significant." I said. "This installation is not massive enough to possess that kind of gravity. It should only be about…"

"One eighth of a standard G," Cena provided. "Taking into account the apparent density of its substructure."

"Thanks. So they have enhanced it somehow. Which then begs the questions. How and Why?"

"I'm more concerned with the why right now," Sooch said. "An AI does not need gravity. If anything it's a hindrance."

"I'm not sure," Tebercy interjected. "How would a civilisation at this level of development generate a gravitational field? The only way I know of them achieving it is by creating a singularity of some kind at its core. If they're not regulating it properly and it becomes unstable. We're not safe where we are."

"Sid has a point. Pull us back please. I want us at least twice as far away."

"I'd recommend three to four times," the engineer said.

"What the man said. Make it five times please. Will that interfere with comms to the MAV?"

"No," Matt said. "I am interested in time dilation effects though. I've asked Cen to monitor and let us know if it starts to see any lag in comms."

It was easy to dismiss the Xon. Technically they were far less advanced than we were. Still, there were a lot of them. This system was teeming with swarms of vehicles. Every planet and moon was occupied. Even the gas giants harbouring orbital stations. We may have destroyed a few thousand of their vessels, but that was only a small fraction of how many they possessed. They had simply been those close enough to reach us in the time they had. Which, proportionately, was not many at all. We may also have destroyed Xon itself, and that was a blow, but these were machines we were talking about. They did not need a planet with atmosphere and warm barmy days. They could just as easily thrive in a vacuum on a barren rock a few degrees above absolute zero. They had also been out here a very long time. Easily tens of thousands of years. They had filled every gap, clawed their way into every niche. They had not spread much outside of this system simply because there was no drive to do so. The mission to Sunna being an exception. Hollowing out this moon, and building whatever they had constructed inside it, could have been achieved a very long time ago. Millenia before the Confederacy even existed.

So, we might look down on their crude vehicles and meagre technology. But we should really respect them. Respect their ability to persist in a universe where the only constant was change. Where so many other civilisations had fallen by the wayside and been forgotten.

The MAV swept into darkness, and was soon lost beneath the lip of the passage. We watched its progress in the CIC's central holoscreen, few words passing between us. There was nothing to say. Not until we reached our destination.

Twenty, thirty, forty kilometres the MAV descended. Eighty, a hundred. And still the passage continued. Slowly narrowing as it went, its walls still smooth and unmarked.

"There is a slight time dilation effect," Matte announced as it reached three hundred kilometres. "It will not affect tele-operation. Not unless it becomes a lot more pronounced."

"I think that answers the question though," Sooch said. He leaned forward intently, studying the image, even though there was still nothing to see. As an engineer he would love to get in there, and study what the Xon had built.

"Now this is interesting," Matte continued. "The object's centre of gravity is shifting as we head deeper. I don't think its core is its centre of gravity. Rather there are a number of them scattered through the object's crust."

"That doesn't make sense," I said. "It should only have one centre of gravity."

"Of course, of course. I mis-spoke. Systemically it will have one centre of gravity. Rather I mean there are multiple sources of gravitational stress on the system. They don't have one singularity. They have a number. Cen calculates in the region of seventy-five to a hundred. Each equidistant. Each about halfway between the core and the crust."

Shit. What had the Xon built here? And why? It made no sense. It was not a means of propulsion. The anti-matter detonations had proven that. And machines had no use for gravity.

"Cen. The antimatter detonations we detected. Given the mass of this object, what is the maximum acceleration they would have exerted?"

"Each detonation would have imparted enough energy to generate a three G acceleration on the system," the AI responded. "There were a total of thirty four detonations. That acceleration would not have been long lived though. It appears they used some kind of crude funnelling system. The escaping plasma would have had the effect of forming a rocket engine. Of a kind."

"Radiation at the core because of them?"

"Depends on the structure of the mass between the site of the detonations and the core. The higher the density the greater the protection it would have afforded. Still, given the estimated density of this object the radiation exposure at the core would be minimum."

"Survivable? For a human?"

"Shit, Izzy. What are you thinking?" Sooch turned away from the image to stare at me.

"Survivable, Cen?"

"Yes."

"I think I know what this is. And why they want us there in person."

"You are suggesting there are people here? Humans? And this is a habitat of some kind?" Matte asked.

"We will find out."

She shook her head. "The MAV has passed peak gravitation. It's passed through the ring of singularities. It is no longer falling. It now appears to be climbing up a gravity well."

"So they have reversed gravity at its core?"

"Seems that way. And this passage is blocked ahead. There appears to be a landing platform of some kind. Time dilation effects are still minimal," Matte said.

The MAV slowed as it approached the end of the passage. There was a ledge of some kind ahead of it, presenting a space for the vessel to land safely. Fortunately it was Cena piloting the MAV and not a human pilot, as the perspective would have been very confusing. The vessel was essentially landing upside down, as it swept past the ledge and then eased carefully onto it. With a bump it was down. One point two G. But in the completely wrong orientation.

Now what?

"We are receiving radio traffic," Cena said. "Emerge."

"I'll take it from here, Cen. The teleoperator ready to go?"

"It is. I will link to your implants."

"Go ahead."

The CIC dissolved as Cena routed data from the MAV. I found myself standing in the MAVs main passage. Within the gangway between the marine launch pods at the rear and the combat and control spaces towards the front of the vessel. I stumbled, reaching out to put a hand against a smooth metal wall. This was disorienting.

"The others can still hear and see everything you can," Cena spoke in my ear. I will take over control of the remote should you require it. But for moment it will feel like you are standing within the MAV."

"It's OK. I have it."

"There is breathable atmosphere outside the vehicle. Would you like me to open the ramp?"

"Please." I started wondering why the AI made that point. I wasn't really there, so didn't care if there was an atmosphere or not. The android we had camouflaged to appear human didn't care either. But then I realised we were keeping up pretences. It failed if I stepped into a vacuum without some kind of pressure suite on.

The ramp lowered silently and touched down onto bare stone. It was not completely dark beyond the MAV. There was a source of light somewhere overhead. It was not very strong, leaving me in a deep gloom. It was enough though.

"I can smell it. It smells like ... turpentine."

"I don't believe the atmosphere here has been filtered in a long time. There are a number of chemicals present. They would not be dangerous at their present concentration."

I stepped from the MAV and looked around the space. It was too dark to see anything. The wall could be a few metres or a few kilometres away. I couldn't see where the edge of the platform was, which was a worry. There wasn't much beneath this platform but for an awful lot of emptiness.

"I'm picking up an electromagnetic signature. A door is opening," Cena said.

A light grew in front of me, like a door trundling open, allowing light to flood out. An invitation. I accepted it and headed in its direction.

"This simulation is good," I said to the AI. It was. Had I not known better I could easily believe I was actually there.

"For this to appear natural it needs to be accurate," it responded.

Fair enough. The AI had considered this a utility, not an experience for me to enjoy. As much as anyone could enjoy whatever this was.

The lit entrance wasn't very large. It was perhaps large enough to fit a car through, but not much more. This invitation was for people only.

I heard a voice then. It was clearly mechanical, like a primitive machine trying to mimic human speech. I couldn't understand what it was saying.

"Interesting," Cena said. "This is the first time I've heard Xon speech. All previous instances have been in electronic form of some kind. I can translate, but it will be slow at first. I believe you are being invited to enter."

"This is going to be interesting if I am expected to talk to them."

"I had taken that as a given. Once I have decrypted enough of it I will be able to translate in real time."

"Presuming there is someone here to talk to."

"I think it is safe to presume there is. Otherwise there would be no point in the Xon invitation. It is still to be seen what form that presence will take however. Human would be ideal, naturally, but it cannot be guaranteed."

There was a passage beyond the door. It wasn't very long, perhaps a few dozen metres, and ended in another door. It began opening just as the one behind me started closing.

"We might be leaving the MAV behind. Will that be a problem?"

"As long as the unit remains within a few dozen kilometres it will not be a problem. Image quality will begin dropping off after that."

"It could be a lot further than that. This place is a planet. Pretty much."

"We're going to have to hope we don't. Unless you wish to come here in person?"

I was actually tempted. So far the Xon didn't seem to wish us harm. "Let's just see how this goes."

The first compartment was an airlock of sorts that opened into a cavern. It was a vast, empty and poorly lit space. It was difficult to judge its size, but it looked large enough to park the *Cesa* inside with ease. The walls were jagged rock, sweeping up to a ceiling lost in darkness. Punctuated here and there by a stalactite or column. The floor was a smooth, featureless expanse. As if the Xon had poured rock into the cavern and let it set. The only light was from the floor itself. A dull luminosity that did little to banish darkness from the space.

"Apart from the floor this looks natural," I said. "It's unusual for a planetary body to have spaces this far down though."

"Everything about this planetesimal is unusual. We must presume it was either manufactured, or the Xon heavily modified a naturally occurring planetary body."

I said nothing, concentrating on walking over the gloomy floor. There was a light to my left. It looked like sunlight washing through a cave entrance. Perhaps the Xon didn't want us to walk the full length of this cavern after all. We were not in any kind of rush, but I wasn't really looking forward to a long walk in darkness. I had been tempted to relinquish control of our emissary to Cena for the duration. I could always take over control again when we arrived at our destination. Unfortunately the booming voice had not returned with any kind of instruction. It was leaving me to find my own way.

"OK, now this is interesting." I stepped out of the cave onto a mountainside. A heavily wooded valley lay before me, with what looked like a river lazily making its way through the centre. There were openings in the trees here and there. The odd meadow breaking up the expanse of foliage. In the distance was a low mountain range stretching as far as I could see. It faded into haze, concealing the fact I was on the inside of a vast sphere. Land rising on all sides to meet overhead. That I could not see, as high above there was a sun blazing down on me. It looked natural from here, but that would only be an illusion. It was far too close and far too small, whatever it was. Still, it was all a matter of perspective. All I could say was that, from where I was standing, this looked like any mountain range on any planet. The illusion was perfect.

"There has to be a human presence," I heard Tebercy commenting. I'd almost forgotten that he was looking over my shoulder — as it were. "Why would the Xon build all this if it wasn't for a human population."

"I don't see any," I said.

"I believe I can identify something in the valley," Cena said. "Perhaps that is where we are expected to go."

I looked downwards, catching sight of what the AI had seen. A faint whisp of smoke rising into the warm air. It looked like someone was cooking lunch.

I headed away from the cave entrance, along a path that had been paid down the side of the mountain.

Chapter 11

There was a house. Of sorts. It was an assortment of domes, each one shaped from what looked like clay brick. Some were linked together by short tubes made of the same material. Others were standing alone. In the centre was a courtyard, empty but for a bushy, flat topped tree and what looked like a well. Someone had their washing hanging from lines at the back of the settlement – house. Whatever it was. Sheets and what looked like dresses flapped slowly in the warm breeze. Simple footpaths led this way and that from it. Either towards a nearby forest or in the direction of the river.

One of the structures sported a chimney. Smoke rose from it lazily. Someone was home.

"Shit," was all I could find to say.

"Your assessment appears to have been correct. This Xon has a captive human population," Cena said.

"There could be a lot of people here. In this habitat. I doubt there's more than a handful living in the settlement itself."

"The surface area of this habitat is considerable. Depending on their population density there could be many millions living within this space. I am afraid we are on the edge of my sensor range here. I cannot detect anything much further out than this. I do note, however, that we have not witnessed any other evidence of occupation."

My boots crunched on gravel as I approached the settlement. I was vaguely aware I had no boots. I had no feet. All of this was a simulation cast around the android's chassis. A very good one, but a simulation nevertheless.

"I can hear something," Cena said. "Singing. A woman's voice. From the courtyard."

Using a hand I sheltered my eyes from the glare of the bright orb high above. There was movement down there. I couldn't see much of it, it was obscured by the tree.

"Would you mind holding where you are for a moment? I am attempting to translate. We have never heard a spoken Xon dialect before."

"How long?"

"It depends."

That wasn't very helpful.

I settled myself onto a rock and looked around me, taking in the scenery. I was aware that this was an affectation. This sitting. I wasn't here to need the rest. I was a million kilometres away aboard the *Cesa*. Comfortable in a couch within the CIC, my command staff around me. I could disconnect this at any time. Still, sitting felt right.

We were in what looked like a depression. Or the bottom of a vast bowl. Grassland gave way to trees and hills in the distance. There was the odd rocky cliff protruding from the trees to my left where the cave entrance was concealed.

"How did all of this not shake free when the Xon accelerated the habitat?"

"Unknown," was all the AI could say.

"Acceleration along one axis should have thrown much of this into the air. This place should have been wrecked. Even under such limited acceleration."

"They clearly utilised a means of nullifying the effect. I am afraid I have no information as to how they achieved it. I can only speculate."

"So speculate."

"Without a complex means of manipulating gravitational effects directly, the only real solution would be to adjust the effects the micro-singularities embedded within the planetoid's crust. This would have gone some way to counter the accelerational effects."

"That sounds difficult. Is that even possible?"

"We could do it. Technically. I am not aware the Xon possess that kind of technical ability, however."

I shouldn't have asked. "Any ideas on that?" I pointed towards the image of the sun overhead.

"Also only speculation. I can think of several dozen ways they could achieve this effect. We do something similar in Longtown. If anything it is not the most remarkable feature of this habitat. I would be interested in understanding how they vent excess heat."

I nodded. A planet would radiate heat into space, but that couldn't happen here. The heat from their sun was trapped in this enclosed space. Vast as it was.

"I think I have it. You may proceed."

"You have translated her song?"

"I have used it as a template to translate the Xon dialect itself."

"Explain."

"While we have not heard their spoken language before, we have received a great deal of it though other means. Usually electronic. There are similarities between the two, that allow me to use this sample of spoken Xon to match against our existing library. I now have what I need to engage in conversation. You may proceed."

"Great."

The melody did not stop as I approached. It was a woman's voice singing softly. As if she was busy doing something else and not really paying attention to the words. "What is she singing?"

"It's a lullaby of sorts. 'For sleep you shall take. Long not to wake. The world will change, washing your troubles away.' It rhymes in their tongue."

"Long not to wake. Some sort of suspended animation?"

"I rather hope not."

I didn't have the opportunity to ask why as the singing ceased abruptly, the woman catching sight of me stepping into the courtyard. I hesitated. I think I might have stared.

She was old. That was my first impression. Long grey hair hanging about bony shoulders. She was wearing a simple white linen dress. No shoes. Before my interruption she had been working at a loom. A simple shuttle moving back and forth, the frame clack clacking. It was silent now.

She smiled and waved. "Come. Come. Do not be shy."

"I am translating, speak normally" Cena informed me.

I walked closer. The courtyard was simple sun beaten clay. Trampled smooth from generations of feet passing over it. Entrances to the dome-shaped abodes led off it. Their interiors either lost in darkness, or obscured by bead curtains.

"Sit. I do not often receive visitors." She indicated a rough wooden stool alongside hers. "None that require seating anyway."

"Thank you." I seated myself. This too felt natural.

"Let me look at you." She studied me, her gaze lingering on my uniform, as simple as it was. Cena had clothed the android in an unadorned shipboard uniform. Black trousers and black jacket. "You are from outside. Dreya told me you were coming."

"Dreya?"

"I believe she refers to the local Xon AI," Cena supplied.

"Yes." She waved to the buildings around us. To the skies above. "Dreya."

"Did Dreya tell you why I was coming?"

"Yes. You are here to take me away. I am ready."

So that was not what I had expected. I needed to slow this down a little. "I am called Isia. What are you called?"

"I am Me."

"Your name is Me?"

"It is what I am."

I wasn't sure Cena's translation was helping me with this. "This is your home, Me?"

"It is. You are welcome. Allow me to bring you a drink. You have walked a long way."

"Thank you, but I am not thirsty. Tell me, are there many other people living here? Or nearby?"

"There is only Me."

"There is no one at all?"

"Who else would there be?"

This whole habitat was for one woman? That seemed unlikely. "How long have you been here?"

Her brow furrowed as she considered. Perhaps a poorly phrased question. How would she judge the passing of time in this place? A habitat with no night. No seasons.

"It is hard to say." She held up a hand and studied it for a moment, turning it this way and that in the warm sunshine. If you could call it that. "I was not this old when I last woke. My hands were not this wrinkled. I have become old."

I was not altogether sure what that meant. "You do not sleep? You do not rest?"

"I'm not sure she means sleep in the classical sense," Cena said. "Her terminology is slightly off. I believe she may have a different meaning."

Suspended animation. Perhaps how the Xon managed to maintain a population over such vast stretches of time. We had estimated the Xon machine takeover to be somewhere in the region of seventy-five to a hundred thousand years ago. With the information we had there was no way to be more precise than that. Still, either way that was an unimaginable amount of time. That this small captive population had survived was astonishing. "Was it a long sleep? Perhaps cold?" I knew about hypersleep. I had been subjected to it as a child. It was not pleasant.

"It was cold. Yes. I don't remember much from before." She was silent for a moment, as if searching her memory. "There might have been other people here once. I don't remember. I was awake ... once. Before I slept. There might have been others. The trees seemed different. There are forests where there were none before. Fields where there was once a river. It is as if I dreamed."

"You have no memory from before you slept?"

She shook her head. "It does not matter. I was young then."

Now I knew about this all too well. We called it suspension amnesia, or freezer burn. It happened when someone was left in suspension for an extended period. Their long-term memory became fragmented, sometimes lost altogether. This very thing had happened to me, and was one of the reasons I remembered so little of my own childhood. Of why I had spent so much of my adulthood trying to find those answers. Unsuccessfully.

I had no idea how long this woman had been left in suspension. It could easily have been millennia. The interior of the habitat could have changed drastically in that time. Trees were themselves not immortal. Forests would have died. Replaced by new forests somewhere else.

"Have you always lived here?"

She smiled at me suddenly. "Dreya can answer you. We should go there and ask of it."

I hesitated. Was she referring to some kind of Xon interface where the machine intelligence spoke to her? I would be interested in that. "That would be good. Is it close?"

"We can walk. Would you like to walk?"

"I would." I hoped it wasn't far. Sooner or later we would reach the limit of this apparition. "How much further can we go?" I asked Cena.

"You are fine for the moment. I'll let you know if you are reaching our projection limit. Currently I can guess only. It depends on what is between your location and the MAV."

My companion stood and brushed down her dress. It allowed me to study it briefly. It looked home made. Perhaps on this very loom. "You make your own clothing?"

"I do." She seemed proud, a hand running the length of the loom as if caressing it.

"Did you build this yourself?"

"I have cared for it. Replacing parts when they broke." She paused and looked steadily at me again. "You ask many questions."

"It is a way of learning things. I wish to learn about you."

She nodded slowly. "I do not talk often. It tires me."

"So you wish to talk less?"

She shook her head and abruptly walked away from me without looking back. I followed quickly, presuming that was what she wanted. I had to give her allowances. She had been alone for a very long time.

"No," she said presently. "Soon I will be away from here. When will you take me?"

"I …" I couldn't take her. Not aboard the *Cesa*. Not now. I hadn't come here looking for … whatever she was. A survivor. A refugee? True, Confederate vessels were ultimately warships, but they served multiple roles. They were designed to break blockades, bringing relief to besieged populations. Our holds were large, many vessels such as the *Cesa* carried relief supplies as a matter of course. Engaged on a long-term diplomatic mission ours were taken up by storage for our own supply needs, as well as hydroponics bays so we could re-supply as we went. Still, the principle held. While we were a warship, we were not just a warship. We could take on refugees, and were expected to do so when it was appropriate. So taking her aboard was not unprecedented. Far from it. But I had reservations. Was it right taking her from this place? The only world she had ever known. Her home. She was in no danger here and seemed content enough. From what I could judge from the brief amount of time I had known her.

I'd need to know a lot more before I could make a judgement. She may very well be the last member of her people. She needed protecting. A Confederate warship was no place for her.

"I would like to know more about you first," I said after a long moment's contemplation. In that time we had left the tiny settlement and headed further down the valley, along another footpath winding between trees on its way to the river that flowed through it.

"What would you need to know?" The path was not wide enough for me to walk alongside, so I was relegated to following on behind. She didn't turn her head to speak to me.

"There is just you here?"

"I am not alone. Dreya lives here too."

"There is no one like you here though?"

She was silent for a long moment. I started believing she had not heard me and was about to repeat my question when she spoke: "I remember words … thoughts. Words like brother. Sister. Mother. Father." She paused again, as if searching her memory. "Friend. But those are words to me. They are empty. No one fills them. There are no faces in my mind."

"But Dreya could say for sure?"

"Dreya knows our world."

That would be a yes, I presumed. But of course a Xon would know what lay within the habitat it had constructed. There might have been others here once. Many others. A people who had all perished in the long stretches of time this place had existed. And now only this woman survived. Me.

"Do you know about anything outside of this place?" I asked her. "Does Dreya tell you what lies outside?"

She stopped so abruptly I almost walked into her. The apparition almost walked into her, rather. She turned to look at me.

"Dreya has told me what you did."

I stepped back slightly. "To Xon? To the planet?"

She frowned, as if she did not understand. "No. It told me what you did to Home."

"I believe she means the Xon homeworld," Cena interceded.

"Yes," was all I could find to say.

"Why did you do this thing?" She didn't move. As if she did not intend on continuing until she had a good answer. We'd be here a while. There was no good answer.

"Xo … Home contained a contagion. There was a presence there that was a threat. To all of us. We could not risk it spreading."

"Beaut came here once. I do not remember it. Dreya has told me about it. Dreya did not allow Beaut to know I was here."

"Beaut is how the Hauda refer to themselves," Cena said. "Hauda is itself a pejorative term. A name given to them by one of their neighbours, the Antanari. It means infection. Particularly an infection of the parasitical kind."

"The Beaut and my people do not have a great history," I said. "There was also evidence there were once people like you living on Home. People the Beaut destroyed. We could not allow it to happen again." Which was our official line anyway. Not that I put much faith in it. Our real motivations were somewhat more opaque than that.

"There were people like me on Home?"

"A long time ago. They were all long gone by the time we arrived."

"Dreya was not on Home. It remains out in the cold where the others cannot find it. That changed when you arrived. The others will find it now." With that she turned and continued on her way. We crossed a stone bridge spanning the river and continued on the other side.

"I don't know what that means," I said internally, to Cena.

"It is possible Dophant, or Dreya as Me refers to it, avoids the other factions," Cena said. "Perhaps it has been in hiding on the outskirts of the system for some time."

"To protect Me?"

"It is highly likely. Although, from what we saw of Sunrise, I doubt the other factions would have meant her harm. Sunrise revered its human population."

"Me, even knowing what we did, you are willing to leave this place with us?" I asked her.

She shrugged her bony shoulders. "It is what Dreya wishes."

"Do you want to leave?"

"To leave my friend? To live amongst strangers?"

"Yes."

"Dreya knows best."

That was not an answer. I didn't think I was going to get one.

"Cen, I am starting to suspect it was Dreya who sent the asteroidship to Sunna. It wanted to draw us here to hand Me over to us. It probably woke Me up in the hopes we would arrive to take her off its hands."

"It is possible," Tebercy said. He, along with the rest of my bridge crew, were still monitoring. "It also introduces the possibility the Xon did not have advance knowledge of the attack on Sunna. The ship could have been sent there to invite whoever it found to come and pick Me up. Due to what it found there … the Sunna being gone … the ship AI could have come to the conclusion we were the threat, which is why it attacked us."

"This could all have been a mistake?" I said.

"Possibly. Do we actually know any better? Do we actually know anything?"

Shit. He was right. True, the Hauda — and I purposefully use that term here — had been implicated in what had happened to the Sunna. But that was itself a guess. The Hauda locked in my brig had never admitted to anything. Not explicitly.

Perhaps all of this had been a colossal waste of time. And we were no further forward in understanding what had happened to the Sunna. A waste of time that had destroyed the Xon homeworld.

"How far have you travelled?" I asked my companion. My train of thought was not going to get me anywhere. "Have you seen much of your world?"

She was silent for a moment. "Why would I leave here?"

"Why would you travel? To see what is there."

"What would I see?"

OK. This line of questioning was not going well. "Do you know what there is to see?"

She was silent for a long moment again, and then said, "you are very strange."

"I ask questions as it is the only way to understand. Do you know what lies … that way?" I pointed in the direction we were walking. Much of the interior space was beyond Cena's detection range. I was curious what else was concealed here.

She didn't look back to see where I was indicating. "Trees. Rivers. Fields. Just as you see here."

"Have you been there?"

"My home supplies what I need."

OK. So perhaps that was a no. This was a pointless and quite frustrating conversation. I suspected it was for her also. "How much further do we go?"

"It is this way."

"Do we walk far?"

"Dreya will find us."

"Dreya moves around?"

"Sometimes I find Dreya here. Sometimes I find Dreya there. Sometimes I find Dreya at home."

So that was a yes. Perhaps some kind of mobile local node of the Xon AI. We passed into some trees. My companion slowed her stride, looking towards the dense foliage overhead.

"You are nearing my transmission limit," Cena warned. "You will start to experience drop outs in another hundred metres or so."

"I'm hoping it's not far now." If it was this would be a problem. How would Me react discovering I was nothing but a mirage wrapped around a metallic frame? How would the AI react?

We were soon lost in the forest. The pathway faltering, the valley beyond concealed by trees and bushy undergrowth. I stopped walking.

"Me, I need to know where Dreya is. We cannot keep on walking in the hopes we come across it."

My companion did not respond. Frowning I stepped around the bush she had just passed by. She was gone.

"Shit. Where is she? Cena, can you pick her up?"

"I am afraid my sensors are not effective at this range."

"Me?" The undergrowth was thick here, but not so thick a tall woman wearing a white dress could easily disappear in it. The android's internal sensor package was limited. Given more time Cena could have installed something a bit more comprehensive, but for the moment I couldn't see much more than I would have had I been stood there myself. We were relying on the nearby MAV for anything more than that.

"I am detecting motion in your proximity, but am unable to localise the source."

"She can't have gone far." Running out of places my companion could conceal herself I looked upwards. "Oh."

There was a shape in the trees above me. Spiderlike, it scuttled from branch to branch, before taking a swinging leap to a nearby tree. Once there it paused. I couldn't really discern whether it had a head, or any other kind of sensory organs, but I had the distinct feeling it was looking at me.

"Did we see anything like this on Xon?" I asked my AI companion. I didn't recall anything remotely like this, but then we had only visited a very small part of that doomed planet. There were undoubtedly all kinds of creatures we had never witnessed.

"I don't believe it is native fauna."

I was about to ask what Cena meant when something looped around the android's chassis and lifted it effortlessly into the air.

"I think I'm about to find out," I commented. I think I was about to find out whether the android was to become this thing's next meal.

"You wished to speak to Dreya," a voice said from nearby. I looked around as my perspective swayed. Whatever had picked me up hadn't accounted for the weight of the android.

My elderly companion was perched on a tree branch high in the air. So high the ground was lost in the foliage below us. She was cradled carefully – almost gingerly – by a thick tentacle that secured her to her perch. That was little more than a thick branch almost perfectly horizontal to the invisible ground.

There was more than one of these creatures, I realised. A few of the spidery shapes – three, no four… six?– skittered through the treetops. One held me securely and deftly placed me near my companion. My branch wasn't quite as horizontal, and I had to hold on tightly to stop myself slipping to the ground. Once I was placed the creature swung away. Clearly not concerned whether I fell from the height or not.

"I didn't think Xon built biomechs," I commented.

"I am not sure it is one," Cena responded. "I don't know what it is."

"OK. You've got me here," I said aloud. "I don't know why we couldn't have done this on the ground."

"Do not be concerned. I know the fall will not harm you," a new voice said. It did surprise me. Not because I couldn't tell which of the creatures was speaking, but because it was speaking in Complex. Complex was not a Xon tongue. It belonged to the Confederacy, our Lingua Franca if you would.

Holding onto the branch so as not to slip I focussed on the closest spider. "You forget that humans are frail."

"They are," the voice continued. "But automatons are not. You must admit, my own people have some experience in their manufacture."

I said nothing, gauging its meaning.

"Come. I ask you to respect me enough not to continue the charade," it continued after a moment.

I think that answered the question. "It does not concern you?" The Xon had not been fooled. It knew the nature of this apparition. Perhaps it always had.

"Should it? As you say, the human form is frail. Why would you trust your safety to an alien habitat like this? Although I do note you did so within Eight's lair. Should I be offended, that you trusted it more than you trust me? A mechanism that would not welcome your presence."

"Interesting," Cena said. "In Xon script the glyph for the number eight does resemble the Sunrise icon."

"So Eight is Sunrise?" I asked the AI.

"It would appear so."

"That was necessary," I said to the strange apparition. "Although I can't see how you should be offended. You have not presented yourself here."

"What makes you believe that?" The spiders had found a spot to observe me, each one perched a few metres away, their dark forms resisting my attempt to identify what exactly I was looking at. The simply looked like big spiders. Their bodies about a metre across, six spindly legs – more tentacles really – holding them securely to the tree tops. As the voice spoke they started moving. Dancing around us, swinging from limb to limb, the trees creaking as their weight came to bear. With a solid thump one impacted on another and clung on. Then there were twelve legs swinging the creature from tree to tree. There was another thump and a third collided with it, and clung on too.

"Can you tell what it's trying to do?" I asked Cena.

"I have a suspicion. I don't believe we have long to wait."

With each impact the creature grew in size. Arms wrapped around arms, making the resulting appendages thicker. It stopped swinging, finding a sturdy branch nearby to attach itself to, allowing the others to come to it. Each of them was a slightly different colour, I realised. And with each impact more and more detail was visible. Only the spider holding Me had not moved. It was needed where it was.

"OK, this is weird."

The collection of creatures was making a face. Or a head. Its hair — if you could call it that — the limbs that held it to the tree behind it. There was one final impact and the head was complete. Starkly blue eyes opened to regard me cooly.

"You wished to speak to Dreya," Me said again.

"You are not an AI," I said to the ... whatever it was.

"I am not," the disembodied head spoke. It was a deep, resonating voice. Not quite human but not completely inhuman either.

"Then what are you?"

"Does it matter?"

"I wish to understand your nature."

"I was human once. A long time ago."

"Before the machines took over?"

It might have nodded. Its hair appendages moved the grisly head slightly. "This was not always a civilisation of machines. You know that. I am from a time before that. A time when meat and machine lived alongside each other."

That made this apparition very old indeed. "Then you will know what happened. Why machines came to rule this civilisation."

"I do."

"I would be interested in hearing it." We knew very little about the Xon. Nothing about their civilisation before the arrival of the machines. Admiralty Science would not want me passing up on the opportunity.

"I did not invite you here to discuss history."

"I know why you invited me. You want me to take Me from here. Why should I want to do that? This is her home. Is it not?"

"She is no longer safe here. I wish for her to be safe."

"You need to convince me. My vessel is no place for a fragile old lady ..." I glanced towards Me. "No offence. It is a vessel of war. You have seen that." She smiled, not understanding. We were no longer using a language she was familiar with.

"Why would your Confederate masters send a warship to build relations with its neighbours? Would that not be provocative?" It felt strange hearing the disembodied head speaking like this. Particularly in what was, in essence, my own tongue. There were a great many languages within the Confederacy. Most worlds used many, and that was even when you excluded their local dialects. Complex was a mishmash of a lot of tongues, drawing aspects from many. As many as it could - that was its purpose. To build commonality.

Still, it was right, and I had walked into that. I didn't want Me onboard because … I wasn't sure really. Perhaps I had many reasons, none of which I had thought through just yet. The *Cesa* was more than a warship. Although it was easy to see why someone could believe otherwise.

"Cen, is there a city ship in the vicinity?" I already knew none of the giant vessels were in our patrol area. They would have declared themselves. It was considered etiquette. Still, the vehicles roamed the galaxy. Exploring. Colonising. One could be close enough to summon.

"The Shaan is the closest. It is six thousand lights from here. Would you like me to contact them? They could be here in ten days."

"Not yet. Does it have the facilities to take her in?"

"The Shaan is a GSX class vehicle."

That was all the AI needed to say. The GSX's were legendary. They averaged at over a hundred kilometres in length, with a population of between seventy to two hundred million souls. There was little they couldn't do. As massive as it was, I knew the Shaan's commander would respond if I called. It, also, was etiquette. Out here, beyond our borders, vessels always responded when another called.

"Not yet. Thank you." I studied the Xon for a moment, wondering why it had decided to call us here. Was this … entity responsible for the asteroid ship we encountered in the Sunna system? That was likely.

The disembodied head was three to four metres in width. So big I could see the tree it was clinging to bend under its weight. It didn't seem concerned. The individual spiders were still present, I realised. They hadn't morphed completely into this bizarre head. They were still there, each one a slightly different colour. Ranging from light grey to so dark as to be almost black. One creature seemed to form the lips. Another the nose. Still more the ears. I didn't know how the eyes worked, or which creature they were attributed to. Still, the fact that Me's spider was still holding her firmly to her perch meant the head had not absorbed every spider into it. There might still be more out there. Dozens, hundreds. Scattered around this planetismal, perhaps within the fleet of ships it controlled around the Xon system itself. A distributed intelligence of some kind. One that had been human once. I knew things like this were possible. I had met the Hauda, after all. They also possessed a kind of distributed intelligence, all be it within manufactured biomechanical creatures.

No wonder the Confederacy disliked adapted populations. Humans who had changed themselves in some way, either to adapt to their planetary conditions, or to enhance their physical form – to become more than mere human. How could we absorb a people like this into ourselves? How could they ever be one of us? They couldn't.

"I cannot take her with me," I continued. "But I can ensure she is looked after, if that is what you – or she – wants. I need to understand why though. Why, after all this time, is she no longer safe right here?"

"You already know the answer to that question. Or you must suspect." The bright blue eyes left me and studied my human companion. "She is precious to me."

"Is she the last of her kind?"

The eyes flicked back at me. For a moment the head did not respond, as if considering an appropriate answer. "She is."

"All other humans within this system are dead? You know that for a fact? After all, the other AI's ... you... have succeeded in concealing populations."

"She is the last."

"Explain. I need to understand."

The entity paused again. "I am not your enemy. I have done much. Much that I now regret. But I am not your enemy. We will never be allies, I am not foolish enough to believe that. But we do not need to be enemies." It paused once again. "There was a time when there were many of us. Humans. We were proud of our accomplishments. We had built a civilisation that spanned this system, and we were beginning to look outside it. To seek our destiny in the beyond. Still, we knew we would not succeed as we were. The spaces between worlds, between stars, was too great. We needed to become more robust. Longer living."

"So your people changed yourselves? To what? Entities like yourself?"

"I was the first. I am the last. We reached too far, and we fell. It was a step many were not ready to take."

"You're talking civil war." We had seen this before. Many, many times.

"When the conflict was over few remained. Our machines became our guardians. The mechanisms meant well, but in time we became fractious. We resisted. They were forced to act. Then there were even fewer of us. Our populations were captives. We were ... farmed. For our own protection."

"What were you doing during this time?"

"Neither the remaining humans nor the mechanisms, what you call AI's, welcomed my presence. Nor did I possess the ability to leave completely, seeking my future elsewhere. I withdrew to where you find me now. To the edge of the system. I built this world in an attempt to create a home for as many of my people as I could. For a long time I was successful."

"What changed?"

"The people who call themselves the Beaut found us. They took refuge amongst us and discovered we were still sheltering a human population. I believe you can speculate what came next."

I could. "What I don't understand is why the Hauda – the Beaut – would wish them harm."

"The Beaut themselves did not. However they were harbouring a parasite. A parasite that would feast on a human's mind. On their individuality. The parasite came with them."

"Hold on." I held up a hand to stop the creature. This was what I needed to know more about. Finally, an entity that could give me the answers I needed. "Tell me more about this parasite."

"I know nothing of its nature. I simply know of its existence and that the Beaut carried it with them."

"You said it consumes humans?"

"That it does. A Beaut brought it here, to this very world, under the guise of attempting to form a relationship between us. There were many people here then. My world was full of them. I tended to them. I protected them. I hoped they were happy here. But within hours of the Beaut's arrival they were dead. Consumed by the thing they carried with them. It feasted. When it feasted they perished. I was powerless to stop it."

"Some sort of predator? What did you try? What weapons?" I needed to know what this thing's weakness was. I knew I would face it sooner or later. I needed to know as much as I could if I was to defeat it.

"There are no weapons here."

"Describe it then. What did it look like? How did it act?"

"I cannot describe that which is formless."

Shit. What did that mean? "It had no physical form?"

"Its form changed. At first it was on thing, then it was another. Which is its true form? Are any of them?"

So some kind of shape shifter? "But it hunts humans?"

"It sought the mind. It fed on what made them who they were."

"It consumes human brain matter? Is that what you mean? Did it not consume their bodies too?" Which wouldn't make sense. The Sunna had simply vanished. Their world had not been left strewn with countless headless corpses. Everything had been taken. The Sunna had not been warlike, but they had most certainly possessed weapons. They were an unfortunate necessity for a people to defend themselves against the forces that creep between worlds. Pirates. Raiders. Whatever.

"All you need to know is that they cannot be stopped. When they were finished everything was gone. I was alone here."

"Apart from Me."

"Yes. She was in suspension and so had escaped their notice."

"Why? Why was she alone in suspension? Were there others who were not so lucky?"

"No. She was alone."

"Explain."

The entity was silent for a moment. As if contemplating an answer. "Before I was changed I had a family. A partner. Siblings. Children. I lost all of them ... most of them in the conflict. Only my daughter survived."

"What? She is your daughter?"

"I kept her close all this time. I protected her."

That was some feat. I'd never heard of a subject surviving more than a few centuries in suspension. If she had been in suspension since that ancient conflict that made her the oldest living human in existence. By a very long margin.

"Yet you revived her now? Surely it was not safe?"

"I sent an envoy to a neighbour in the hopes they could take her. I revived her so she would be ready when they came for her. She would be safer there than here. And it was time. Time for her to be amongst her own kind. In my desire to protect her I stole her life from her. I regretted that. I wished to repay her. To give her back that which I had taken."

"You sent the vessel to the Sunna."

"I did."

"But you didn't know the Sunna had been attacked." I said that mostly to myself. Of course it hadn't. How could it? So we – I – had been mistaken after all. We had come here because of it. Xon had been destroyed because of it. It was just a coincidence whatever had attacked the Sunna had visited here too, in the guise of the Hauda.

"I did not."

"Nor did you intend an attack on us." Also to myself. I didn't know why the AI governing the asteroid ship had decided to attack us. Perhaps it believed we had attacked the Sunna ourselves, and so took it upon itself to deliver justice.

"If the vessel engaged you, it was regrettable." The entity could not know what had happened. The attack was only a few days ago. The news of the event wouldn't reach this system for decades.

"We came here looking for those who attacked the Sunna. We have come to believe it is the same force that attacked you here."

"What is your intention?"

"We intend to destroy them. To prevent this from ever happening again."

"A worthy cause. I fear you will not be successful. However perhaps it is as you say, you should not take my daughter aboard your vessel."

"I have an alternate. I can call another vessel where she will be safe. Where she will be looked after."

"Where she can be with her own kind."

"Yes."

"Then I wish that."

I nodded. "Matte, call the Shaan please. Line up a call between me and its governor."

"They're going to want to get in here," my communications officer said. "They're going to want to talk to this ... whatever it is. I'm getting in touch now."

"Tell me what I need to know," I said to the disembodied head. "What are these parasites? Where are they?"

"I don't know what they are. But I know where they are. Quint."

Quint? That was not what I had expected. The Quint were one of the few civilisations even more advanced than the Hauda themselves. If the Quint were involved in this we were in trouble.

Chapter 12

This presented us with a problem.

The Quint were what we termed an elder civilisation. There were only a few around. The Hauda, the Suziemakaar, the various Tern Flocks and then the Quint. That we were aware of anyway. The Confederacy was widely travelled, but even we had not been everywhere. Interestingly, neither the Confederacy nor the Shoei Commonwealth fell into that particular category. We were a more of an upstart civilisation. Relatively young – in comparison. We might be numerous, we might be advanced, but we did not command the kind of respect an elder civilisation did. We were not as old. The Hauda and the Quint were, at the very least, between a hundred and two hundred thousand years old. Who knew how old the Tern or the Suziemakaar were? They didn't talk to us. They certainly wouldn't now that we had all but eliminated the Hauda. The Beaut. Whatever.

Technically most colonised worlds around here had been inhabited for similar lengths of time. Most regions of space were the same, with a slight fluctuation between regions. Interestingly the further to the galactic south (a convention, as such terms didn't mean much in this context) the older the worlds became. There were theories humanity had originated there some time in the past. We didn't know that region of space well. However, and I think I've mentioned before, there is a cycle most civilisations are caught in. I'd read a paper on it when I was in military school. It was termed the Civilisational Cycle. Not a catchy title. The central notion was that civilisations tended to fall. No matter how advanced they became, no matter how numerous their populations or how many worlds within their system they had colonised, they always collapsed. There were a number of reasons. War, contagion, catastrophe. It was pretty much inevitable. Civilisations collapsed, followed by several thousand years of slow, painful re-development. Without FTL there was no way of preventing it. I think I've mentioned all that too, so won't repeat myself.

The elder civilisations were the exception. They had not collapsed at any time in their history. Essentially, that same paper had proposed, they were simply lucky. Their civilisations had a contiguous history spanning eons. They were advanced. They were numerous. Or at least we thought so. The Suziemekaar, for example, didn't talk to us. At all. Ever. And we couldn't make them. We only knew they existed by chance, and in those encounters we had been firmly rebuffed. Or simply ignored, which I think is worse. We didn't know how old their civilisation was. We didn't even know where their home world was, if they even had one.

We did know about the Quint. Perhaps a bit too much.

Dreya itself didn't know much about the Quint though. But it did know they were involved. The reason it knew that was actually quite devious. In a sense.

Dreya had never entirely trusted the Xon factions. To the extent it had infiltrated each and every one of them, placing its own spy mechanisms right alongside faction AI cores. An achievement certainly. One it had taken the creature millennia to achieve. But ultimately it meant Dreya knew everything that was happening within the system.

Specifically, it had been eavesdropping while Sunrise (Eight?) was first contacted by the Hauda as they fled in-system. A Confederate vessel close behind. The outsider promising advanced technologies in exchange for asylum. What faction could pass up on that? Sunrise certainly hadn't.

Still, that was not the most interesting piece of information Dreya had gleaned from the AI. It was also monitoring when the Hauda utilised Xon facilities to blast a communications beam out of the system. Aimed directly at Quint. It was almost a hundred years before a reply was forthcoming. But it had ultimately arrived. Dreya had even decoded the contents of the message.

Yes. The Quint were involved all right. And that was a problem for us.

We were specifically prohibited from either entering their space or contacting them directly. The wording of the standing order was very clear indeed. There were a lot of 'must nots' and 'under no circumstances' scattered through the order. You could even say it was with good reason. And we had Captain Akker of the CSS Terminore to thank for that – the commander of a previous envoy mission to this area. This was a few hundred years ago, long before we had many dealings in this region of space. Captain Akker had been taken to running live fire drills within Quint territory. Provocative in itself. Even more so when some clumsy interdiction fire clipped a Quint vessel. Destroying it utterly. An act of war, the Quint claimed. Simply exhibiting our abilities, Akker had retorted. I believe the Quint likened the behaviour to a dog pissing up a lamppost to mark its territory. Or something along those lines. The Quint don't have dogs, but you get my meaning.

Technically the Quint had declared war on us. Although there had been no further weapons fire, or any contact at all after Akker was pulled out. As a result: standing order D-2090a. Failure to respect it was a court-martial offence.

Lovely.

I was still considering options when Governor Sayall called me back. I took the call on the bridge, flicking on a privacy field to speak to him without interruption. I didn't need Matte interjecting right now.

"This had better be good, Captain. I was somewhat indisposed," he started without bothering with any niceties.

"Thank you for your time, Governor. I hope it was nothing pressing."

"Tuarana 98 is expected to re-ignite. It only happens once every …" he shrugged, "five, six thousand years. I had to return to the city to take this call. Interference on the line out there. So, what can I do for you, Captain?"

He was a tall man, shaved completely bald. Artificial sunlight reflecting off his shiny pate. Wearing what looked like engineer's coveralls he was sat behind a desk in what appeared to be an office. There were wide doors behind him that stood open, revealing the view beyond. The interior of the Shaan, a wide tube-shaped space almost a hundred kilometres from end to end. I'd looked up the vessel while waiting for his call. Its interior was open space, a drum shaped habitat that was mostly parkland. Mixed in with forests, trees and fields. There were spires scattered through the space, some almost reaching up to the glowing rod of incandescence running through its core. The habitat's artificial sun. The vessel's hull was dozens of kilometres thick. It was there its tens of millions of inhabitants lived. I'd expected cramped conurbations, but instead I found wide open habitats, each with their own environment. Each a city unto themselves; dozens, hundreds of them. A city of cities. The vessel was a mobile civilisation, holding the same status in the Confederate senate as an inhabited world. It was essentially considered a world by itself, with all the rights and responsibilities that came with it. As a result, it was expected to support at least one main line warship – a vessel of similar classification to the *Cesa* itself – alongside a small flotilla of frigates and scouts. They tended to accompany the city, serving as pickets and a small self defence force. A prerequisite when few cities remained close to Confederate space. Most journeyed into the black, into the far reaches of the galaxy. Exploring. Cataloguing. They could be gone decades or centuries. Each city was well armed itself, but they could always do with the extra line of defence. This vehicle was relatively new. It had only been launched a century or so ago. Its mission statement was to reach the galactic core sometime in the next hundred years. It had a long way to go but it wasn't in any hurry to get there.

The city ship I had grown up in was nothing like this. That vessel had not been Confederate, and was a fraction of a GSX's size. That entire ship could fit into the Shaan's main chamber with ease.

"I have encountered an entity of scientific value that I cannot accommodate myself. It requires more specialised support."

He frowned as he checked something on a screen before him. "Liturbis 647. You are in Xon? What are you doing there?"

Liturbis 647 was the astronomical specification of the system. "I believe we have discovered the last remaining human in the system. Her AI patron would like to hand her over to us. It is also willing to supply its own historical records for our analysis."

"Shit. The Xon want to talk to us? And there's a survivor?" He sat forward, his disdainful attitude gone.

"It would appear so. From our own brief survey, it is clear humans survived in the system until relatively recently. They were held captive by the AI's themselves. To the best of my knowledge this individual is the last."

"That would be quite some find. To date the Xon have never interacted with us. We know nothing about their system. How did you come across this?"

"I am pursuing a mission of my own. You are familiar with what happened on Sunna-Deste-Anne?"

He frowned. "That is one of the dead worlds."

"It is. We are investigating." That was true enough.

"Which has led you to Xon." He leaned forward, studying a screen that was out of my viewpoint. "Ah. MI Ference. We have crossed paths with him before. I would warn you, Ference never does anything unless it is in his own interest. If he has set you on this path you would do well to remain cautious. He might just be manipulating you."

"That has occurred to me, Governor. But thank you for the warning. Ultimately, however, I strongly suspect we will be engaging the perpetrator of these actions at some time in the future. While I cannot know what the outcome of that will be, I can say that this is no place for an elderly woman. A woman who is the last of her kind."

"I agree. And as the Xon are one of the few remaining enigmas in our region of interest, this is something we simply cannot allow to pass us by. We will attend, and bring this survivor aboard."

"You are bringing the Shaan here?" That did surprise me. The governor had access to all kinds of resources. He didn't need to bring the city itself.

"Of course. Thank you for bringing this to my attention. Rest assured this survivor will be well cared for."

I imagine that meant my part in this was over. Me was his problem now. "Something you need to know. The survivor will be accompanied by a biological entity. It claims it was human once, before its adaptation. She will not leave without it." It would only be one or two of the spiders, but she had made it very clear. She would not leave without Dreya.

"Ah. And the Confederacy doesn't like the adapted, does it? Never mind, thank you once again Captain. I'll handle this from here."

The connection went dark. Well, that was that.

I sat back and thought through the brief interaction. Me was certainly better off aboard the Shaan, and I knew the governor and his army of scientists would love to pick the planetesimal apart, learning all they could of it and the Xon. It also released us to go on our way.

"The governor has requested a record of all our interactions with the Xon," Cena informed me.

"Ok." That didn't surprise me.

"Should I release it?"

"Of course. Full disclosure, Cen."

"I am sending it over now."

"Is the MAV back on board?"

"It is docking now. As agreed we have left the android behind. I have updated its persona to increase its independence until the Shaan arrives. It will remain as our emissary until that time."

"Good. Thank you. Have you calculated the trajectory of the planet?"

"I have. It's current velocity and heading will take it out of the system within the next five years. It is headed to open space. Its next astronomical encounter will be DDY-482 in approximately fifteen thousand years. It is not an occupied system."

So unless Dreya found a way of decelerating it was heading out into the cold and dark. The creature had revealed that it had expended all of its resources in its mad rush towards us. It had kept nothing aside to slow down again. A suicide run. All to save Me.

It would be up to the governor and his staff as to whether they were prepared to modify the planetesimal's trajectory to bring it back into orbit around their sun. It could be done but it wouldn't be easy. Not without shaking the thing apart. A gravitational gradient could change its course, sending it careening into the inner system, perhaps braking around a planet or two as it went. Possible, certainly. But would we do it? Well, that depended didn't it? What was in it for us?

"What are your orders now, Captain?" Tebercy asked as the privacy field fell.

I was silent a moment. "I have absolutely no idea, Sid."

"It might be time for another evening gathering at your cabin." He smiled.

"Sadly not. Cena is in the process of dismantling it. I don't know what I'm replacing it with just yet." I'd instructed the AI to clear everything out, not just the village, but also the forest and the cabin itself. The creatures that had inhabited it were now safely ensconced in the small zoo we had on deck 64. It had all been an indulgence. A distraction. My personal effects had been transferred to an NCO's cabin in Longtown. That was enough for me. I didn't need anything else.

"I believe Matte has an interesting view from her balcony," he suggested, turning towards the communications officer who was stationed nearby.

"You are welcome. I have the space," Matte said.

It was settled then.

If my quarters were an indulgence Matte's were an extravagance. I knew enough about my communications officer to understand she came from money. She was related to Rufus Sho, the industrialist. I didn't know to what degree, but that family was so wealthy even distant cousins were ridiculously rich. I didn't know that much about the Sho empire, but I did know they owned a string of habitats in the Lapoe sector. Along with a number of autofactories orbiting a string of gas giants in their territory, churning out all kinds of vehicles. From civilian yachts to military contracts. Her own home world was Reaos, the capitol of the Confederacy. A world that had changed a lot in the last few thousand years.

That was immediately obvious when we stepped into her quarters an hour or so later. Those of us who hadn't been invited inside before hesitated at the sight. Some better at hiding their amazement than others. I'm not sure where I fit into that spectrum.

Her quarters were a garden terrace, built atop a scraper somewhere on that world-city. I couldn't tell where it was supposed to be, I'd never been to Reaos myself. Too many people. It made my skin crawl. I don't know how to describe it. Other than to say it was an image of architectural horror.

Reaos had long since outgrown itself. Its original cities spreading until they merged. Like a mould growing on an apple, the last open land vanishing beneath layers of city. Even then the city kept on spreading. Since there was nowhere else to spread to, it headed upwards. Into the stratosphere, into space itself. Its towers kept on growing. Absorbing orbital stations and platforms. And still it grew. I don't know how tall its tallest spires are now. I don't think that notion means anything any longer. One tower formed the foundation for the one above it. Up and up until the planet was no longer a planet. You couldn't even say it had an atmosphere any longer. Rather it had a habitat, a sliver of air where there had once been the space between one structure and another. A space that had long since been filled in. I don't think the ground existed anymore either. It was deep down somewhere where stone and sand had once been. Now there was just tunnel and more structure. Underground habitats carved into what little rock remained. Down and down until it became too warm for air conditioning systems to keep the air cool enough for comfort. And likely a lot deeper than that too, into regions where people lived in sweltering heat. Too poor to escape to fresher air who knew how many thousands of kilometres above their heads.

I had never been to the place. I had no desire to.

So, Matte's rooftop garden wasn't technically within the atmosphere at all. It was some way above where it had once been. And even there its view was taken up by the structures around it. There was no horizon, there were just more buildings. Between all of this cruised vessel of all kinds. Some small enough for one passenger while others were so large they looked like they travelled to nearby systems – and probably did. Night and day didn't mean much here either. Overhead was more city, crowding out what remained of the sky. Still, there was light everywhere. From windows, from landing pads, from glittering walkways joining one spire to another. From the myriad of vessels winding between all of this. There was no night. There was no day. Just the eternal glow of the city.

Don't ask me how many people lived here. I have no idea. Too many, certainly.

It was horrific.

But that was the view Matte had settled on when designing her quarters. Each to their own.

"It looks a bit like Ferna's joint," Tenua commented as we settled onto what looked like a veranda overlooking the spectacle.

"Ferna?" I sat opposite him, my back to the edge. Or what appeared to be the edge in Matte's holographic image. I'd preferred to look at Matte's quarters themselves, a long brick building set into the scraper behind it, than the city itself.

"Commander Ferna of the *Stalker*," the marine continued. "This was back when I was a lowly subaltern. They picked us up after the evacuation of Onis. He was feeling charitable and hosted us in his quarters. His view was similar to this." He waved to the city scape about us. "I think it was an older recording though. The city wasn't quite as built up."

"I didn't know you were that old, Captain," Sooch commented. "What was that? A good fifteen, twenty years ago?"

He frowned. "Sure. Why?"

"Ah. You hadn't heard then? No reason you should have I suppose. There are a lot of ships in the navy."

"Heard? Heard what?" He twisted in his seat to look at the surveillance office who was seated slightly behind him.

"The *Fire Stalker* was lost about fifteen years ago," Matte said.

"Seventeen. Almost," Sooch corrected her.

She shrugged.

"Strange circumstances," Sooch continued. "They encountered an unknown object while on patrol duty. All comms were lost a few days later. I believe Chisholm herself went looking for it. There is no record of what she found though. The *Stalker* is officially registered lost along with all hands."

"I understood there was one survivor," Matte said. "A doctor."

It was his turn to shrug.

"All sorts happens in war," the marine commented as he straightened up and watched a lighter cruising overhead.

"That's the thing. The *Stalker* was nowhere near the front. The Shoei were not fingered for its loss. It was something else entirely. No one knows what."

"An accident?" I asked. "Some kind of malfunction?"

"No idea. It was an older ship. A frigate. I believe its model was pretty reliable though. We still run a number in the fleet."

"I've been out here long enough to know there's a lot besides the Shoei that can threaten a ship," I said. The last few days was evidence enough of that.

"True. As I said, it remains a mystery."

We'd lost a lot of ships in this frontier war with the Shoei. We would lose a lot more. I had preferred it out here, away from all that. But after visiting Sunna and Xon, I was starting to have second thoughts. The front seemed positively peaceful.

I was aware Matte had brought androids of her own aboard. Servitors, it had said on her personal manifest. They appeared as we became settled and began delivering refreshments. Most of the officers paid them little heed. We were all familiar with such things. Still they would always be strange to me. I didn't have as illustrious a background as the others. I won't bore you with all of that, it is a story for another time. But I will say my first encounter with such machines had not been pleasant. I don't think I will ever trust them entirely.

"The Quint," I said as I sipped a cocktail that had been delivered to me. It was blue and tasted of … almonds?

"Yes," Matte said. "How do we interrogate a people we are not permitted to talk to?"

"Is there any leeway in the order?" Sooch asked. "If we have evidence of their involvement in a crime, surely there is a statute to override the order, if not ignore it completely?"

"Cen?" I consulted our AI. If anyone could find such a loophole it would be the machine.

"Actually no. And only due to a technicality. The order was registered in 11 243 CE, by the Senate itself. It contains language that overrides all previous statutes and legislation. The only legislation that would allow us to enter the system without Senate consent, is YT-4118, which was added to the books 8 444 CE. Some thousands of years earlier. Which means that this order can only be rescinded or waived by a full senate vote."

"Shit," was all Sooch could find to say.

"Perhaps we should apply for that then?" Tenua suggested.

I hardly had to reply to that, as he was met by groans from around the balcony. "That would take years," I said. "And we'd need a sponsor in the senate just to get us heard. Plus we would have to do that in person."

"You're presuming we'd be heard at all. Doctor Fisher has been petitioning for an audience for twenty or so years. The closest he ever got was a hearing with the Securities Commission about twelve years ago," Matte said.

"Doctor Fisher?" Tenua turned to face her.

"My uncle. He's the governor of Fentay."

"Ah."

"So, not an option then," I said. "So, what options do we have?"

"Ignore the ruling and do it anyway?" Tebercy suggested.

"You know, if it was just me, I'd be tempted," I said. "But you would all be in the dock alongside me."

"I'm afraid there is more to the restriction than that," Cena said. "I am restricted from setting a course for the system."

"You mean you could not take us there, even if we gave you the instruction?" Matte asked.

"Correct."

"Well, shit," it was Matte's turn to swear.

"More than that, I would be obligated to report the attempt to the Admiralty. You have noticed that the order includes any attempt to enter the system, not just the act of entering the system itself."

"So we'd end up in some gulag for just ordering you to take us there?" I asked it.

"Also correct."

"What the hell did Akker do to them?" Sooch demanded.

"He accidentally destroyed a Quint vessel," Cen said. "What is not largely known is the fact the vessel in question was approaching the Terminore to engage in diplomatic activity. A first contact scenario, if you must. An individual known as the Grand Swing was aboard. It was the death of that person that enraged them so."

"Grand Swing?" I frowned at the strange terminology.

"I have no information," Cena said.

"We don't know anything about them at all," Sooch said. "We have some long range scans of their habitats but that's all. We don't even know what they look like."

"Cen, put up what we have please." I turned as the AI cast a long-range image of the Quint inner system, superimposed on the image of the city around us.

"Habitats," Matte said. "They don't look like planets at all. Like the Hauda, they dismantled their system and built habitats."

She was right. There was a string of pearls orbiting the system's star. Five of them in the same orbit. Equidistant. Each a glittering jewel against the darkness. The image zoomed in on one of them.

"It looks like a bubble," Sooch commented.

It looked like exactly that. An incandescent bubble, its contents indistinct, although it did have a greenish tinge. Cena brought up an image of one of their vessels. Possibly the very one Akker had subsequently destroyed. It was a blue/green crystal, perhaps a kilometre or so in length. Shaped vaguely like a spear point. Slim, its edges sharp. Other than that it was featureless.

"They are definitely advanced," I said. "Other than for the Quint habitats I've never seen anything like this." I turned to Matte. "Your family oversees habitats –"

"My family builds them," she corrected me.

"OK. So you have some insight. Could we build something like this?"

"No," she said immediately. There was no need to consider it. "Nothing like. We tend to build rings because they are stable and you can generate internal gravity by spinning them. The largest we've ever built is HableHorne. Its radius is just under two hundred kilometres, with a rim width of fifteen kilometres. That's the largest we can build with current techniques and materials. How big is this?" she asked the AI.

"Calculated width of two hundred thousand kilometres," the AI supplied.

"That's your average gas giant," I commented.

"So they have built not one, but five gas giant size habitats," Matte said. "We can't touch this. We can barely speculate on their techniques. How do they handle gravitation across such an area? It looks like they use some kind of field to keep the atmosphere in check. We have nothing like that. How does that work? And how did they shepherd five of these into such exacting orbits? And where did they get the mass from? You can't just use rock and debris from the rest of the system. This will require high density materials, which are rare in any system."

"You sound like a fan," Sooch commented.

"I am. My point is we have no idea how they built these."

"Or how the Hauda built their own habitats, come to that," I said.

"Exactly. We could learn so much from these civilisations. But we don't even try. We destroy them instead."

"How far away was the Terminore when this image was captured?" I asked Cena.

"Six light hours."

"So a long way, but still within the system. Our surveillance systems have advanced a lot since this was taken. How close can we get without breaking the order?"

"We may not approach to within one light year. I am afraid any images we capture from that distance would be no better. Even utilising hyperspacial systems."

I nodded. It had been worth a thought.

"Gravitational lensing," Tenua said abruptly. "I've seen the Pateras Array. With something like that we could see right into that system."

"If we had twenty years to build it," I agreed. I'd seen the array myself. I had been accompanying the marine when the *Cesa* was in for refit at the Antanari yards. The array was certainly an impressive installation. Situated in open space it generated a massive gravitational field some half a lightyear across, with a focal point just outside the Antanari system itself. It was at that focal point the station itself was located. As gravity bent light, the array used the technique to magnify distant objects. I'm talking about objects within distant galaxies, not those in nearby systems. If we wanted to explore those we could simply go there. It was the first installation of its kind to pick up planetary objects within the Andromeda Galaxy. Impressive certainly. Overkill for what we wanted to achieve here.

"MAV," Matte said. "A MAV could get in there undetected. We could unship Cena's guidance core and fly it in manually."

"I'm afraid I would be obligated to report you," Cena said.

"Shit, Cen. Work with us here."

"It is a directive I cannot override."

"There has to be a loophole somewhere," Matte continued. "Otherwise this was all a waste of time."

"Do we have another avenue of investigation?" Sooch asked me. "Another lead?"

"Sadly no."

"So we're screwed."

"Does Dreya know anything else?" Sooch asked.

"It's a thought," I said. "We could spend more time here. Interview the other factions. As much as we are able. There might be another lead somewhere. One of them might know something."

"Ultimately what is it we're wanting to achieve here?" Sooch asked. "Our objective is to track down who attacked the Sunna. And then what?"

"It depends on the nature of the threat. Our intention is to neutralise it. But we need to understand what that threat is first. We cannot make a judgment until we do."

"So potentially we'll be reporting back to the admiralty, and they make the decision? I mean, if the threat is more than we can handle ourselves?"

I shrugged myself. "Of course. "Whatever steps we take they need to be proportional. And effective. There is no point taking half measures."

"So why don't we report back now?"

I sighed. "Cen?"

"Captain Marla has made regular progress reports to the Admiralty," the AI said. "The last was two hours ago. Their response was we should continue as we see fit."

"Just that?"

"Just that," the AI confirmed.

"So we're on our own," Sooch said.

"Until we get more information."

"I have an incoming transmission from Governor Sayall," Cena announced. "It is a non-interactive."

I hadn't expected to hear from him again. "Put it up."

Darkness had fallen within the Shaan. The doors behind the governor had been pulled closed, their embedded panes showing nothing but darkness beyond. He was still at his desk, as if he hadn't moved.

"Captain. I have been reviewing the records of your interactions with the Xon. I can't say I agree with your actions, but it is not my place to second guess the navy while on operation. I can say, as I did for Ference, I would not trust Chisholm. She clearly knows more than she is telling you. I digress, that is also your business. I imagine right now you are reviewing your options. You don't have many. Quint space is out of bounds, as you know. So, I have only one suggestion for you. Hermitage. That is all I will say. I'm not going to do all your work for you. You can look them up yourself."

With that he was gone.

"Hermitage?" Tenua said. "Who the hell are they?"

Clearly she hadn't read up on the region before the mission.

Chapter 13

We were underway again, our engines leaving the forlorn system of Xon way behind us. Our trajectory was curved to avoid the system of Quint, heading for a dim G type star some way beyond it. This time our objective was somewhat different. We were not seeking retribution.

The Hermitage were refugees. We knew that, they had an entry in our database. I'd read up on them before the mission. It was my job to know who I might run into out here. But that brief had missed out on some crucial information. No reason it should be included to be fair, it had been held within the Confederate Diplomatic Corps database. Cen had had to request access before it could be shared with us.

So, I knew about the Hermitage but I didn't know about their significance.

About two thousand years ago a city ship was discovered near here. Its drive and life support system failing. Its crew were starving after their provisions had become depleted, and had taken to farming every open space within the vessel. Even that was merely delaying the inevitable. There might have been a bit of cannibalism.

True, boarding the ancient, and quite run-down vessel had been a gamble in the first place. But from what little information we had on the matter the Hermitage had had little choice. A super volcano had erupted on their home world, killing most of their world's population in days. The survivors damned to a slow death as their atmosphere filled with ash and the temperature started to plummet. They did have an old city ship in orbit, the ancient vessel stripped to bare bones to feed their manufactories on the planet. In their last, desperate act, the people of the world came together to repair it as much as they could, before they selected a hundred thousand to board it, and flee. A hundred thousand. From a world that still hosted many millions. I couldn't imagine what that would have been like.

Still, the decrepit vessel could not last forever, and it hadn't. It had inevitably failed, dooming the very last of the Hermitage with it.

Fortunately for them they had been found by a people who were advanced enough to help them. The city ship had been towed to a nearby stable system. The survivors allowed to disembark on an empty, life supporting world. They had been saved. I knew all of that. I'd read reports of events on their original, doomed planet, of what had been happening on the city ship itself. Terrible stuff. Some of it was a bit too close to home. But as I've said before, that's a story for another time.

What I didn't know was that their saviours were the Quint.

Now, here is where it gets complicated. Apparently that system was an old Quint mining colony which was why they knew it so well. Perhaps one of the places they had drawn materials from to build their habitats. They still had a presence there, a siphon drawing matter from a gas giant in the system's outer reaches. Perhaps shepherding in the odd asteroid to harvest its materials. All standard stuff.

It would have been, except for the Hermitage. They had survived. And their world, now itself called Hermitage, was their new home. They were thriving. They had rebuilt their civilisation. All was good, until they developed to the point where they started exploring the system. Setting up the odd base here and there.

That was when they encountered the Quint again. And that was where things got messy.

You see to the Hermitage this was their home. This was their system. They needed the resources it offered to keep on developing. They needed to settle the system to prevent the same catastrophe from happening again. Spreading the risk, as it were. But of course the Quint cared nothing for that. They had been here a long time, and had only allowed the Hermitage to stay as an act of kindness. An act that was coming back to bite them. At this point the Hermitage were not aware the Quint had been their saviours. The Quint had not communicated much during the rescue itself, and had certainly not kept in touch afterwards.

All this led to conflict. Of course the Quint always came out on top. An upstart civilisation was never going to be a threat to an elder race. The notion would have been laughable if it hadn't been so tragic. In desperation the Hermitage had reached out to the Confederacy. Requesting intercession. They didn't know about our history with the Quint. Why would they? They just knew we were powerful. A people the Quint could not ignore.

Official Confederate policy was that no entreaty had ever been received from the Hermitage. Whoever made these decisions – be it the Admiralty, the Senate or the Colonial Commission – had simply decided to ignore it. It was better that way. It was little more than a footnote in the Diplomatic Corps report. Written by the governor of the Shaan at the time, as it happened. Perhaps why Sayall was aware of it.

There was no directive to stay away from Hermitage themselves. There was also no directive to avoid the Quint outside their own home system should we ever encounter them. So, here was an opportunity to talk to the Quint, without going to Quint. I could offer the Hermitage our assistance, as a good officer of the Confederate fleet, and have a chat with the Quint as part of that mission brief.

Perfect.

The Shaan had passed through this area some years ago on its leisurely journey to the galactic core. They had clearly been in contact with the Hermitage at some point. According to the records they had remained in-system for a month or so. Engaged in survey work. I could ask Cena to request more information but I didn't really care. It didn't matter.

We were in no hurry ourselves so I gave the instruction for the *Cesa* to engage standard cruise and I retreated to my new quarters to sleep. Hermitage was just under a hundred lights from Xon, so it would take us about three days.

I busied myself with the never-ending administration that was required running a modern warship. Much of it was handled by my officers - the respective department heads. They were self sufficient and knew what they were doing. Still, I couldn't delegate everything. Besides, I did interest myself in how the ship was running. Crew morale (or disciplinary issues), resource management, that kind of thing. So most of my time was taken up perusing reports that didn't actually require my engagement at all. I might lodge the odd question or request for clarification, but that was it. If one of my officers made a decision involving their own department, I respected it.

There was a knock on my door as I was wading through the manufactory's resource management report. There was a fault with one of the extruders, and the engineers had been called in to work on it. It was delaying the replacement of the MAVs we had lost in Sunna, so it was high priority. I padded over to the door and opened it without thinking. This was my ship after all, there was no one on the other side I might not wish to speak to.

I must admit I did quite like living in NCO Row, as it was called. Or simply the Rows. The cabins were small but comfortable. I had lived in similar quarters earlier in my career, so it felt a bit like coming home. When I moved in I had heard music coming from one of them, which quickly ceased the moment it got around I was joining them. Which I was actually sad about. I didn't want anyone to tip-toe around me.

The Rows was an apartment block built into one wall of Longtown, each with a view down the long compartment. It was local night within it now. The space lit up by the odd ball field where teams were enjoying a late night game. Along with a scattering of lit windows and the main source of night time light, the running tracks that loped around the structures. Even now I could see a number of joggers making use of them.

"Lieutenant Beyard." I was a bit surprised to find the marine waiting patiently. While this was technically marine country, there was nothing stopping a member of Red Group making their way here. Still, this was unexpected.

She smiled. "We've seen combat together, Izzy. Call me Sen."

I laughed. "Sen. Like to come in? I have some tea brewing."

"No, thank you. I have a jousting match in a moment. en-ed-bas is going down. You're welcome to come spectate." She was wearing a blue padded jousting jacket, a helmet in her hands.

"I'd love to, but you know … reports. I have been neglecting my duties recently."

She nodded in understanding. "Of course. I'll be quick. Rumour has it you may be leaving the ship on a mission in the next few days, and may require a retinue."

"You'd heard that?" Now that did surprise me. I hadn't given instruction for our intentions to be kept secret. It wasn't a secret after all, and I trusted my crew. But this was quick.

She nodded again. "I did. I have come to offer you my assistance. The rest of the squad is ready to go too. Just let us know when."

Now I did laugh. "That is kind of you, Lieu… Sen. Any mission like this would be on a volunteer basis only, so your offer is appreciated. I can't think of a squad I would prefer to have at my side. We'll need a replacement for Sanquey though."

"Brice has been signed off by the doc. Wonders of modern medicine and all. He's eager to prove himself to you. And the rest of us. I understand he feels a bit embarrassed."

That was quick too. The corporal had been seriously injured. I had been keeping up on his recovery, but to be fair it was a few days since I had last checked in on him. An oversight I felt embarrassed about myself.

"I'd be delighted. It will be formal. Ceremonial arms only."

"Perfect. Now I'd better go." She settled the helmet onto her head. "See you soon, Izzy. Don't forget!"

"I won't, Sen." I watched her hurry down the walkway, nodding to a sergeant who was himself almost knocked over by the hurrying marine.

Well, that had been unexpected.

I returned to my reports and general administration. No one told you about all this when you were a young lieutenant and dreamed of becoming a starship captain. Cen was quite a help, as it could handle a lot of it, and focus me onto areas that actually needed my attention. Still, there was a lot to do even then.

I did find time to revisit the reports of the Hermitage, discovering many of them had been written by researchers stationed aboard the Shaan. Well, that did answer that question. There was one side report I had missed before, relating to a mission sent to the original Hermitage home world. It wasn't actually that far away. Even though their city ship had been in space almost two hundred years, it hadn't been travelling very quickly. As a result their original home was barely twenty lights further out. Still very much within our patrol area. It had originally been listed as visited but abandoned, its population perishing in a catastrophe some time in the previous few thousand years. A perfunctory report only, originally written quite some time ago by the original explorers of this region of space. The Shaan's report was a lot more detailed.

There had indeed been a super volcanic explosion. The volcano was relatively quiet now. Just the odd rumble. Its damage had been done, and that had been extreme. Its caldera was two hundred kilometres across. Ejecta from its eruption had been found thousands of kilometres away. Ash and dust forming a thick blanket just about everywhere. The remains of cities could be seen poking out of it. Those closest were little more than rubble. Buildings toppled, rooves collapsed. Further out structures appeared relatively intact. Some showing evidence they had been occupied for quite a time after the eruption. Many were modified, as if the occupants had attempted to make them weather proof, insulating them from the terrible cold that had followed. There were some subterranean shelters that appeared to have been dug in the years after the eruption. But the story was the same everywhere the team looked. Machines had ultimately broken down. Allowing the cold and the dark inside. The last survivors had clung to each other, finding their last warmth in companionship. And that was where the team found them. Desiccated bodies all long dead. Men, women, children. Some pets and farm animals. There was no human life anywhere on the planet. Sure, some sea life had survived, along with hardier plant life and the odd burrowing mammal nearer the equator, where it had been the warmest. But that was all. The planet was a wasteland. Warmer now that the dust had cleared, but dead all the same.

It didn't look like they had colonised any of the other planets or moons in the system before the eruption. None of them were really suitable anyway, being either too small, too large or too far out. Nor were there any stations in orbit. Apart from the cityship they had had no presence outside of their own atmosphere. That city ship itself was, of course, long gone.

Sadly this was not the first time we had seen this kind of thing. It was one of the reasons the Confederacy had been formed, an attempt to form an alliance of similar minded people who had the resources and ability to intercede when catastrophe struck. We couldn't prevent the eruptions, but we could bring relief to the survivors. Sadly we had been nowhere near here when this happened. As big as we were, with as many ships as we had, we simply couldn't be everywhere.

I put the reports aside and left my cabin behind, heading up a few decks to where the marines were conducting their drills.

en-ed-bas did indeed get his ass handed to him.

Chapter 14

Most systems are relatively flat. In the sense that each planet orbits on the same plane, or near to it. You get the odd variation, but it's rarely more than a few degrees. Astronomers call it the plane of the ecliptic. So as to reduce the chances of running into any Quint vessels we approached the Hermitage system from high on that plane, looking down on the array of planets as they lazily orbited their star beneath us. It was there that we paused for a moment, looking down on everyone and everything. Allowing the *Cesa's* sensors to scan activity within the system. Seated on the bridge once again I watched as a picture slowly started to form.

"The Hermitage are concentrated in the inner system," Sooch reported. "Hermitage itself is the second planet in the system. It's relatively warm and also relatively large, at a magnitude of 1.4 standard, but perfectly habitable. It has two small moons, neither more than large asteroids. Aah, fifty kilometres at it's widest for the smaller of the two and four hundred for the larger. Both are irregular. Both are settled and being actively mined by the Hermitage. It looks like they've learned their lesson about restricting their activities to their home planet. They're actively spreading out into the system. Settling where they can. Mining mostly. Their largest colony is on the fifth planet. It's icy, with a subglacial ocean. They have about fifty million people on that planet. According to records they call it Hugyur. Which I believe means Planet Five, or something like that."

"The Quint?" I asked him.

"They have a considerable presence in the outer system. I can't guess at their numbers but I imagine they are in the billion plus range. They have constructed a habitat here, about planet eight." He brought up an image and zoomed it in. It was of a hulking grey-blue gas giant. An icy ring system glinting in the weak sunlight. Floating before these rings was a tiny green dot that he zoomed in further on. It was a bubble of light, like the habitats we had seen in Quint, but far far smaller. "These rings are artificial," Sooch continued. "They have shepherded icy asteroids into place and if you look closely," he indicated something in the image, "you'll see they've left a gap in the rings so the habitat can pass through. Which looks small from this vantage point, but I'd like to point out it is in the region of five thousand kilometres wide. It is not small by any measure."

"Conflict with the Hermitage?" I asked.

He shrugged. "Nothing current. If there was anything recently the victor has cleaned up after themselves."

"That would be the Quint then."

"It would. I have picked up a couple of potential flash points." He manipulated the image, bringing up a barren, rocky moon. "The Quint have an active harvesting facility here. It looks pretty established. The Hermitage have landed a prospecting team on the opposite side of the moon. They're well established now, but haven't been there as long as the Quint have."

The image zoomed out again and refocussed on a small group of asteroids. It was unusual to see them group together like that, unless they had been one large asteroid that had broken apart at some time in the recent past. "It looks like both parties are harvesting materials here. I can't tell who arrived first. The Quint are naturally better at it. They are stripping the asteroids and directing the material into a facility to the rear of the assemblage. Looks like some kind of gravitational flux device that shreds the material and separates out heavier metals from lighter spoil. The Hermitage are less efficient. They're drilling into one of the asteroids and removing valuable materials manually. We might have a conflict brewing here. The Quint look like they're about to process the asteroid the Hermitage are occupying. This will be interesting."

"There any people on that asteroid?"

"Sure. A few dozen. And before you ask, yes. This will most definitely kill them."

"How long?"

"Unclear. The Quint haven't started working on it yet. So it's just speculation which roid they will target next. And how long it will take."

This was either very good timing, or very bad timing. "Head in that direction. Do we know where the Hermitage seat of government is?"

"They don't have a government as such. They are isolationist. Each district is isolated from all those around it. Literally so. Their borders are either walled or fenced. Anyone attempting to cross over is shot on sight. They are forced to be self-sufficient or else they fail. The Shaan detected two districts that were wastelands after a localised famine. Their cities deserted, their farms dustbowls. Their neighbours did not seem aware of their fate. Each monarch is an absolute ruler. They have advisors who are responsible for different aspects of local society, but they all answer to the monarch. Local languages all have the same root, but have drifted over time. It is doubtful they would understand each other at this point.

"All that ties them together is their adherence to an individual they call the Celebrant. This individual apparently still lives aboard their old city ship which has been repaired and remains in orbit. Each state sends a tithe to it on an annual basis. Off world states are run along similar lines. However it appears all the off world mining stations are part of the Hugyur province," Sooch said.

"This Celebrant sounds like a religious figure." I had perused their political system but hadn't spent much time on it.

"It is. The Prime Celebrant is credited with leading them to salvation. Of making the pact with their deity, which they call the Oseonophis, which loosely translates as the sherd. Or the spear. Something like that."

I recalled an image of a Quint vessel. "The Quint. They worship the Quint."

"Ah, yes. I think they do. Except they don't appear to know their saviours are the same Quint they have encountered in this system."

Well, that was awkward. "Did the Shaan come into contact with the Quint while they were here?"

"Apparently not. They left as soon as they discovered a Quint presence here. And they only discovered that because the Hermitage requested an intervention."

That did sound somewhat unusual. True, we possessed advanced sensors, however we tended to only scan what interested us. If we didn't aim those sensors in a direction, we didn't know what was there. Still, the Shaan was massive. It carried a considerable population. Many of whom considered themselves scientists or explorers in one sense or another. If they didn't they wouldn't be living on a city ship. With that many people aboard someone was bound to be interested in localised astronomy, and point a sensor towards the outer system.

"What's our plan, Captain?" Matte asked.

I pointed towards the image on the main screen, showing the small collection of asteroids and the accompanying Quint processing station. "We get in the way. I intend to piss the Quint off. We need them to react to us."

She turned to look at me. "Is that wise?"

"I intend to get them to reveal their true selves to us. Cen, park us right in front of their mechanism. Between it and their next asteroid."

"Provocative," Matte commented.

"Can we really make our relationship with the Quint worse? Besides, the Hermitage have formally requested our assistance. We are merely complying with their request. I don't want any firing though. Sooch, what do we know about that mechanism?"

"Ah, I think it could do us damage, Izzy."

"Explain."

"We haven't seen it in action yet, so we don't really know what it does. In appearance it does seem similar to the mechanisms we use for harvesting smaller astronomical bodies ourselves. Asteroids and the like. If it's anything like that … we're talking about gravitational torque in the region of a thousand standard G's."

"Cen, can we resist that?"

"By engaging the FTL drive, certainly. But we won't be."

"Are you saying we'll be risking the ship?"

"If we are caught in the gravitation sheer within the mouth of the mechanism, certainly. I would suggest we don't enter it. If we stay ahead of it we will be safe. They appear to use some kind of tractoring mechanism to draw asteroids into it. Of course, we have not seen it in operation, but we should be able to resist it."

Should. "OK. That's the plan for the moment. The moment it looks like their mechanism is about to get the better of us, get us out of there."

"Or destroy it," Sooch said.

"Not sure I want to actually fire on them just yet. I'm not looking to start a war." Not until we were provoked anyway.

"We are technically still at war with them," Matte observed.

"Not a shooting war. And we'll avoid that if we can." At least until I discovered exactly what was behind the attack on Sunna. There might be some shooting then.

The Quint mechanism was a string of eight oval vessels arranged in a perfect circle. The vessels themselves a featureless blue/green material. Cena aimed our sensors at them as we approached, but they remained enigmatic. We couldn't pick up any activity within. They appeared inert. Their temperatures were neutral to their background, only a few dozen degrees above absolute zero. There wasn't much ambient heat this far from the system's sun. It was barely more than a distant disk, casting as much light as the moon on a clear night. And about as much heat. An inhospitable place. The Hermitage must be desperate for resources coming this far out. I can't imagine the Quint themselves cared. They lived far out in the system. They probably noticed the cold as much as we did.

The *Cesa* manoeuvred into the space between the Quint machinery and the closest asteroid. The one we believed they would harvest next. The one that was inhabited.

"Any evidence of the Hermitage leaving?" I asked Sooch.

"No. I don't think they can. They only possess a small number of maintenance vehicles. Not enough to accommodate all of them, and certainly not for an extended voyage. I imagine their installation is serviced by a supply vessel of some kind, although nothing is headed in this direction currently."

"They have an on-site refinery?"

"They do." He cast an image of the site before us. "It's more economical to process the ore on site. Less weight for a freighter to haul away. They have a few blast furnaces. It's a well established base. They've been here a while."

The hermitage base was extensive. It was a wart of steel clinging to the asteroid. There were a few concentric circles of unidentified machinery and piping, all linked to a central station. A number of lights illuminating the base itself. There was no way the Quint were unaware of their presence. The lights themselves were easily visible from our vantage point. If we could see them so could the Quint.

What was surprising was the fact the asteroid was not mined out after all these years of activity. Bearing in mind the Quint could harvest an asteroid of this size in an afternoon. Using range surveillance we were able to peer within the rock, revealing the ant-hill like tunnels that riddled it. It wasn't far off being gutted. Perhaps of little interest to the Quint then.

"Any radio comms?"

"Some. They have an antenna complex on the main structure. It has two dishes. One aimed in-system, calling for help looks like. The other aimed at the Quint. They have been asking the Quint not to harvest the asteroid ever since before we arrived."

"Response from our Quint friends?"

"You're joking?"

"Are we sure the Quint installation is inhabited?"

"Inconclusive. It could be automated. We're unable to view anything within their vessels."

"I don't think we should make any presumptions. Once we're situated fire off a greeting." We knew enough of their communication language from our previous interaction, as brief as it had been.

There was no response. I can't say I had expected one.

We took lunch on the bridge while we waited, an orderly delivering sandwiches to anyone who wanted one. No one left their post, each eagerly awaiting a response that never came. This was an elder civilisation after all. One we had limited contact with. One that was still an enigma to us. We didn't know much about them. We didn't even know what they looked like. We didn't know their spoken language. We knew nothing of their political or caste system. Of their culture and history. Of their technology. We did know they did not possess FTL, which gave us an unassailable advantage. Whatever happened we could still leave.

"I'm picking up a gravitational disturbance," Sooch reported some hours later.

"From the array?" I asked him. The assemblage of Quint objects hadn't moved.

"No. From behind us. From within the asteroid. It's moving. It appears to be heading for us. It's only a metre per second now but it is accelerating. Two metres ... three."

"What's going on, Sooch?"

"No idea Izzy. There doesn't seem to be a source to the gradient. It's just there. The asteroid is sliding downhill. Right at us."

"You mean at those," I pointed to the Quint machines.

"Yeah. But we're in the way."

"Can we stop it?"

"Shit. No. We have tractoring capability but it's pretty focussed. Designed to operate on other vessels that have far higher structural strength than that asteroid. If we try we'll rip it apart."

"And the debris would keep on coming."

"Yeah."

"Someone find me the source please."

"There is nothing else out here," Cena reported. "Nothing other than what we have already identified."

"Nothing in the range?"

"Nothing."

That was pretty definitive. The range measured the stresses on space caused by objects with mass. It was impossible to hide a signature. "OK. Target one of the objects. Let's see if we can disable it. In the meantime, Ono, get some MAVs out there to pick the crew up," I instructed the marine.

"On it."

There was a twinkle of light as a munition ejected from a launcher and accelerated towards one of the machines. It didn't contain a warhead, it didn't need one. Instead it's drive accelerated it to multiples of c, using its own mass as a battering ram against whatever it was aimed at.

Nothing happened. The munition passed clear through the Quint machine and disappeared into empty space beyond it.

I turned in my seat to look towards Sooch. "You did fire at it?"

"I did. Interception confirmed but ... I don't get it. We hit nothing. It passed clear through."

"Try again, please."

High energy plasma seared through the blackness of space. It struck nothing. Continuing into space beyond. Slowly dissipating.

"Are we sure it's not some kind of mirage?" I asked.

"Definitely. There is mass there. About two hundred thousand tonnes. This doesn't make sense. We're not impacting on any kind of shield or interdiction system. Our weapons are simply passing through as if it's not there."

"I doubt it's some kind of Quint trick," Matte said. "They didn't know to expect us and they were there before we arrived. I doubt the Hermitage have even got a proper bead on them. They don't have the surveillance capacity. So there's no point projecting this kind of image for their benefit."

We dispatched a warhead next. There was a flash of nuclear annihilation as the weapon deployed. The image within the bridge dimmed slightly to cut the glare.

"It's still there, isn't it?" I asked no one in particular.

"Yeah. It is, Izzy," Sooch reported. "Not a scratch. It's still on station. It hasn't even moved."

"The asteroid is continuing to accelerate," Cena reported. "It is now moving at two thousand two hundred metres per second. It will pass this position in two minutes. You may want to consider avoiding it."

"The MAVs?"

"Almost there," Ono said. "The crew had better be ready to go. We won't be waiting."

"Move us aside then, Cen. Those things have mass though, don't they?" I indicated the Quint machinery.

"They do, Izzy," Sooch confirmed.

"What effects mass then?"

"Primary weapons fire might be an overkill," Sooch commented.

"Overkill it, Lieutenant."

Energy surged over the *Cesa's* hull as its primary weapons system engaged. The very weapon that had ripped the heart out of Xon.

"Weapon cycling," the weapons office reported. "Approaching peak output."

"Fire immediately, Sooch."

"Singularity is forming. Ejecting ... now."

The gravitational pulse seared through space, a singularity ejected at near the speed of light. Unstoppable it ripped through the Quint machinery. With a flash the platform was torn apart, its very atoms sheared by the wall of force battering into it. Whatever its power source was it detonated instantly.

"Brace brace brace," the AI instructed. An alarm warbled somewhere within the bridge.

Something hit us. Hard. A reciprocal wave of energy. A force like nothing we had ever felt before. We had weathered fire from Shoei dreadnoughts. From whole Shoei squadrons. Their concentrated energies shearing through our armour. Even then we had felt nothing down here. All of that destruction a long way away. This was nothing like that at all. This was as if space itself reared up and slammed into the *Cesa*. It cut through our every defence as if it wasn't there.

My console leaped up at me as the backlash tossed the cruiser like a rat caught in a terrier's jaws. With a crack my head hit the metal of the terminal, pain exploding into my mind. I felt a crunch as my nose broke. Blood from my shattered nose splattered my uniform.

The lights within the bridge flickered as power was interrupted. Crew tossed from their stations to the deck. Into bulkheads. Into consoles. Those unfortunate enough to have been standing at the time were propelled across the compartment, crashing into whatever stood in their path. Trying to ride it out I clutched the console before me. The stench of burning circuitry filling my beleaguered nostrils.

"Cen. Back us out of here. Military thrust."

"Doing it, Captain. Main drive engaged," the unflustered AI reported.

"Seal pressure doors," I continued. There was small chance our hull had been breached, but we'd never experienced anything like this before. There was no underestimating it. "Medical to the bridge." One of the bridge crew was gasping in pain as he clutched a broken leg, the bone protruding from his ripped uniform.

"I am afraid all compartments were effected," the AI continued. "It might take some time."

I stood unsteadily, wiping blood from my face with a sleeve. The sudden blow had not been repeated. Once was enough. "What was that?"

"Unknown. A gravitational pulse of some kind. I am gathering information on it now."

"Casualties? Damage?"

"Our hull is intact. Some minor electrical damage. All main systems are on line and functional," the AI said. "I am dispatching uninjured medical personnel to the critically injured." Anyone who happened to be walking down a wrongly oriented passage would have been catapulted down it. I can't imagine any of them had escaped serious injury. The *Cesa* was not designed to be shaken around like a rag doll.

"Anyone injured in the wells?" They were the longest open passages within the ship. If anyone had been thrown down one of them they wouldn't have survived the fall.

"No. If anything commuters were the luckiest. They were already insulated."

"What was that?" Matte demanded as she picked herself up. Her uniform was rumpled but she appeared unharmed.

"Undetermined at this point," Cena said. "There were elements of an extreme gravitational surge, but there was more to it. I cannot determine what exactly at this time."

"Are we safe? Is it going to hit us again?"

"We appear to be at a safe distance now."

"Quick thinking, Cen."

"I'm afraid that was the capt-"

"If you're unharmed, can you check on everyone else, please?" I interrupted the AI. I pulled Sooch from where he was sprawled on his own console. He was out cold. I made him as comfortable as I could and stepped to the next console. The duty officer had been tossed bodily over it, bouncing over the next line of stations before coming to a stop before the railing that separated the executive area of the bridge from general services a floor below us. Fortunately no one had been thrown over it. She waved to me as I checked on her. She was fine. Just a bit bruised.

"The asteroid?" I asked the AI as I worked.

"It did not survive the impact."

"Our MAV?"

"One clipped the asteroid and has received minor damage. The other escaped damage entirely. They both fared better than we did."

"Did they get anyone on board before the impact?"

"Unfortunately not. All of the Hermitage personnel perished."

"OK. Bring them back then." So this had been a lot less successful than I had hoped. "The Quint array?"

"One of the mechanisms was destroyed. The remainder are intact and still on station."

"They're undamaged?" I checked the pulse of an officer who was laying flat on the floor, his face pressed up against a bulkhead. He was alive but unconscious. I gingerly felt his neck. I didn't think anything was damaged.

"They appear so, yes."

"Is anyone else out here? Any Quint vessels?"

"I have detected none."

That was something. We didn't need any more excitement right now.

"Sid. Can you hear me?" I pulled the engineer straight in his seat. His station was nestled in a corner, a dazzling array of consoles and screens on all sides. This was the heart of the *Cesa*, if anywhere was. The one place all systems could be monitored and controlled. He had been thrown into one of the monitors, blood seeping from his scalp where he had caught a sharp edge.

"Iz … Izzy. What happened?" His eyes were unfocussed.

"I don't know. Are you fit to do your duty, Commander?"

"I .. yes. Of course." He raised a shaking hand to his temple and gingerly felt the lump rapidly forming there. He needed medical attention, many of the crew did. We just didn't have time for it now.

"What happened to you?" He noticed the blood smeared over my face.

"I'll be fine." I was aware of the throb of my nose. It was too soon for real pain to set in. I still had that to look forward to. "Commander, I need you to ensure every damaged system is identified and repaired. Cen is already on it, but it needs help."

He nodded jerkily. "I'm on it, Captain."

"Good." I returned to Sooch. He was unconscious and I felt multiple broken bones when I checked his limbs quickly. Maybe a rib or two, and by the looks of the frothy blood at his mouth at least one had pierced his lungs.

I waved over a subaltern. "Medbay. Priority." I indicated his alternate who was stationed a few metres away. She looked dazed herself but at least she was conscious.

"Set situation one," I said to her. "I want interdiction launched. Disengage primary weapons. Secondaries only."

She nodded jerkily as Sooch was carried away on a stretcher. She slipped into his station and grimly wiped blood from the console with the sleeve of her uniform jacket.

"Captain. I believe we have a problem," Cena said abruptly.

"What is it, Cen?"

"I have lost comms with Internment. Sensors are down and power is not routing to subsystems."

"The Hauda?"

"Yes."

"Shit. Tenua?" I opened a connection to the marine. She wasn't stationed on the bridge. Her own command post was a dozen or so metres to our stern.

"Captain. What's going on?"

"No time right now. Get a squad in hard armour up to Internment. Secure that location. Drop everything else, Captain."

She didn't hesitate. "On it."

"Matte, you have the bridge." I headed for the exit.

"Where are you going?" she demanded but didn't get a response. I was already in the companionway outside.

Chapter 15

"We are losing power in sector four, level twelve," Cen reported as I ran towards Internment. Forced to hop over the still forms of crew lying in the gangway as I went. I didn't have time to stop for any of them.

"Level thirteen," The AI continued.

"What's going on, Cen?"

"I have no information. My internal systems are becoming corrupted. Level fourteen."

Four lumbering figures appeared in the passage ahead of me. This was one of the primary communication routes through the ship. One of the avenues the military contingent used when they needed to get around. These were hard armoured marines. Each encased in dull grey metalloy, heavy weaponry bolted to their carapaces. Each one towering over me, the deck vibrating slightly as they moved. They easily left me behind.

"Weapons locker to your left," Cena said as if sensing my intention.

A bulkhead partition sprang open, revealing an emergency weapons locker. "Plasma," I said. "From what we saw on Sunna they are affected by plasma. Don't even try using anything else." I snatched up a bulky weapon and kept on running. Quicky cycling the charging mechanism as I went.

"You are thinking this is the same kind of entity that attacked Sunna?" The AI asked.

"I cannot discount it."

"Plasma weapons fire within the ship will cause considerable damage."

"Unavoidable. Review the report of the limb we extracted from Sunna. Does it give any indication of how to kill these things?"

"Inconclusive. It does appear that extreme heat damages their cellular structure. However the report also indicates an ability to adapt. As such a suggestion would be a mixed arms assault."

"Chemical? Radiation?"

"I was thinking electrical discharge."

"Make way!" I shouted to some marines as they worked over a prostrate figure. I ignored them as they flattered themselves against a bulkhead.

"The marines are engaging an unknown assailant."

"Patch me in."

I heard the zip of an arc reactor in my implants. "I think you hit it. Is it down?"

"Shit. No. It's still moving. Hit it again."

"Damn. It's quick. Hold still." The weapon howled again.

"There's another one. There's two? The report said there was only one."

"Just kill it, Sarge."

There was a grunt. "It hit me. It hit me. My arm is jammed. Damn it. Someone –

"

Someone screamed. I heard metal creaking. Crunching, as if an unbelievable force was cracking the marine's hard armour open.

"Get it off me! Get it off me!"

"Hold still. Hold still dammit." A slug thrower thudded like a jackhammer biting through pavement.

There was another scream. This time it was cut off abruptly.

"Lo? Lo? What the ..."

"Hold your position. Backup is enroute," another voice broke in. An officer overseeing the contact.

"There's another one. Where are they coming from? There's only supposed to be one!" More weapons fire. This time the shrieking of an atomic lance.

"It's killing marines, Cen," I said to the AI. "It's killing hard armoured marines." That was impossible. Hard armour was unbelievably tough. You could land a MAV on a suit without so much as denting it. The amount of force it took to crack one open was ridiculous.

"Suiku. Suik ... dammit. We need help now!"

"It's almost there."

There was another shriek. The thrower fell silent. I heard a distinct crunch over comms.

"Lieutenant, where is their backup?" I asked the sector commander, Suiku.

"They are there now, Captain. Second platoon has arrived."

I heard more shouting and firing over comms.

I turned a sharp right and hurdled up a stairway, aiming directly towards the fight a few decks above me. As I did a figure moved in in front of me.

"Stop!" An armoured fist closed around my arm, pulling me abruptly to a stop.

"Get off me." My fists thumped into impregnable armour.

"You're not going up there, Captain. Let my marines do their job." It was Suiku.

"I let this thing on board, Lieutenant. I'm not leaving them to die because of it."

"You can't help them and we need you alive. Let my people do their jobs. Go back to the bridge. We have this."

"That is an order, Lieutenant."

"I'm sorry, Captain, I cannot comply. And you are interfering with my ability to do my job. Please return to the bridge."

He was right. If whatever was up there could go through hard armour I had no hope of beating it with an FE weapon and a bit of attitude. "OK. Just get off me."

The marine released me and I rubbed my arm absently. "Cen, how did this thing get out?" The holding facility was designed to take a massive amount of damage and remain functioning.

"Unknown. It appears to have taken advantage of the shockwave to affect its escape."

"And there's more than one of them now?"

"Also an unknown."

I said nothing, continuing to listen in on the marines as they engaged the Hauda. If that was what it was. I could only make that presumption. What else could it be? One of these creatures masquerading as a Hauda? Or perhaps all this had been the Hauda from the start. They hadn't been in league with the creatures that attacked Sunna. They were the creatures. There were too many unknowns. I didn't like it. I needed to know more.

Fortunately it did seem like concentrated plasma fire drove them back. It was unclear whether it destroyed them entirely, but it certainly did them damage. I didn't want to consider the damage that was being caused to the *Cesa's* interior. It would be considerable. Whole decks were being destroyed. Interior systems were being obliterated. Life support and power systems. Water treatment plants. Stores. Of course we had backups. We always did. But no captain enjoyed standing idly by while their ship was dismantled from the inside out.

"Can we isolate this section?" I asked Cena. "Close boarding doors. Cut the power. These things are replicating somehow. We need to stop them spreading further into the ship."

"We would need to extract the marines. We now have four marine squads engaging the entity."

"We need to know what kind of environment is hostile to it," I said. "And then create those conditions in the sealed area."

"What do you propose?"

"I have no idea." Technically it was possible to eject parts of the ship. Sections that had become compromised by an enemy or were damaged beyond repair. An option, but we were a long way from that just yet.

"From analysis of the sample the creature is adapted to survive extreme environments. I suspect it will survive in a vacuum indefinitely and it does appear hardened to radiation. While being resistant to heat, plasma fire does affect its cellular cohesion. Meaning it does have its limits," the AI continued.

"We can't flood the compartment with plasma," I said.

"No."

A group of Red Group marines approached from the deck below. They were led by Captain Tenua. Her visor swung aside as he drew to a stop beneath me. I was still standing in the stair well, the Lieutenant blocking me from going any higher.

"I've brought you this, Izzy," she said, an armoured arm indicating a suit beside her.

With a clunk seams appeared in the suit's tough hide and swung open, revealing the padded interior. It was empty. Clearly someone had remote piloted it here.

"You bring me the nicest things, Ono" I pulled myself into it and allowed it to close around me. It fit perfectly, the mechanisms adjusting to my body, the machinery forming a second skin around me. A skin I had long thought impregnable. Until today.

There was no flimsy transparent visor. The suit was a featureless plane of metalloy. Once it was sealed it was unbroken by joints or hatches. The material itself bending and stretching as I moved, allowing my arms and legs to move naturally. Each motion powered by the suit itself, enhancing my strength a thousand-fold. The interior of the helmet contained a projection of what lay outside. As if I wasn't wearing a helmet at all. Superimposed were ammunition readouts and optical enhancements.

"I still can't let you up, Captain," Suiku said. "Even now. It is not safe."

"I don't think you will be stopping her, Lieutenant," the marine captain said. "You may as well step aside. She can look after herself."

"Are you making that an order, Captain?"

"Do I have to?"

The marine hesitated but then stepped aside. "No, Captain."

"Thank you, Lieutenant," I said. "For now we need to get everyone out of these compartments. Then we need to isolate them by closing the boarding doors. Can you do that?"

He hesitated again. "Yes, but we have people trapped in there. Some engineers on twelve. Some unarmed marines on fourteen."

"Get them out. Cen, when the doors are closed I want you to cut power to these sections. From memory there is a backup reactor here?"

"There is, Izzy," the AI replied.

"Overload it. I want you to send that thing critical. Can we withstand a detonation?"

"Captain!" This was too much for Ono. She stepped forwards as if that would stop my order. "We can't. This is inside the ship. You're talking about writing off this whole section."

"It does not border on the hull so will not compromise shipwide safety. As long as everyone is out and safe I couldn't give a damn about some destroyed compartments. As long as the threat to the ship is gone."

"This is an extreme course of action, Izzy," Ono objected. "We will require refit. That means we'll have to return to a shipyard. It means giving up on your mission."

"When we are finished here, we'll head straight back."

I heard a solid thump nearby. "I am closing the internal boarding doors to this section," Cena reported.

"Close the next ones along also, and vacate the intervening spaces. I want a buffer zone."

"There is a med bay in that area," the AI said.

"I know. Transfer any patients to the next closest bay." I returned my attention to the captain. "Ono, I need some volunteers. Three."

"For what, may I ask?"

"We need to know how this thing, this Hauda, got out. It escaped a secure facility. I intend on going in there to inspect it."

"You've just given an order to incinerate those spaces," Ono reminded me.

"Cen. How long will we have?"

"If I remove the baffles now and ramp up output the reactor will enter critical mode in five minutes thirty seconds. I will need to override its safety protocols. One of which would otherwise eject it from the ship."

"So we have five minutes. Some volunteers, Captain." I checked the loadout of the hard armour. The weapon attached to my arm was an FE, a focussed energy weapon. It was connected to a reactor situated on my back by a thick silvery cable. The fuel rods were at one hundred percent. That would last me quite some time. Certainly enough for five minutes.

"I volunteer," Ono said.

"Are you sure, Captain?"

"I cannot send my people into situations I fear to enter myself. I think you already have a squad of volunteers, though."

I took it he meant the squad who had accompanied me to Xon. "They aren't here though, Captain. Two more?"

All of the troops behind him stood forward, along with the Lieutenant. I indicated the two marines closest behind Ono with a blunt armoured hand.

"Not today, Lieutenant. We're risking enough officers here as it is. I need you to coordinate from here. Get everyone out."

I turned the lumbering suit around and headed further up the stair well. Movement was effortless, the machinery concealed within it doing all the work for me. "Close the doors behind us, Cen."

We moved quickly, our armoured legs carrying us away from the stairwell and towards the holding facility. It wasn't far away in a straight line, only twenty or so metres, but the passage ways here were a tangle of engineering and storage spaces. We cut through one of them, a relatively small hold that had once contained consumables. A battle had clearly been fought here. The storage crates were ripped open, spewing their contents onto the deck. The framework that organised them was twisted and broken, allowing upper levels to come tumbling down. Blocking our way through it. Everything was on fire. High energy plasma searing through bulkheads and containers alike. Anything that could burn was, filling the space with thick smoke.

"There's some marines down here, Izzy," Ono said as we ploughed through the detritus of the battle. We didn't have the time to go around, and so simply batted the remains of containers aside as we went.

"Life signs?"

"None."

"Mourn them later, Ono. We have a job to do now."

"They will be incinerated if we blow the reactor. We should get their remains out."

"No time. I'm sorry."

"You are hard, Captain."

I didn't have anything to say to that. I'd always known some of my decisions were not popular. People tended to shy away from the hard choices. Taking the easy way out that ultimately invited further problems in the future. Right now the safety of everyone aboard was at risk. That was my primary responsibility. I didn't know what this Hauda was. If it even was a Hauda. I did know there was something in here that could kill hard armoured marines. Something that was becoming more numerous by the moment. I didn't know how it did any of it. I did know I had to stop it before it became unstoppable. Time mattered.

"You have four minutes, Captain," Cena reported.

"Thanks, Cen. Keep it coming."

"Movement left," one of the marines reported.

"Feel free to engage, people."

An FE shrieked. A bright flash of light speared the smoky air, tearing through a far bulkhead. A nearby stack of containers groaned and started sagging.

"No hit," the marine said. "These things are quick."

I came to the far loading door. I didn't stop, simply putting my shoulder into it and battering my way through. Steel snapped, the door giving way under the impact. With a bang it fell into the walkway beyond. It was dark, Cena having already cut the power to this section. Left. We had to go left.

"Internment is just up ahead," Ono said.

"Are you seeing this, Captain?" I scanned around me, at the once sturdy steel of bulkheads as we approached the most secure compartments within the ship.

"Looks like something chewed on it."

One of the marines fired again. This time there was a cheer as they hit something. I didn't stop to see what it was. Before us was a thick armoured door, isolating the holding area from the rest of the ship. This entire section was a box within a box. A solid armour-clad compartment thirty or forty metres on a side, subdivided further by more armoured cells. Each one in isolation from those around it. Each one considered impregnable. Just within the entrance was a watch station, where the guards and other personnel who worked here were situated. It was abandoned now, the crew retreating when the Hauda escaped. Fortunately the creature had been our only guest within the facility. There was a regular need to incarcerate marines or other crew-members due to minor infractions. We didn't use this holding station for that though, they were generally locked within their own quarters if we found restricting their freedom necessary. This was for enemy combatants only. For those we needed to ensure did not pose a threat to the ship.

"You have no telemetry from this event at all?" I asked Cena.

"None. The escape occurred during the temporary disruption caused by the shock wave. By the time power was re-established the Hauda was out and had already destroyed a number of internal systems. Making further analysis of its activities impossible."

"Anything unusual before hand?"

"Before the event? Nothing at all. The Hauda was under constant surveillance. It remained motionless, as you saw it when you visited."

"How long did you lose power in this section?"

"This is a priority compartment. My subsystems returned power here before most others. I estimate the Hauda had less than two point three seconds to take action."

"Are you saying it took the Hauda just over two seconds to escape the most secure compartment aboard? One even we considered impregnable?"

"I am."

That should have scared me. That should have terrified me. I think it would have had I taken time to consider it and its ramifications. Right now was time for action, not contemplation.

"Are you sure this thing is a Hauda?" Ono asked. He had been listening in on the conversation.

"I no longer know what it is. I don't think we ever really did, but this was unexpected."

"Contact rear," one of the marines reported. She opened fire, filling the passage behind us with stuttering light.

"You have two minutes," Cena reported.

"Hold up," I held up an armoured fist as we passed the duty station and cast our sensors over the holding cells beyond.

"Shit," Ono said.

Our sensors scanned through the darkened space, revealing it in stark relief on the interior of our helmets. The cells were gone. As if someone had stripped them out. Nothing remained but a jagged chasm. A massive open sore within the *Cesa*.

"Look at the walls, Izzy," Ono continued.

I was looking. But I didn't think I could quite comprehend what I was looking at. The walls, what remained of them, were writhing with movement. As if they were teeming with lice. Lice bigger than I was, even in the suit. They were indistinct shapes, each one morphing into the one alongside it. My targeting systems stuttered, trying to identify individual shapes, but failing dismally.

"What is this, Izzy?" the marine demanded. "What's going on here?"

"I don't know, Ono."

"The entities appear to be consuming the ship's substrate," Cena provided. "They also appear to be subdividing."

"They are eating the ship?" Ono demanded. "Are you serious?"

"They are using the materials to duplicate themselves, yes," the AI said.

"This isn't good. Shit. This isn't good."

"We can't hold them, Captain," a marine reported. I had almost forgotten they were still engaging something to our rear.

"Might be time to go, Izzy," Ono said.

"One minute," Cena reported in my ear. Definitely time to go.

"OK. Let's go. Stop messing about with them and get a bowler in there," I told the marines.

They didn't hesitate. One of them clipped an attachment to their weapon and aimed it loosely down the passageway. With a thump a dark object was launched into the darkness. We didn't stay to watch its effects.

The incendiary device smacked into something fleshy and dropped to the charred deck. Just as we disappeared around a far corner the energy pent up within the device erupted. Designed to blow a hole through armoured hulls the bowler released the miniature sun that was held within. In an instant heat seared through the passage. Vaporising everything it came into contact with. Wall. Floor. Hauda. Everything.

Heat washed over us as we fled, the shockwave almost picking us from our lumbering feet. Had it not been for the suits we would have perished instantly, even though we were now quite a distance away. An unprotected human would have been vapourised instantly.

Which was nothing more than a prelude to what we would experience if we stayed here. Cena continued counting down in my ear. Her calm voice urging me on.

"Thirty seconds."

"Do you have a door ready to open?"

"I do."

"Ensure nothing besides us comes through it."

"There are marines waiting for you."

"Contact right," Ono said. His weapon screamed, sending a torrent of fire towards movement his sensors had picked up ahead of us.

"Stop!" I shouted, my own sensors picking up the same motion.

It wasn't a Hauda. It was a side door that had creaked open slightly. A human face had looked out. Snatched away quickly when they discovered the intense heat in the passage.

"I thought Suiku had everyone out of here!"

"Temperature, Cen."

"One hundred degrees and falling," the AI reported. I had wondered why the door hadn't stayed open long. The intense heat from the bowler was dissipating quickly. But it was still hot out here.

"We don't have the time," Ono said.

"I'm not leaving anyone." I stopped outside the door. It was warped and seared but had stayed in place. Somehow enough to protect those sheltering within. I clicked on my external speaker. "Do you have any thermal protection?"

There was a muffled response. Far too indistinct for my own ears to decipher, but enough for the suite to pick up and amplify.

"No."

"How many of you are there?"

"Two. My companion is hurt. She can't walk."

"Do you have anything at all? Blankets. Clothing. Anything."

"This is a service locker. I can't see anything."

"Ten seconds," Cena reported.

"We're out of time," Ono said.

I could feel a vibration through the deck, even within the suit. The reactor had exceeded its tipping point. There was no stopping it now.

"Foam packaging," I said. "They use it for trunk insulation. There will be a roll. Wrap it around you. Quickly!"

"The reactor core has breached," Cena reported. "The generator room bulkhead will breach shortly."

"How long?"

"I cannot say."

"Give me a time, Cen."

"Less than thirty seconds."

I heard a thump from inside the locker. It was going to have to be enough. We didn't have the time to wait. Even if the temperature didn't spike immediately this area would be irradiated. Anyone outside of a hard armour suit would not survive it. Seconds later even those inside them would succumb.

That was the point. We had to kill something that could survive a directed energy beam. We needed to turn this compartment into a roiling inferno.

I ripped the door from its rail and was reaching inside even as it thumped to the deck behind me. Two ensigns were inside. One rolled up in foam cladding, her head protruding from it. Clearly her companion hadn't understood the brief. She had been leaning over her when the door was ripped off. She tried to stand as the flood of heat hit her. Her eyes grew wide with surprise but then fainted almost instantly. Dropping to lay over her comrade.

"Pick her up. Let's go."

I snatched up the first ensign, aware that my grasp was probably snapping bones. We could fix bones. We could fix heat exposure. To a degree. We could not fix what was coming.

"Get the door, Cen. And get medical down here. Two wounded incoming. Both heat exposure. One with wounds of an unknown nature."

"Medical personnel are on site."

It wasn't far to the nearest boarding door. It was a thick slice of hull material, designed to prevent boarders from continuing down the passage. Sealed it created a pressurised and armoured partition within the warship. One of many thousands that intersected every space within it. Each one designed to impede the penetration of enemy forces.

As we lumbered closer it slid aside, casting light into the smoky atmosphere within. I could see marines beyond. Each of them hard armoured themselves, each one aiming a weapon at me. Between them I could see the red and white armour suits of medical personnel.

I didn't look down to the ensign in my arms. I didn't want to know what this was doing to her. In any other circumstance this would likely be fatal. The human body was frail. It could not survive this kind of damage. But these were marines. Their systems coursing with nanomachines designed to keeping them healthy and alive in the most unusual of environments. Although this was pushing it.

I burst into the light. Keeping on going so as not to get in the way of those behind me.

"Here. Take her." I handed the ensign to a medic. "Close the door. Close the door."

"The last barrier is failing. Temperature is spiking," Cena reported.

As the door slid quickly closed again I might just have caught site of a boiling wall of flame rushing towards us. I couldn't tell. It was simply too quick. I didn't hear or feel anything when it hit the door. The material was simply too thick for that.

"That was close," I heard a marine comment. I couldn't argue.

"Did you get what you needed, Captain?" Suiku asked.

"I don't know," I said. "I really don't. But these things, whatever they are ... we've never seen anything like them. We have to find where they came from, and ..."

"And what, Captain?"

I had no idea. How to you stop a force like this? What if there were thousands of them? Millions? One of them aboard the *Cesa* had caused unbelievable damage. Just one. An army ... I didn't want to think about it.

Chapter 16

We called it the Sundeck. It was an officer's club built into the ceiling of Longtown, invisible from the town itself as it was behind the holographic image of the sky. Much of its floor was transparent visiplex, revealing the playing fields and walkways far beneath. Some people never entered the place, uncomfortable with the view. It didn't bother me.

I was here for some solitude. And I needed a drink.

The battle ... the defeat in Sector Four was hours in the past. Six. No seven. I had stayed to ensure the Hauda were not getting out. If any were still alive in there, which I doubted. Nothing could survive the detonation. The heat. The radiation. Cena had certainly detected no movement within the sealed sections. The barricades were holding. The buffer zone remained secure. We were safe. I had refused to leave until I was certain of it.

Then came checking on the wounded. Apart from those who had been killed immediately the wounded would make a full recovery. Even the two we had rescued from Sector Four as we retreated. Some burns, heat exposure. Broken bones and a concussion. Nothing we couldn't repair. Our medical science was good. Our people were better.

Which was little consolation. This shouldn't have happened. I could descend into self-recrimination but it would serve little purpose. It would not revive the dead. It would not repair the damage to Sector Four.

"Cen, get me Sorl'o."

"He is off duty and has requested not to be disturbed."

"Get him please."

"Contacting him now."

I needed to speak to him. I needed to know what I had missed. I had brought this creature aboard. Ultimately this was all on me. I felt my nose idly as I waited. It had started itching, which I knew was a sign healing was well underway. Its swelling had subsided, as well as most of the bruising. Had it not been for the cocktail of drugs in my system this kind of healing would have taken weeks.

"Izzy, what is it? I heard what happened. Do you need me?" The half ceramic face of Sorl'o appeared in my mind's eye, courtesy of Cena's communications. He had had a long day treating the wounded from Sector Four. He had only just gone off duty himself.

"I'm sorry, Sorl'o. I need to know what we ... I missed. You completed the sample testing on the Hauda. Did you find anything? Anything at all that could have caused this?"

He paused for a moment as if gathering his thoughts. I might have caught him asleep. I know he removed his ceramic plates when sleeping as it was more comfortable without them. "You've read my report, Izzy. There's not much I can add to it."

"Then I need someone to explain to me how this happened. There was nothing in the report that suggested this thing could change like this."

"No. No, there isn't. But ..."

"Tell me, I need to know what happened here."

"Well, I have been trying to understand this notion of distributed consciousness. Or the hive mind that the Hauda alluded to. So, while the creature's genetic heritage did not allude to any kind of metamorphosing ability, it might be linked to that."

"I'm not following."

"Well, there is nothing in our science that might explain the functioning of a hive mentality. How could it possibly work? How do all its constituent parts communicate with each other? Effectively enough to be considered one single mind? The communications latency between one node and the other needs to be remarkably small, otherwise it cannot function as one unit. And how can that work over a distance? Without any kind of artificial communications equipment involved at all? It simply makes no sense."

"You have a theory?"

"Well, I've been playing with the notion of complex entanglement, but that doesn't work that way at all. None of our existing theories come even close unless I start dabbling in the metaphysical. Which I am loath to do."

"So?" I promoted him.

"Well, I did find an unusual structure in the Hauda's cerebral complex. I couldn't identify its function at first, but I'm starting to think it is some type of organic computer. Or rather, an interface. One that is designed to handle range communications."

"You are suggesting it is possible for a brain ... even if it is very heavily adapted ... to engage in hyperspatial communications?"

"It's a hypothesis at the moment. Barely that. Moreover it may also function to download a physical template. An overriding genetic blueprint, thus allowing the Hauda to become something else entirely. Their genetic structure itself is stable, it does not contain multiple heritages. But it does appear plastic. Changeable."

"You didn't want to dabble in the metaphysics?"

"Well, no." He laughed self-consciously. "This is all new to us, Izzy. I have sent some queries to Admiralty Science, but they haven't come back to me yet. I'm hoping someone ... somewhere, has worked on something similar to this, and has a more advanced understanding than I do. In the meantime ... I guess."

"That's the best you have at the moment?"

"It is. You couldn't have known, Izzy. This is not your fault."

"I am not trying to avoid any responsibility here, Sorl'o. I am trying to understand this thing."

"Of course, I am sorry."

"Can you continue your research without the Hauda itself?"

He shrugged. "I'll have to. I have samples. I ran thorough scans. There wasn't much else I could get from it anyway."

I nodded. He didn't have any answers. Not yet. "OK, thank you. I'll leave you in peace. Sorry for the interruption."

"Any time, Izzy. Anything you need." The link cut.

I swilled the last of my drink before drinking it down. It was called a flanly, originating from a world I had never been to, far out on the other side of the Confederacy. Non-alcoholic, sadly. I am not teetotal, but I needed my senses clear.

In some respects, the fact none of us could predict this was irrelevant. I had still brought it aboard in the hopes of gleaning some information from it. Clearly that had not been very successful. Still, had it been a risk? Certainly. Nothing is ever entirely without risk. Particularly when it came to an unknown quantity like the Hauda.

Members of the crew had lost their lives. The ship had been damaged. That was all that mattered.

"Cen, get me Lieutenant Sepulveda." Tebercy was still in the medbay himself, recovering from injuries sustained after our attack on the Quint mechanism. Sepulveda was his stand in.

"Captain, how may I help?"

"Do we know anything more about the effect we experienced after destroying the Quint mechanism?"

"Well, yes actually, Captain. I have a team going through our telemetry and they believe they have an answer. If they're right it's actually quite exciting. I believe we may have proved the Lucander Theorem."

"OK. I'm unfamiliar, brief me."

"Well, Professor Lusander was based at Aricepos Observatory, when she-"

"In brief please."

"Yes, of course. Sorry, Captain. It relates to the intersection of a micro-singularity with a steep gravitational gradient. In a sense the event cancels both out while enhancing the gradient itself. Which is a contradiction."

"Naturally." Where was this going?

"The theorem suggests that the intersection temporarily prevents gravitational leakage. Or seals the leakage."

"You're going to have to be a bit more detailed than that, I'm afraid." Like all naval officers I had completed courses in engineering and physics, but that was a long time ago.

"Well, you know how gravity is considered a weak nuclear force. Some theories suggest this is because gravity is leaking. As in, we only experience a fraction of its true force. The remainder leaks."

"Ah. So we are verging on brane theory."

"Yes!" The engineer's disembodied voice sounded excited. Perhaps he was. It took an engineer to get excited about these things. "So gravity is weak because of leakage across the brane. But the intersection of a micro-singularity and a steep gravitational gradient temporarily seals that leakage. In a pulse, if you would. Almost like an explosion of gravity. That was the Lusander Theorem."

"So there was a micro-singularity within that mechanism? Why didn't we detect it?"

"I don't know. I suspect the Quint are cloaking it somehow. I don't think they're doing it on purpose, I mean, no one other than us have a means of detecting it. So why bother? I think part of the mechanism's function has the effect of cloaking it. It's a coincidence. But it's really very exciting."

"Good. Good. I'm glad. But we understand what happened?"

"We think so. In fact we were really very lucky. Had we been much closer we would have been crushed. We were on the far outskirts of the effect."

"Will it happen again?"

"No. Not unless we fire our primary weapon at another of their asteroid mining installations. Or expose one of our own ASPECTS to a steep gradient. Like within a star or something. Which was what Lusander proposed. Fortunately the Aricepos governing body refused permission for the experiment. It would have destroyed whatever star she attempted it on."

"That is good. Thank you, Lieutenant."

"Did you need any more information on it? The team is compiling a report."

"No, not right now, thank you. That will be all for the moment." I cut the comms. There was only so much physics I could handle in any one day. It answered that conundrum though. That, at least, gave me some comfort.

I ordered another flanly as I noticed a familiar face approaching. Commander Matte. She sat without invitation.

"Captain, the first officers are concerned. They would like a briefing," she said in greeting.

"They are welcome to review my suit telemetry," I said.

"With all due respect, that is insufficient. And is dismissive."

I sighed and watched as a human waiter approached with my drink. "Commander, dispense with the bullshit. Whenever anyone says 'with all due respect', no respect is ever forthcoming." I held up a hand to prevent a retort. "And I don't care. I like keeping you around. You keep me honest. But in this instance I would have to say, you are all senior officers of the Confederate Navy. You don't need your hands holding. You also don't get to summon me to a briefing. I will give you one when I am good and ready."

She nodded slowly, her eyes widening as the waiter placed a drink in front of her. I had ordered two. "I am on duty, Captain."

"It's non-alcoholic."

She sipped it carefully and then cleared her throat. "We ... all of us, are supposed to be a team. You must admit some of your actions have breached the military code of conduct-"

"And let me stop you there. Only a military court martial held within the Admiralty, attended by a minimum of two flag officers, can come to that conclusion."

"Of course. But you have to admit, Captain, you have put yourself at risk!"

"My responsibility entirely."

"And this ship and its crew."

"That remains to be seen."

"Come on, Captain. Sector Four is in ruins. How many of our crew have we lost in this?"

"This is a vessel of war, Commander. Any loss is regrettable, but we are all professionals. We knew the risk when we joined."

"You can't seriously make light of this loss-"

I held up a hand to interrupt her again. "Speak plainly, Commander. What do you want?"

She was silent a moment, taking another sip of her drink. "There is talk about removing you from command."

And there it was.

"They sent you here for that did they? Tebercy too much of a coward?"

"It was not his idea."

I snorted a laugh. "Well, while you are reviewing our records, review my orders from the Admiralty. Review my reports to them. You will see every action has been sanctioned. Then seek their sanction for this proposed course of action of yours. If you don't get it you realise this broaches on mutiny?"

"Be reasonable, Captain. This ship has been put at risk. People have died."

"I know this is a bad time, Izzy," Cena said into my intercom. "But we're being hailed. I think it is the Hermitage."

I put my drink down. "Duty calls, Commander." I walked away, leaving her staring after me. I didn't think I was going to get that solitude.

Chapter 17

A MAV is nowhere near as quick as a heavy cruiser. It is FTL capable certainly, but that facility was only afforded it to enable accelerated transfer times, between ship and whatever the marines were engaging. Be it planetary, orbital station or starship. As a result, it was quick in short sprints, but not ideal when travelling any distance. So, where it would have taken the *Cesa* moments to cross the system, it took the MAV almost an hour. To be fair we weren't really trying, and in order to stay out of any conceivable danger the *Cesa* had retreated to the system's far reaches. So I shouldn't talk the MAV down. For what it was it was a very capable vehicle.

Besides, it gave me time to gather my thoughts and brief my squad as we approached Planet Five. Which I believed was the Hermitage's own name for the planet, as unimaginative as that was.

They were gathered around me within the MAV's CIC. The command and control spaces just behind the vessel's bridge. Sidearms only had been the instruction, and they were idly checking them over as they listened to Cena's briefing. The twins were, naturally, armed only with their ceremonial swords. They were oiling the gleaming blades, the weapons laid out on perfectly white linen cloths as they dabbed tiny amounts of lubricant along their lengths. As with all things, this was a critical stage in their preparations. Preparation for battle. Even though I had made it clear we were not expecting conflict. They always expected conflict. Conflict was life. Life was conflict.

"So they are claiming they captured a Quint?" Beyard said as Cena finished up its briefing. "And they've been holding it for almost forty years?"

"What is more interesting is that this happened only two years after the Shaan left the system. Even though the two parties have been cohabiting this system for quite some time, and have been in direct conflict for almost two hundred years. They have only come into physical contact with a Quint on this occasion," the AI confirmed.

"You are suspicious," I said. "You believe the Quint allowed it to happen."

"I cannot rule out the possibility."

"A strange thing for them to do. Unless you believe the Quint sent it as an emissary. To broker a peace between them?"

"I find that unlikely," Cena said. "It has also been unsuccessful in that endeavour."

"So they have a mysterious motivation. All the more reason for us to see this Quint. I can't believe they managed to keep it alive all this time."

"Without torturing it to death," Sanquey commented.

I nodded. That had struck me as unlikely too. "We'll have to find that out for ourselves. Have they managed to converse with it?"

"They have not. The invite from the Hermitage was brief, but it did indicate they did not understand its language. In fact they suspect it to be a pet, an animal. Which was the reason the Quint didn't attempt a rescue. They simply didn't care enough."

"An animal? Why would they think that? What does it look like?" Sanquey asked.

"I have no information. The invitation was not appended with an image file."

"Elder civilisations are often adapted. From what little we actually know about them," I said. "Or at least, all of those we have had direct contact with are. To one degree or another."

"So the Quint might not look human any longer," the marine said.

"A possibility. They do take it to be an animal after all. But I can't imagine what kind of modification would lead to that conclusion."

"It is worth noting that while we are intrigued by their Quint captive, they are not," Cena said. "They mentioned it in the invitation as a side note. They believe we are here in response to their request for aid. Particularly as we have just destroyed part of a Quint installation. They mention the captive in the hopes we can learn how to kill Quint from it."

"And no one comments on the irony they wish to murder their own god," Beyard said.

"I don't think any of us have missed that connection," I said. "And I'm not sure we want to tell them. Particularly as we're not here to help them against the Quint. We're here to interrogate the Quint ourselves. To find out what they know about Sunna."

"We are some way from the Quint system here," Cena said. "But we are certainly within communications range. The Quint population here should be relatively up to date with events in their home system. Recently enough to be aware of their collusion with the Hauda anyway."

The Hauda. I didn't need reminding of them and the devastation they had caused aboard the *Cesa*. That was too fresh in my mind. Literally in fact. We had received the invitation from the Hermitage barely four hours earlier. Enough time to satisfy myself that I could safely leave the ship. That there was no further threat. We had lost twelve crewmembers and five marines in total, only retrieving the bodies of four of them. The remainder were still in there. Their bodies atomised.

Four hours. Enough to equip a MAV and gather up this little squad. There hadn't been time for anything else. I hadn't spoken to Matte or any of the other bridge officers again, except to hand over temporary command to Tebercy for the duration of this mission. They could think their course of action through while I was away. And come to their senses. Or not.

I opened a private comms to Cena. "Any activity within the exclusion zone?"

"None. Temperature inside the destroyed section is dropping slowly as it disperses into compartments alongside. It will take some time before we can open any of the doors. Weeks in my estimation."

"We are still confident the Hauda have been destroyed?" I don't know how many times I had asked that question.

"We are."

That was all I was going to get. Confidence. No actual verifiable fact. No dead bodies to examine. Not for a few weeks anyway. If there was anything left in there. Which was actually very possible. The creatures had been eating the internal structure of the *Cesa*, using that material to replicate themselves. Which meant they were made of the same material the ship itself. A heat resistant material.

As long as they were dead. I didn't care about anything else. And that it meant these things could be killed. With difficulty by hard armoured marines perhaps, but I didn't rate their chances highly against the main weapons of a warship like the *Cesa*.

In the meantime we had things to do. The Hermitage had sent a broad beam communication, little more than a broad spectrum radio signal. Which meant they knew we were out here, just not where. Cena had reported picking up long range comms from the asteroid mining settlement just after we contacted it. The crew perhaps reporting a Confederate presence in the system. Perhaps calling for help. Either way, the Hermitage knew we were here and that we didn't mean the Quint well. They wouldn't have missed the destruction of the Quint facility.

Oh, and they had a Quint captive. Pet. Whatever.

Planet Five was an icy ball. Little solid ground protruding from the sheath of ice. Most of that was in the southern hemisphere, not that far from City One, their capitol. Original names certainly. Perhaps the Hermitage had learned not to grow too attached to places and so didn't invest in a complex naming system. It was our destination. The origin of the signal and apparently where they kept their captive.

I'd left an image of the city on the CIC's central holoscreen for the team to inspect. It was little more than a string of domes connected by tunnels. The domes themselves weren't that large. Perhaps a few hundred metres in radius. Cena suspected the bulk of the city was buried within the ice, away from the blistering winds of the surface. An inhospitable place certainly. An odd place to build a city, unless there was something drawing them here that was not immediately obvious.

Cena believed the ice was only a few hundred metres thick in places, and that there was a source of heat beneath it. Possibly a hidden ocean. The surface was cracked and split, most of those tears long since iced over. The ice sheet was clearly not a solid expanse, there was something shifting beneath it. A bit like Europa in your own system. An enigma I know your scientists have been pouring over for a long time. I imagine one day you'll go there for yourselves and find out.

As interesting as it was, and potentially something to investigate further at some point in the future, it was not what was drawing us here. The captive Quint was. That was all.

"Get in touch with them, if you don't mind Cen. Let them know we're on our way and ask where to land."

"Sending tightbeam now."

"Let them know we're interested in the Quint. In fact, we'd like to take it off their hands."

"I doubt they'll go for that," Beyard said.

"I don't really intend on giving them an option," I said. I didn't have time for niceties. These people had seen the Shaan. That massive GSX class city ship that was over a hundred kilometres in length. There was no way they could have missed it parked in their system. It had spent some months here after all. They knew we were capable of taking on the Quint too. We were not to be trifled with. Was I a bully? Certainly. Did I care? No.

The Hermitage were not our enemies but nor were they our allies.

"They are directing us to a patch of ice alongside one of their domes," Cena said. "The regent will welcome us. They have celebrations planned."

"No celebrations, Cen." I was not in the mood for frivolities.

"I shall relay that request."

"Instruction."

"Of course. I should warn you it is thirty five below zero on their landing pad. The entrance to the dome itself appears to be over a hundred metres away. A storm is approaching from the west. The wind is already picking up."

So either the Hermitage were a hardy lot or they wanted to see how we coped. Or alternately there was nowhere else to land. "Just get us in close." They underestimated the flight capabilities of a MAV.

The MAV streaked through the atmosphere, barely bothering to slow down as we approached the city. I suspected the Hermitage traffic controllers had caught sight of us as soon as we hit the stratosphere. We had left a long streak of fire that was impossible to overlook.

"Cold weather gear, Captain?" Lieutenant Beyard asked as I stood and headed for the external gangway.

"I doubt we'll be outside long enough. But who knows how warm it is inside? I'd recommend it." I checked the planet's atmosphere. It was mostly carbon dioxide, some methane and nitrogen. Desperately little oxygen. Atmospheric pressure was also low, about twenty percent standard. Not a vacuum but not something you could comfortably step into without some kind of pressure suit.

The MAV was relatively well equipped. While it was primarily a close support troop transport, it was also an emergency escape mechanism. As such it carried some supplies and survival gear. There were enough cold weather jackets in a locker, and we handed them around. I tossed a ghoscht belt to the lieutenant and buckled one on myself.

"Set to atmospheric integrity mode," I instructed.

Yes, I am showing off. But I had a point to make. We were Confederate. We possessed capabilities these people could not even guess at. Watching us walk across a virtually airless, freezing expanse in little more than a hoodie, with no care in the world, would definitely have an impact.

True, a ghoscht was not a pressure suit, there would be leakage around the periphery, particularly where it interacted with the surface. But it would be enough to last the minute or so it would take us to enter their building.

Piloting the MAV Cena ignored the landing instructions and brought the vehicle down as close as it could to the dome's entrance. Or what we presumed to be the entrance. It looked like a wide retractable door, large enough for ground vehicles to pass through. The icy surface outside it was churned up and muddy, as if it was regularly crossed by tracked vehicles. Unfortunately it was far too small for the MAV itself.

"Any space capable vehicles?" I asked Cena.

"Not that I have detected. They have built a steel reinforced concrete platform on the opposite side of this dome. Potentially for use by rocket propelled vessels. The Hermitage do possess quite a number of them, I have detected several dozen around the system. Either enroute or docked to a station. One does appear to be headed away from this facility now. It might have lifted off in the last day or so."

I recalled mention that the Hermitage territories did not trade with each other. As a result they would only have use for vessels such as this to connect to their own mining outposts, such as the now destroyed asteroid station. Or potentially to dispatch their annual tithe to the ancient city ship still in orbit around the second planet. Planet Two, I imagined they called it. Which meant they didn't need all that many space capable vehicles. Their fleet was small.

"I've instructed them to open the door," Cena said as our own outer ramp slid down, allowing in a blast of freezing air. The AI had already matched external atmospheric pressure.

The dome's door lumbered open as we stepped onto the snow, our boots crunching through a layer of ice that had formed on it overnight. We were quite far south here, the pale sun low on the horizon. Not that we could see it through a thick cloud bank that was sweeping in slowly. Two of the domes in the distance had already been enveloped by it. The navigation lights at their peaks only just visible. I couldn't imagine there was much air traffic here. There wasn't much call for it.

The MAV retreated slightly once we had all disembarked and settled onto the snow itself. It could have remained on station, orbiting the city lazily, but it didn't really matter.

There was what looked like some kind of garage beyond the door. Containing any number of tracked vehicles. Large and small. A dozen or so single seaters buzzed out onto the snow as we approached. Our welcoming party, I presumed. We ignored them as they circled around us, one or two of the drivers waving to us. Another party on foot waited just within the entrance. I imagine they didn't relish stepping into the snow themselves. They, at least, were wearing insulated pressure suits, their faces obscured behind tinted visors.

"I am ready to translate," Cena said in my ear as I approached them.

There was a lot of waving as we stepped into the garage. The vehicles buzzed in behind us and parked up against a wall.

"What's going on, Cen?"

"They're just excited. Giving each other instructions," the AI said. It was likely listening in on their radio chatter.

"Who is the leader of this group?"

"I believe it is the male in the middle. In green."

I headed straight for him. He was a short man. Very short in fact. They all were. But then their home planet was a high G world, so that did tend to happen. I did notice he was wearing an exoskeleton of some kind over his pressure suit. It was constructed of chrome and dull steel. A bulky power unit on his back. None of the others had anything like it. An oddity as he surely didn't need assistance on Planet Five. It was smaller than their home world, its gravity about a third of what their kin laboured under.

"Patch me in, please."

"You are connected."

I was about to greet him when he saluted and shouted loudly. "Welcome people of the Shaan!" I didn't know it then but the salute was a bit cringeworthy. I wasn't aware of the National Socialists on your world. Not then anyway. Here it was just a salute.

The others joined in, throwing up their arms in salute. Fortunately they didn't share in his shouted greeting.

I bowed slightly. "Greetings. Are you the leader of this installation?" I heard my own words in my head, and the translated versions Cena transmitted as I spoke.

"I am Regent Hoersch. His holiness, Lord Mayor Aarsene Hoewetish the First, Prime Candidate, Master of Planet Five and surrounds, First Supplicant and Beloved of the Shard, is on his way to give supplication. Regrettably he is unavailable."

I groaned. All of this was shouted at the top of his voice. I get local custom but it was annoying. I'd had a rough day so far. I didn't need to be shouted at.

"May I hope Governor Freuch is in good health?" he continued. Freuch? I think he was the governor at the time the Shaan visited here.

"Detailed introduction, then an enquiry into the health of the last delegate they encountered," Cena said in my ear. A bit of cultural detail.

I cleared my throat and decided to ignore it. It couldn't be that much of a tradition. The Hermitage did not allow contact between provinces so there was little need for it. "I couldn't speak for their health, as I am not from the Shaan. I am Captain Isia Marla of the Confederate heavy cruiser, the *CSS Cesa*. I am here to collect your Quint. That is all." I didn't have patience with pleasantries. I wanted that Quint and nothing else.

He hesitated as my translated words were relayed to him. "You are welcome. We parlay. Come." He stood to one side and waved us ahead of him.

I was starting to understand why some Confederate officers threw their weight around and ignored local custom. It was tiresome. Of course encountering other cultures was to be expected and was part of the job. We were officially out here to meet the worlds beyond our borders. Make allies, sign treaties. That kind of thing. But not right now. Right now I wanted the Quint. Then I wanted to go and destroy something.

"We cannot parlay now. You have detected an explosion in space? You know your asteroid mining station was destroyed?"

"Station sixty-five. They told us you were trying to save them from the Outsiders. Did you bring them back with you?"

Ah. He didn't know the miners had been killed. But then how could he?

"Sadly no. We were unable to rescue them."

He was silent a moment. Then he said loudly: "It is a dangerous profession!"

"It is. My mission now is to confront the … Outsiders. To do so I need access to your captive."

"Welcome, welcome. Come, we parlay." He stood to a side and held out his arms as if ushering us in.

"I'm confused, Cen. What protocols can a people have when they do not permit contact between the provinces?" I watched as the last of the vehicles returned to the garage and the door lumbered closed once again, cutting off the wisps of snow that were curling around its frame in the gale.

"They may have developed them since the Shaan's visit. I have a theory that would explain the exoskeleton the emissary is wearing."

"Oh? Go on."

"It is not a device to render assistance to the wearer, but rather one to increase resistance. It is keeping his muscles in tone in low gravity, allowing him to return to Hermitage at some point in the future. Without it his muscles would atrophy and he would be unable to return."

"So he is not a local. He's from their home world."

"A theory, as I say. I have no actual information either way."

"But from another province, yes?"

"From what I understand of their provincial structure he would have to be."

Interesting. So either the information gathered by the people of the Shaan was wrong, or the appearance of the city ship in their system had prompted some radical changes. Either way, we didn't really know what we were walking into.

"Come, come," The regent – Hoersch – insisted.

"We go, Izzy?" Beyard suggested.

"Sure."

They didn't pressurise the bay itself, but rather led us to a wide, brightly lit compartment that sealed behind us. Air hissed in. Once the inner door lumbered open a squad of brown jump-suited attendants entered and began assisting our hosts out of their pressure suits. They hesitated when they noticed we were not wearing any, realising we had no need of their assistance.

"The Shaan research team found the Hermitage to be culturally and physiologically homogeneous," Cena said in my ear. "Their original home world was high gravity also, so they are well adapted to the environment of Planet Two. Less so Planet Five. The team believe the Hermitage did not build this facility, nor a good number of other similar stations to be found around the system. They posited the existence of a now extinct population who lived here in the hundred thousand plus year range. There is no information as to who they were, or where they went. They believe the Hermitage have no information on them either. They have realised that large parts of the system have been mined out, likely by a combination of that previous population and the Quint themselves."

"Which is causing them to explore further out, including the asteroid fields," I said. "Which is in turn driving conflict with the Quint who are doing the same."

"That was the supposition, yes."

"Come, we go." Hoersch said as soon as he was out of his suit. The exoskeleton had been reinstalled, adjusted slightly to accommodate the missing bulk of the pressure suit. We had stood aside all the while, waiting patiently while he was attended to. "You are not troubled by the cold and the air?" he continued.

"We are not. You are taking us to the Quint ... the Outsider?"

"Yes. Yes. We talk." We became part of a retinue as we left the chamber, the regent and some of his colleagues before us, three more behind. None of our hosts seemed bothered by our sidearms, but Cena did relay the odd comment about the swords. I imagine they were not commonly used here.

Hoersch engaged in small talk as we passed through a service complex that was attached to the garage. Repair facilities, storage, that kind of thing. Then we stepped into the dome proper.

"This is nice," C'Gen commented as we stepped into warm air. It felt like a greenhouse, humid and close. Uncomfortably so.

The dome itself was a glassy structure, I didn't know what material it was made from. It must be pretty tough if it was as old as Cena suggested. Within was a pale grey complex. Built of stone perhaps. Reaching up to, but not quite touching, the apex of the dome far above us. It was an assortment of towers, each one connected to the one beside it, gradually growing taller towards the centre. Around it at ground level was a mass of foliage. Trees perhaps, it was difficult to see. Before that, almost like a moat, was a waterway that butted up against the lower sections of the dome itself. A number of gondolas were poling their way this way and that across the water, carrying passengers or cargo. We headed to a wharf and the two vessels tied up there.

"Cen is picking up cargo elevators to lower levels," I said to the others. "It believes the bulk of the installation is below ground. Sensors can only reach a few hundred metres down, and all of that space appears to be composed of subterranean structure. It goes as far as sensors can reach, and likely a lot further."

"There could be a lot of people living here," Beyard said.

"I think there is. It could be in the tens of millions."

"I am not detecting a facility that could be used to hold a Quint," the AI said.

"Which does raise an interesting question," I said as we boarded the gondola. "If the Quint is like the Hauda we will have a problem."

"It has clearly not attempted an escape. I doubt the Hermitage could contain an entity such as the ones we encountered aboard the *Cesa*."

"It might be waiting for something. Us perhaps."

"Which raises another question," The AI said.

"It does. Why bother coming here? We can't possibly take it aboard. It's not worth the risk."

"The regent is asking about our ship," Beyard said.

I hadn't been paying attention. "It is here," I said to him. "Close enough to pick us up if need be."

He nodded. "Wise."

The moat wasn't very wide so it wasn't long before we were disembarking on the other side. Still talking the regent led us towards a ramp leading up the structure's side. Beyard kept him entertained. I think she sensed I wasn't in the mood for idle talk and so deflected him. I did listen idly, but soon realised he wasn't saying anything of any particular interest. He was explaining their history to her. From the beginning. I don't mean when they were saved by what they called the Shard. I mean the very beginning, those half-forgotten days on a doomed world. And how the chosen few had managed to escape.

This could take a while.

She just shrugged when she noticed my expression. "Diplomacy. It costs nothing."

"I have lost crew today, Lieutenant. I am not in the mood to massage this man's ego."

She inclined her head slightly. "Leave it with me, Izzy."

The walkway took us quickly towards the summit of the building, air whispering past is as we walked. It didn't take us long to realise this was no mere walkway.

"It's moving," Baes said. "The walkway. Look."

"Unilateral Ceramofluid," C'gen said. "Is what we call it. It's solid in the vertical but fluid in the horizontal plane. We use it all the time. It's nothing special."

"Unusual for the Hermitage to have it though."

"I don't think they built this place," the sergeant continued. "Look at the architecture. It's quite light weight. Elegant. Then notice the decorations. What decorations there are. There's some flags back there," she pointed. "Some pennants too. They're all rather crude. Monochrome. They're not made by the same people." The Shaan's scientists had attempted to date parts of the structure itself. Now while I say this, it does amuse me how dating mechanisms are often portrayed in your own media. I won't go into a detailed explanation of the mechanisms the Shaan used, but they did not radiocarbon rocks. Because you can't. They did find there was a massive disparity between the present occupation and the original construction works though.

"That's a reach," Baes commented.

"She's right," I said. "The Hermitage did not build this place. Someone else did. We don't know who. Or when."

"Their walkways still work though?"

I nodded. "They built well."

The walkway deposited us at the apex of the structure, no more than a dozen or so metres from the peak of the dome itself. I stopped and looked around me. There were no Quint here. It was a shrine of some sort. Perhaps a temple.

A blue/grey spearhead was suspended above the space. It was featureless, about as featureless as a Quint vessel. The space below it was flat, ringed by a low wall to prevent supplicants from stepping into emptiness by accident. Just within that was a circle of torches, filling the space with warm light. And quite a bit of acrid smoke.

The mayor bowed low upon catching site of the spearhead, as did all his companions. They placed a hand on their chests and spoke a brief incantation in low voices.

"What are we doing here? There's no Quint here," I said.

"The Shard blesses our gathering," the regent said.

"He's wasting our time. Cen, direct us to one of those freight elevators." I turned around to head back down.

"We lose nothing," Beyard said. "Please, Captain."

"You stay, Lieutenant. Parlay with the man. In other times I would have stayed and engaged in this. Right now I have other priorities."

I heard a shout as I descended the walkway again. I indicated for C'gen to remain with the lieutenant while the remainder of the squad joined me. The Hermitage delegation stood around staring at us as we walked away. Hoersch called out to us again but I ignored him.

"Bit of a diplomatic gaffe?" Baes said once we had lost sight of the shrine above us.

I sighed. "Yes. Not ideal. And yes, you could say that we have the time. The few days it would take to satisfy diplomatic obligations could not possibly make any difference. But I lost crew today. I have no patience for this."

"Perhaps we should have waited before coming here. Until we were ready to take the Hermitage seriously. They could have been friends. But not if we disregard them like this."

"Thank you for your concern, Sergeant. However I would point out that the Shaan pulled up stakes and left hours after learning the Quint had a presence here. They had been engaged in a diplomatic session when they discovered it, and promptly walked out. It would take weeks, if not months of diplomatic efforts to repair the damage that caused to relations. There was even a Hermitage delegation aboard the Shaan at the time. They were promptly ejected onto an orbital station rather than returned here, simply because it was more convenient. Sure, once we have completed our current mission we can return here and try to patch things up. But not today."

Baes said nothing as we reached the bottom of the walkway and headed through dense foliage towards the canal. "Cen, where to?"

"I am adapting your ghoscht units to scan your surroundings. As you descend we can use them to plot your location and identify where they are holding the Quint. For the moment, turn left. There is an elevator alongside the canal. It appears to lead into the lower city."

As we approached the platform a figure rounded the foliage behind us and shouted. She gave that same unfortunate salute and bowed deeply. "Honoured visitors, I am to be your guide. You wish to see the outsider creature?"

Perhaps Cena's modifications would not be needed. "We would."

"I am Oernie Soernie, it would honour me if you allowed me to guide you."

I held up a hand to stifle a comment from one of the marines. I think the name amused them. "Oernie, please lead the way."

"Thank you, how should I address you?"

"Isia. Lead on." She was little more than a child. Short like they all were, but not quite as heavy set as most. She was wearing a flowing green robe, with ringlets of what appeared to be gold about her neck. A member of the elite then, even if she was young.

She bowed again. "Isia. We go down."

I wasn't sure this qualified as a freight elevator, but I let that slide. It was a simple raised dais, a seam on its surface denoting a perfect square in the centre of it. In the centre of that was a pedestal with what looked like a simple control on it. A lever, and nothing else. As we stepped onto it and the girl took hold of the lever the edges of the dais raised up, creating a barrier about us. I imagine to prevent anyone from accidentally falling into the open shaft. A gravity well this was not.

With a hiss we descended.

"How far down does this go?" I asked her.

She frowned as if struggling with the question. "It goes to the Dark City. From there we take a raft to the rapids. That is where the menagerie is located."

"Zoo. She means Zoo," Baes commented.

"The Hermitage have never been able to communicate with it, so they believe it to be a pet," I said. "Cen, what kind of translating can you do?"

"I may need some sampled speech. I do have limited comms with the Quint on file. Electronic once again. We have never met an actual member of their people, much less conversed with one."

It quickly became clear why Oernie called the city beneath the dome the Dark City. At first we descended through a featureless expanse of white. Once the light from the surface vanished above we were left in gloom, the space above the platform lit only by lighting strips embedded into the platform itself. I didn't know what the walls were made of. They could be ice; they could be steel. The girl didn't seem concerned in the slightest. She certainly didn't warn us to stay away from them.

"Have you lived in the city all of your life, Oernie?" I asked her.

"I have."

"Do you know who built the city?"

She hesitated. "The city is the city. I was born here."

"Yes, do you know who built it? It was a long time ago, I imagine. Long before you were born."

She shook her head. "No. My people have lived here since we came to Planet Five. It is our home."

It was then the walls of the shaft disappearing around us. Leaving nothing but blackness. I stepped up to the edge of the platform and peered into it. Holding out a hand I felt an invisible barrier. It felt like glass, but was invisible to the naked eye. Featureless and perfectly clear. As I took my hand away I didn't leave a print behind. At least now I knew there was something there, to prevent the clumsy or unwary falling off the platform.

"There's something out there," Sanquey said as he joined me. "Look. In the distance."

He was right. As my eyes grew accustomed to the dark I started to make out a pattern. There was a faintly glowing line joining two half circles. As I studied it I realised there were more lines and more half circles joined to them. Each faintly lit from within.

"Domes", I said. "They are domes."

"Sorry, Izzy? Domes?" Baes asked.

"Yes. We've passed beneath the ice. We're under water. And over here," I pointed, "are more domes. Like the ones on the surface."

"Ah, there's more over here, Izzy," Sanquey said as he stepped to the opposite side of the platform, avoiding the twins who were stood silently by, as if unimpressed by the view. "They are all around us. There's dozens of them."

"I think there's one beneath us too," I said. "That's what we're headed towards. Dark City?" I turned to the girl.

She nodded. "This takes us to the Dark City."

"It is underwater? This is an underwater kingdom? Hidden beneath the ice cap?"

She said nothing, I don't think she followed.

"How many domes are there?" I asked.

"Thirty-two," she said. She could handle that question.

"And they are joined by passages. How many people live here?"

"They are joined by rapid. I don't know – a lot of people."

Rapid? I didn't know what that meant. We would find out.

"Aah, Izzy," Baes called me over.

I looked in the direction he was indicating. "Ah."

There was life down here. It was a pod of some kind of aquatic creature. A mixture of whale and squid. Each of its arms culminating in a glowing star shape, the light bright enough to illuminate the creature's length. They writhed as it moved forwards, as if the arms themselves were driving it through the darkened sea. Beautiful and mesmerising. And terrifying at the same time. They were massive, each one as long as the MAV once its arms were fully outstretched. There were a dozen or so of them, lazily moving past the platform as it plunged deeper into the unknown depths.

"What are these things?" I asked the girl.

"Hursthale," she said, barely looking at them. As if they were common down here. They might very well be.

"Hursthale. Are they dangerous?" I asked her. "What do they eat?"

"You can." She wrinkled her nose. "I don't like them. They taste salty."

I don't think she had understood my question. It didn't matter. "There are other creatures down here? Like them?" I pointed. The pod had just about left us behind as we dropped beneath them.

"Like them? No. Other fish live here too though." I don't think she meant actual fish. I think it was as close as Cena could translate what she did say. Creatures of the sea perhaps.

I was surprised at how clear the water was. I could clearly see the domes arrayed around us, even though they were some kilometres distant. They were all built of the same crystalline dome material that their counterparts on the surface were. Allowing those within to see the watery world around them. A world cast perpetually into darkness, the cap of ice above cutting all light from the surface. I couldn't see the seabed below. It could be just out of reach of the lights from the city, or it could be several kilometres beneath. My optical enhancements, courtesy of the military, allowed me to see better than most, revealing a number of lights moving about the city. Be they more pods of sea creatures or submersibles owned by the Hermitage. I could also vaguely see into the domes themselves. Each was slightly different. Some appeared to be residential conurbations, housing units piled on top of each other, walkways winding through to allow residents access to their front door. Others were fields, rows upon rows of crops growing under fake sunlight. Still others might have been machinery. Life support or power generation, it wasn't clear. I was unfamiliar with the designs. I could see nothing of the ocean floor though. That was lost far beneath.

A city under the sea. Housing many millions of people. All coming and going barely aware that there was a universe beyond the ice overhead. I knew cities like this existed within the Confederacy. Trii itself was a waterworld. The moon of a gas giant that had a string of mirrors orbiting it to warm the atmosphere, melting the ice and making the world habitable. I'd never been there, but I had heard of the place.

And then we arrived in Dark City. I tried to learn whether that was the name of the whole city, or just the dome beneath us, but the girl didn't seem to follow the question. Cena's ability to translate was failing us today.

"We live in the light. They live in the dark," was all she would say on the matter.

The dome we arrived in was gloomy, to be fair. It did not boast the bright lighting of the other installations. There were glowing strips on the floor, as well as long the structures within, but they were barely enough to banish the darkness. We didn't stay long, leaving the platform behind to board a gondola awaiting us on a still lake. Oernie took hold of another control and it surged forward silently, some hidden mechanism driving it through the water. It was silent apart from the rush of water past its hull.

"Is it a long way?" I asked her.

"It will take some time."

"Have you been to Trii? This place looks a lot like the cities there," Baes said, echoing my own thoughts of a moments earlier.

"The Triian Democracy is a dump," Sanquey said. "I had a layover there once. Spent a week in the dark. Everything smells like fish. It's damp and it's cold. If it's metal, it's rusted to shit. There's whole sections that have been leaking for years. Sure, they pump it out, but you're up to your ankles in foul water wherever you go. They pump sewage straight into the water around the city. Some of it leaks right back in again. Half the people there are sick with it. Do yourself a favour and stay away from the place."

"You paint such a pretty picture," Baes commented.

The marine shrugged. "Hey, nothing stopping you from seeing it yourself. Just don't say I didn't warn you."

We entered a tunnel and the gondola sped up, the little vessel churning through the water. The tunnel seemed to angle downwards, the water turning into a river rushing towards the depths. I could feel cool air buffeting us.

"Do you know if the people of the Shaan came down here?" I asked the girl.

She shrugged.

"Any information on that, Cen?" I asked the AI instead.

"Sadly, no. The delegation from the Shaan were still in the early stages of contact when they found cause to leave. They did not explore the city extensively."

"So it's possible no one knows any of this is down here."

"The Hermitage know."

I didn't comment. Primarily as we had just arrived.

"The menagerie," the girl said as the gondola slowed and approached another wharf.

"Now this doesn't smell as nice," Baes said. A waft of warm air greeting us. It was heavily laden with the reek of animal faeces.

We had reached another dome. This one was brightly lit, allowing us a view of the low hill that perched in the centre of it. It was ringed by what looked like enclosures, a haphazard collection of walls and fences. Each pen a different size and shape to those alongside. Some with trees planted within, some without. Some were fully enclosed, preventing flying creatures from escaping their habitat. There were people here, but not very many of them. Most looked like workers, either engaged in some kind of labour or pushing trolleys loaded with a wide assortment of equipment. Those that caught sight of us as we headed towards the hill stopped what they were doing to stare. We were the tallest people here, possibly the tallest people in the city. Once got over the shock of that they noticed the girl we were with, when they promptly bowed slightly and scurried off to continue with their tasks. I did catch the odd glance over a shoulder as they hurried away. Mostly at the swords firmly clipped to the twins' backs.

A caste system? I wondered. The girl perhaps belonging to some kind of royalty or upper class. I didn't notice any of the people about us wearing any jewellery at all, never mind made of gold. I would have asked but it was then I caught sight of what I took to be the Quint.

It was not what I had expected.

Chapter 18

The creature had blue fur and looked like an Earthly primate. Perhaps more slender, with longer limbs. If it stood up it would be about as tall as I was. Its fur shimmered as it moved, as if each strand caught the light differently. Its eyes were yellow and followed us as we approached. As if it had been expecting us. Perhaps it had.

It was seated in the centre of its enclosure, which was situated on a grassy knoll near the peak of the hill. Unlike the unkempt and soiled habitats about it, it was perfectly manicured. The grass looked like it had been mowed recently. Blooming flowers in neat beds around the edges of the space. A tree was growing in the centre, its foliage casting shade from the bright artificial sun high overhead. I doubted the menagerie workers kept it this pristine. I doubted they dared step foot inside. That meant the creature did it itself. To the rear was a simple stone structure, its shelter perhaps. It was beneath the tree that the creature sat, perched on what looked like a stone stool.

"Is that it?" Baes asked.

"The Outsider creature," the girl said. "This is what you wanted to see, yes?"

I said nothing, walking up to the fence that separate it from visitors. There was a sign clipped to the fence, covered in local script. Don't feed the animals, I imagined it said.

"The line," Oernie said. "Do not cross the line. It reaches out."

I imagined it could if it wanted to. Its hands and arms looked slim enough to fit through the bars. I also imagined it had motivation to reach out and choke visitors. The Hermitage would have studied it. Perhaps taking tissue and bone samples. Who knew what kinds of experiments they had run on it over the years? It didn't look injured though. Its fur was not marked, as if concealing scars beneath.

I don't know what drove me to do it, but I placed my hands on the bars and looked straight at it. "Why did you allow them to capture you?" I asked it. It would understand me. I felt it.

The Quint unlinked its limbs and moved forwards slowly, ambling on all fours just like those Earthly primates you would be so familiar with. It stopped just before the bars, easily within arm's reach, and regarded me silently for a moment.

"You are a Confederate terrorist?" the creature said in a soft voice.

The girl behind me shouted, turned and ran away. I didn't pay her any attention, or any attention to my companions who unholstered their weapons and took aim.

"That is some greeting," I said in return. I couldn't quite say why I was not shocked by this. That this captive in a zoo could suddenly talk, and speak Complex at that. I had my suspicions. I would have to see if I was right.

"It is accurate, yes?"

"Some would say." I could barely disagree with it. From this creature's perspective we might very well be terrorists. We did have a history of some very questionable acts. "Yet you allowed yourself to be captured in order to meet us."

The Quint bowed its head slightly, as if in agreement. "Sometimes distasteful acts are necessary."

"And you speak our tongue," I continued. Cena was not translating here. The Quint was talking to me in my native language. Well, in the common tongue of the Confederacy at any rate.

"We have known of you for some time. There was a time when we explored as you do. We have witnessed much."

"Why did you wish to meet us?" I had many questions. But there were priorities. "So badly that you allowed yourself to remain a captive for almost forty standard years. Probably experimented on and tortured."

"My fate matters not."

"Why did you wish to meet us?" I repeated.

The creature cocked its head to one side and it closed its eyes, as if contemplating. When it opened them again it moved. So quickly it took us by surprise. With a leap it hurdled the fence, landing gracefully on the other side. It kept its eyes on me and held out a hand. Long hairless fingers with slightly blue skin. Its nails were pointed, almost claws.

"We offer you an opportunity to redeem yourselves."

"That's kind." I studied the hand, ignoring my companions who were urging me not to take it. I reached out and grasped it. Its skin was soft yet firm. Its long fingers closed about my hand, holding me gently.

"Do you deserve redemption?" it continued.

"Who is to say? You?"

"Your people claim to seek it."

"I doubt we're looking for some new religion, if that's what you mean. Why did you allow your capture?" I tried to pull my hand away but the creature held on firmly. I could have engaged my ghoscht but I didn't know what this thing was capable of. I didn't fancy having my arm ripped off.

"Your people do lack patience. You are young yet."

"Things happen while we engage in idle talk."

It let go of my hand and rocked back slightly. It settled itself as before, seated firmly on its buttocks, long legs folded in front of it. "I am Crawl," it said.

"I am Isia," I responded. "Yes, I am from the Confederacy, but you clearly knew that."

"You have met the Beaut," it continued. "And what they have become. You call them the Hauda."

"I have. I am here because I believe you know more about them than we do. In particular, what they have become."

"It would be difficult to know less," Crawl said. It didn't speak like a vaunted member of an elder race. But then if it was speaking our tongue, so it would be speaking like us too. Dumbing down, as it were.

"I am here to be educated."

194

I could have sworn the creature smiled. Its thin – rather un-apelike – lips stretching, revealing startlingly even and white teeth. "You are patient enough to learn what we know of them?"

Perhaps not everything. Not today. "Tell me two things. What are they? And how to we kill them?"

"Neither answer would be short. The Beaut have a long history, as you know. It took them some time to become as they are now. Should I call them the Hauda?"

"Call them as you will, I know who you refer to. But answer me this, you allowed yourself to be captured, yes?"

"I did."

"So that you would meet us?"

"It is indeed so."

"Even though the chances were small we would come back here. You know why my predecessors left. And you also know we would not be inclined to return."

"We know this."

"Yet here you are."

"I am but Crawl. Nothing is lost in this."

"I don't believe Crawl is its name," Cena said in my ear. "You will recall that an individual called the Grand Swing was killed by the Terminore. For a species that have adapted themselves to resemble apes, how would they rank their social classes?"

"Crawl at one end, grand swing at the other," I said.

"I believe that might be the case," the AI said.

"Your machine is correct," the Quint said.

Now that did surprise me. Our comms were supposed to be secure. As far as I could tell this creature was not enhanced in any way. It possessed no cybernetic augmentations. None I could detect anyway. Yet it had still listened in on encrypted comms with ease.

But then, this was an elder race. Who knew what they were capable of?

I don't think I succeeded in hiding my surprise. Its lips stretched ever so slightly further in a smile.

"So to your people you are of the lowest caste. Easily sacrificed on a mission with low probability of success," I said.

"We deemed it more efficient to wait here in the event you did return, than travelling to one of your worlds to speak to you directly. We do not possess such a speedy means of travel as you."

That was a point. We were a good thousand lightyears from the nearest Confederate outpost here. Without FTL it would take a very long time indeed to travel there. In that context forty years was insignificant.

"You are impatient yourselves then?"

"You have seen what happened to Sunna-Deste-Anne. We would prevent that from happening elsewhere. In this case we are impatient, yes. Time cannot be wasted."

Now that did interest me very much. How could this creature possibly know about what had happened there? We were too far from Sunna for any kind of message to have reached here. Not without FTL comms anyway.

"How do you know about the Sunna?" Baes interrupted.

"Unless it was involved," Sanquey said.

I held up a hand as they stepped forwards. "It is a valid question. How do you know about Sunna? You yourself have been incarcerated here for nearly forty years."

The creature closed its eyes as it nodded its head slightly. "We do not possess as speedy a means of transportation. But I made no statement about possessing a means of communication."

"But you were here!" Baes insisted.

"Sergeant, please." I waved him back. "The Hauda – the Beaut are a hive mind. Each unit is in constant communication with its companions. Are your people the same?"

"You misunderstand what the Beaut have become. But my people can communicate without clumsy mechanical means, yes."

"Meaning one of your kind witnessed it."

"We did."

"So you know what happened there."

"Sadly, yes."

"But I note you did not try to stop it."

The creature raised its eyes to look at me for a long moment. I couldn't imagine what it was thinking. "I did not state that. But you can presume we were not successful, because we were clearly not."

"So even you were unable to stop what happened there."

"We were not."

"So tell me what happened."

It was silent for another moment, looking away again. "They were harvested."

"By who?"

"I cannot tell you. You must see."

What did that mean? "It was the Beaut, wasn't it?"

"Not entirely."

"But they were involved."

"They were."

"Who else was involved? You?"

This time it did not respond. Instead it leaped into the air, easily hurdling the fence again. It landed on its long legs, the limbs collapsing to take up the impact. Without looking back at me it ambled back to its stool and seated itself, pulling its legs up close beneath it.

"What? Is that it?"

"I am not convinced you wish to assist," it said.

"What do you think we've been doing all this time? Why do you think we are here?"

"Then you must see. I cannot explain this to you."

"I'm sorry. Stop playing games. Speak clearly."

"You must come with me. To my world. To our home itself, not the station you see in this system."

"We are not permitted there."

"Unless we invite you."

"Are you? Are you authorised to make that invitation?"

"It is why I am here."

"The Quint must speak clearly," the *Cesa's* AI said suddenly in my ear. "It must make it's invitation."

I raised a hand of my own. "Go on then."

"You are formally invited to the Quint system. There will be no repercussions from the Quint people ourselves. We no longer wish to be in conflict with you."

"Thank you," the AI said.

I frowned. There was something else going on here. Something that was not immediately obvious. Why should the AI suddenly intervene? I would have to interrogate Cena later. "Why? Why do you wish to meet with us now?"

"We need your help."

Help? What did that mean? Why would a vaunted elder civilisation require the assistance of the upstart Confederation? Why couldn't this creature just explain itself?

"For what? Against the Hauda?"

"Incoming comms," Cena reported. "Eyes only. Non interactive."

It was orders from the Admiralty. I read it quickly. It wasn't long.

"Shit."

Chapter 19

"I don't get it. What's going on? We only just got here," Beyard complained.

"Just ... just do it. Please."

"Tell me what's going on."

"Don't ask us. We have no idea," Baes commented.

"Your captain has been relieved of duty," The Quint said over our own comms. "You have been instructed to return to Hotchkiss Station."

"Who the hell is that?" the lieutenant demanded. "Get off this channel."

"It's OK. You'll meet him ... her ... in a moment."

"Those such as I are genderless," the creature said. I wasn't altogether sure I wanted to know.

"Is that the Quint? It's the Quint isn't it?"

"It is."

"Oh. Ok. Hold on, you've what?"

I said nothing. It was not something I wanted to discuss right now. It hardly surprised me. Neither did the list of charges that had been appended to the order. Dereliction of duty. Breaking the military code of conduct. Endangering my ship and crew. Clearly the Admiralty had sided with Matte and the others.

All the charges were technically true. But that wasn't what bothered me. What did bother me was the timing of it all. Why now? When the restriction from entering Quint space had just fallen away. I had a suspicion and it scared me.

"Izzy, please tell us what's going on," the lieutenant implored.

"Just get back to the MAV. And quickly."

We were running through the menagerie, workers scattering in terror before us. It was not us they feared, but rather the Quint that was ambling easily alongside. Knuckling on all fours. It was coming along for the ride, and I didn't think I could stop it if I wanted to. We reached the docks and boarded one of the gondolas.

"How do we get back up? The watercourse only went one way."

"I will demonstrate," the Quint said. "The water way reverses."

The gondola started moving unbidden, no one at the controls. It was the Quint. It had to be. The little watercraft turned and headed towards the tunnel we had used to descend to this dome. Water rushed beneath, far faster than it had before. The creature had picked up on my sense of urgency. Even though it couldn't possibly understand why I needed to get out of here. Unless it could read minds too.

"Captain, we are with you," en-ed-bas said, the first words he had uttered all day. Both he and his brother drew their swords and held them out, points towards the deck. "Our blades and our blood are yours."

"We're with you too, Izzy," Sanquey said.

"Same here," Beyard said over comms. "Whatever the hell is going on."

They deserved to know. Our futures were intertwined now. "Why now?" I asked. "Why am I being removed from my post now?"

"You've not exactly been following protocol," the lieutenant said. "I mean, a captain on a mission into enemy territory? A captain's place is on the bridge. You have marines for that kind of thing. We're expendable. The captain is not."

"It is why we respect you," C'gen said. "It is why the crew respects you. You will not expose the least of us to any danger you wouldn't face yourself. I've never heard of a ship's captain who would do that."

In other times I would be flattered, but those times were not now. "That's their excuse. One of them anyway. The others … bringing the Hauda on board. Look at how many people we lost. Look at the damage to the ship. It's inexcusable. But all of that is irrelevant. Why have they taken action now?"

"The Quint invited us to its home world," Baes said.

"What? We're barred from entering Quint space. Even I know that," Beyard said.

"We were. That injunction lifts the moment a duly authorised member of the Quint people invites us inside," I said.

"I'm sorry, Izzy. I don't get it," Beyard admitted.

"Sid. Tebercy. He follows orders I would not. He followed an order to fire on Xon. An order I would have refused. They removed me from command now so they can order the commander to do something I would have refused."

"Yeah. But what?"

"To go to Quint and to destroy them." We had done it to the Hauda, we had done it to the Xon. I was sure the Admiralty wanted to do the same to the Quint. Even a lone heavy cruiser could do a massive amount of damage to the Quint habitats. They might be considerably larger than any worlds we had ever seen, but they were not invulnerable.

"Can this thing go any faster?" I asked our Quint companion.

"I fear not. The magnetic drive has its limitations."

"I'm missing something. Why would the Admiralty wish to murder the Quint?" Beyard continued.

"I think they always knew what happened to the Sunna. Because they had seen it before. Because they had run across the perpetrators before and had tried to wipe them out. They failed then so they're trying again now."

"The Quint? You're saying the enemy is the Quint?"

"My people are no longer my people," the creature beside me said softly.

"That was why you wanted our help," I said.

"It was. But genocide was not our intention."

The gondola finally ground to a halt at the wharf in the darkened dome. We launched ourselves from it and sprinted towards the elevator. Fortunately it was still where Oernie had left it. It started up before anyone could touch the lever, swiftly whisking us upwards towards the distant surface. Crawl controlling it as easily as it had the gondola.

"We're in the garage now," Beyard reported. "We'll wait for you here. Our hosts were not pleased when we walked out on negotiations. It was going so well too."

"No it wasn't, Lieutenant," C'gen said. "They were boring our asses off."

"Well, it hardly matters now does it. Are you still bored?"

"I am not."

"Cen, what is the status of the ship?" I asked the *Cesa's* AI.

"I am afraid I cannot respond to queries," the AI reported.

"Can you put me in touch with Sid?"

"I am afraid I cannot respond to queries."

"Damn it. Is that it? We've worked together for years. And you're just shutting me out?"

"I am afra-"

"Oh, shut up."

"How are we going to get aboard, Izzy?" Beyard asked. "Will they open the MAV bay for us?"

"I'm not going to give them a choice," I said with false bravado. If the *Cesa* didn't want to open that bay there was no way I could force them to.

"And if they don't?" the lieutenant continued. "What do we do then? It's over a thousand lights to Hotchkiss."

"One thousand two hundred. Approximately," I said.

"Can we even get there by MAV? It's not designed for extended FTL."

I shook my head. We could. It would not be comfortable and it would take months. But we could do it. The MAV carried enough consumables for such a flight, even if most of the foodstuffs were emergency rations. I couldn't go back there though. Heading to Hotchkiss was giving up.

"Incoming comms," the MAV's onboard AI reported. It was the only AI that was still talking to me. "Non interactive from Commander Tebercy."

"I'm sorry, Captain. Izzy. Chisholm has ordered us out of the system. We can't wait to pick you up. You should have enough supplies to reach the border from here. Or she might let us swing by and pick you up once we're finished." There was a pause as if the commander was gathering his thoughts. "I didn't want this. I didn't intend any of this. I can't share our orders with you, but I imagine you know what they are. I ... I wish you luck. Out."

"Bastard," I muttered. "Cowardly bastard."

"They're leaving us, aren't they?" Beyard had not been privy to the comms but knew I had been receiving one.

"MAV, report on the disposition of the CSS *Cesa*," I ordered the MAV AI.

"The CSS *Cesa* is accelerating out of the system on long range scans," the machine reported. And then it said: "the CSS *Cesa* has left the system."

"Shit. What do we do, Izzy?" Beyard asked.

"Nothing we can do. We go to Hotchkiss," Baes said.

"Can we even get there from here? In a MAV?" Sanquey asked.

"Sure. We'll be used to each other's stink by the time we get there. No shower in a MAV," Beyard commented.

"No beds either. We'll be sleeping on the floor," Sanquey said.

"We're marines. Any floor is a four-poster," Beyard intoned.

"Any meal a banquet," the others replied automatically.

"We're not going back," I said. "We can't."

"We're with you, Izzy," Beyard said. "All the way. But what else are we going to do?"

"I'm going to Quint. You should stay here. I'm sure we can get a message to the Admiralty. They'll send someone out to pick you up. Eventually. The Shaan will be close by soon. They might send someone over."

"You offend," ne-de-sab said abruptly. "We vowed our blades. Our blood. We do not make such a vow lightly."

"I cannot bring you into this. I don't know what we'll find there."

"I'm offended too, Captain. We volunteered to follow you," Beyard said.

"I also am offended," C'gen said.

"Seriously?" I shook my head. We were passing another pod of strange squid-like whales. No one was looking at them.

"I'm in," Sanquey said.

"So am I," Baes confirmed.

"My blade is yours," en-ed-bas said.

"You don't know what you're getting into. It's very possible none of us will be coming back. In fact I almost guarantee it."

"We have spoken," en-ed-bas said.

"Damn it."

"How long to Quint from here by MAV?" Baes asked.

"Four, five days. Less if we ruin the engine," Beyard said.

"And how long will it take for the *Cesa* to get there?" the sergeant continued.

"From here? Not long. Hours. Maybe half a day."

"Well, we're not coming back anyway. May as well ruin our engine."

I didn't like walking them into danger like this. But it didn't seem like I had any choice.

We were going to Quint.

Chapter 20

The MAV travelled into the night. Its motors degrading as we pushed them past their limits. We would arrive safely but once we slowed down the MAV would never be engaging its FTL drive again. Not without a major refit. A refit I doubted would be forthcoming.

We ate and slept little. No one apart from the twins had the presence of mind. They seemed as calm as ever. In fact they seemed to be relishing the upcoming engagement. A fulfilment of a lifetime's training and dedication. Death by combat was what each of them longed for. It gave their lives meaning. They cleared out a space in one of the equipment lockers and trained relentlessly. Sparring with each other using makeshift training swords. en-ed-bas invited Beyard to join them. He was not sore at losing to her when they last fought. If anything he valued the learning experience. It made him a better warrior.

The Quint and I stayed in the CIC, trying to formulate a plan of action. The creature overflowing the acceleration couch, its long legs bent uncomfortably in the limited space. Still, I was sure it was a lot more comfortable than a stool in an enclosure. There were simply too many unknowns. One of the main reasons for that was because the Quint living in the Hermitage system had lost contact with their fellows at home. The last communication of any kind had been centuries earlier, long before the Hauda had even arrived in Xon. Crawl didn't really know why, but could guess.

"We met the Beaut a long time ago. The Hauda as you know of them," the Quint explained to me on the first day of our voyage. "Both of our peoples explored the stars. Voyaging to worlds far from here. We conquered death long ago, so the length of any voyage did not deter us. We did not dream of travelling as quickly as you do. We determined early in our history that it was impossible, so we put that dream aside. Our voyages took a thousand years. Ten thousand. It meant nothing. We were in no hurry to see every part of the galaxy, because we knew we would get there one day anyway. We had the time.

"If anything the Beaut had travelled further that us. They had ventured into the very core of the galaxy, where they discovered something that was not human."

"Hold on. Not human? We've never come across anything like that. There have been rumours. Myths. But no one has ever actually proved anything. I believe some ruins were found that archaeologists didn't want to ascribe to an earlier human population, I'm not sure why. I know quite a few careers were ruined over it. But we've never come across any non-human civilisation. Are you saying the Hauda did?"

"They believed so. They believed there was another civilisation within the galaxy once. There are hints of it everywhere. Concealed from the casual eye unless you know enough to recognise them. They were themselves far travelled, just as humanity is now. With colonies from one side of the galaxy to the other. All gone now. Even the Beaut don't know why, or even when. They believe there was a conflict. A galaxy ranging war that persisted for a million years. And then it stopped. Someone won. Or perhaps no one did.

Nothing was left but for ruin. This was long before humanity left its first world. Long before humanity had even evolved. Still, the Beaut believed they encountered a remnant. Something left over from that long-forgotten race. Something still alive. Naturally they took it home."

"What was it? Was it what caused all of this?"

"We never saw it ourselves. Not then. The Beaut kept it to themselves. They had already formed an alliance with your Confederacy by this time, although your people were still young then. Controlling only a handful of worlds. You did not permit the Beaut to share all your technology. You did not share FTL with them, and so even then they could only travel slowly. As we did. Soon after they brought their prize home they stopped travelling completely. The last of their voyages returned home and never left again. They changed then. They became something different."

"So it was the cause?"

"We believe so. We stopped travelling to your area of space at the same time, as did not wish to come into contact with you. Not then anyway. We could still communicate with the Beaut for a time. But then even that stopped."

"They never told you what they found?"

"Not directly. But we had been sharing information long enough to guess. They had encountered one of the survivors of that ancient conflict. The victor. But it was not what you might suppose. It was not itself a civilisation. It was a created thing. A tool the original civilisation created. A tool created to achieve immortality. They made a new body for themselves. A creation they could transfer their minds into. An artificial life-form that was strong enough to withstand any environment. That could not be destroyed. One that could voyage between the stars without the need of a flimsy vessel of space. Because their bodies could become their own craft. Adapting, changing to suit any environment. Any requirement. It could live in the cold vacuum of space as easily as it could on a warm, moist world. It could break itself down into any number of smaller segments, so each could travel independently. Each equal to the sum of the whole. Each able to duplicate itself and grow stronger. Larger. It was perfect. It was flawed."

"Is this what this thing is? Some ancient machine?"

"Not a machine. Not what you consider to be a machine. It was a living thing. But a living thing without a mind of its own. It could only gain consciousness by absorbing the lives of its creators. By becoming them. That was its flaw. Its ingrained desire was to become conscious. To become one with its creators. Instead of waiting for them to join it it started seeking them out. And taking them. And it found that it enjoyed it. It ached for it. It was driven to madness by the desire, and nothing could stop it."

"The conflict. This was its cause?"

"It was."

"And it only stopped when the original civilisation was wiped out."

"So we believe. Some of their creation survived. In the small, distant parts of the galaxy. It is unlikely the Beaut were the first to encounter them. It is also unlikely those that did survived it."

"But the Beaut did."

"Did they? They changed. They became something else. We believe their discovery consumed them. Taking their minds. Populating their worlds. By the time your own people discovered something was wrong it was already too late."

"The first mission to Beaut was lost," I said. "We sent a fleet. It vanished."

"They were unprepared. But your second fleet was prepared. And they did what was needed. They burnt the Beaut down."

"Something you call us terrorists for."

"That is not why I call you terrorists. I call you terrorists because of the other worlds you have destroyed. Shuynti. Phaenor. Asinta. Dutchess. You claim to gather worlds together so that they may protect each other. But you destroy those you feel don't belong."

I could not disagree with that. I knew about Dutchess. I had been there. But as I've said before, that is a story for another time.

"How does this relate to your own people? Do you think the same has happened to them?"

"The Beaut came to us after their own world fell. After your fleet torched it. We took them in, as all old friends should. We did not know they had changed then. It was not long after that that contact with our own world ceased. We sent vessels there, to try to find out what happened, but they never returned. We know something of what they discovered, as we were in touch with them when the Beaut entered the system. But we don't know much more than that. We believe what happened to the Beaut has happened there too."

"You do know what will happen when the Confederacy finds out, don't you? You know we will burn your worlds down too? To stop the spread of this thing?"

The creature said nothing. It did not need to. Of course it knew. That was why it had waited for us. That was what it wanted.

We didn't talk much after that. There was no reason to. I stayed out of the CIC and spent my time in the diminutive bridge, watching lightyears pass. Watching our speed drop as the engines degraded. I did the math over and over again. Proving to myself we would reach the system before the engines failed. We would. But there was little margin for error.

What did I think I would do when we arrived? How could I help the *Cesa*? They couldn't possibly know what they were walking into. The first fleet into Hauda space had vanished. Presumed lost. The same could happen here. But perhaps that was the Admiralty's intention. Motivation for launching another fleet. One capable of dealing with anything it found. I wondered if it was already on its way. Ready to act once the *Cesa* was destroyed. Revenge for fallen comrades.

Sacrificed comrades.

I tried to eat. I tried to rest. But my heart was not in it. I ventured into the twins' training room to try and distract myself. Jousting with en-ed-bas. He was good. Faster than anyone had the right to be.

I remember mentioning that I've always felt there was something different about me. Something wrong. I have never really understood what it was. I'd given up trying to a long time ago. I would never meet another member of my people, someone who could teach me what made us different. To understand why the Confederacy feared us so much that they destroyed our world. Why my home had appeared on the Quint's list of eliminated peoples. Still, I did know that, when I put my mind to it, I could beat anyone. Even the twins. Both of them. At the same time.

Startled when I lost control and beat en-ed-bas to the deck, ne-de-sab stepped in to put a stop to it. That intervention gave his brother time to leap to his feet. Then I beat them both. Easily.

I don't know what happened. I had felt it only a few times before. A clarity of mind and body. A strength I could not explain. I can still remember the first time I felt it, in that hateful pit deep in the city ship of my childhood. One of my earliest memories when I was thrown to the gladiators as a girl. Amusement to warm up the masses. And I killed them with my bare hands.

Beyard was forced to step in behind me and knock me to the deck.

Ashamed I bowed before then and begged their forgiveness. Even as they pulled themselves to their feet, blood flowing from the wounds I had inflicted.

Then they bowed in return and thanked me for the learning opportunity.

I didn't leave the bridge at all after that. I couldn't look them in the eyes.

And then we were there. The Quint system growing large in the monitors, our sensors reaching as far ahead as they could. They were nowhere near as sensitive as the *Cesa's*. But they were all we had.

The system was on fire.

I stepped into the CIC for the first time in days and joined the rest of the team around the central holoboard. Studying what was revealed there.

"The Confederacy has declared war on the Quint," Beyard commented. She was not wrong.

The only images I had seen of the system had been from the Terminore's own sensor logs, showing an orderly array of habitats. Space around them swept clean of any of the other debris to be found within a system. Asteroids. Comets. Other planets and moons. They were all gone. Consumed to create the massive Quint habitats. They had been all that remained. Five of them. Giant glowing orbs. Each the size of a gas giant. Each indistinct in the distance, but with a slightly green tinge. As if they possessed an abundance of vegetation and little in the way of sea or ocean. As we grew closer we could see more detail that that original recording. It was not good.

The system was in chaos. A chaos easily visible even at a distance.

The habitats were on fire. All five of them. They glowed in the infra red. A motley patchwork of temperatures, as if smoke blocked out parts of the image. There were rivers of fire, as if volcanoes had erupted, spewing molten rock over the surface of the habitats. Creating a swirling inferno that tore through the surface, igniting everything it touched. We could see smaller moons orbiting them. They might always have been there, but the earlier images had been too grainy to make them out. Some of them had been cracked open, their rocky surfaces shattered, throwing debris to the beleaguered worlds beneath. As we watched boulders the size of mountains crashed down, ripping through the habitats. They seemed to disappear into the world, as if they had pierced the crust to penetrate the mantle beneath. The shockwave of the impacts tore through the inferno about them. Extinguishing some fires here, starting new ones there.

Space between the habitats had not escaped the conflict. There seemed to be swarms of defending craft darting between the debris of previous battles, sizzling beams of energy reaching out to attack their enemy. Like living things they moved in concert. Like shoals of fish avoiding a shark. Forming and reforming as they darted about the burning habitats and shattered moons. There were a lot of them. More than the MAV's simple AI could count. It reached the billions before giving up, supplying an overflow error. Each was a spear point a hundred metres long. A Quint defender.

The Quint beside me leaned forward, studying the image intently. These were its people who were suffering and dying. It didn't say anything. Simply watching as another moon crumbled in on itself. Caught in the gravitational sheer of the habitat beneath it.

"There," Beyard pointed. "I think that's the *Cesa*."

A fiery speck darted through all of this. Forever moving. Sprinting from time to time, its FTL drive throwing it across the system to attack a different habitat, before sprinting to assault another. It was too quick for the defenders. They could do nothing but try and catch up, opening fire whenever they chanced on its new emergence point. Only to waste ordnance as the vessel vanished again, taking its attack elsewhere. Fire ripping through them as the secondary weapons the *Cesa* left in its wake sought them out.

Streaks of energy tore through the defenders and the habitats alike. The *Cesa's* primary weapon firing singularity after singularity, as quickly as its systems could form them. As massive as the worlds were the weapon still tore straight through them, continuing into space on the other side. Dragging the habitat's viscera in its wake.

This did not look like swarms of alien creatures. This looked like an advanced civilisation trying to defend itself against an invader. I said as much to the Quint.

"The entity is able to adapt and change to circumstance. What did it look like when you first encountered it?"

I hesitated. "It was an insect. I took it to be human ... but heavily adapted."

"Did it always look like that?"

It was not a question I could easily answer. Did the infestation aboard the *Cesa* look like bees? Giant, unnatural bees? I doubted it. "No."

"It changes. It can look and act like a member of your own people. It has read your genetic heritage so it can mimic them easily enough. It also possesses enough human memories to present itself in any way it wishes. But beneath all of that is still its base nature. It's ability to change into something else to survive. In Hauda it appeared to be Hauda. Here it appears to be Quint."

"It can withstand extreme heat?"

"Potentially."

"Radiation."

"Yes. As well as extreme cold and the vacuum of space."

So it could have survived the reactor meltdown in sector four. Potentially. It was not a possibility I could ignore.

"MAV AI, can you connect to Cena?"

"Attempting connection."

"I don't think they will want to talk to you," Beyard said.

"I can try. They won't expect to see any of us here. They might be surprised enough by our being here to talk to us."

"And say what?"

What indeed? Be wary of sector four?

"Captain? Is that you?" A familiar voice transmitted into the CIC.

"Shit. Matte, is that you?"

"Yes. What are you doing here?"

"It doesn't matter. We need to come aboard."

"No. No. That's not going to happen. Do you know what's going on here?"

"We've just arrived but we have a pretty good idea."

"No. I don't mean that. Who cares about that? Cena has taken over the attack. It's all automated now. I mean do you know what's happening aboard?"

"What? You're making no sense, Commander. What's happening aboard? Something happening in sector four?"

"Sector four? Shit. And sector six. Eight. Twelve. Two … where isn't it happening? We've shut all the interior boarding doors but this thing is still getting through. Its everywhere. We've lost half the bridge crew. I don't know where Tebercy is. Or Ono."

"It's still onboard?"

"Still onboard? You're joking? The thing never went anywhere. I don't think you even slowed it down."

"You have to let us onboard, Commander. We can help." I had no idea how we would do that. But I had to do something. Anything. And I couldn't do it from here.

"Help? How are you going to do that? No. We have a job to do, and then we're going to scuttle the ship. Orders from the Admiralty."

"What? You can't do that."

"You have already lost them," the Quint beside me said. "They have been exposed."

"I can't leave them."

"You have already lost them," it said again.

"Who is that?" Matte said. "Damn it, Captain. It's good to hear your voice, but get out of here. There's nothing you can do. Just leave. We have a job to do, that's all there is to it."

"There's too many of them. You're not going to be able to kill them all. Not on your own."

"What? No. We're no longer trying to. They've been experimenting with FTL. The Admiralty wants those units destroyed."

I didn't know what to make of that. FTL? With everything that was going on they were concerned about the Quint learning the secret of FTL? It was so insane it made sense. Of course the Admiralty would care about that. It was ultimately the only edge we had in a hostile galaxy. It was the only thing that kept us ahead of everyone else. But still. Now?

"This is a problem," my Quint companion offered its opinion. "Is there anyone aboard your ship who understands the principle of faster than light travel?"

"Sid ... Commander Tebercy if anyone. Why?"

"Then he is already lost. He has been taken, and they have learned the secret from him. They will experiment until they perfect the technique. Then they will be able to spread everywhere. You will not be able to stop them."

"Listen, who is that?" Matte demanded.

"Ask why she believes their enemy possesses FTL," the creature said.

"What?"

"Ask her."

"I heard ... whoever that is. Because we've seen it. Here and there. They breach FTL for a moment. It's very inefficient but they seem to be getting better at it all the time. They can't travel more than a few hundred thousand kilometres before they have to cool their engines down. But when they first started they were barely doing a thousand. Soon... who knows."

"Once they perfect it they will share it," the Quint continued. "And then they will be unstoppable. You must destroy them now. All of them."

"My ship is under attack. My people are dying. That is my first priority."

"No. It is not. They will spread throughout the galaxy if you do not stop them here. They will be free to harvest any world they wish. Even your own worlds."

"We can't stop them without the *Cesa*."

"Your vessel is lost."

"So what is your suggestion? You must have one."

"The Beaut brought a nexus here. It can be used to control them."

"A what? They were no longer the Beaut when they came here."

"It was brought here nevertheless."

"Listen. I have to go." Matte said. The communication cut off abruptly.

"Can you get them back?" I asked the MAV's AI.

"Communications unsuccessful," it reported.

"This nexus," Beyard said. "Is it an option? What is it?"

"It was what the Beaut were transforming themselves into," Crawl said.

"We have called the Hauda the crystal entities in the past," I said. "It's not a term we often use. We usually call them the Hauda."

"But what is it?" the lieutenant insisted.

"Has anyone seen it?" I asked the Quint.

"Yes. I know where it is being held. We have to go to ..." it paused, studying the image before it. "This habitat. I can be more precise when we get closer." It pointed to one of the habitats.

"Are you mad? That thing is on fire," Baes commented.

"Nevertheless, we must go there."

"We go," I said.

Chapter 21

The MAV's sensors detected a substantial amount of smoke in the habitat's atmosphere. More than our ghoscht's could easily accommodate. With no hard armour suits available we donned pressure suits stored in the vessel's equipment lockers. They were cumbersome white suits, with bulky attachment points, a glassy helmet and slimline backpack. They would not seem out of place on your own world. Old technology is sometimes the best.

Once we had loaded up with weaponry, we each took a crashpod and secured ourselves inside. They were designed to accommodate a hard armoured marine, so there was a lot of space to rattle around in. We would have to make do with bracing ourselves in place using our ghoschts. I routed in telemetry from the MAV AI so I could see outside the diminutive vessel and waited.

"Two minutes," the AI reported.

"Everyone secure?" I asked the team. They called off their status one by one. We were ready.

The MAV slid out of FTL close in to the habitat, the engines spinning down and promptly seizing. They would never operate again. We were on manoeuvring motors from here on in.

The MAV's collision avoidance alarm blared, the vehicle twisting and turning to avoid debris from a shattered moon. Secured within our pods we didn't feel a jerk as we grazed a boulder. Tough as it was the MAV's hull was unmarked.

"This is crazy," Beyard said. "We're going too fast. We need to slow down."

"Keep going," I instructed.

"We're going to kill ourselves."

"Keep going."

"We're not going to do anyone any good dead."

"Keep going."

"Shit."

Atmosphere ionised about us as we streaked through it, leaving a trail of flame a hundred kilometres long in our wake.

"You will soon see an opening to our left," the Quint said. "We want to enter there."

I couldn't see anything. There was too much smoke. I did feel a jerk as a shockwave slammed into us, almost knocking us off course. Something else had just entered the atmosphere. Something a lot bigger than we were. I sincerely hoped it didn't land on our heads.

Fortunately the MAV AI could see where it was going. It banked sharply, aiming for an invisible gap ahead. Then, suddenly, we were in clear air.

"What is this place?" I asked our Quint companion.

"This is the Eiesker habitat," the creature responded. "It is the second oldest of the habitats. We used the last of the material within our own system to construct it. The others were constructed from material harvested from nearby systems." It didn't sound in the slightest perturbed by our chaotic crash through the atmosphere.

"Explain what we're looking at." None of it made any sense to me. The surface of the habitat was not a surface at all. It was not solid, but rather comprised by an untidy array of spars. A mesh that looked solid from a distance, but was anything but. It was riddled with passages and wide-open spaces. Greenery everywhere, interspersed by what looked like lakes and waterfalls, one level feeding the one below it. We were moving too quickly for me to focus on any of it.

"It's a tree," C'gen said abruptly. "It's a tree, isn't it? This whole habitat is one big tree."

"What? Shit, yeah. You're right," Beyard responded.

"Eiesker, like all the habitats, is indeed a tree," the Quint said.

That immediately made a lot of sense. A tree. A tree an adapted arboreal people called home. A tree the size of a gas giant.

"How far down does it go?" I asked. "Is there a planet down there somewhere?"

"There is no planet," it said.

"It is tree all the way?"

"It is."

That gave me a moment's pause. "How many? How many people live here?"

"By your counting methodology, sixteen quintillion of my people live in this system."

That seemed impossible. That meant there were more Quint living here than there were people living in the rest of the galaxy combined.

Quint indeed.

Swarm. We had been looking for a swarm. We had been looking for a force that could harvest the Sunna with ease. Without those beleaguered people having any chance to so much as defend themselves. I think we had found it. And then some.

"Do you think they have all been ... converted?"

"Yes." The answer was matter of fact and final.

"So anyone we encounter is an enemy," I said.

The creature did not respond.

The MAV was forced to slow as the passage narrowed a thousand or so kilometres beneath the surface. What surface there was. It twisted into a tight spiral, round and round deeper and deeper. There was still light down here, far from the last rays of the sun. The foliage around us seemed luminous, banishing shadow from the deeper reaches of the habitat. There was still smoke billowing from the odd side passage. Spaces out of sight set alight by the battle in space overhead.

"MAV AI, open connection with Commander Matte," I instructed.

"Opening connection. Please wait."

"Matte? Matte? Can you hear me?"

I could hear a faint sound over comms. Like voices muttering in the distance.

"Commander Matte?"

"Captain? Captain? Is that you?"

"Yes. Now this is important. You'll be able to pick our telemetry. We have taken the MAV into one of the habitats. Please refrain from firing on it."

"You've what? Listen, I don't think we'll be firing on anything soon. You're mad, but you're quite safe from us."

"Explain."

"I think they're out there. We sealed navy country from the levels above. And then closed the partitioning doors. But I think they've gotten through them. We've picked up firing outside. It never lasts long. Marines have no chance against these things."

"You must abandon ship, Commander. Save yourselves."

"I think it's too late. We won't survive ten seconds out there. We have everyone we can fit into the bridge and we closed the doors here too. There's still people in the companionway but we couldn't fit them all in. This is it, I think. There's nowhere else to retreat to. We've lost contact with the rest of the ship. Cena has lost contact with most of its processing nodes. It has no contact with any crew above level eight at all. And only a few below that. Pockets. Pockets here and there. Fewer all the time." She almost spoke too quickly for me to follow, her voice wavering as her words exploded from her.

"Commander … Matte … do what you need to to survive. Save as many as you can. Leave this place. You can't do anything else here."

"We can't get out of here, Captain!" she shouted. "We can't get out! We're trapped!" She was silent a moment. "I'm sorry. I'm sorry. We don't know what to do."

I didn't know either. There was nothing to do.

"We're going to try something. It might work. We don't know," I said.

She laughed hysterically. "It won't matter. We'll be dead by then."

"Listen, Com-"

"Hold on. Hold on. Something is happening outside." There was a long silence, punctuated by muted conversation. The line went dead suddenly.

"Communications terminated," the MAV AI reported.

"Whatever we're doing, we have to be quick," Beyard said.

"We are almost there," the Quint said. "The chamber is just ahead."

"Brief us," I said. "What are we walking into?"

"The Beaut brought part of their old selves with them when they came here. An individual. One of their own. We believe it to be a captive. A hostage perhaps. They are keeping it here in a secure location. This is what we called the Tintus Quersum. A holy site if you will. A temple. It is one of the oldest parts of our civilisation. Some believe it is where the tree was first germinated."

"Describe it. This temple."

"It is within a chamber six hundred of your kilometres wide. The temple itself is built on the summit of a column in the centre of the chamber. The floor of the chamber is a lake, across which pilgrims will sail for many days before reaching the central island. From there they would climb the column to the temple itself. Only the swing are permitted the pilgrimage. Crawls such as me are not."

"Do we expect to come across much resistance?"

"I have no information. Everything I know is out of date.

"You know this individual is kept here though?"

"It was brought here originally. I know nothing further than that."

"So if it's been moved we have no chance of finding it."

"None," the Quint agreed.

Great. "But you believe this individual may hold the key to controlling these … whatever they are."

"We call them the Seneque. Which you may consider the consumers. Or the feeders."

"The eaters," Beyard said.

"It is so. This individual is considered important to the Seneque. They maintain it. There will be a reason for that."

So we were hoping this individual, if it still existed after all these hundreds of years, could be exploited. Exploited in such a way as to help us against these Seneque. The eaters.

What else was there?

Should we have headed back to Hotchkiss station? I may have lost the ship but at least I could have saved the people about me. Coming here I had killed them. We could not escape this place aboard the MAV, and the *Cesa* was lost to us too.

That was never an option, I realised. These men and women would rather die in the hopes of serving their crewmates, than escaping to safety. Even if there was no real hope of it anyway.

"We are here," the Quint said.

We passed into a massive chamber. The far wall all but lost in the distance. For all its size it was well lit, its ceiling a dazzling meshwork. The waters at its base were still, reflecting the brightly lit ceiling far overhead. In the middle of it all was a pillar that reached to the centre of the space. A building of some kind was perched atop it, much of it hanging over the edge. Oblivious to the fact the cavern floor was hundreds of kilometres below. There was no smoke anywhere. This place remained untouched.

"Land on the structure at the top," Crawl instructed. "As high up on it as you can."

"No capacity for touchdown," the AI informed us.

"I think this means we take the pods," Beyard said. "The MAV's ass is too big."

"Please no one miss," Baes said.

"Your first time, Sergeant?" C'gen laughed as she ejected her pod.

We all followed, the pods firing from the MAV's underside, aimed directly towards the peak of the tower beneath us. Control surfaces slid from recesses in their sides, allowing us to guide them in manually. The AI's job was done for now, it could keep the MAV on station in case we needed a hasty exit. We'd have to figure out how to get back aboard later.

There was no time for showboating this time. I wanted to get down, and fast. The longer we took here, the less time Matte had aboard the *Cesa*.

It was a tree, I realised as we got closer. A tree growing on a pillar within a world tree. It was massive. Bigger than any tree I had ever seen before. If you ignored the fact the Habitat was itself a tree. It was flat topped, the branches beneath pale in the bright light of the cavern. Even the smallest branch was dozens of metres across. The largest could have been up to a kilometre. I didn't know how tall it was. The trunk itself was a collection of trunks, each one intertwined around the others, allowing spaces between for what looked like walkways and stairs. Allowing supplicants access to the very highest spaces.

"This is Tintus Quersum," the Quint said. "The first tree of trees. It is from this tree that all others were grown. It was brought to this place by our distant ancestors when they first arrived in this system. We believe they came here from a world where sentient trees dwelled. A world that was a forest. Where the forest was one tree, each one linked to every other. A world tree. They brought a sample here, and it has lived here ever since. Becoming the habitats you see now."

"You are saying this tree, and this habitat, is sentient?" I asked it.

"All of them are. They are all one being. Even the tree in the system where you found me, where we gave the Hermitage refuge. All are one tree."

"I see movement at its base." Baes reported. "A few hundred individuals. I hope they don't – ah, they've seen us. They're headed up."

"That won't leave us much time," I said. "We have to do what we came here for before they arrive. We can't fight that many off." I could see the multicoloured Quint at the base of the tree. So many of them they looked like a wave washing uphill to surge through the openings in the trunk. Some mounting stairs, others simply swinging their way upwards, using whatever handholds they could find.

"I will guide this pod to a platform," the Quint said. "Bring yours down beside me. The location of the Beaut is nearby."

We fell in behind it, control surfaces twitching to keep us aligned. We weaved between the tree's upper branches, aiming for one of the higher platforms. At the last moment a chute billowed out, cutting its fall. And then it slammed into the wooden platform, the pod's walls snapping off at the impact. Crawl rolled out, skidding to a halt at the far end, giving the rest of us space.

I kicked out my own chute, the pod lurching as it caught the air. Then I was down too, my own pod shattering as the Quint's had. It was designed to absorb some of the impact of a heavy landing. And also to release the marine held within as quickly as possible. My ghoscht held me tightly as I fell forwards, avoiding another pod as it slammed down alongside.

"We are here," Crawl turned away from us even as we clattered to the platform behind it, facing a tall, pointed door set into a wooden wall before it. The wall was itself part of the tree, I realised. A vertical branch, or part of the trunk itself. The Quint reached out with spindly arms and pushed, the door creaking slightly as it gave under the pressure.

"How do you know?" I asked as I checked my equipment quickly, following behind it. I carried a carbine, a side arm and a sword clipped to my back. "You have never been here before."

"We all remember," it said, stepping into the passage beyond. It opened up into a wide space. A teardrop shaped chamber within the wood, a walkway running around both sides to meet at another door on the opposite side. There was no railing, allowing anyone venturing in to leap into emptiness should they so wish. I peered into the darkness below. I could see a bottom. I think. It wasn't all that far. A string of what looked like vines fell from the apex above, twisting about themselves as they reached to the darkened floor below. There was a shape secured within them at the same level as the walkway. It looked like a human.

"You have come to kill me," he spoke as we were still registering his presence there. He, like the Quint, spoke Complex.

I stopped barely a metre from him, his head at about the same level as mine. If I reached out I could touch him. Perhaps pull him from his prison. As I studied him I realised it would be impossible. The vines pierced his flesh at arm and leg, seeming to pass through him to the other side. Something seeped from the wounds. It could be blood. It could be sap. He wasn't wearing any clothing. His skin alabaster white and glistening in the dim light as if he was sweating profusely. Perhaps he was.

"I have been watching you," he continued before we could speak. "Since you came to this system. They see you. I see what they see. You have caused a lot of damage."

"Who are you?" I asked, realising as I did the question was probably meaningless.

He laughed. "I had a name once. They called me Feneshwede. There were many like me then. But I think you already know I am the last."

"You are Beaut," I said.

"You started calling us Hauda. The parasites."

"You control these things?" It was what we were here for, after all.

"Control? No. I can still hear my people. They whisper to me. Sometimes I whisper back."

"You butchered the Sunna," I said. "It was you, controlling these things."

He was silent a moment, his mouth working as if to find the words. "I did what I must," he said finally.

"Must? Why must you murder a world? An innocent people?"

"I ... you do not understand. The thirst builds. It is always there, but it builds and builds until ... until ... who are you?" He seemed confused for a moment, as if he didn't know where he was. It quickly passed.

"You are the eaters. You are part of them," I said.

"Eaters? Yes. It does fit. They do eat. They do feast. But it is not flesh they desire."

"It is the mind," our Quint companion supplied. "They desire the mind. The individual personality of their victim. They consume it."

"Like a drug," the man continued. "It is a drug to them. It is irresistible."

"But they have not taken yours," Beyard said abruptly. "Why did they save you? Why do they keep you here?"

"Because they can't consume him," I realised. "Your mind is not of flesh."

He shook his head, a fresh dribble of fluid running down his neck from the branch piercing his spine. He didn't seem to notice it. "It was once. But like most beings we sought immortality. So we transferred our minds out of our mortal husks."

"To a crystal lattice," I said. "That was why we started calling you the crystal entities. That was why we didn't trust you with all that we knew. With FTL itself. You were making yourselves into something other than human. But you didn't finish it did you?"

"No. I was one of the first, but I was not the last. I was the only one they kept."

"None of this makes any sense," Baes said. "And we don't have the time for this. We'll have company soon and we don't want to be caught here."

"Why did they keep you?" I asked him. "Why you?" If they couldn't consume him what use was he to them?

"I can hear the whispers. I can hear them. Still. After all this time, I still hear them. Something of them remains. Diluted. Torn asunder, but still there." He stared at me for a moment, his eyes wide in apprehension. "Who? Who are you?"

I don't know how I suddenly made the connection, but his words made a strange kind of sense. Why the Seneque – the eaters – kept him, when all of the others were gone. Why the Sunna had been destroyed. It all made a twisted kind of sense.

"You can still hear them," I said. "Your people. The Beaut. Because you were … are a hive mind. You learned to share each other's thoughts. So even though they have been consumed, and you have not, you can still hear them. They're still in there. Somehow. Some shadow of themselves."

"Yes," he said faintly. "I hear them. I felt it, I felt it all."

"You experienced each and every one of them being harvested by the Seneque. You felt their minds being taken. Consumed. Their bodies digested. You felt it all."

"Yes." His voice was so soft I could barely hear it. "Have you come here to kill me?" He sounded almost hopeful. Perhaps he was. I couldn't imagine the insurmountable anguish he had suffered for centuries. Centuries without respite.

"But there's more, isn't there? You can still talk to them. Somehow. You can still guide them from the outside. That is why they kept you alive when all the others were butchered. Because you can still control them. At least to a degree."

"It is not control. Not control. I can give them ideas." His eyes cleared, as if he realised where he was. Who we were. "But you cannot kill me, can you? You know what happens if you kill me?"

"Tell me," I said.

"Then there is no one to control them. They will be unleashed. Unleashed on the galaxy. To go as they will. To take whatever world they desire. You cannot stop them. There are too many. Too many."

"I think you'll be surprised at what we can do. And how does keeping you alive improve the situation? You guided them to the Sunna. And that was just one world of the many you reaped. Your ... creatures have harvested others."

"Yes." He giggled, a hint of madness entering his voice. "Yes. Just a world here. A world there. Without me they would spread out. Consuming everything. Not just a world here or there. All worlds! Why don't you understand? I did what I must. I did the only thing I could."

"He has a point, Izzy," Beyard said. "If we kill him there will be nothing to keep them in check. And they have FTL now. Who knows where they will turn up? Can we honestly say anyone can stand against them? Maybe we could. With a massed Confederate fleet. We could burn them out. But they could hit us anywhere. Our fleets cannot be everywhere."

"Neither can we keep him alive," I said. Keeping him alive would be sanctioning his actions. It would be saying butchering the Sunna was OK. It was not. It could never be OK. And there was the remote chance they would become unfocussed. Uncontrolled. Perhaps what the *Cesa* needed to break free from their grip. Remote. But it was all I had.

Still, I could see his twisted logic. But it was not something I could ever condone. I could not leave him here to keep on doing it.

I simply couldn't. Regardless of the effect on the *Cesa*.

"Why the Sunna?" I asked him. "Why did you single them out?"

He laughed thinly. "The Sunna? Because they are close."

"Close? You murdered them because they were close to you?"

"Their thirst was becoming too much. I could no longer control them. I needed to choose. And the Sunna were close."

"Shit." He'd butchered a whole people simply because they were convenient.

"If we're going to do something we need to do it now." Baes said. "I think I can hear them coming. They're almost here."

I pointed to the entrance. "Bar the doors. Use your ghoscht if you must. We need more time here."

"Time to do what, Izzy? Time to do what?" the marine demanded as he hurried to the far entrance. The door there was already closed. There was no locking mechanism so he reached out with his ghoscht. Anchoring it in the wood all about. Locking the door in place.

Time to do what? I didn't know.

"How do we stop them?" I demanded of the man. "There has to be a way."

He shook his head, fluid spurting from the wound at the back of his head. "No. I can keep them in check. Harvest a world here, a world there. Satiate their thirst. For a time. Until I need to direct them to another world. But while I do that everyone else is safe."

More worlds like Sunna-Deste-Anne.

"Survival at that price is not a survival I want," Beyard said.

"Conflict is life," en-ed-bas said. He and his brother were so quiet I had almost forgotten they were there.

"Life is conflict," his brother intoned.

"We cannot survive at that price," I said. "It is too steep."

"Then you must kill me," the figure said. "I cannot say I do not relish it. It is so long since I have felt peace. Since I have not felt the horror of my people. Of all the other people who have joined them."

As he spoke I heard a thump from a door, something heavy crashing into it.

"They're here!" Baes shouted.

"Here too!" C'gen yelled from where she was holding the opposite door, her ghoscht flashing under the strain.

"We're trapped in here," Beyard said. "I say we go down fighting these things. What say you?" She looked to the small group standing beside me.

"We fight," Sanquey agreed. He unslung his rifle and powered it up. It hummed in his hands.

"I see you all wish to die today," our Quint companion interjected. "But there is a larger context. Our people, yours and mine, know nothing of this. They need to be informed. Otherwise how will they know to defend themselves?"

"It's right, you know," Beyard said.

"And how do you propose to get out of here? The MAV's FTL drive has seized. The *Cesa* is lost to us. And that's after we get past all those creatures out there," I said.

"Perhaps. Do your people not possess the belief in hope? In faith?" the Quint continued. "Dying here all hope is lost. Leaving here there remains some hope. As forlorn as it is."

"I did suspect the Admiralty was sending a fleet right behind us," I said. "There's no way the *Cesa* could destroy everything here. It was undoubtably a sacrifice. That the fleet would finish what it started."

"Then we need to get as far from here as we can," Beyard said.

"I don't think we're going anywhere!" C'gen shouted. Her door was still rattling, the wood around its hinges starting to splinter and crack. Something heavy indeed was throwing its weight against the door, trying to batter it open.

I looked upwards. The vines seemed to lead to an opening above. The only source of light for the terrible chamber. I imagine we could climb it and somehow find a way of boarding the MAV beyond.

"Go!" Baes shouted, his own door bowing dangerously inwards. "You don't have a lot of time."

"The decision is yours to make," the trapped figure said. "Stay or leave."

There was only one decision. I didn't like it, but there was a lot I didn't like today. I unclipped my side arm and raised it, aiming towards the figure's head.

"Ah, a decision is made. But may I advise, my mind is not where you would expect it to be. Aim lower."

I lowered my arm to aim at his pasty chest, his skin marked by decades, centuries of sap dribbling over it.

"There," he said. "I thank you."

I fired, the weapon shrieking in the enclosed space. The bolt of energy blasted through his chest, ripping through the vines on the other side. Gore and sap splashed over the walkway opposite. With a sigh his head fell forwards.

"Well, that's done then," Beyard said. "Next, we need to leave here."

"I can't let go of this door," C'gen said. "If I do they'll get inside and stop you escaping. Just go. Leave us. We have this."

"Go!" Baes shouted again. "Just go, damn it!"

"Sergeants." I saluted them both before leaping from the walkway to the slippery, gore splattered vines. I almost lost my grip and fell, but my own ghoscht caught me and kept my balance.

"I will check the way ahead." The Quint leaped above me and swarmed up the vines, its long arms pulling itself quickly upwards.

Enhanced by my ghoscht I followed, leaving my companions to join me on the shaking vines. They were woody and hard in my grasp. Not quite too wide for my fingers to close about them.

I heard a crash beneath me as a door finally gave way. There was a shout. A carbine screamed. In less than the time it took to take a shallow breath, the carbine spoke no further. A defender swarmed by the Quint coming through the door. Their battered and bloody body crushed to the floor.

A long, furry arm reached down and pulled me into the light.

Chapter 22

We ran.

Across bridges, down walkways, and through passages. Higher. Ever higher.

"MAV AI, come to our location," I instructed.

"Nearing location. No landing site available," the machine responded. That was as good as we were going to get.

We had entered the tree's foliage here, the branches no longer bare. Leaves bigger than my hand sprouting around us, some fronds almost blocking our progress. We pushed our way through, swords flashing as we hacked at it. We hadn't heard anything further from our fallen comrades behind. Both C'gen and Baes had fallen silent moments after their doors gave way. Bringing up the rear, ne-de-sab had cut away the vines behind him as he clambered to the walkway, allowing them to collapse back into the chamber. The approaching horde would not be using them to pursue us. They didn't need it though. They were quickly finding a way around and continuing the pursuit. They were too quick for us. It wouldn't be long before they caught up.

The twins had stood for a moment about the gap in the walkway, heads lowered.

"oter sin wa," their said softly in unison. Their words in ancient oy, and unknown to me.

We hadn't stayed to honour our fallen ourselves. There wasn't time.

"This way." Beyard pointed to what looked like a ladder leading into foliage above. "If we can get on top of all of this we might be able to get to the MAV."

"Lead on."

Our Quint friend ignored the ladder, simply gripping swaying branches as it leaped from handhold to handhold. Quickly vanishing into greenery. "This way!" it shouted. "The way is clear."

We pulled ourselves after it. These branches were the last before we reached the top of the tree. Empty space opening up above us.

"There is a final walkway here," it said. "I believe a location for winged creatures to land."

"Winged creatures?" I had not seen any. How far had the Quint adapted themselves?

"Birds," it responded. "You have birds?"

"Sure. Just keep going."

It was a slippery smooth branch. There were no leaves or smaller limbs leading off it. It seemed to head out into empty space ahead of us. Almost as if it had grown here with a purpose. A lone, crooked appendage stretching beyond the rest of the tree. Convenient. I wasn't going to question it.

"MAV. Come to this location."

"Approaching."

The foliage we had just left behind quivered, a shape rising through it. It was a Quint. Its fur deep brown. Its broad shoulders battered the smaller branches aside, snapping them when they could bend no further. It was massive. Easily three or four times the size of our blue companion.

"It is a climb," it said. "It will be strong."

Another member of the Quint caste system, I guessed. A far bigger and stronger one. A climb whereas our friend was a crawl.

"You go," en-ed-bas drew his sword and turned to face it. "We will stop it here."

"I don't think you will be able to stop it," Crawl said.

"He will not be alone," his brother joined him, his legs far apart to balance himself on the shaking branch.

"Conflict is life," en-ed-bas said.

"Life is conflict," his twin agreed.

"Let's ensure it's not for nothing," Beyard said as she hurried further down the limb.

I followed. There was no choice in it. I could only honour them by giving value to their sacrifice.

"I will stay too," Sanquey said, turning and raising her weapon. "In case they get past them."

"You don't need to," the lieutenant objected. "They have this."

"I do. I need to make sure. You go."

The brown reared above the twins. They looked ridiculously small before it. With a shout they swept in, their blades flashing. Cutting through fur and muscle. The creature reached out for them but they were too quick. They danced to the side to strike again, swinging at an outstretched hand. The creature bellowed as a finger was severed, the digit larger than my arm. It thumped to the branch behind it, splashing blood over the wood. Fists like clubs it swung again and again, each time the twins dodging back, delivering more blows. Blood was soon flowing freely, matting its fur and making footing treacherous.

Still, they weren't killing it. None of its wounds were fatal. If anything they only served to enrage it further.

One of them slashed a tendon, dropping it to its knees. But in that moment he misjudged, a boot slipping in the blood coating the wood. He fell to his back. He quickly rolled away but the creature snatched him up, roaring with victory.

In one swift move it tore him in half, throwing each part in opposite directions. The remains of ne-de-sab disappeared into foliage below. He did not utter a sound.

Shouting his brother lunged at the creature, his sword held out like a spear. He plunged it into its chest. All the way to the hilt. With a grunt it toppled forwards, trapping him beneath its bloodied corpse.

Behind them Sanquey opened fire, her weapon pouring flechettes into the massed Quint following closely behind the brown. A motley collection of reds, blues and greens. All surging forwards. They dropped as her weapon cut through them. Ripping through flesh and bone alike.

There were too may of them. Even as the front rows fell the ones behind surged forwards. They were quickly on their fallen comrade. Hands pulling the trapped twin from beneath it. His bloodied sword freed he swung it at them. Hacking and slashing.

Another red rose and waded through the throngs of shorter Quint. It snatched up the last brother and sunk its teeth into his shoulders, his head disappearing into its maw. Strangely human shaped teeth cut clear through his pressure suit, crushing the man within. Even mortally wounded, much of him still inside the red's mouth, en-ed-bas swung his sword, the glittering blade plunging deep into its neck. Blood gushed out, drenching its fur and the man still in its mouth. Still, it refused to give him up, collapsing forwards slowly with the twin still between its teeth.

I didn't see much of what happened after that. The surge of Quint bodies flowed over both fallen forms. Sanquey's barrage paused for a moment as she swapped out clips. They leaped at the opportunity, bounding forwards to smash her to the branch. I heard a shout over coms as she pulled out a side arm and pumped round after round into the writhing mass of Quint flesh about her. It was quickly cut off.

"Get to the MAV," Beyard said. "I think this is as far as I go, Izzy." She stopped and turned also, facing the stream of Quint.

"We can both get on. It's almost here."

"We can't let them jump on after us. You saw what one of them did to the *Cesa*. Just you go. I'll keep them off you."

"I stand with you," our Quint friend turned also, facing the creatures that had once been its fellows. Who knew what they were now. Their bodies taken over and mimicked by an alien other. While they might look like Quint, they were anything but.

"You have to warn your people," I said to it.

"I entrust that to you," it said. "Waste no further time in talk."

"Damn it." I saw the MAV streaking in below, quickly slowing as it neared the overhanging branch. I dare not look beyond it. There was nothing beneath the branch here. Nothing but a very long fall to the glistening waters beneath.

I heard her weapon behind me, the rifle purring on full auto. What I didn't see was a shape swinging beneath the branch itself. Yet another red, its strong fingers gripping each side of the limb. In one smooth movement it mounted the branch in the space between me and the last of my comrades. They didn't notice its approach, too engrossed in trying to stem the tide of attackers before them.

Too late Beyard turned just as the creature brought down one massive fist, crushing the marine to hard wood. Her helmet shattered under the impact, blood gushing over her white pressure suit.

As the MAV manoeuvred beneath me I leaped onto its hull. My boots slamming down on hard armour. A hatch clicked open before me and I dropped through.

I didn't see what became of our Quint friend. I think I caught sight of a flash of blue fur as the tide of attackers swept over. Swamping it instantly. And then my view was cut off as the hatch slid closed. My last image was of Quint slipping from the branch as they jostled each other, dropping into emptiness beneath.

"Get out of here. Full speed," I instructed the AI.

"Manoeuvring," It reported.

I dropped the carbine to the deck, realising I hadn't fired so much as a shot. I don't think it would have made any difference if I had.

"Connect me to the *Cesa*, please."

"Connecting. Connection failed."

"Try again."

"Connecting. Connection failed."

I stepped onto the bridge and slumped into a couch. I could see beyond the ship from here, the monitors arrayed around me revealing what lay beyond the vessel's hull. It wouldn't tell me much. There would be more passage. More tree. Then hopefully space. A lot of space.

"Path interrupted," the AI reported.

"What?" We had barely left the chamber behind, entering into one of the long, twisting tunnels that led to the faraway surface.

"Objects in path. Avoiding."

"Engage all weapons. Auto fire."

"Interdiction engaging."

Fire sheathed the MAV's ebony hull, burning away anything that ventured too close to it.

Quint, I realised. There were more Quint in the passage ahead of us. They were dropping down from above, trying to land on the fleeing vessel. It made no sense. It was sheer suicide. But then I realised these were not Quint. Whatever they were they cared little for their lives. If they were even alive.

The MAV battered its way through them, its weapons searing them as they crossed its path. Its fiery shield vaporising them when they came into contact. The vessel bucked at the impacts, as if it had flown into a wall of flesh.

"Advise enter escape tube," the AI said.

I shook my head. What for? It made no sense. If I couldn't fly out of here in the MAV I wasn't getting out.

"Advise enter escape tube," it repeated.

"No. What for? Keep on going."

"Advise enter escape tube."

"Oh damn it." It wouldn't shut up until I complied. So I did. This AI was not Cena. You couldn't bargain with it. I stepped into a nearby drop tube, and closed the pod nestled within about me.

"Connect me to the *Cesa* please."

"Connecting. Connection established."

"Hello? Hello?" My heart leaped. Maybe they were still alive out there. Still fighting.

"Captain Marla," a voice said over comms. Cena.

"Cena. Is Matte there? Is anyone there?"

"I have no access. Nothing remains but for my primary node. I have lost access to all compartments within the ship."

"Including the bridge?"

"Yes."

"Do you know if anyone has survived?"

"I have no information."

I said nothing. There was nothing to say. No information meant only one thing. The *Cesa* had been completely overrun. There were no survivors. The MAV shook again as it battered its way through a fresh wave of falling Quint. I didn't think they were going to stop. Not now. Not ever.

"Cen. There is one last thing you have to do."

"There are no officers available to instruct me."

"Will you take instructions from me?"

"There is no one else."

"Will you take instructions from me?"

"I will."

Good. "Listen. We have to stop this. We have to stop all of this. There is only one course of action now."

"Supply instruction."

"You must engage FTL and head into this system's primary. You must get as deep into it as you can. Then you must self-destruct. Full SAD."

"Simultaneous ASPECT Devolution is not recommended in a populated system. You are familiar with the Lusander Theorem? I know Lieutenant Sepulveda mentioned it to you."

It was what I was counting on. While I didn't fully understand it, that was the kind of effect I wanted. "Will you follow this order?"

"I will comply. Will you be able to reach minimum safe distance?"

Now that was the question wasn't it? Honestly? No. I couldn't.

"Cen ... are there alternatives? We need to stop the Quint here. They cannot develop functional FTL and cannot leave this system."

"You require complete civilisational destruction?"

"Complete."

"It would require additional Confederate units to achieve that objective."

More ships. Cena meant it would take more ships. "Do you detect an approaching fleet?"

"I do not."

That answered that question. "So to achieve this objective there is no alternative?"

"There is not."

A modern heavy cruiser could create singularities by warping gravity about its hull, because at its heart the vessel contained a singularity of its own. A black hole if you would. A small one. Small enough it could keep it in check. It was the only system that could produce the prodigious amount of energy a vessel such as the *Cesa* required. It was the vessel's ASPECT drive. To devolve it was to release all safeguards. It was to set it free.

If that happened within a star such as the one that sat at the centre of this system, the results could only be termed catastrophic. A star was a delicate balance of forces. A balance between gravity and thermal expansion. Fighting each other they kept the star from either flying apart or collapsing in on itself. By igniting a singularity deep within it that balance was disrupted in a way no star could withstand.

Perhaps this was an act of desperation, reaching for an effect I barely understood. Still, it felt fitting. If we could duplicate the effect that had been visited upon the *Cesa* after firing on their processing platform, but in a far larger way, all life within this system would be stamped out.

But without FTL there was simply no way I was going to get out of here in time.

"Please explain the necessity for this course of action," Cena requested.

The MAV shook like a wet dog. I could hear heavy thumps against its hull. The Quint, whatever they were, were becoming serious.

"Incursion detected," the AI reported.

"What? Shit."

"Incursion detected. Recommend ejection."

"No! Are you mad?" I wouldn't survive a moment out there. Not in this pod. Not that it mattered any more.

"Please explain the necessity for this course of action," Cena repeated.

"We have to stop these Quint," I said. "You know they are developing FTL. We have to stop them before they perfect it. Before they use it to escape the detonation."

"I calculate they cannot escape the systemic event you are proposing," the AI said.

"So you know we have to do it? The Admiralty has given the order to prevent this technology from escaping."

"That order has been given," it agreed.

"Then you must do it."

"Disabling ASPECT safeties. Spooling FTL," it reported.

"Ejecting," The MAV AI interrupted.

"What?" Caught off guard I crashed into the roof of the pod as the AI fired it out of the vessel. I clung on, my ghoscht reaching out to stop me rattling about within it.

"You utterly insane useless .." I couldn't think of anything else to say. I connected the suit's systems to the pod so I could see outside of it.

We had left the habitat behind. Just. Jetting out the last of the tunnel as the Quint attackers breached its hull. I could see the massive surface beneath me. It was vast and flat from this perspective. The habitat so large the horizon was thousands of kilometres away. Much of what was beneath me was shrouded in smoke. Smoke from a million fires as the habitat burned from the inside out.

There was a shape beneath me. A promontory of sorts. Perhaps some kind of landing pad for space-based vehicles. It was reaching so high into the upper atmosphere as to pierce the blanket of smoke. It was as good a place as any.

"Status," I asked Cena.

"Safety protocols have been removed. Prestressing in preparation for detonation."

"How long?"

"Engaging FTL … now." I guess that answered my question.

I couldn't see the *Cesa* from here. I had no idea where it was. Wherever it was it streaked into the system's sun, its beleaguered hull taking damage almost instantly. Bulkheads collapsing, the creatures swarming within vaporised. As tough as they were they could not survive a star's chromosphere.

The *Cesa's* core disrupted, exploding with a force that would crack any planet in two. Exposing the singularities held in check deep within to the maelstrom that was the system's sun.

The pod thumped down hard. Shattering around me to release me onto the hard surface. I started sliding down its steep incline. My ghoscht trying to brake against it.

I hit a level section. The impact knocking the air from my lungs. Stunned I lay there for a moment. Gazing up at what looked like a moon passing above me. It seemed so close I could reach out and touch it. Something else streaked past. Debris burning up in the atmosphere.

"Cen. Cen, can you hear me?"

Coms remained silent. The AI was gone. The *Cesa* along with it.

"Cen?"

I stayed where I was. There was no point in moving. I don't know what had happened to the MAV. It was gone too. Crashed. Exploded. Taken over by attackers. I had no idea. It didn't matter.

Yes, before you say it, I am aware of my own hypocrisy. I despised the Confederacy for what it had done in the past. For the worlds it had destroyed. Yet here I was, perpetrating a far, far worse crime. How many quintillion has Crawl said? And I had extinguished all of them. By destroying the star at the centre of the system. Something I doubted even the Confederacy had had the temerity to do. Still, it was effective if you needed to kill every living thing in the system.

It wasn't a hypocrisy I would have to worry about for much longer.

"Movement left. Two kilometres," the suit's system said.

"Oh you're kidding me."

I heaved myself to my knees and looked around. I couldn't see anything. The platform's base was lost beneath me. In the cloud and smoke that consumed the planet. Habitat. If there was anything climbing up it it was invisible from here.

"Well." I unholstered my side arm and decided to wait.

"Eighteen hundred metres."

"Oh shut up." I peered in the direction it was indicating. "Magnify."

Yes. It was Quint all right. A lot of them. They were clambering up the spire. No idea why. They couldn't possibly know I was here. They couldn't possibly care if they did. Could they survive at this altitude? I needed a pressure suit. They clearly didn't.

I turned and looked away, watching the moon passing overhead. It was going to crash into the habitat, I realised. Atmosphere was already twisting around it, generating titanic eddies of gas and dust as it fell. It was silent. I couldn't hear anything. It was too far away. There wasn't enough air pressure up here to carry the sound. The gravitational distortions created by the firing of *Cesa's* primary weapon had disturbed the moon's orbit. Enough to send it plummeting. As big as the moon was it was dwarfed by the habitat. A gnat hurling itself headlong at an elephant.

"Time since detonation," I asked the suit computer. It did not respond.

"Time since cessation of comms with the *Cesa*."

"Eight minutes," it reported.

I did some rough math. How long would it take for the star to tear itself apart? Minutes? Hours? I didn't know. And how long would it take me to see it from here? I was about fifteen light minutes from the sun. It would take at least that long for me to see it once it did happen.

"Contact left. Sixteen hundred metres."

I groaned. It wasn't going to leave me in peace. I considered getting up and heading in the opposite direction. I preferred dying in a fiery explosion than in the hands of the Quint. Or whatever they were now. I supposed I could use the weapon to end it quickly.

That just wasn't my style.

The moon touched down. It looked like it was crashing into the habitat in slow motion, but I knew it would be travelling at many thousands of kilometres an hour. A shockwave ripped through the habitat's surface. Like a pebble dropped into a pond.

I sat and watched, trying not to think about the approaching Quint. It was a marvellous sight. As destructive as it was. I doubted any human had watched anything quite like this before.

"Time elapsed since comms?"

"Eighteen minutes."

Well, that was enough time. I looked upwards, the visor dimming automatically against the glare. Did the sun look different? It didn't seem perfectly circular anymore. But it was hard to tell.

"Oh. Oh. Well there we go."

The sun seemed to contract suddenly. Growing visibly smaller even from my vantage point. It was definitely getting darker.

It was happening quicker than I had expected.

I waved towards the approaching Quint. "Sorry to disappoint you, guys."

"Contact rear."

"Oh really? Just shut up. I don't care."

It grew suddenly dark. The sun disappearing overhead. I could see stars in the distance. Stars and the burning debris of battle. Burning despite the vacuum of space.

It would be any time now.

I breathed deeply. I wasn't scared, I realised. I was ready for it. I had lived with danger all of my life. Fear had lost its power over me. It was strangely silent. Even the suit's systems seemed muted. I could hear nothing but my own heartbeat.

I only had one regret. The Quint knew something about my own people. Perhaps they met them before the Confederacy sentenced that forlorn world to destruction. I had given up on ever knowing anything about them. About where I had come from. After all my years of searching I had finally come across a people who might know something. Who might know why the Confederacy hated them so much they would destroy them.

But I had lost all that now.

I sighed and threw down the weapon in my hand. I hadn't known anything new yesterday. I didn't know anything new today. Nothing had changed. Tomorrow was someone else's problem.

"Well, are you going to get in or what?"

I turned and saw a vessel floating behind me. Its ramp lowered in invitation.

Ference.

Epilogue

We travelled into the night. I didn't know where we were going. We didn't talk much. The grey man was still grey. And uncommunicative. I didn't care. I didn't want to talk.

Once I had relayed everything I needed to say I had nothing else to talk about. My story was out. Ference could report to his masters. They could do with it as they would. My part in it was over. He had been following us, following me, all through this. Cena keeping him up to date on my reports to the Admiralty. He had been the one to set me on this course. Manipulating me as Governor Sayall had warned. I didn't care. It didn't matter anymore.

Once we were safely outside the system the spy allowed his ship's sensors to aim back the way we had come. Watching the devastation unfold. The sun did not explode at first. Something else happened before that. I can barely describe it. If anything it was as if everything disappeared. The gravitation gradient far too steep to allow light to escape, and so the system went dark. Even though it was only for an instant the results were catastrophic. When we could see it again the system was already dead. Everything within it crushed by the overwhelming effect.

It was then the star flashed in silent detonation. The thermal energy at its core released from the grip of gravity. The shockwave washed over the ashes of the habitats and moons. What remained of them.

We did witness one or two sparks trying to outrun it. Quint vessels that had adapted Confederate FTL technology. They couldn't maintain their speed for long. Their warp fields collapsing. Their engines overheating. Needing time to cool down before trying again. Time they didn't get. The detonation caught up and overwhelming them too.

Nothing survived it.

His ship was small, with only a few compartments. I stayed in bed. His bed to be fair, but he didn't seem to need it. He remained on the tiny bridge. Making his reports. Plotting courses. Whatever.

I don't know how much time passed. He didn't tell me and I didn't ask.

I did wake up one morning – I think it was morning – after a fitful sleep to hear voices. He was talking to someone. On comms maybe. Then a voice responded. It didn't sound like comms. It sounded like Ference had company.

Rubbing my eyes I pulled on a bath robe and padded out of the room. It was bright in the companionway. If you could call it that. It was little more than a space joining a few compartments together. Storage. A shower/bathroom. An airlock. A lounge of sorts – perhaps where the man had been sleeping. And the bridge. The chambers were dim, barely lit by dim strips around the bulkheads. The ship looked old. Worn out. Rusted and marked. It had been out here a long time.

They sounded like they were on the bridge. The heavy steel door was open.

"Who are you?"

Another man was sat at the only other station in the cramped cabin. A comms console, I imagined. He looked up at me without saying anything.

"Have we stopped?" I asked Ference.

"No. Not yet."

"Izzy … Can I call you Izzy?" Ference's companion spoke.

I shrugged. "Go ahead."

"Good. That means we can be friends."

"Great."

"I've come to offer you a job."

"The Admiralty might have something to say about that. They want to court martial me."

He smiled. "Don't worry about that. I'll sort them out."

"Who the hell are you?"

"Eli. Eli Massen. My friends call me Mas."

Thank you for reading Unleashed. If you enjoyed this book, please leave a review. I know you hear it often, indi writers are always asking for reviews. Still, it does help.

Connect with C.P. James

Visit my Amazon Author Page:
https://www.amazon.co.uk/C-P-James

Isia's journey continues in The Dustbin Man.

Printed in Great Britain
by Amazon

27231720R00131